*The Be*

"Fans of *The Best Man* films and Peacock series are in for an absolute treat with this soulful, sexy, fast-paced new read! What a delight, catching up with beloved fan favorites Harper, Jordan, and Robyn (and a dazzling supporting cast) as they navigate relationships and their careers all around the world—only to discover that some bonds can never be broken. *Unfinished Business* is an utterly propulsive, stylish read with so much heart."

—Tia Williams, *New York Times* bestselling author of *A Love Song for Ricki Wilde*

"This felt like catching up with a group of beloved friends I hadn't heard from in a while. The complicated relationships, angsty passion, and doses of humor I've come to expect from *The Best Man* franchise . . . it's all here! Such a treat! This new story is just as cinematic as the movies themselves, maybe even more so."

—Farrah Rochon, *New York Times* bestselling author of *Pardon My Frenchie*

"When you're as close to the characters as I have been, you think you can predict what's coming around the corner, but this kept even me on the edge of my seat. *The Best Man: Unfinished Business* dives deeper into the lives of these characters, revealing what has made them who they are, the good and the bad. From a second-chance romance to wrestling with heartbreak and purpose, Malcolm D. Lee and Jayne Allen have given the best men and women new life. Emotionally engrossing. Seductive. Impossible to put down. It's the perfect summer read, full of heat!"

—Taye Diggs

"Not only are fans of *The Best Man* films going to fall in love with this book, which goes deeper into the emotional lives of characters we have loved for decades, but readers new to the canon will be swept up in the interpersonal dramas between Harper, Jordan, Robyn, and their crew in a story that spans from Brooklyn to Ghana. I believe in second acts—in life and in love. *The Best Man: Unfinished Business* gives us a front-row seat to the challenges of grown folks' love and the sometimes bumpy ride to becoming your most authentic self."

—Tembi Locke, *New York Times* bestselling author of *From Scratch*

"When I met these classic characters twenty-five years ago, no way did I think they'd have the longevity that they've had, but Malcolm D. Lee keeps elevating the storytelling. *Unfinished Business* is the characters you love like you've never seen them before! You will laugh out loud and possibly shed a few tears, so read this with your crew. A must-read for new and old fans alike. You will keep wanting more."

—Morris Chestnut

"*The Best Man: Unfinished Business* contains every element that we love about this franchise. It's full of heart, vulnerability, and most important, love, mixed in with a few delicious surprises. These characters continue to deliver new dimensions as they navigate the tricky process of real growth."

—Jemele Hill, author of *Uphill*

# *The* BEST MAN

# *The* BEST MAN

## — Unfinished Business —

Malcolm D. Lee

with Jayne Allen

NEW YORK

STOREHOUSE VOICES
An imprint of the Crown Publishing Group
A division of Penguin Random House LLC
1745 Broadway
New York, NY 10019
storehousevoices.com
penguinrandomhouse.com
crownpublishing.com

A Storehouse Voices Trade Paperback Original



ISBN 978-0-593-97425-4
Ebook ISBN 978-0-593-97426-1

Editor: Chelcee Johns
Production editor: Craig Adams
Text designer: Andrea Lau
Production: Heather Williamson
Copy editor: Shasta Clinch
Proofreaders: Pam Rehm and Robin Slutzky
Publicist: Gwyneth Stansfield
Marketer: Chantelle Walker

Manufactured in the United States of America

2 4 6 8 9 7 5 3 1

The authorized representative in the EU for product safety and compliance is Penguin Random House Ireland, Morrison Chambers, 32 Nassau Street, Dublin D02 YH68, Ireland, https://eu-contact.penguin.ie.

*To my late mother, Nancy Jean Reid Lee, who* loved *to read. An aspiring writer, she was proud of me, and she would be proud of this one. She would have read it immediately. Love you, Mommy. I know you're with me every day.*

*My cousin Donald P. Stone, who was one of the first writers in the fam, and my great-grandfather, William James Edwards, who laid the foundation with Snow Hill Institute and twenty-five years in the Blackbelt.*

*The displaced citizens of the Altadena and Palisades fires.*

# *The* BEST MAN

# ACT I

# CHAPTER ONE

## Harper

Harper Stewart stood in the mirror of the generous room labeled TALENT and squared the tailored wool of his Brioni blazer across his shoulders. The fit was immaculate, giving "Pulitzer Prize–winning author" for days. He was freshly shaven, and the smooth chocolate of his chiseled face looked just right in the reflection ahead as he mouthed the practiced words he'd soon speak before the television cameras. He'd made it a point to look his best, color-matching the blazer to his form-fitted turtleneck underneath in just the perfect dark navy blue to complement the deep brown of his skin. The mirror validated his decision. *The blazer-turtleneck combo was the right one,* he thought.

"Five minutes to air, Mr. Stewart." A headset-wearing production assistant ducked his head through the doorframe and just as quickly was gone down the hall in a blur of all black and a quiet squeak of rubber-soled shoes against the floor. The behind-the-scenes bustle of the show was a beehive of dozens of producers, technicians, and cameramen rushing past Harper's temporary oasis of calm. Every one of the passersby reminded him of the enormity of the opportunity—national broadcast television. He was at the tipping point of becoming a literary tastemaker. Harper took a deep breath and ran his palm across the top of his perfectly smooth head, careful not to disturb the light dusting of face powder applied by the station's makeup artist. Harper hated makeup, all that fuss, but the high-definition camera would tell no lies, especially this early and yes, at his age. Even the best Black can crack eventually, but today was the day to look his finest.

"You good?" Cassidy, Harper's longtime publicist, entered the room. Harper turned to her, nodding with an "Mm-hmm" and a smile. It was Cassidy who'd booked this appearance on the second hour of *CBS Mornings,* maneuvering him out of TV bookers' first suggestion of the "natural fit" during Black History Month. Cassidy did not play. Harper was a Pulitzer Prize winner now, so any month was a "natural fit." She was always advocating for her talent to get face time in prime slots. And today it was Harper's turn to make book recommendations to a national morning audience. Cassidy got shit done and made sure that when it came to Harper Stewart, everyone came correct.

"It's almost time," she commanded. Her nod toward the door meant that they needed to begin their walk to the soundstage. Harper wanted everything to flow perfectly. And so far, it had. He'd spent too long as a literary afterthought—present but still invisible. *Everything is under control,* he reminded himself. He was prepared. And when the cameras hit, he'd be charming, memorable, and, most important, worthy of a return invitation.

A short walk and they arrived. The morning show set looked warm, like someone's living room, with cozy yet generic décor of creams, oranges, and yellows and flowers that were so perfectly placed on the table they seemed fake. The station signage for

*CBS Mornings* glowed in the background, a reminder that this was a place for important conversations. America would be up and watching, catching him making tastefully considered book picks over their morning coffee and eggs.

Harper heard the anchor call his name from the other side of the room in a polished female voice that made him sound official. "And coming up after the break, Pulitzer Prize–winning author Harper Stewart joins us with his must-read books for spring and to maybe get into some *Unfinished Business* while we're at it. Stick around. . . ." Harper smiled and sighed with pride and relief. *Pulitzer Prize winner.* He still hadn't quite gotten used to that being attached to his name. He had been a *New York Times* bestseller before—his debut work, *Unfinished Business,* placed him on "the list"—but it felt asterisked. The novel was too easily dismissed as *Black* ***and*** *successful,* an anomaly, a fluke. Not even a box-office-smash Hollywood adaptation of his work gave Harper the kind of cachet that he now owned.

His Pulitzer Prize–winning *Pieces Of Us* put Harper on the map. No longer the unknown, under-acknowledged Black author—Harper had been fully Christopher Columbused now. The "literary elites" had "discovered" him, only twenty-five years into his career, and made him a household name. Finally, he had the world's attention. And that alone drove him to another deep breath. *Great . . . right?* It wasn't so clear. In fact, nothing this morning was. He didn't get nervous at interviews, but for some reason, he was . . . off. He hadn't slept well. Bailey had kept him up.

"Two minutes to air!" another all-black-clad producer shouted from the brightly lit soundstage, barely looking up from her clipboard. Harper thought to check his phone, and reached for it just as it started buzzing. It was already on silent mode, but also, now it was ringing.

He pulled the phone out of his jacket pocket, and seeing the number of his alarm company, he figured he'd better answer. "Hello?" he whispered.

"Hello, may I speak to Mr. Harper Stewart?" The voice on the other end was formal, a bit Southern, matter-of-fact and businesslike.

"This is he. Who's this . . . ?" Harper whispered hurriedly.

"This is Summit Security. There's a fire alarm alert at your home."

"What? *My* home? Are you sure it's me?"

"Yessir." The attendant on the phone repeated Harper's address perfectly. The swell of panic rose into his chest. That smoke alarm was sensitive as fuck, but it never resulted in a call from the security company, unless . . . it was . . . *real*?

"Well, I'm—I'm not at home. I'm about to go on live television. I—I have an interview. . . ." Harper stuttered the words, looking around wildly for Cassidy. After he finally met her eyes, she slid quickly over to his side.

"What's wrong?" she whispered.

"There might be a fire at my house. . . ." Harper imagined his four-million-dollar condo burning to ashes while he droned on about the best spring reads.

"What?" Cassidy looked perplexed and mildly annoyed. Harper noted the terrible timing. *Especially if* . . .

"The fire department has already been dispatched," the voice on the phone continued. "Is anyone home?"

"Ummmm . . ." Harper didn't really want to answer while this Southern dude and his all-business publicist were hanging on his every word, but the truth was . . .

*Bailey.* Harper left her sleeping as the dawn hadn't even broken when he departed this morning. *Was she okay? Was* . . . The unmistakable deep tone of call-waiting pressed his eardrum interrupting his thoughts. He pulled the phone away from his head to look at the screen and saw Bailey's name and photo displayed on the caller ID.

"Yes, I think so. Maybe . . ." Harper turned the phone away from Cassidy's gaze as he went to swap the line. "Could you just hold for one sec . . . and maybe not call the fire department. . . ."

"Mr. Stewart I cannot—" Harper's finger stabbed at the screen before he heard the rest.

"Bailey—?" Harper said into the phone with an urgent whisper. "Are you okay? Is there a fire . . . ?"

Bailey's voice floated through the air over the screeching sound of the fire alarm. The panic in his chest had reached his throat by now, closing the passageway. "Oh, Harper! I was just making some toast—that fresh sourdough looked so yummy I just had to cut a slice . . ." Her explanation seemed way calmer and less urgent than he needed. Still, she continued, "But all of a sudden there was smoke from the toaster and now . . . your alarm . . . and—"

Harper cut her off quickly. "Bailey, is there a fire?"

"Well, no . . . no, I don't—know, I mean I opened your balcony door to let the smoke out, but the alarm's still ringing . . . I don't know how to turn it off and—"

"Mr. Stewart." The clipboard holding producer was suddenly at his elbow. "We're ready for you on set, sir." Harper's eyes widened as his head swiveled on its own accord to his right. "Forty-five seconds to air."

Harper willed his feet to move. "Okay, okay, I'm following you," he said in an attempt to reassure the producer. In step, he remembered the alarm company on the other line, waiting—and fuck! the fire department! And . . . Bailey. He turned his attention back to his phone. Cassidy was right in lockstep with him and all up in his convo. "Bailey, I need you to turn the alarm off."

"Okay, sure. Where is it?" *Shit.*

"It's a panel right at the front foyer." He tried to remain even-keeled, but he was already starting to perspire despite the subzero temps in the studio.

"Okay, okay, I'm sorry . . . I'm headed there now . . ." Bailey's breath on the other end confirmed that she was in motion.

"Listen, the fire department is on the way—" Harper warned her.

"Oh my God, no. I'm naked in here. . . ." Bailey gasped. Despite the circumstances, *naked* immediately made Harper recall the image of Bailey's beautiful brown body with those round areolas and that plump firm booty hustling around his living room. What was also inopportune and certainly distracting was the sound or rather the non-sound of her movements, all breath and no rustling of clothes. *Naked, like she said.* They both needed to focus.

"It's okay. Just go over and turn it off—" Harper calmly yet urgently begged into the phone.

"It is so *loud.* Freaking me out. I don't see any numbers. . . ."

"Just put your hand on it to activate it."

"We're thirty seconds to air!" the stage manager bellowed.

"Nothing's happening, babe." Bailey's voice hinted at her mounting frustration.

"Just take a deep breath and place your palm on the panel and the numbers will come up."

"Does it matter if it's my left or my right?"

*Seriously?* "No!" Harper snapped, and then tried to recover. He needed her to be calm. "I mean I don't know—I'm right-handed—" he delivered with a change in tone.

"Well, I'm a lefty. And please don't yell . . ."

"I'm sorry, but I'm in the middle of—"

"Twenty seconds, Mr. Stewart." The stage manager was clearly losing patience.

Cassidy snapped her fingers and quickly beckoned at his ear. "Give me the phone," she commanded. *Just one second,* Harper thought, holding up one finger and pleading with his eyes. Cassidy's glare was incredulous, screaming, *Are you serious right now?* "We can't show the audience an empty seat, Harper . . ." she said through gritted teeth.

On the other end of the phone, Bailey's triumphant voice sailed into his ear. "Okay. it came up," she said. "What's the code?" *Oh damn.* Harper couldn't help but hesitate. *If I give her my code* . . . he thought. *I'm not feeling this girl like tha—*

"HARPER!" Cassidy was full voice now.

"Okay." Harper exhaled. "Twelve, twenty-eight, thirteen . . ."

"What . . . ?" Bailey asked.

Harper's frustration peaked. "It's Mia's birthday! Fuck, I gotta go. I'm giving you to Cassidy for the code. . . ."

"Who's Cassidy . . . ?" Bailey asked. "And who's Mia . . . ?" *Is she serious right now with the jealous vibes . . . ?*

"Fifteen seconds to air, sir." The stage manager started the countdown from there. "Fourteen . . ."

"My publicist . . ." Harper hissed. ". . . Hold on."

"Thirteen . . ."

He flipped the call back to the alarm company. "Listen, it's a false alarm. Kitchen issue, toast . . . smoke . . . call off the fire department . . ."

"They're already on the way, sir. . . ." *Fuck.*

"Give me the phone," Cassidy said, reaching for his hand. "Give me the code. *Go.*" Swiftly, she ripped the phone from his grasp and practically shoved him with her other toward the set where the show host was getting settled into her seat.

"Ten . . ." The stage manager then switched his countdown to a silent indication with his fingers.

Harper picked up his walking speed, laser-focused on the empty seat ahead. With a quick look back to Cassidy he said, "Mia's birthday . . . twelve twenty-eight thirteen. Give Bailey the code."

"Who's Bailey?" Cassidy mouthed. *Who is Bailey indeed. . . .* Cassidy still looked confused, but she put the phone to her ear. Harper spun again toward the set, to bridge the impossible distance, and started a quick step toward the producer who had already doubled back to guide him, physically now, toward the stage. He turned his head to Cassidy. "Mia's birthday . . . !" he said again. And the last thing he saw in that direction was Cassidy with the phone to her ear, mouth moving frantically. In front of him were the five extended fingers of the stage manager turning to four and the contorted faces of the hosts as he, in three paces, made it to the empty seat ahead and slid into it. Three . . . two . . . one.

"And we're back with Pulitzer Prize–winning author Harper Stewart, whose Hollywood plans for his book sequel aren't the only excitement he's had this morning. Welcome, Harper."

Harper felt the sweat beads trailing down his back, past his waist, pooling at his crack. *Jesus.* He hoped he didn't look as hot as he felt. So much for a dope-ass look. He smiled sheepishly at Gayle King, his interviewer. She was all perfectly set makeup, pristinely positioned hair, and a smile frozen on her face while her eyes looked concerned, if not a slight bit judgmental. "Did I hear something about a fire at your house?" she asked. "Is everything okay?"

"Yes. Thank you," Harper managed to say. "False alarm. Evidently sourdough is very combustible. All good now." A little more at ease, Harper turned directly to the camera and flashed a megawatt smile. "Shout out to the New York Fire Department—I'm gonna owe you guys some coffee and bagels."

"Wow, that's quite a morning!" Gayle's face relaxed a bit as she continued. "We're glad everyone's safe and that you're here with us to discuss something exciting in its own right—the world of characters that you'll be bringing back to the screen. What can you tell us about the highly anticipated sequel to *Unfinished Business*? Word is you're writing the screenplay?"

Harper thought about his answer to that. What could he actually tell her that was true? That he was nervous about it? Because he was. That he desperately wanted it to go better than the last disaster of a film adaptation that was *Unfinished Business*? Because he did. That the first one almost cost him his friendships and, arguably, his marriage? That the stakes were so much higher in this round? That he needed to make it right?

"Yes," he said, trying to sound much more confident than he felt. "I'm really looking forward to having the opportunity to expand upon the story that was started in *Unfinished Business* and writing the screenplay is giving me the chance to finish out that journey."

"So, in writing this sequel, does that mean we should expect to see your future work on the screen rather than the shelf?"

Harper shifted in his seat and crossed his ankle over his knee. "I'd like to use the medium to keep the integrity of the novel, the story, and the characters . . . in an elevated way." *Jesus, did he just say that bullshit?* Harper perceived how quickly the drivel he was forced to spew at countless lunches and creative calls found its way out of his mouth, even here. He added quickly, "Screenwriting is giving me a chance to exercise a new muscle. But my bread and butter is still the printed page."

"And we're all clamoring to see what comes of those pages," Gayle's co-host, Nate Burleson, interjected.

Gayle continued. "*Unfinished Business* was a huge box-office success. We just love those characters. Especially Jackson and Kendall. They've got that serious will-they-won't-they thing."

"They do indeed," Harper responded.

"So will they or won't they, Harper?" Nate chimed in again with a probing smile.

Harper couldn't help but think of Jordan, at the most inconvenient time—in front of millions of viewers, and he hoped the thought wouldn't show on his face. In his writer's view, the future could be written, even if reality was a world apart. So he answered with what was true for now. "I guess we'll have to wait to find out," Harper remarked.

"Spoken like a true artist," Nate teased. "Keeping things close to the vest."

Harper smiled. "But what I will say is . . . everyone likes a happy ending."

"That's what we're all hoping for."

"Me too," Harper said. "Me too."

"Okay, let's get to those must reads for spring. . . ."

# CHAPTER TWO

## Harper

Harper's interview went by in a blur, only to place him all too quickly back in the plush leather seat of a chauffeured black Escalade heading home. New York City rush-hour traffic seemed extra thick this morning. The Dominican brother with a razor-sharp haircut was doing his best to navigate Manhattan's aggressive commute—the large volume of vehicles and risky lane switches, all going south on FDR Drive. Harper was ready to get back to work but tried to settle himself into the wait, resigned but definitely frustrated as they made their way back to his Brooklyn Heights residence.

Last night was the first time that Bailey had chosen to sleep over until morning. Usually she was out the door before dawn. Her online marketing company kept her on her toes and Bailey seemed to be about her business. She'd suggested the Brioni. And the turtleneck. Through half-mast eyes and a raspy morning voice she gave a "fire" and a "perfect" approval of his attire with a gesture of her thumb and forefinger, before she said, "Hey, do you want me to get out of here?" *Um, yes.* But at 4 a.m. it felt like a trick question.

So, he responded with "Oh. No. It's cool." And she seemed

happy about that. Too happy, snuggled in his one-thousand-thread-count Egyptian cotton sheets and Frette duvet. Thankfully she said, "I just need another hour. I'll set my alarm," before she rolled over and hugged one of his thick pillows. "Good luck, baby."

Were they at the pet name stage at this point? They'd been flirting, dating, fucking for the better part of two months. They weren't exclusive, though. At least he wasn't . . .

Harper hadn't even fully stepped into the car leaving the television studio when Bailey's name popped up in his text messages. "You did so great, babe!" Already "baby" from this morning had shifted to "babe." It wasn't any better. Harper resolved to stop and get her a latte and send her on her way for the day before she got too comfortable. The interview reminded him of the stakes for this project, the responsibility for the sequel to *Unfinished Business,* his redemption. Against his longtime agent Stan's best advice, Harper had given up a lucrative potential payday in exchange for the exclusive shot to script write. It wasn't easy doing battle with the studio suits and their best efforts to persuade Harper to leave this project to the "professionals." No way. He might've been a novice when it came to screenwriting, but he'd pay for the opportunity to get it right. "Keep the money" was Harper's stance. Stan worked overtime to protect Harper and his bank balance, always got the best deal he could. He wasn't in agreement with taking less money up front, but knew how much the *Unfinished Business* title meant to Harper, and most important, *why.* Harper had gotten a rare shot he owed to himself and others not to blow.

Stan's ears must have been ringing at Harper's thoughts, because his name was now buzzing his phone.

"Hey, Stan," Harper answered. "Did you—"

Stan's enthusiastic greeting took over the call. "Harper Stewart. Setting the world on fire," he began.

"So you *did* see the interview," Harper said wryly. Of course Stan had seen it. Harper Stewart was a major client—and had been since Stan snapped him up right out of Iowa's graduate writing program. A promising young writer who he'd helped blossom into "the voice of a generation."

Stan chuckled. "Yes, I did. You are quite the polished writer, my friend—made the book picks sound interesting. It was a great hit. Congratulations."

"Thanks, Stan."

"I'm sure once the West Coast wakes up, they'll be watching it as well. And I want to be ready when I get the eventual calls about all the *Unfinished Business* sequel talk."

"How'd they even know I was writing it?"

"Mehhh, you know, it's a hot property. Someone's assistant probably leaked it. Who knows?" Stan opined. "More importantly, how's it going? I'd love to be as confidently cagey with the studio as you were with the CBS crew."

Harper bit on his bottom lip, choosing a response.

"Yeah . . . about that," he said finally. "Can you buy me some more time?"

"You mean, 'more time' like more than the week between now and the studio meeting in LA?"

Harper felt the heat rise in his face. "Yes."

Stan released a dramatic sigh. "Look, Harper, we can't keep pushing this meeting. It took us a month just to get the schedules coordinated . . . *again.* . . . Don't overthink this. All you need is a pitch. A *convincing* pitch. You go in and sell the room on the pitch and I can get you the creative space you need to work on rewriting the college sequel you wanted to do, or even a whole new idea. You know they can do whatever they want without you—"

"Yeah, Stan, they already did!"

"And that's why we need to make sure this opportunity works. These are *your* characters, Harper. No one knows them better than you. No matter how successful the movie version was, you can tell their next chapter better than anyone."

Harper sighed.

"That's what we fought for. This is what you wanted."

Stan was always good for a pep talk—one part encouragement and two parts pressure. Harper had hurt his friends by losing control over their depictions. He should have known the movie studio would take liberties; they always did. But his friends had placed their faith in him, given him their confidence when he'd asked for it, blessed the book when he'd needed it. Hell, his best friend and retired NFL All-Star, Lance Sullivan, had even given him unprecedented access to his life and legacy to write his biography. The least he could do now was take this opportunity seriously. But Harper wasn't as focused as he needed to be with this project. Even he could admit it—he was distracted. Especially so if "distracted" meant the three rounds of vigorous sex that had kept him up far past midnight the previous night, and even later nights before. But it wasn't Bailey's fault. And it wasn't the fault of the string of women that he'd been dating either. The problem was Harper feeling untethered with this new stage in his life. He had to figure some shit out, and quick.

"Yeah, I got it," Harper said, his tone lower and signaling defeat. "This screenplay thing is tricky."

"Listen." Stan's coach mode was in full effect. "I'm just as new to this Hollywood way of doing business, but it's not nearly as complex as what you do. What they care about is 'the big idea.' You solve that, you'll have them."

"I got you, Stan," Harper declared. "I'll be ready."

The chauffeured car pulled to a slow curbside stop in front of Harper's condominium building on Front Street. To his relief, the entry could not have looked more pristine. The fees of his HOA were already high enough without add-ons for damage. He briefly imagined the arrival of the firefighters, with their boots and gear, marching through the immaculate marble and carved chestnut–paneled lobby. It must have caused quite a scene.

The elevator ride took him up sixteen floors to the single floor two-bedroom, two-and-a-half-bath showplace that he'd purchased following his divorce. Fourteen hundred square feet was a lot of luxury living for just one person (and occasionally his eleven-year-old daughter, Mia). The views of the river had been a huge selling point for him, but more than that, every time he saw his brown hand lying upon the polished brass knob to open the wood-panel door, he remembered the years of toiling and under-compensation, the unrecognized years of scraping a dollar here and there, stitching together gigs to make ends meet. Well, now times were good. Real good. And opening the door to his crib reminded him that the sacrifices had been worth it, seeing the perfect blend of industrial charm and modern opulence inside. From its vaulted ceilings with white crown moldings, oversized windows that flooded the space with morning sunlight, to its neutral furnishings and sleek hardwood floors, his home was an incarnation of the kind of aspirational worlds Harper created in his novels. And back in his familiar entryway, he didn't even smell smoke. It was home, just as he'd left it.

"Bailey?" Harper called out. Aside from a slight echo from his own voice, the calm sparked curious suspicion that she may have already exited the premises. But as he made his way toward his open-plan kitchen with the cardboard tray of cooling lavender lattes, he could hear the TV on in the bedroom and the faint sound of a buzzing motor coming from inside.

"Hiiiiii!" Bailey's voice caroused through the hall in response. *Damn.* Harper thought. *She's still here.* And then instantly, he felt bad about his disappointment. "I'll be right out!" she sang happily.

"All right." Harper made an effort to sound cheerful as he put the lattes down in the still intact kitchen and clocked the time: 9:17 a.m. Time to get this day started; the clock was ticking and a week could pass quickly. Sometimes his best ideas were slow to arrive. He picked up the closest cup and took a sip, appreciating the view of the East River glistening through his living room window. *Relax, Harper, take a breath. Be a good host.* "I got you a latte," he called out.

"Awww. So sweet . . ." Bailey was laying it on thick. And then, just one second later, "Juthonesecond, babe, immjuthbrushinmahteeh," she replied in a jumble of garbled words. Toothbrush talk, for sure . . . but wait. *Brushing her teeth?* Harper wondered. *With my toothbrush? Awww, hell naw.* He hadn't signed up for this. Not the debacle at the station, not the extra time away from work, and for sure not the intermingling of his toothbrush with her mouth . . . Or maybe she brought her own? Harper's thoughts on which scenario was worse were interrupted by the bedroom door opening.

"Good morning, superstar!" Bailey exclaimed.

She appeared, standing in the bedroom doorway, hair in a ponytail and body in Harper's favorite Westmore University T-shirt. Faded and stretched, it had a neckline that hung low, exposing her naked shoulder. The rest draped to only barely cover the remainder of her seductive hourglass shape. The outline of her nipples revealed that absolutely nothing was underneath. The undercurve of her ass peeked out from below the hem as she leaned backward to turn the light off behind her. "I watched the whole segment. And you were *brilliant,*" she purred. Bailey advanced toward him seductively until she was so close that he could smell her minty breath. With outstretched arms, she embraced him tightly against her and planted her full lips on his. Harper's own body responded despite the protest of his mind, reminding him of the two cooling lattes still on the counter—one for his work, and the other to say a polite goodbye to his present company.

Harper reached behind him to grab Bailey's cup to hand it to her. "Lavender," he said, a half-hearted attempt to keep to the earlier plan, a gracious but imminent goodbye. *But damn . . . she's fine. . . .*

"Awww, thank you, babe." Bailey looked up at him with doe eyes set in a beautiful face with a natural glow, absent any trace of makeup. *Was she planning on staying longer?* he wondered. She took the cup and sipped, closing her eyes to savor the lukewarm goodness. "Mmmm . . ." Her eyes opened again slowly to smile at him with the cup still at her lips. "You brought me a gift and I was being so careless," she said coquettishly. "I want to make it up to you."

"Ehhh, that's not necessary." Harper shrugged. "It's not that big a deal."

Bailey pressed her body closer to his. "It's a big deal to me." Her non-latte hand made its way down his side, across to his cashmere clad stomach, and reached the crease of his leg and his pelvis. "Very big," she said. *Oh boy.* Harper's head was gearing up for a day setting descriptions, character motivations, and three act structures. Harper's manhood, however, immediately rose to the occasion with a rigid betrayal of his work ethic. He shook his head; this was not how things were supposed to go.

"Bailey . . ." he began in protest.

"There's my friend," she said reaching her hand down farther. "Mmmm . . . hmmm . . ." she said into his neck. The heat from her breath was arousing. Her hand had reached the front of his pants, rubbing across the zipper, with pressure and warmth that started to stiffen him into a protrusion pushing back against her palm.

After a hard swallow, his voice came in a whisper into her hair. "You don't have to do this," he managed to say.

Bailey pulled back and met Harper's eyes with her own in a gaze of long eyelashes and full-throttled temptation. "Oh, I know," she said. "I want to." Her hand had already managed to snake past his waistband and belt, and into his zipper, where her fingers firmly wrapped around his developing wood. She smiled at him mischievously before seamlessly lowering herself down before him in a nimble squat. She set the latte cup fully aside and with both hands undid his belt buckle, unbuttoned his slacks, and slowly slid the expensive fabric down his strong legs and thighs.

"Oh, we're doing this?" Harper made a half-hearted playful protest.

"Don't worry, I'll take excellent care of him," Bailey spoke into Harper's midsection. Her balance was impressive—with knees bent with her heels squarely on the ground, she brought her hands up to Harper's waist. *Damn, Pilates does that?* Harper thought. *And I was a dancer,* she reminded him often. She pulled down the waistband of his boxer briefs, releasing his penis to spring toward her chin. Exposed and sensitive, Harper felt the slightly cool breeze of the room's air flow across his bare crotch and looked down to examine the top of Bailey's head while she got reacquainted with "her friend."

"Hi, buddy. You miss me?" Bailey murmured softly, just before enveloping him fully into her mouth. The reception felt like an overwhelming rush—inviting, warm, and wet.

"Mmmm," he moaned.

"Mmmm," she moaned back. A call and response began between them, exchanged between both sides of pleasure.

Harper could not resist the vigor and enthusiasm Bailey always brought to embracing him in this way. She treated it like a craft she was eager to perfect. That sense of desire for him she conveyed was just as intoxicating as the act itself. Her purposeful eye contact made it clear she enjoyed it.

Pleasure started to build in Harper's body at Bailey's insistent rhythm. She was taking it seriously. Now he was too. He bent down toward her nipples to caress them with his fingertips. He was getting close now, very close, and this wasn't how he wanted his release to happen, even though his body was yielding to the urge. Already his hips started to move along with her back and forth in rhythm. She looked up at him with mischievous determination. She knew she was in control of him, his time, his desire. And that shit was *hot.* This was life, his life, after divorce, being single—a life well-earned. An intense hunger tingled its way through his entire body, a crackling energy building up, so tense his muscles began to twitch. He needed her naked.

Harper gently undid her ponytail and then moved his hands to her shoulders, grabbing the fabric of the T-shirt she was draped in. He tugged it up, springing her arms skyward. Miraculously, she still held him in her mouth until the very last moment, shirt completely inverted above her head. She finally released him from her mouth's warmth and the shirt fell to the floor. Her hair cascaded down over her seductive eyes and lightly parted lips.

"Come here." He guided her up toward his mouth and she

raised her now fully naked body to stand in front of him. Her backside's reflection in the mirror and her full-on frontal nudity was giving a complete boyhood fantasy. Harper pulled her close and kissed her. She pushed her lips onto his and opened them, this time to receive his tongue and join her mouth with his in exploration. His hands rose to her chest as he took her full breast in his mouth to tease her nipple, entirely devouring her areola.

"Mmmmmm," she moaned. "Yesss, Harper." Encouraged, he rubbed her other breast. It felt firm and heavy in his hand as he squeezed the soft flesh in deep massage. Bailey was less in control now, more in rapture. He loved hearing pleasure in her voice. He could see it in her face as her eyes opened, looking down at him suckling her, kneading her breast with his hand. And just then, her face registered something more, a furrowed brow, a naughty and lustful look. "I'm so sorry I stressed you out today," she said in a sweet voice. "I'm such a bad girl. . . ."

*Mmmm. I kind of like bad girls.* He was down for the role-play.

"You are. . . ." Harper growled back. And in proper bad-girl fashion, as he continued his work of sucking, licking, and caressing her body, he freed one hand to move to her round soft ass and to caress between her legs, surprised at how slick the area already was. *So, she really does enjoy giving head.*

"Mmmm, yes, baby . . ." she moaned as Harper rubbed her opening, taking his fingers up to her mouth. She played along, sucking his fingers sensuously, rearing her head back, closing her eyes as if she was tasting something delicious. Her confidence and adventurousness stimulated all his senses and his creativity. He explored inside her, enjoying the muscular walls that seemed to contract around him, while observing the effects of his efforts in the full-length mirror. Her ample backside sexily gyrated to the movement of Harper's keyboard fingers. "Yes, baby. Yes. Right there . . ." she instructed breathily. Harper kept up consistent work in the front, but used his other hand to squeeze her backside and cover it with caresses. "Oooh, Daddy, you gonna make me come with all of that." *Oh yeah?* Harper swiped her left buttock in a swift, firm upward motion with an audible smack. It lifted in the reflection and landed with a bounce.

"What'd you say?" Harper was ready for more role-play.

Evidently, Bailey was too. "I said you're gonna make me come . . ." she repeated huskily. *Whap!* The sound rang through the air as Harper slapped her cheek again and continued the play of his fingers inside her.

"I don't know if you deserve to come," he chastised. "You think you do?"

"I don't know," she whined, her voice sexy and full of yearning. "I waannnnt to. . . ."

*Whap!* The noise again filled the room from Harper's hand connecting with the tautness of her skin. "Say it again," Harper's confidence began to build.

"I wanna come . . ." she whined. And again came another firm *whap!*

"OOOH, Daddy," Bailey cried out. "Yes, punish me!" Harper's eyebrow lifted. *Oh hell yeah.* Harper grabbed the back of her hair, giving her a firm but playful tug. Her head fell back with a sexy gasp. In control, he pulled her by the waist, spinning her voluminous backside in front of him now, pirouetting her by her tresses, so they could both face the mirror.

Harper met her eyes in their reflection, giving himself over to the moment with his commands. "Now watch me hit it, naughty girl. And you *better* come."

Bailey loved it. "Oooooh, yessss," she purred. "Bad girl likes to come, baby . . ." And Harper liked what he heard. Suddenly, even "baby" sounded appropriate. She pushed herself against his torso.

"Hold tight while I grab . . ." Harper began to maneuver, but Bailey turned to pull him back, producing a condom in her hand.

"Where did—?"

Bailey turned to face him with a smile. "Bad girls stay ready, Daddy." She tore open the wrapper and proceeded to strap up her "friend."

"Are you ready?" Her eyes held his, matching the challenge of her words, even more of a turn on for Harper.

"You about to find out," he said, grabbing Bailey by the waist to spin her back into position. He liked this role. Dominant and assertive suited him. He was still hard and ready to bring out a release for both of them. It excited Harper to see her, bent over, in the reflection in the mirror. There in front of him, her ass was soft, wide, and spread against him. Her hair slid across her back and stuck to the places where the sweat had begun to gather. Harper entered her slowly through the slippery parting of her lower lips, taking his time to enjoy the sound as she let out a guttural, throaty exhale of pleasure.

"Ohhhhhhh. Yesss. Give it to me, Daddy," she said, looking at his reflection.

Harper did so, deliberately holding her hair and her waist. "Take it."

"Yesss . . ." she said as her body started to glisten.

The sound of dense skin-on-skin smacking continued, as did more bawdy talk, mirror glances, and heavy breathing. When Bailey began to verbalize her building orgasm. Harper thought, *I want to come too* . . . He was ready, too ready.

"Ohh God, yes." As Bailey rocked back against him reveling in pleasure, Harper saw their reflection in the mirror, deep in the moment. He could see the swinging of her breasts and the slapping of her perfectly toned, round, brown gloriously massive ass up against him. This was the moment of his fantasies. The kinds of fantasies he'd written about, seen in porn, and heard about back in the day when Lance would regale the crew with his own college sexcapades. But this wasn't college. Harper was a grown-ass man and she was a woman. A sexually adventurous, brown-skinned hottie who he was banging in front of a full-length mirror in the living room of a palatial DUMBO apartment with a panoramic view of his favorite city. Living the dream, everything he'd ever wanted. At least that he'd ever *thought* he wanted. But seeing it for just that one brief moment felt . . . empty. He saw it when he met his own eyes, a second's pause that lasted for an eternity of reflection. But he shook it off, quickly, in part because Bailey was not giving up her role.

"Fuck, Harper. Fuuuuuck!"

Back in the moment, Harper began to thrust himself forward.

She shut her eyes. "Feels . . . so good. I'm so close," she whispered on top of heavy breaths. Her hand slipped down to rub between her thighs. At this, Harper thought he was going to come too—the stimulation was overwhelming, but the feeling wasn't there. He kept going, more vigorously. "Ohh . . . baby . . . dick so . . . good," she pushed the words out between his strokes tapping up against her. Between the accelerating sounds of her mounting orgasm and the sporadic *whap!* of Harper's smacks to her ass, he was thankful for the soundproof walls, the expensive home, the adult shit in his life. He fantasized about the end of this, with Bailey being on her way for the day. But somehow he knew that wouldn't happen. And that's when he lost it. Completely. The feeling, that wave of arousal he'd usually ride into his release . . . was gone.

Still, he picked up the pacing—a vigorous *thwapthwapthwapthwap* against her as he felt the slickening of her insides and the quivering within her. "I'm cominggggg! I'm cominng, baby!" Bailey's body squeezed around his penis in quick releases letting him know this was true.

Harper gave a few more quick thrusts and then did something he didn't expect to do. Not part of the fantasy, but very much of the moment, of *this* moment. "Aaaagghhhh!" he exclaimed and immediately wondered if it'd been too loud. After all, he'd just faked his own orgasm.

# CHAPTER THREE

## Harper

*Damn.* In the living room, Harper stood still in disbelief as Bailey walked toward the bathroom and even after she'd closed the door behind her. At the sound of shower water, a deep sigh left his body. And that sigh, filled with the weight of confusion, was his first moment of any release. *What the fuck?* He'd been living out the fantasies of his youth, the recompense for all the times he'd been too studious or not suave enough or was left out of contributing a salacious story to entertain his boys. He could relive his fantasy as many times as his memory would recall it, but in no version of what he imagined would he . . . *pretend to come?* Something was off. Way off. Maybe it was Bailey, but she'd given her all. A rousing performance. No, it was something else. With his trousers pooled around his ankles, Harper duckwalked his way to the kitchen where he dropped the dry jim hat in the trash. As the highlight reel of his tryst danced through his mind, he shook his head at his fortune. Empty condom or not, that shit was still hot, a bachelor's dream.

*You a nasty nigga, Harp.* He imagined Quentin's voice in his head as he reached down to pull his unbuckled pants up from the floor and across his knees. He hadn't even fully removed his shirt. He'd shower later—as soon as he was alone again. It'd be a perfect way to refocus and dive back into work. Thoughts were already swirling—an overflow of ideas for the script, storylines for Kendall and Jackson, memories really, and a growing sense of general unease he acutely felt as the seconds ticked away from him for the day.

Beyond ready to get started, Harper walked over to a nearby end table and pulled out a journal, one of the various replicas of the same leather-bound notebook all around his place. His morning "brain dump" journal was in the bedroom nightstand, but he wasn't about to retrieve that one and be caught by Bailey anywhere near his bed. The journal he had in his hand, for various chicken scratch ideas, would do just fine. His brain dumps weren't ever supposed to be read, understood, or even make sense. Writing everything down allowed Harper to clear the decks and empty his head of his plethora of distracting thoughts. Get it all out, meditate, then ideate on this fucking screenplay.

He counted down—ten . . . nine . . . eight—in deep breaths with his eyes closed until he reached one, then he opened his journal's leather cover and wrote the first thing that came to mind.

Bailey in the shower . . . she wanted to apologize . . . With a hummer . . . Mmm-mmph . . .

Interview went well . . . Nate and Gayle were very cool . . .

That false alarm charge will be $$ . . . Fuck it. whatever

Stan and Cassidy said it was a good hit . . . studio meeting still happening . . .

I need more time . . . can I do this . . . ? Unfinished Business indeed . . .

So many cooks in the kitchen. Never needed that when writing a novel. Just my ideas on the page. No wonder the kitchen caught fire this morning . . . while I was on national television. Stop it . . . she's leaving soon . . . then you can dive in with the "BIG IDEA" sigh . . . WTF???

Why did I insist on writing it? This form of writing is so restrictive. The studio executives, the producers, the director, and the actors all have a say too?? ? I just wanna write . . .

Sigh. Why? Because I can't let this next movie—based on my closest friends—get out of my control . . . not this time . . .

Harper stopped writing and looked around his living room. He didn't really see the trappings of a life well-earned anymore. All he saw in his mind's eye was Murch lighting into him: "*Every time you have the opportunity to choose yourself over doing the right thing, you always choose* ***yourself***," he'd said. Or, better yet, *yelled.*

Harper never forgot Murch's words. Ones that were said when the tumult of his divorce from Robyn was at its highest. Even through the pain of ending a twenty-one-year marriage, he felt the sting of Murch's words then and still did. He'd hurt one of his best friends, a dude who loved him unconditionally. Harper readjusted his pen and recommenced writing.

No not this time. I can't let my peeps down. This project is going to be different . . . it doesn't have to hurt anyone. I have control this time.

"Are you writing state secrets?"

Harper snapped the journal shut and whipped his head around. Bailey was standing at his elbow. He hadn't heard the shower stop, or even her footsteps as she approached for that matter. He shifted to look at her. Still beautiful, wearing a matching bra and thong set. Still sexy AF. And still, he was ready for her to go.

"Yeah. State secrets . . . something like that . . ." Harper made the effort toward a good-natured chuckle.

"What are you up to today?" Bailey casually inquired while rubbing shea butter into a glow along her thigh. *I'm doing it,* Harper thought, trying to stay focused.

"Couple projects that need moving forward," he replied. In an attempt to channel genuine interest into his voice, he volleyed, "So, um, how about you? What are your plans today?"

"Well, my morning meeting just canceled. I'm actually free! You hungry? Wanna do brunch?"

"Um . . ." Just then Harper's stomach growled, loudly. *Fuck.*

With the menu in his hands, Harper examined the food selections at JAMZ in Brooklyn Heights. A Black-owned old-school diner bumping old-school hip-hop, with black-and-white photos of the Source Awards and vinyl albums with their colorful labels decorating exposed redbrick walls. Plants sat in pots on shelves and hung down from celling beams in macramé holders. It was the coolest living room you'd never get invited to and supposedly the hottest seat in the borough. But, worth a forty-five-minute wait in the middle of the week? Harper was dubious. This was just supposed to be a momentary detour to get him home by noon. *Don't all these people have someplace to be?* Evidently not. Already it was 11:45 a.m. and they hadn't even placed an order. At least Jay-Z's "Girls, Girls, Girls" was providing a meal for the ears.

"What're you thinking, babe?" Bailey looked up at him from the other side of the table. *Babe? Again. Really?* Harper squirmed. Bailey smiled. She'd put herself together well, assembling a choice selection of his clothes—a vintage *Vibe* magazine T-shirt with a faded cover image on the front. And the leather jacket draped around her shoulders that, incidentally, his ex-wife Robyn gave him for his forty-fifth birthday. Not waiting for Harper's reply, she continued with palpable enthusiasm. "The Country Breakfast has my name all over it. What about you?" Bailey had good taste in fashion. In food, perhaps not so much.

*Did we just wait fifty minutes for some scrambled eggs and bacon?* Harper had been having a hard time finding something that met his tastes on the menu. He'd lived with a gourmet chef for a wife for over a decade. So Country Breakfast was far too basic now; he'd learned to expect more. Maybe the specials would have something to offer. "I don't know yet," he said finally. "Let's see when the server comes around."

"Take your time, babe. I already told my assistant to block out my morning. I didn't want us to be rushed."

"Babe" again and the threat of leisure time prompted Harper to speak. "Babe" was like saying "I love you" prematurely, when you should be saying "I miss you" still, or how about just "goodbye"? "I have—" Harper started to just tell her he had a deadline.

"I just have to tell you guys—" A random Gen Zer stopped by the table, cutting him off. "You guys are the cutest, most stylish couple in here."

"Awwww." Bailey smiled big. Her perfectly contoured red

lips stretched open to reveal her gleaming white teeth. "That's so sweet! Thank you! Harper, you hear that?"

"Yeah, that's nice," he muttered, and then tried to recover. "Thank you. That's . . . that's very nice." Harper willed his mouth to smile again. The young Gen Zer formed a heart with her fingers and held the display like a camera pose.

"Hashtag couple goals. Enjoy, you guys." And just like that she left the restaurant with her multicultural crew of similarly clad girlfriends. Harper turned back to Bailey, who seemed to be basking in the compliment.

The girl probably wasn't wrong about how they appeared together—Harper still looked good for his age and Bailey was a confident and accomplished woman. On paper and Instagram, they couldn't be beat. But something wasn't right, and he knew it. It was more than wondering what his friends would think, although he did wonder. His reputation was the serial monogamist, all the way back to college, to high school even. He was a one-woman man, but did that translate to a dependence on always being with someone? He liked the stability, but did he like it too much? And why? Harper had analyzed these questions through thousands of dollars of post-divorce counseling and purposeful meditation—another Robyn influence. But he stopped having reasons to go. A never-ending stream of companions would make you think that all your problems were solved. At least, for a while. Plus, he'd been consistent with his own journal writing—something he'd done since undergrad. Yet, he still couldn't quite answer the question that came up so often no matter who he'd been with since Robyn. *Why don't I want to be here?*

True, *on paper* this thing with Bailey should work, but life was much more trees than paper, growing and evolving still, a forest of complication. And it all made Harper uneasy.

He smiled at her—with his mouth, but not his eyes—his lips stretched and closed. They'd eat, she'd be full, and he'd be on his way home to work, where he wanted to be. Instead, at the end of breakfast Bailey suggested another stop at a great coffee spot she knew. "It's just on the way back to your place," she said. "The barista is my girl!" *Seems reasonable,* Harper thought. It was on the way home.

At 12:48 p.m., while walking on the cobblestone streets of DUMBO, Bailey was talking, and Harper was thinking about his sequel's first draft and what about it had earned the label "existentially indulgent and tonally boring." It "lacked the fun of the original," he was told. But no matter how he tweaked the draft, he only found himself digging a deeper hole. He needed a "big idea," not some to-go coffee and now a suggested ride on the Brooklyn carousel.

"It'll be fun," Bailey promised. "Clear your mind." As Harper sipped, somehow this idea seemed like a reasonable option to jolt his creativity. So, he agreed.

At 2:17 p.m., the walk from the carousel turned into a stop for ice cream, again "on the way," and idyllic under other circumstances. Harper knew the day was wasting away, but there was something charming about catching melting chocolate with his mouth until they reached the end of the park at 2:48. Something in him liked being with Bailey, but that thing was fading quickly. He tried to satisfy her whims, to enjoy her easygoing excuses to procrastinate, but it was wasting time. The distraction didn't help—his ideas weren't flowing.

At 4:35 p.m., they still hadn't made it back to Harper's. By then his mind was a mess of thinking, of swirling deadline worries mixed with disjointed ideas. Still "on the way back," they passed a cookware store and stopped to taste a demo that ended in Bailey offering to cook dinner, if they just popped into the specialty grocery at the end of the block. Harper wondered how so very much could be packed in under Brooklyn's iconic bridges. Entire worlds of experiences, distractions that he normally never noticed, preferring his usual places and tight schedules. This meandering was not part of his day's agenda and the sun setting on his best writing hours would be a failing grade on the day's productivity. By now, one thing was clear: the excursions weren't helping at all, and he had to make a choice.

"So . . ." Bailey cajoled, "I could make some of that tagliatelle . . . and you could make . . ." Harper yawned. "Oh. Am I keeping you up?" Bailey chuckled but seemed a bit taken aback. Her hand froze mid-caress on the side of his face.

"Nah, just . . . I *did* wake up early. And girl, you kinda wore me out today. *And* last night." Harper's charm was down to fumes.

"Plenty more where that came from." Bailey offered a smile. He didn't smile back. "Maybe you need a nap . . ." Bailey smiled coyly. "I wouldn't mind that . . ." She brought her body closer to his, lining herself up against his torso. He felt himself getting excited (again). *Damn.* The temptation began to snake its way through his body, but his mind was already on overdrive. It was time to go to work. In the middle of the pasta aisle, surrounded by bags of dried noodles, Harper managed to put some air between him and Bailey.

"Hey, look . . . dinner sounds amazing, but I'm sorry, I have a deadline." There he said it, "deadline." He had a deadline.

"Oh?" For a second Bailey paused, like she was hurt, or concerned, or puzzled. And then she seemed to shake it off just as quickly. The smile returned to her face. "Oh, I get it, you need to get work done. Of course . . . I will totally be quiet. And whip this up with some vodka sauce, fresh parmesan, or maybe some fresh ricotta . . ." With every offer, Harper became more anxious. "Plus, I want to see your process. I want to get to know you, Harper—how you work, produce your bestsellers. But I won't intrude. I'll work with headphones on and let you do your thing. And *then* . . . you can do your thing on me . . ."

*That's it, Harp. She doesn't get it.* He had to make it plain.

"Bailey—No, I'm sorry. I need . . . I have to be alone right now. I mean, I need to work alone. That's my process. And I have a deadline." Harper finally said something with certainty and conviction. And Bailey became silent with a blank stare. She bowed her head introspectively and incredulously. It was like the entire shape of her head morphed into someone he barely recognized. *Oh shit, I done did it now.* And braced himself. This was going to be awkward. *She mad.*

"Oh, you have a *deadline,*" Bailey said, as if the word were not in English. "Why didn't you just say *that*? Look, Harper, don't worry. I'm a big girl, not some fragile delicate flower. It's okay. So cut the bullshit." Bailey put the full basket of grocery items on the floor in between them. *Fuck.* Momentarily, Harper deflated. Bailey turned on her heel and marched down the aisle toward the sliding glass entrance.

"It's—it's not like that . . ." Harper stammered to an entire audience of silent jars of tomato sauce. He was alone in the grocery aisle. At the front of the store, Bailey was briskly approaching the door. With that much intention behind her strides, she wasn't just walking out of the store. If he moved quickly though, he could catch up. Harper decided to take off after her. Maybe this could be smoothed over?

By the time he caught up to Bailey outside, she was already halfway down the block with her phone whipped out, typing intently as she stomped down the sidewalk. "Bailey!" Harper called after her, half out of breath. *Damn, she's moving fast,* he thought. *Where was that urgency earlier?* "Listen, let me call you an Uber Black car, okay? We can maybe link later . . . ?"

"I'm calling my own car, Harper. Thank you." She replied with attitude. "And no, I'm going home . . . to *stay.*"

"Are you sure . . . ?"

"UMMMM, YEAH. You just said you needed to be alone. The fuck?" By now she'd stopped and whipped around to face him.

*She's definitely mad-mad,* Harper thought. He hated drama.

"Two minutes away," Bailey said definitively, slipping her phone back into her bag.

"Look, I'll wait with you."

"Oh, thaaaanks," Bailey's tone dripped with sarcasm. "Don't bother." She wrestled Robyn's birthday jacket from her body and shoved it into Harper's torso. Harper took it reluctantly.

"You're sure you don't want to wear it until your ride comes . . . It's kind of cold . . ."

"You know what, Harper?" Bailey began. "You really need to grow up. You're a brilliant writer but you're full of shit and you *suck* as a human being." Harper had expected some nasty retort, so he was going to take it. "You suck as a man. No wonder you're divorced. Fucking selfish prick," she spit.

"Listen, I'm sorry. I should have been up front—"

"Yeah, you should've. Not just with me, but with anyone else you're sharing your fake orgasms with." *Whoa. What?* "Yeah, I could tell. What fucking man does that? Who *are* you?" Passersby were tuned in to their lovers' quarrel and Harper didn't like the visual of two Black folks—no matter how stylish and sexy—having a public spat. No longer #couplegoals.

"Hey, Bailey, can we not do this here?" Harper attempted to evenly intervene, but she was on a roll.

"You should just come to terms with who you are." Bailey stepped in close for emphasis. "A middle-aged *fuck boy.*" Harper was frozen and dumbfounded. He forced himself to close his mouth and swallow that one. *Wow.* "A middle-aged fuck boy who doesn't even really wanna fuck. Where do they *make* you?"

Though it was rhetorical, the intensity of her stare and the tone of her voice demanded an answer. Harper didn't have one. *Fuck boy.* That stung, but was it accurate? Harper didn't know, but he didn't like the way it sounded. She meant that shit. Harper began to open his mouth to articulate something, but she said what she said, raised her hand as if to say *Don't say shit else,* rolled her eyes, and walked down the block.

*Damn, I really liked that T-shirt.* Harper watched her switch away. Even pissed off she was still sexy AF. But *fuck boy?* That one was hard to come back from. *It was likely over anyway,* he thought . . . *just like the others.*

# CHAPTER FOUR

## Harper

Details for Tomorrow Night Fellas . . .

It was 7:30 p.m. by the time the text came in from Murch about Candace's birthday dinner. Harper had been home for only an hour and a half—which meant just twenty minutes of decent writing. The argument with Bailey had thrown him off. He'd been hiding his truth all day while she told hers right there on the sidewalk. *But, fuck boy? Really?* He filled out more of his usual daily journal pages, picking up where he left off when Bailey materialized from the shower. *I knew it was a bad idea to let her sleep over,* he wrote.

> I never sleep well with someone new in my bed. It's unsettling and I don't know why. Maybe because I'm worried they'll post up and never leave. Looks like my concerns weren't that far off today . . . Bailey isn't "new" but she's not Robyn . . . no one is Robyn. We always slept well together. Even before we were married. breathing patterns, rhythms . . . funny how that works . . .

It had been a mistake to let things linger all day with Bailey, and it would have been a mistake to try to fit another square peg into the round hole of his life. Now he faced another life event with the entire crew—alone. Candace's fiftieth birthday dinner would be sure to draw them out in loving pairs: Murch and Candace, Shelby and Quentin, Lance and Jasmine. Harper didn't like being an appendage on a symmetrical gathering. Work would be as good of an excuse as any to sit this one out.

Harper's fingers hovered over the screen of his phone as he watched the text conversation unfold before him. Eventually, he'd be expected to chime in. But the reply in his mind wasn't likely to be the one the others were expecting of him.

The text from Quentin appeared next.

Shelby's been buggin' me about it all week. We'll be there.

Then Lance.

You know it. Me and Jas will be there!

Lance and his Caribbean Queen, Jasmine, married and happy. Since tragically losing the love of his life, Mia Morgan, to cancer a dozen years prior, Lance had recovered from tragedy and found a new mate, a great partner and someone the entire crew respected.

And, as Harper expected, less than a minute later came the text from Murch.

Harp??

*Damn.* It was almost as if they knew his exact stance, phone in hand, fingers hovering, ready to deliver an expertly crafted excuse. After all, Candace had always been closest to Robyn.

Sure, she was part of the crew and Murch's wife, but what did Harper know about Candace, really? What was it for him to be there, without Robyn, and in the middle of an important deadline? Plus, where were they going? Tatiana? That place wasn't cheap. If Murch was footing the bill he could save a few dollars by taking Harper off the list.

Harper began to type, carefully considering each word. I will. No, he deleted "will." I intend to be there. Harper hit send.

Awww shit, Harp is trying to jump ship. Lance's reply appeared immediately.

Then Quentin's. Yeah nigga, come up for air. You been swimming in that ass for a minute.

Um, fellas, I'm in the car with Candace, Murch wrote.

*Damn, now she's seen my reply.* Already, things weren't as simple as he would have preferred.

Man, detach from the car! Get off the Bluetooth, Quentin replied. Moments later Murch responded.

Fine, I'm off. Harper, Candace says she
wants to see you.

Harper had a good reason to hang back, to pass on the festivities. Especially since things had gone so far left earlier. Would Bailey have been his date? Probably not. He'd tried before to introduce new "friends" to his old ones. None of that worked. It was like an incongruous note in the right song. Maybe they all had too much history together. But Lance *had* found Jasmine. So there was reason to hope, but reality hadn't been particularly kind.

Today didn't go so well. Harper decided to reply. He wouldn't make an excuse so much as he would just be transparent. The fellas would get it.

Great night, bad morning with Bailey. A brotha's got a deadline. I tried to be nice and do brunch, but that turned into a walking tour of Brooklyn. And when I tried to head back to the crib to hit this work shit, she got pissed.

Harper hesitated. Then he spelled out the rest because these were his boys, and good or bad, it was true.

So she called me a fuck boy and bounced.

Dots appeared immediately; replies were about to fly in.

LOL!! came from Quentin. And then, Aye joe, if I was you, I'd be that.

Murch wrote, "Fuck boy." It's ironic how women were slut-shamed and now this is our scarlet letter. I'm sorry, Harp. But Fuck Boy or not, we still want to see you tomorrow night.

Lance added: Yeah, fuck-boi! Come on out! LOL!!

As Harper smiled and shook his head, contemplating the text and how to respond, Quentin's face appeared on the full screen, an incoming call. He answered.

"What's with this 'intend to be there' bullshit, man?" Quentin came into view, poised against black leather cushioning, appearing to jostle gently in the back seat of a chauffeured car in the city. "These times are sacred. We don't know how many days we're gonna get. You gotta mark these milestones, joe." Even since their high school time together, Q was always a voice of conscience, of reason. He wasn't about to let Harper get away with some weak excuse to bail on a chance for fellowship with the crew.

Harper knew Quentin was correct. He'd made a bad choice earlier, not setting a firmer boundary with Bailey. He didn't know how to keep it casual. It was never *just sex,* even when it should have been. So now when he should be there for his friends, he'd blown his schedule. Even if Candace wasn't so much *his* friend, her milestone birthday meant that all his friends would be gathered in one place, an important convergence of schedules, priorities, and other obligations that far too often kept them apart. There was plenty of reason to be there, of this Harper was sure.

"I know, Q," Harper admitted. "I really do have this deadline, though . . . and plus what do I look like being a third wheel? I should probably just sit this one out."

"Nigga, you'd be a seventh wheel, but who cares? Stop with the excuses, Harp. When have you ever *not* gotten your work done? Call homegirl, invite her to come with you . . ." Quentin said.

Harper scoffed. "I don't think that's gonna happen—"

"Look . . ." Quentin continued, "Call her up, invite her tonight. She'll take it like an apology. Sometimes you just gotta fall on the sword. Plus, we're used to you bringing a sidepiece. We already takin' bets on how the wives are gonna react. And she can't be worse than the last one." He chuckled. Suddenly, like a shadow, Shelby's stunningly crafted face slid over Quentin's and into Harper's view.

"Nope. No random bitches, Harper!" She looked at him with wide eyes, all long lashes and eyeliner, waiting for his confirmation.

He had to laugh. "Hi to you too, Shelby." Harper greeted her with a good-natured smile. Clearly, she'd been sitting next to Quentin in the car, listening the whole time. "Thanks for the heads up, Q." Harper could hear him snickering behind Shelby's head before she slid back out of view.

"Hey, I don't keep no secrets from my wife. . . ." His look in the direction of Shelby's seat made it clear who that comment was for. Harper shook his head while Quentin slid over for an audible kiss. *These two . . . not in a million years did I imagine this was possible,* Harper reflected. Quentin and Shelby once *hated* each other. Like feral animals. And now they played, laughed, and joked like they had always been made for one another. With the ease that he'd only known once for himself . . . with Jordan.

"Okay, I'll be there. Tomorrow night. No random *acquaintances,* Shelby," Harper confirmed.

"Excellent. See you there!" Shelby said.

"Later, joe," Quentin added before he hung up. At the end of the call, Harper set his timer. Ninety minutes, no distractions, no email, no internet, no porn. It would be just him and his words, writing in one of the leather journals, or even his voice recorder would suffice. In times like these, a good idea was nothing to waste. And the time was right, at the end of the day, with the sun setting, ducking down below the Manhattan skyline just beyond his wraparound balcony. Stepping outside, he took a deep breath of the crisp air that lingers in March. Spring was being elusive thus far. Hence the rut in which he found himself. The seasonal transition, the reinvigoration of coming change, was energy he thrived off of, but it was in a holding pattern.

Back inside, after finding his thinking chair, Harper sat with his journal folded in his lap and willed the ideas to come. He set a guided meditation to play, and the soothing voice immediately filled the room.

"Let's take a full inhale for five counts."

*Yes, inhale.*

"And exhale for five . . ." Harper released the air in his lungs and tried again to focus. But instead of new ideas, he kept thinking of old ones. His mind showed him a string of images, each an example of why he'd rather be a seventh wheel at dinner the next evening, than endure another painful attempt of trying to mesh his dating companions with the crew. His day with Bailey had already been painful enough, and worse, distracting. "Fill the belly," the recorded voice continued. "Be present in this moment . . ." But again, his mind only showed him the past. With his eyes closed, a smile crossed his face. He was thinking of Jordan now. Jordan again . . . She'd think the "fuck-boy" experience was hilarious. She'd probably even agree. But she had a way of telling him about himself, of showing him the truth without the harshness of Shelby. In a way they could both laugh, but still pulling no punches. Boy did he miss her; their communication had slowed. *I'll hit her up* . . . he resolved. *But only after I knock out these ten pages.*

# CHAPTER FIVE

## Jordan

Jordan Armstrong turned to glance briefly through her own reflection and out the window of the forty-second floor of the Manhattan high-rise that she used to call her office. A very different woman was looking down now at the nine-to-five bustle on the streets below, and yet it was still invigorating. She missed the energy of the city, but the constant grind she did not miss at all. At least now that she'd developed as much of an affinity for her feet touching sand as she used to feel for a pair of killer stilettos. Two nights ago, she'd been in her spacious Malibu home, breathing the salt air of the ocean. Yesterday afternoon, she'd touched down in New York expecting the mildness of spring and the turn of seasons, but outside it still looked very much like winter. Thirty-six hours in Manhattan was passing quickly, especially with a schedule crammed with meetings.

The frenetic motion of the city below reminded her of her past life as the executive vice chairman of MSNBC, a position she'd left almost three years ago. The constant stimulation, the on-the-go energy, for the first part of her career at least, had been the fuel that she thrived on. Now this view wasn't as satisfying, even perched on the top of the world. She loved the life she'd created in Malibu, doing things at her leisure—self-care for sure, plus her unbeatable view of the Pacific. This trip was just a quick detour, a necessary one to set the wheels of her next chapter in motion.

"Ms. Armstrong, we have the podium and microphone all set for you." A soft voice behind her brought her back into the room. Jordan turned and smiled, instinctually smoothing her already immaculate beach waves into proper place along the shoulders of her power suit.

"Great, let's go." She stood and followed her wrangler down the hall as the young woman continued to contort herself trying to walk and talk at Jordan's pace.

"Thank you again for agreeing to speak to the ladies," she said effusively. "We couldn't waste an opportunity knowing you'd be in town. I mean, when we sent the email to the junior staff, that you'd be coming, we had a flood of responses. I hope you don't mind, but there were a few ladies who agreed to stand in the back just to be in the room."

"It's not a problem," Jordan said. She wanted as many junior staff to attend as possible. She meant to bring her best here, her full attention. As hard as she had to work for where she'd gotten, it was important to give back, especially in rooms like the one she was entering, filled with the eager faces of young women of color just starting their careers, full of energy and ambition like she was.

Jordan pushed back a single tendril of hair from her immaculately set face, flawlessly finished, with red lips for both power and presence. Now reset into a perfect middle part, the cascading waves of ebony satin showcased her face like open draperies. It was important to look good and feel better. Her power suit fit perfectly, her blazer opened just so. *Yes,* she thought, *these girls should see and hear from me.*

The door opened to a completely full meeting room, and Jordan let herself be guided to a podium that seemed far too formal to be just "stopping by for a quick lunch with the interns and juniors" between the pitch meetings she'd set for her new show concept. When she stepped to the podium and looked out at the dozens of sets of blinking eyes staring back at her from mostly brown faces, she felt overwhelmed with everything she wanted to say. How she wished to tell these women, so young still, that success goes hand in hand with regret. Already they were so willing to give so much of themselves to a corporation and an industry that would never so much as thank them and would happily let them give their all until there was nothing left. She wanted to tell them to take care of themselves. To tell them to say no instead of just thinking it. To set boundaries and take weekends, to make self-care actually mean something, and to never lose sight of their friendships and relationships that matter (especially that part). But that last bit would be slightly ironic, because Jordan was in town for work, and not a single one of her friends knew. Not even Shelby, not Harper, not even her godchildren.

Hands in front of her, placing one on each side of the lectern, Jordan cleared her throat before leaning forward into the microphone. All the talking in the room had stopped. It wasn't even clear she needed a mic. The way these girls leaned forward, Jordan could have whispered and they still would have picked up her every word. This is how her afternoon meetings needed to go. All eyes on her, listening and nodding around the conference room table to her pitch of her own show. Especially Evelyn, who she'd met in a room just like this, ten years ago. Evelyn, who she'd helped climb the ladder into the positions that made up the executive levels of her own career. It was Evelyn now who had the power to listen, to decide, to green-light. And it was Jordan who finally had something of her own.

"Ladies," she began. "I started my career in positions like those that many of you hold now. I answered calls, set schedules, hoped that maybe just a few of my suggestions would make it to air. And then I earned my boss's job, and then my boss's boss, and finally when I was *the* boss, when I'd made it to the top of everything I dreamed of, you know what was waiting for me there?" Jordan paused, catching the eye of some of the girls so eager, they sat suspended at the edge of their seats with bated breath, waiting. She wanted to make sure they heard her, especially the young Black women present. "What was waiting for me was even more . . . more hours, more pressure, more expectations. And the life I'd set up to meet those demands wasn't serving me. So, I took a new position. I become the CEO of my own life, a role I should have held from the start. One that you should hold for your own life. Maybe this is your dream job, but it should be part of a much bigger picture. Ask yourself, how is it serving you? In this room today, you are the greatest natural resource that this country will ever produce. And you need to act like it. To treat yourself like it. That's how I see you and that's how you need to see yourselves."

Jordan had more to say, but as she took a breath to continue, the room broke out into applause. And she looked out again at those brown faces, young women in whom she could see herself. She hoped they heard her and that some of them would wake up and take the advice she wished she'd been given. But anyway, that's what her next meeting was for. She'd make them hear her, just next time with a much bigger microphone.

"Success doesn't mean just being successful." An hour after the lunch with interns, Jordan sat in the conference room four floors higher, presenting the well-considered opening lines of her show pitch. She was seated across from Evelyn Castro, EVP of programming and three less senior executives. Beyond her role at the network, Evelyn had been Jordan's friend for years. Just a few years behind her, Evelyn had followed Jordan up the corporate ladder, and Jordan had certainly reached back to help her climb, making it nice to see her in the decision-maker's seat. This was supposed to be a low-pressure, familiar setting, but as confident as she felt, she loved this idea enough to still harbor a bit of nerves. She wanted the best for it, and for herself. Jordan had been on the buyer side for many years, wielding power, cultivating relationships, smiling, power hugging, and giving firm handshakes. Her hard work had taken her to the mountaintop, a huge accomplishment that she was proud of herself for. But still, she didn't miss this room one bit. In front of yet another audience, her sixth of the day.

Jordan let the words of her show pitch float through the room and settle upon the executives seated around the conference room table. She was ready to place her concept—wellness for Black women. She wanted to get specific, relevant, and meaningful because by now, she realized that if you're talking to everyone, you're speaking to no one. She would center Black women with intention and address all aspects of wellness that were too often overlooked while they (and she) "got the job done." Her own exit from MSNBC was well-chronicled. And she'd set the record straight for those young women earlier today, just as she had for those who'd known her professionally in the years prior—Jordan Armstrong was no quitter. Why the exit? That type of grind wasn't her anymore. She'd needed a change, made one, and it had worked for her.

Now she was on a mission to help other Black women begin their own wellness journey. Her pitch deck was flawless and her sizzle reel looked like a movie trailer. The scene had been set, and she was in the presenter's seat now, all business. Evelyn, her contemporary, was at the head of the table, in the decider's seat. This would be her ace in the hole. Everyone in the room knew that they were friends, that Jordan had even mentored Evelyn through the ranks, but they had no idea of the strength of the relationship, one that Jordan was counting on to make this last meeting her best.

*Success doesn't mean just being successful. . . .* She surveyed each person's face in a split second, gauging if they were following along and nodding. She'd said something profound, the payoff of what she'd learned after a very costly sacrifice and perhaps equally expensive therapy sessions. Now it was time to take what she had learned and do with it what she did best. Turn it into a smash hit, Emmy Award–winning broadcast show.

"I see," Evelyn said, uncrossing her arms and settling into the cushions of her executive swivel chair. "Very intriguing. Can you expound, Jordan?"

Jordan looked to the other faces, seeing some nods to her left and to her right. She understood Evelyn's directive; make *them* understand.

"Of course." Jordan made it a point to make and keep eye contact as she slowly turned to look around the table, bringing everyone along with her, fully in control. Satisfied that she'd taken all the air in the room, she continued. "We are at an inflection point in corporate and career culture. People are unplugging, adjusting, taking inventory. COVID was a wake-up call. We've had years of political instability and an insurrection. And now the reelection of a divisive and polarizing figure in our nation's highest office. Who bears the brunt of that divisiveness? You know who. After generations of striving for a corner office, it's become absolutely clear there is something to pay attention to outside of boardrooms like these. And *urgently,* with more at stake now than ever, that *something* is the rest of our lives. Women, and in particular *Black women,* are no longer willing to show up just to pay the price of success and expect nothing in return. They want . . . no . . . they *expect* more." *I do too,* Jordan thought, and took a breath to reset herself. She felt this so deeply it was easy to get worked up about it, to have her passion bleed through and have it mistaken for anger. There was always such a thin line between a Black woman's enthusiasm and some kind of misinterpretation. So she was being professional, deliberate with each syllable, each pause, each turn of her head, each set of eyes that she met. This was her sixth meeting of the day, and intentionally so, making her pitch well-rehearsed by now. It had been repeated all day long in rooms just like these, full of suits and cynicism. But this one was different. She'd saved the best for last. She had good connections with all the executives in the room and her reputation was still stellar. But having Evelyn in this room, with real power now, was worthy of her best performance and she was happy for the questions. Evelyn for sure would get it.

Jordan wound up for the big reveal. "It's time now, for wellness to go mainstream. Black women are ready for a show that centers all aspects of wellness—physical, mental, spiritual, and environmental. The host for this show will bring in guests each week for a panel-style discussion to center the latest developments and discoveries of interest on the topic of health." In her career, Jordan had already heard more pitches than she'd ever be able to remember. Today, she was ready for anything. Each question that even *might* be asked as a follow-up she already held in her mind. *Who's this show for?* She didn't even need to think about that answer.

"This show is for Black women, particularly now—feeling

betrayed and let down, tired of shouldering the burden of everyone else's work, who are thinking about the changes they need to make," she added. Jordan knew this woman, these women, well. This woman was her. She'd walked away at the pinnacle of her career. She'd made a choice and the choice was for a change, a different life, one with herself at the center, where she could enjoy the fruits of her work.

Fully in her flow, she concluded. "This network's core business is to sell access to consumer buying power. In order to do that, you do need forward-leaning programming that addresses the needs and interests of key viewer demographics. And the wellness economy is the largest sector in the world, led by the United States. That's a $1.8 trillion market. So people are getting the message—success can't be enjoyed if you've compromised your health. Yet Black women are still dying to succeed. Yes, we're killing it. And it's killing us. We're the growth sector within the growth sector."

Jordan winced slightly at her use of the personal words "we" and "us." She hadn't meant to bring it so close to home. This pitch wasn't personal. It was about the right thing to do right now, a business opportunity for an audience of millions, not a vanity project.

She surveyed the faces around the room. They looked interested, intrigued perhaps, but not as excited as she expected. They were processing. Evelyn was the big boss in the room, so the junior execs wouldn't say anything until she'd said her piece. But for an extended while, she was quiet.

After a moment, just before Jordan started to ask for questions, Evelyn started to speak.

"Thanks so much for this, Jordan," she said. "As I'm sure you know, we're focused more so on news and covering measurable developments relevant to our viewer. This seems like we'd be doing something outside of our core competence. A new format, a new approach, and a topic that's interesting, but still niche, as it would target just a portion of our audience. Who do you envision as the host?" Evelyn asked her follow-up, leaning forward toward Jordan against the table, an indication of the importance of the question.

*The host?* They'd just hire a host, of course, like they'd hired so many hosts of so many shows before. It wasn't about the host; it was about the concept. One five-hour flight, three hours of sleep, and six meetings in, six times that she'd done this pitch, this was the first moment that it occurred to Jordan that things wouldn't be as easy as she thought they'd be.

"The host?" Jordan repeated. There were so many other much more important questions they should be asking, like who would be prime advertisers, and how would they penetrate their core audience demographic targets. Questions they'd ask, if they were interested. Was Evelyn just throwing her a line? Was she drowning? Was this a prelude to no? But, unfazed, she listed a litany of well-known camera-facing personalities. Anyone would be glad to helm a Jordan Armstrong show. She'd generated hundreds of millions of dollars over the course of her career in advertising revenue, maybe even hit a billion.

"Hmmm . . ." Strangely, Evelyn seemed far less than satisfied with the answer. While "hmmm" wasn't a proper word, it was as much of a response as any, and Jordan knew it. Something about her pitch was unconvincing and Evelyn was trying to convey that to Jordan—she hadn't sold the room. They were humoring her, according her the respect her long career and experience had earned her. This wasn't what she'd come for. She wanted them to recognize the value in the concept she'd brought forth, and more important, the value in addressing the audience this concept was for.

Jordan leaned down and placed her fingertips on the table in front of her. She had no hesitation to meet each one of the executives straight in the eye, Evelyn too. Nobody was going to bullshit her in a meeting. Not like this. She'd been here too many times, charged with the same kind of decision-making. She'd brought them a great idea, but if they didn't get it, then they didn't get it.

"How about you tell me what you're thinking," Jordan said, looking straight at Evelyn now.

Evelyn shifted, looking much less comfortable than she had earlier. She cleared her throat and then seemed to find her grounding. "Well, Jordan, what I think we need to do is circle up on this on our end to discuss and—"

"Ev, let's not do this." Jordan cut Evelyn off quickly. She knew where it was headed. She'd been in five meetings prior and the responses had been similar. Tepid. Perfunctory. Any warmth in the room was for Jordan herself, but not for her pitch. It was already obvious that was the case here too. "Listen, if you like the pitch," Jordan continued, "then say so. And if you don't like it, then say that too. If you're going to pass on this, then I'd like to hear that now, in the room. Let's not waste each other's time. You can be straightforward with me."

Tension thickened the air in the room. Jordan could feel it herself but made no sign to show it. She wanted them to know that she meant business and didn't need to be babied. She'd been on the other side of that table. Even held the position of each person who sat across from her. Hell, she'd even been the executive that these executives would need to seek approval from if they *did* decide they were interested. Evelyn looked unsure, and the others shifted uncomfortably. Surely they hadn't expected confrontation, and maybe thought that she, like everyone else they saw daily, would simply accept their soft-balled rejection and slink out of the room just glad to have had an audience. But she was Jordan *Motherfucking* Armstrong, and that wasn't what time it was. So, she decided to turn up the heat.

"I've given you all the reasons for why this show and why now. You know me and you know my reputation. So I can't imagine what your hesitation could be. Or, actually, I can. You're probably thinking, *Is there a market for this?* And let me answer that question for you *again,* in numbers. Black women are the rocket fuel driving the growth of a $1.8 trillion power base of Black consumer spending. Our hair alone makes billionaires. We aren't just an economy, we are the economy, the fastest growing segment of entrepreneurs, degree holders, and the biggest opportunity this country has to increase its GDP, and that's according to Goldman Sachs."

Jordan was getting her wind now, but Evelyn cleared her throat and spoke up. Haltingly, she said, "Um . . . Jordan, it's not about the numbers. To be frank, and I think I can speak for all of us on the network side . . ." Evelyn turned to her left and to her right, indicating her own power in the room, and then continued, "What you haven't told us is why should we *care*? Why will our viewer care?"

Jordan's voice caught in her throat. On the one hand, it was the most substantive feedback she'd received all day. On the other, it was a swift jab to the gut that she hadn't expected. A weakness in her armor for sure. *Care? Why should they care?* If this had come from the white male executive, she would have gone off twenty ways from Sunday. They would be peeling him off the conference room paneling for weeks to come. *What? You don't care about Black women? The saviors of democracy? The keepers of culture? The purveyors of style, the titans of industry, the champions of education? The hardest-working, baddest bitches to have ever had to hold a country up by their carefully manicured fingertips? You ought to give ALL the FUCKS,* she thought. But across from her, the person speaking wasn't a white person; it was *Evelyn,* someone she'd mentored and helped put in position, a sistah who was smart as fuck. *Okay, Ev, I see you, you're speaking for them.* Jordan took a sharp breath in through her nose. She straightened her shoulders and made sure the waves of her hair were cascading as they should across the shoulders of her tailored blazer. And then she chose her response.

"You know what? Since the answer to that question isn't already crystal clear, I understand that this is not the right home for this project. But thank you for the time today."

Jordan stood and began to gather her personal items. She slid her tablet into her Hermès bag and her phone next to it. By the time the others stood up, she was already across the room, ready to shake their hands. Jordan held Evelyn's gaze for just one beat longer than she usually would before continuing. "It was *fantastic* to see you all again."

She delivered her cordial goodbyes, with special effort, and with that, Jordan *Motherfucking* Armstrong left the building.

At least, she'd intended to, as quickly as possible. But as she pressed the elevator button down once again, she heard her name being called. She turned to see Evelyn walking as quickly as her stilettos would allow, scuttling down the carpeted hallway.

"Jordan," she called out, waving. "I'm so glad I caught you," Evelyn said, pulling her to the side. Jordan allowed herself to be led, even as the elevator door opened for the trip she would have taken down for the quickest escape. "Jordan, I didn't want you to leave thinking I'm not on your side here. I am," she said, touching her arm.

"Then what was that?" Jordan asked.

Evelyn shifted and met her eyes. "Look, I know I don't need to tell you what it's like. But it's gotten so much worse since you left. I go in to get a budget and I'm asked about social media numbers, platforms, existing audience, all kinds of things we never had to think about. But now it's all the higher-ups care about. I was just asking you to give me some ammo, Jordan, something to take up a level and make this undeniable on their terms. Give me a host, a story, something that I can tie this to. That makes it clear that if we miss this, we're missing a moment. I miss you, J. I'd love to be working with you on something like this. But just give me something I can work with?" She looked like she was pleading, sincere for sure. At least they'd gotten down to real talk and not that empty humoring that had been a waste of her afternoon.

"I got you, Ev," Jordan replied. "Let me think on it and I'll get back to you."

"It's a great idea, Jordan. If anyone can make this happen, you can."

As the two women hugged, Jordan wondered just how true that was.

Just minutes later, stuck in afternoon city traffic, Jordan sat in the back of a black Surbarban thinking back over the day. The last meeting hadn't gone as expected, which was only a minimal perturbation relative to now, however. Horns were already blaring, and she could feel the tension of her driver radiating throughout the vehicle, reaching her all the way in the back seat. A sprinkling of light rain started, creating tiny halos of fog around each drop that hit the window. Reminding herself of better weather at home, she whispered a tiny prayer of quiet thanks to be heading back to Los Angeles on the next flight out that same day.

"Don't worry, Ms. Armstrong," the driver said, turning slightly toward her while stopped on Second Avenue. "We should be in good timing for your flight." And then without waiting for her response, he went back to quietly cursing to himself at the other drivers.

Jordan eased back into the crinkling polished leather of her seat and let her eyes close, thinking back to the day's events. She'd arrived with so much excitement and a perfected pitch, ready to deliver her idea into the hands of the ideal broadcast partner. She'd come armed with the research, the stats, the well-rehearsed responses to anticipated questions. But it hadn't landed. She sighed. *This was a stupid idea, right?* What was she thinking trying to pitch a new show idea with a new format, a new concept for a decidedly Black female audience, to a mainstream network? She knew better.

Evelyn felt it would be too tough of a sell and was trying to make Jordan focus on things that were low concept but tended to create confidence for the higher-ups. A social media influencer host with five million followers. A disgraced celebrity who needed a comeback opportunity. Or another Oprah. That was how they thought: just point me in the direction of what's already working, what's been done but give me different wrapping. That wasn't this idea. *I just need to stay in my lane* . . . Jordan thought. It had been Harper who'd convinced her in the first place to try something new.

"You started leaning into your creativity with *From the Culture*," he'd said, referencing the show centering four Black women chopping it up about the news. It had been her brainchild and her idea to feature Shelby. The memory brought a smile to her face and Harper's voice floating back to her. "This is your lane," he'd said. "Lean into your creativity." That was how the idea for this show started. Yes, the original purity of it. Jordan believed in this new idea the same way she'd believed in *From the Culture.* Wellness was a long time coming. Over many conversations, Harper encouraged her, feeding into her creativity. They were bouncing ideas off each other, dreaming like the college kids they were when they met at Westmore. That's how she knew it was real—the ease, free flowing, no pressure. Maybe it was just the comfort of having Harper back in her life, even from three thousand miles away.

When she did share her dreams with him, it always seemed like they landed in fertile ground for the seeds to grow. She had the urge to call him. Being back in the Apple, it seemed like there were memories of him hidden around every corner. Like that day he was being honored at Lincoln Center for *Pieces Of Us*—one of many accolades. He looked like a man who had arrived then. Confident, wise, gracious, and . . . sexy. That had been October 2024. Just six months ago. Countless FaceTimes, texts, email, and phone conversations through the end of the year made it feel as if they had no lag time between their reconnections—despite her move to Malibu and his hermitting to write his masterwork for two years. She was proud of him. The memories made her smile. She picked up her phone. But— *But I'm not fucking with Harper like that right now,* she reminded herself, and motioned to put the phone away. But then it started ringing.

Shelby Taylor-Spivey's fabulous profile picture in all its blond splendor appeared on Jordan's screen, a video call request. Briefly, a spike of apprehension hit as she realized she'd told no one, not even Shelby, that she was doing this day of meetings in New York. Her plan was to slip into the city and slip back out before anyone knew the difference. Of course Shelby would hunt her down, her intuition on overdrive. Jordan considered not accepting the call, letting it go to voicemail, but then Shelby would call back, and again, especially if she wanted something. *Might as well pick up.* But she selected the option of voice only and left the camera off.

"Hey, Shelby," Jordan said breezily into the receiver.

"You're in town, aren't you?" Shelby levied her good-natured accusation.

*How did she know that?* Jordan wondered, swiveling her head to look out of the tinted windows and into neighboring cars.

"And before you answer that," Shelby continued, "I can hear the horns in the background. The sounds of New York traffic are like my lullaby. So, you might as well come clean and turn on the camera." Reluctantly, Jordan hit the button to activate her camera, revealing a well-coiffed Shelby in the backdrop of her airy Manhattan penthouse living room. "Um hum, I knew it," Shelby said, barely cracking a smile.

"It was just a quick trip," Jordan protested half-heartedly. "Just for a few meetings. I'm already headed back to the airport now."

Shelby's face crinkled. "You're *leaving*?! Why would you do that? Candace's fiftieth birthday dinner is tomorrow." And then, as if for emphasis, she added, "Everyone's going."

"Since when are you hyped to go to Candace's birthday?"

"First, it's not just any birthday. It's her fiftieth. And . . . we're close now. Of course we're going. And you're in town? So, you should be there too. I'm going to tell them to add one more . . ."

"Shelby, no, I have to get back." Jordan knew that this wasn't nearly enough to stop the tide.

"For what? Don't act like you have to go to work. And if you did, you can move any meeting. You're Jordan *Motherfucking* Armstrong. Tell them to turn the car around and head back uptown."

Jordan sighed. "Shelby, we're stuck in traffic, my flight is in less than two hours. I'm going back to Los Angeles."

"Nonsense. Change your flight. The city isn't the same without you. Come on, Jordan. We want to see you. Stay here at the townhouse. We just got back from Amagansett, but we still have plenty of room here." Jordan laughed a bit. *Still have plenty of room?* Shelby and Quentin's return to the city from their Hamptons palace probably did feel like downsizing. And yet, their city home had more bedrooms than Shelby could enter in a week. With just one child—who was in college—*why did they need all that space?* Jordan wondered.

Shelby continued her pitch. "We're good for excellent wine and top-tier gummies. You can't tell me you won't have a good time."

"Fine," Jordan said. Shelby was unrelenting anyway. "Let me see if I can move some things around."

"Really?" On the screen, Shelby's face looked genuinely surprised.

"Yes, I will *think* about it."

Shelby narrowed her eyes. "Hmm . . . you're lying. But *I love you* for humoring me." She trailed off with a small giggle to herself. Jordan could only smile. Shelby was a trip, always. "Seriously though, I'd really like to see you. I miss you all the way out there on the left coast. I want you here." Jordan was touched by Shelby's rare showing of vulnerability. She started to feel swayed. "And Harrrperrrr's going to be there."

Jordan snapped back to attention. "Since when do I set my schedule around Harper?" she quipped.

"Oh, you are so full of shit." Jordan could only laugh. Shelby knew her.

"Just think about it, okay? Ugh, I'm done being mushy and soft. It's making my skin sag."

"Okay, Shelby, I'm hanging up now."

"Just do think about it, though, okay? Love you! K! Bye!"

Jordan managed to hang up with only a thin commitment.

And she was thinking, just as she said she would. But she was thinking about Harper and how long it had been since they'd actually talked. *January? No, before the new year. Sooo, was that two, three months ago?* The last real conversation had been about some rando he was talking about taking to Lance's New Year's Eve party. After that, their texting had slowed to one-to-two-word responses: Hit you back, TTYL, Happy New Year, check out this article . . . Regardless, a real conversation had been a while ago. Too long. Too long to know what to expect tomorrow evening. *What if he brings another rando date?* Terrible. And then being forced to sit next to him all night, or worse, across from him with . . . whomever . . . That was something she was going to have to unpack, again, in therapy. She looked at her calendar; her next appointment with Dr. Clark was scheduled for tomorrow.

"Still headed to JFK, Ms. Armstrong?" The driver turned back slightly, awaiting her response while the traffic light overhead burned red.

# CHAPTER SIX

## Harper

On the morning of Candace's birthday dinner, Harper ran along the East River at a good clip. He'd made a fairly successful effort to shake off the drama of yesterday. It felt good to be back in his groove. This part of his life he knew how to do. The running, the writing, the café with his favorite latte. Along his usual path, this part of Brooklyn, down by the bridge, was now as cavernous as Manhattan. This entire area was built up with luxury high-rises, trendy cafés, and boutiques. Harper had the money now to live like he had made it. The area certainly said "successful artist" amid all the hipsters, young families, and yoga pants mamas.

With a much clearer mind after his three-mile run, Harper walked into a French patisserie for that pistachio latte he loved so much, another place Jordan had introduced him to. The cozy atmosphere and buttery scent of fresh baked pastries warmed Harper's senses as he blew on his hands. *Oh yeah,* he thought, *Jordan swore by the almond croissant too.* Harper beelined for a table in the back to put his hat down like other folks reserving shit. *When in Rome . . . or in this case, BK to the fullest. . . .*

This little bite would hold him over until tonight. He was looking forward to top-notch Afro-Caribbean fusion cuisine this evening. And most of all, seeing his peeps. So what that he'd be seventh wheeling it? Better that than hiding behind his work deadline and being a recluse. When he was married, Robyn would have insisted they go—she would have made it so he could be productive during the day and free to enjoy himself at the gathering. They'd ride home recapping the night's festivities, laughing about whatever wild shit Quentin said and snuggle in bed as he warmed her cold feet with his. Tonight wouldn't be like that, but he could still find a way to enjoy himself.

"Pistachio latte and almond croissant, that's my favorite," the cashier said, retrieving Harper's pastry order. "And you got the last one." She smiled. He'd seen her before, but she usually wasn't as friendly.

"Lucky me," Harper responded.

She gave an even bigger smile. "It's room temp but I could give it a little extra heat if you'd like."

"Ummm . . ." Harper hesitated even though he planned to sit, a reflex reaction to the thought of extra time in his routine. As always, work was calling.

"It's no trouble, handsome. It'll take less time than the drink," she assured him. "Go have a seat. I'll bring it to you." She was already headed to the café's toaster before Harper could agree. He decided to take the breather and returned to his seat at the window. Jordan wasn't physically there, but she'd introduced him to this place, told him what was good to order. *I miss her . . .* he admitted, looking out the window. Her imprint was here and everywhere in his life. He couldn't escape her—not that he even really wanted to. When was the last time they'd spoken? *Had it been months ago? Really?* It was hard to remember.

"Here you go." The barista slid into view, scattering his

thoughts by depositing his beverage and a delicious smelling croissant on the table in front of him.

"Oh, hey. Thank you." Harper smiled.

She smiled back at him. "'No problem." Then she gently laid a hand on his shoulder. "You doing all right today?"

"Yeah?" Harper responded, looking at her quizzically.

"You just look like you're deep in thought. Figuring out the next great masterpiece?"

"Oh. Yeah. Kinda," Harper admitted.

"We saw you on CBS yesterday. Definitely gonna pick up that Maverick Wilson thriller. Sounds intense."

"It is. You'll enjoy it," Harper replied.

"Thanks for the tip. What's on the agenda today? You have plans?"

*Oh, shit. There's that word again . . . "plans."*

"I'm . . . uh . . . yeah . . . working all day and then a gathering." He stumbled through his words. Her head-tilt and crinkled forehead in response made him clarify. "A friend's birthday dinner—for her fiftieth."

"Oh, her fiftieth? That's a big one. What're you bringing?"

*Bringing? Oh right . . . shit.*

"Right . . ." Harper had been so focused on work, he hadn't thought about bringing anything at all.

"Don't show up empty-handed," she declared with a wink and shoulder pat before sashaying behind the counter.

*What does Candace even like?* Harper pondered, sipping his latte and looking out the window at the falling drops of rain.

Seeking reinforcements, Harper sent a query text to Murch, who replied quickly with, Hey man, no worries. Just a nice bottle of wine or something. But Harper didn't want to just give something so impersonal. *What does she even like? Red? Rosé? White? Fuck.* Harper messaged Murch again. In a quickly arriving reply,

Murch only reiterated his last suggestion and emphasized that Harper simply "show up."

Julian Murchinson met his wife Candace under inauspicious circumstances. Their first encounter was at Lance's bachelor party when she gave the showstopping performance as "Candy." She and Murch just clicked. It was a meet-cute that just happened to be with her bent over in a G-string. Now that she was "Candace," that image rarely entered Harper's consciousness. She'd since become a wife, mother, PhD scholar of plant-based medicines, and legit part of the crew. Along the way, she and Robyn became close—and remained so.

"I should ask Robyn," he quietly mused aloud. "That's her girl." Robyn would know; she was always great at giving gifts to *everybody.* She had that skill. As it was Robyn's midday in Accra, he debated calling versus texting her. *She really did it, getting away from me.* She'd moved all the way to another continent, and *stayed* there. It was never easy for Harper to admit, especially when he still had a need for her in his life's day-to-day. Her need for him wasn't as obvious. She'd managed to flip her Harlem-based food subscription service into a dope little spot with the same name, Robyn's Nest, with a homey indoor-outdoor vibe perfect for Ghana's tropical climate.

Harper felt good about who he'd become, the voice of a generation that Jordan had long predicted. It's just that Robyn seemed so . . . happy. Without him. *And that's okay,* he reminded himself, even despite their contentious divorce. They were friends. *Friends help each other find gifts for other friends, right?*

Hey, his text to Robyn started. Hope you're having a good day. Candace's 50th's tonight. Need a great gift. Any suggestions? You know what I'm like when left to my own devices. Hence the text. Let me know. Harper hit send. She was probably busy for sure, but it didn't stop him from expectantly looking at his screen.

The three text bubbles popped up. *Always reliable.* The bubbles bubbled, then stopped abruptly. He quickly added: Sorry for the late notice. I'm still me. After a beat, bubbles appeared again, then again disappeared. By the time Harper finished his latte and croissant, there was still no response from Robyn. Harper was on his own.

Outside, the rain continued. *Fuck.* Harper walked swiftly down the cobblestone street on a mission to get a gift and return home as quickly as possible. He'd certainly seen enough of gift options on his impromptu walking tour the day before. *Get the gift, get it over with, go back to work . . .* he chanted to himself with deliberate footsteps, trying to outpace the rain. Certainly, he could find *something.* But gift-giving required a level of being present that Harper hadn't mastered. He began to wonder. *I observe human behavior and write about it for a living, but I don't have a personal connection to one of my closest friends' wives?* How could he find the "just right gift" for Candace if he didn't know her that well? The realization stung sharply in the moment. Harper knew he sucked at this, there was no question. He didn't even know where to start. His 'hood had everything women could want. They were always darting in and out of stores with shopping bags full of . . . everything. But what to get Candace? *I'm already showing up solo. I can't arrive empty-handed. Where's the liquor store . . . ? What would Robyn do . . . ?* She certainly wasn't replying. Harper felt like he was about to make a mistake, but wondered, even two and a half years after getting divorced, if that mistake had started long before now.

Lincoln Center. Once a Black and Puerto Rican populated area of the city, over the years it changed to house classical music, jazz and ballet performances, and most important on this night, celebrity chef Kwame Onwuachi's Black-owned Afro-fusion cuisine restaurant, Tatiana. Harper stepped out of his Uber and shifted the massive package in his hands to walk through the chilly night air across the plaza. A smiling patron held open the twelve-foot-tall glass door so he could enter. The gust of warm air from inside was a welcome contrast to the outdoor elements. From the vestibule in the dimly lit, yet super-chic eatery, the din of buzzing conversation and the driving pulse of hip-hop music, filled the space with high energy and spirited voices. The ceiling was lofty and the space was airy, featuring ultramodern accents, bronze tables, café con leche–colored leather chairs, and a long thick underlit marble slab for the bar. Light fixtures floated down from the ceiling, designed to look like pastel clouds in the sky. It was the perfect setting for Candace's birthday gathering—chic and soulful. And the music was a vibe, the personification of grown and sexy catering to everyone. There was something special about being in an upscale establishment that managed to keep it Black AF, which made it therefore cool AF. Just as Harper approached the hostess stand with his super-expensive, massive "thoughtful" gift, a message from Robyn hit his smartwatch screen. Hey, sorry for the delay. She loves soy candles. You can personalize one to send. She'll love it.

*Fuck. That IS perfect. Why didn't I think of that?* Robyn's message continued. Tell everyone I said hello. Have fun. *A fucking soy candle . . .* Suddenly, his innovative Himalayan salt lamp seemed real lame in comparison. The saleswoman had espoused all the health benefits—relieving allergies, improving mood, and something about better sleep. What fifty-year-old parent doesn't need that, right? He handled the awkward gift, continuing to shift it in his arms. When he reached the coat check and finally put it down to remove his cashmere overcoat, scarf, and camel fedora, he thought briefly about checking the gift too. *Nahh, just give it to her,* he decided.

In his cream-colored fitted sweater and espresso slacks now, he craned his neck around the boisterous dining room searching for his crew and found them quickly.

His six friends were already seated in the center of the restaurant, laughing and having fun. Even in a sea of well-dressed mostly Black clientele, his crew stood out in look and sound. His peeps were the personification of *Black Excellence.* But as he expected, the couples were seated across from one another, three neat sets of two, evenly slotted and spaced, gazing into each other's eyes. *What did you expect, Harp? Boy, girl, boy, girl?* He was definitely the seventh wheel, the odd man out.

Harper shifted the gift once again and headed toward the table of the group that looked like the successful post-graduate members of the tribe of Barack and Michelle. Harper weaved through the room, negotiating tables, servers, and that heavy-ass Himalayan salt lamp. When he reached his friends, they were all transfixed on Quentin, regaled by his animated storytelling. It took a full ten seconds before anyone even looked up at him. Q had always been a great commander of attention.

"Hey, y'all," Harper said by way of announcement. As animated as they were prior to his arrival, the group lit up even further at Harper's presence. He was greeted with a chorus of "Harper! Harp!" The feeling was beautiful. He bent down to kiss the lady of honor. "Happy birthday, Candace." She gave her cheek, and so as not to smear her makeup with his slight scruff, Harper aimed a careful cheek-to-cheek air-kiss around the generous fluff of her hair. Then he handed her the unwieldy gift. "Here you go. It's imported . . . from Pakistan."

"Oh . . . thanks, Harper." Candace reached for the large gift bag with both hands, but once the weight of it transferred,

Harper scrambled forward to help as she narrowly dropped it. Murch swept in from the side to take the package from his struggling wife and to join Harper in placing it on the floor, just in time to save the moment.

Harper gestured toward it awkwardly. "Um, it's a Himalayan salt lamp, supposed to light the room, help with sleep, allergies. Stuff like that. Makes you calm too." Even as he espoused its benefits, Harper wished he could turn it into a simple soy cylinder.

"Maybe you should have gotten one for yourself, player," Quentin commented. Everyone laughed and Harper gave a good-natured grimace.

"Ahh, you could have just gotten a nice bottle of wine like I told you," Murch commented.

"Just trying to be thoughtful . . ." Harper shrugged.

Candace chimed in, "It *was* thoughtful. Keisha has terrible allergies. We can put it in her room." She smiled brightly, looking beautiful in her strapless form-fitting black dress. "Thank you, Harper. It looks great. And so do you, handsome."

"Come on, man, have a seat." Murch directed him to the seventh-wheel seat at the end of the table. To exile, alone, out in the cold.

Lance stood to give him dap, a bro-hug, and of course, his generous smile. "You alright, dawg?"

"I'm good, bruh," Harper assured him.

"Good to see you, Harp." Quentin punctuated his greeting with a fist bump. Harper cheek-kissed and shoulder squeezed Shelby and Jasmine before making his way to the last seat.

"Whatcha drinking?" Murch bellowed over the din of crowd walla and the house remix of Janet Jackson's "That's The Way Love Goes." The way the table looked, all perfectly arranged, with three couples basking in the glow of each other's company, *that's the way indeed,* Harper thought.

"Wine, I guess?" He gestured toward the red blend at the center of the table. Jasmine, the closest to him, took up the bottle and poured for him. Harper tried to protest with, "Oh, you don't have to—thank you, Jasmine." But Jasmine's Caribbean lilt mildly admonished him.

"Ya know I'm in the hospitality business, so ya don't fret." Harper nodded and raised his glass in toast and thanks before taking a sip. "No date tonight, *Hoppa*?" Lance smirked at Jasmine's innocent inquiry. Harper smiled at the pronunciation of his name and told some of the truth about his solo appearance.

"I was forbidden, Jasmine."

"Forbidden?! Oh stop it." Shelby waved a hand of carefully manicured stiletto-shaped nails in the air.

"Facts," Harper pronounced. "But all good. This isn't really the event for someone new. Intimate . . ."

"Hasn't stopped you before," came Shelby's snarky retort.

"Ya seeing someone new, Hoppa?" Jasmine leaned forward with interest.

Harper delivered a high-pitched "Well . . ." He gestured his ambivalence. "Kinda . . . a couple . . . a few . . ." He struggled to find the words to characterize his active and yet struggle-forward dating life.

"What happened to the gyal ya braat to our New Year's Eve paaarty?" Jasmine smiled. "The one with de generous backside."

"Yah, I haven't spoken to her in a while . . ."

"Take ya time, dawg," Lance remarked as he rubbed Jasmine's exposed brown shoulder. She was wearing a simple yet stunning off-the-shoulder jewel-tone top that perfectly set off her skin, turning it copper. Her naturally textured hair had grown out, creating a halo of curls on her head. Both of them looked so comfortable and relaxed together.

Harper sighed. "Oh, no doubt. I know . . . I'm not even really looking like that."

"Yeah, ol' Harp getting his freak on. For all of us!" Quentin's voice carried to the end of the table, creating another round of laughs. Harper cut his eyes back at his oldest friend.

"Shut up, Quentin. You get plenty freak where you stay too, nigga," Shelby said as she gestured toward him before taking a sip from her wineglass. "Don't make me bring one of these Dominican mami waitresses in here to double team your ass."

"That's cool, just no pegging," Quentin joked. Everyone laughed again as Shelby playfully hit his shoulder and Quentin puckered his lips for a kiss. She obliged with a lover's giggle.

"You might like it, boy," Candace chimed in. "Shit, we getting past fifty. You better try some stuff so at least you know!" Candace winked and took a sip of her wine.

"Shiiiit. I know. Nobody playing with this dookie-chute. Save that for Murch," Quentin joked.

"Mine is closed as well. And could we please not ruin our appetite with all that dookie-chute talk," Murch pleaded.

"Shelby said you used to like a little ass play back in the day." Quentin cut his eyes at Murch with a sly smile.

Shelby immediately slapped his arm. Quentin recoiled and cackled. "I did NOT say that!" She turned to Murch. "Julian, get your boy. Candace, I'm sorry." Shelby reached toward them both with a forgive-me hand gesture.

Candace smiled like she'd just been told a secret. "Don't be sorry. Shit. I'm thankful for the information. Things may get spicy tonight." She turned toward Murch and dropped her hand down toward the back of his chair. He flinched noticeably but smiled at Candace. Then he shook his head at Quentin.

"See what you started?"

"You're welcome." Quentin laughed.

Harper took in his friends enjoying their respective partners' flirty gazes, touches, and pet names. He had none of that to participate in. As a reflex, he cleared his throat. "So, umm is this a prix fixe menu? We doing family style, ordering a bunch of stuff?"

"Menu's already planned, Harp," Lance responded.

"Yup," added Murch. "Robyn would be impressed." *Robyn?* Harper hadn't expected the mention of his ex. Murch never failed.

"With what? The menu or the fact that Harp is solo?" And neither did Quentin.

Laughter and smiles returned to the table even as Harper rolled his eyes. When they were together, Robyn was certainly the connective tissue that made these social connections all work with ease. She compensated for Harper's shortcomings. When he drifted away, she was present. Particularly tonight, he felt her absence. He was here alone with no date for distraction, on Candace's milestone birthday, among all the friends they used to share—being here without her felt like having an amputated limb.

"She sends her love by the way," Harper remarked. "Robyn. She texted right before I came in."

"She's so sweet." Candace's face lit up as she spoke of her friend. "She gave me a birthday FaceTime today."

*But too busy to text me back?* Harper thought. *Hmmph.*

"She looks fantastic," Candace continued. "She has really adjusted to life out there." Despite her words, Candace's tone said one thing to Harper: *You fucked up, nigga.* Candace and Harper had always been cool and maybe they even became cooler because of her relationship with Robyn. But after the divorce, there'd been a noticeable shift in their interactions. They were still congenial and warm, but certainly *different.* She'd felt their divorce too. Everyone did. How could they not? They were all chosen family. But Candace was certainly taking some obvious personal satisfaction in her girl doing well.

"Oh yeah. Robyn's Nest is doing great too," Murch added. "Mia's adjusting well. And she's seeing somebody . . . ?" Murch blurted excitedly. And then, "Ow!" A hurt-looking Murch turned to Candace, who returned a classic Black wife "Nigga, are you serious" look.

From the far end of the table, Harper wasn't sure he heard correctly. *Seeing somebody? Really?* Ironically, this was the moment that everyone turned to him, at the end of the table in seventh-wheel "exile." All six pairs of eyes were now focused on him with their full attention. Harper looked at Quentin and Lance to his right. Their shared expression said clearly, *Yeah, nigga, you heard correctly.*

Quentin lifted the table's wine bottle toward him, breaking the silence. "Have some more wine . . ."

Harper watched his glass being filled, knowing the news of his ex-wife seeing somebody shouldn't cause these feelings he was experiencing. And what was he feeling? Surprise? *But also, why didn't I know about this?* Was he jealous? Really? Harper smiled, trying to evoke nonchalance. "Good for her," he replied. "That's great. I hope he's worthy of her."

"He sure seems to be on paper," Candace couldn't seem to help but point out. *On paper? Is she dating a #couplesgoals brotha?* "Anyway, I also got a nice bouquet of flowers from Jordan before she left town."

*Oh, hell no.* "Before she left town?" Now it was Harper who couldn't help himself. There was no poker face to be had. "*Jordan* was in New York?" His shock was obvious.

The bulk of the table seemed genuinely surprised at Harper's reaction. Murch especially. "You didn't see her?" he asked. "I thought you guys were in touch."

"We are. We were. I mean, you know. Life be life-ing," Harper reached for an explanation he could articulate. "We're both pretty busy. As always." His eyes found Lance's. His friend held the look for a moment, and then he pursed his lips before looking away.

"I talked to her last night," Shelby added. "I tried to get her to change her flight, but I guess she wanted to get back to that Malibu life. . . ."

"So nobody saw her . . ." Harper knew the question had made its way into his voice despite desperately wanting to sound declarative.

A chorus of "nos," "nahs," ensued, heads nodding in agreement.

"She must be busy," Harper mused.

"Life be lifing." Lance reentered the chat.

"Word." Harper held up his glass to Lance who returned the impromptu toast with a clink of their glasses. A trio of waitstaff descended on the table with three servings of the first course of egusi dumplings, piri piri salad, and oxtail and crab Rangoon. A refrain of "Wows," "that looks great," and "yummms" ensued as the head waiter explained the dishes, then declared, "Enjoy."

"We will," Murch said with pride. "L, you wanna bless us this evening?"

"Oh, no doubt. Grab hands y'all." Both sides of the table formed a human chain. Murch and Candace held hands across the table at one end. Lance took Harper's right hand, firm and steady, while Jasmine's hand wrapped around his other one in warmth and softness. Everyone bowed their collective heads. Lance began.

"Lord, we thank you for the gathering of longtime friends and found family. We thank you for the opportunity to fellowship, to nourish our bodies, and to fortify our minds and spirit. We thank you for the gift that is Candace and for blessing her and her family with another year around the sun. We thank you, Lord, for her gift of enrichment for her family and for all of us gathered and all the lives she touches. We ask that you bless this sumptuous meal and keep those who are not with us safe and in our prayers. These blessings we ask in your holy name . . . Amen."

A round of "amens" rippled up the table as their hands unclasped.

"Amen," Harper said and attempted to let go of Lance's hand as he had already done with Jasmine's. Lance didn't let go. Harper looked at his hand, then at Lance who met his gaze.

"Amen," Lance said directly to Harper, nodding at his longtime friend. Harper returned the nod and eked out a smile. For a man who didn't believe in God for over half of his life, Harper knew he was richly blessed and this moment of fellowship proved it well.

"You want that oxtail, baby?" Lance attended to Jasmine like the protector that he'd always been.

"Oh yes," she said, relaxed and smiling. "It smells delicious."

"I'ma fuck with that egusi and piri salad," the recent vegan Quentin declared. "Gimme your plate, Harp," he beckoned. Harper handed over his seventh-wheel plate as Quentin, Lance, and Jasmine all filled it with the appetizers.

He understood what they were trying to do. The conviviality, laughter, and warmth of friendship were present at the table. But something else, *someone* else was missing.

"Do women ever get tired of taking photos?" Lance turned to Harper. It was after dinner now and they were in the middle of Lincoln Center Plaza. With full bellies and wine-buzzed brains, they watched the ladies pose for numerous photos in front of the world-famous illuminated fountain. Murch was tasked with the demands of getting the right shot.

"Make sure we look cute! And skinny! Hold it up higher! Duck lips, ladies!"

And Quentin was tasked with impatiently holding purses and clutches. Harper chuckled at Lance's rhetorical inquisition before exhaling his frosty breath. The temperature was in the mid-thirties, making the stilled night air cold but not unbearable—at least for the next ten minutes or so. Or until the ladies felt the cold on their cute and exposed toes. Jasmine was the only sensible one in high boots.

"You alright, man?" With his hands in his coat pockets, Lance pointed his chin at Harper.

Harper turned to him. "Yeah. I'm good." Harper tried to sound reassuring, but his voice hit an unconvincing higher register of trying too hard. Lance called bullshit.

"Don't seem like it," he pressed.

Harper considered Lance's words. Finally, after a long exhale, he answered. "I faked an orgasm yesterday."

"What?" Lance looked genuinely confused. And clearly a bit amused, as evinced by the appearance of his bright, million-dollar smile. "With homegirl? What's her name? Bailey?"

"Yeah," Harper responded.

"Yo, who does that?" Lance asked giddily.

"She asked me the same question."

"Wait, you told her?"

"She just knew. I guess my performance wasn't too convincing." Harper shrugged.

Then Lance let out a laugh. As many sexcapades as he'd had over the decades this was the stuff that could still get Lance's motor going. Harper continued recounting the story, embellishing where appropriate. The storyteller in him couldn't help it.

"In the mirror?!" Lance responded.

"Yeah. Came with the apartment. And it has come in handy," Harper said. "It was like my own fantasy come to life. Straight out of my own imagination and a high-quality porn."

"Dawg, that sounds crazy. *You* the ebony humper now."

"For real. And I'm digging the whole experience, you know? And then, in one moment, I'm just like 'what am I doing? This is stupid.' I didn't even want her to be there. I mean the sex is fire, but I just wanted it to be over. And for her to go."

"So why didn't you just tell her?" Lance's face scrunched up.

Harper considered the question. "Because . . . I didn't want to be an asshole," he said.

"So you became a *fuck boy* instead." Lance laughed.

Harper nodded and chuckled his resignation. "Damned if I do. Damned if I don't."

"You looked a little surprised about Robyn tonight," Lance continued.

Harper shrugged. "I was."

"So, what's up, dude?"

Harper thought about it, but came up with nothing. "I don't know," he admitted. Lance studied him intently. Harper continued, still trying to explain. "Look, Robyn can do what she wants. I don't have any claims on her. She's an adult and a beautiful woman."

"She was also your wife for over two decades. Y'all built a life together. It's not easy."

"True, but she should probably be with someone else by now, whether it's serious or not." The truth was complex and hard for Harper to admit. "She deserves it." He knew that was the adult and mature thing to say, and he had no right to think otherwise. "Hell, I'm out getting mine."

"When you ain't fake bussin' nuts," Lance remarked with a chuckle. Harper laughed too, then exhaled a cloud of vapor after a large breath.

"I just didn't think about it. I didn't think about her . . . moving on. Maybe she's . . . happier without me," Harper admitted. Lance's head tilted, but he didn't interrupt. Harper searched for a better explanation. "I think in the back of my mind I felt like she'd have a harder time. Like, like . . ."

"Like . . . ?" Lance prodded.

"Like me." Harper looked away from his boy to the wives still posing, laughing, retaking photos. "I feel like—like I been kicked out of my life, L." Harper declared. "And I want back in."

"What does that look like for you, Harp? I mean, what are you missing?"

"Companionship I guess?"

"Seem like you got plenty of that."

"I'm fucking a lot. No doubt. I am squarely in my 'hoe' phase."

"You getting your *glory* pussy."

"Right. But I don't know if any of them get me. No one seems to fit. Not with me, not with the crew. And clearly I don't know how to set boundaries."

"You not gonna replace Robyn overnight."

"I don't know that I'm trying to replace Robyn. I don't know that I can." Harper stabbed at the ground with his foot. "We met when I was trying to figure out who I was and what I wanted. She helped me discover those things. I mean she's special and unique and we had a lot of time together, to build a life. How do I replace that?"

"It takes time, Harp. Me and Jas been married a little over a year and I have to remind myself a lot that she's not Mia. She's never going to be Mia. So replacing someone you love, your life, your rib, that's hard. That takes time."

"You guys are cool though, right?"

Lance looked askance, not as if he was avoiding but being thoughtful about his response. His voice lifted an octave as he uttered, "Ehhh, we have our moments. What couple doesn't, right? But we're finding our stride. God willing, we'll get there. The honeymoon never lasts forever and real relationships take work. Communication. Commitment. You ain't there yet, fam."

Harper considered what his best friend said. He knew Lance was right. But he still wanted to be "there," wherever that was, desperately.

Over by the fountain, Quentin began his rebellion against the impromptu photo shoot. He passed the ladies' bags he'd been holding to Murch and walked toward the street in protest, raising his arm in salutations to the fellas. "Catch y'all later," Quentin declared.

Shelby implored Quentin to wait "just one more minute," but her long legs in spike-heels began striding in his direction, each of them like a magnet drawn to the other. She only paused to turn back to Candace with one last air-kiss good night. Jasmine embraced both women separately and then turned to retrieve her purse and an embrace from Murch.

"What's up with Jordan?" Lance inquired as he walked toward his newlywed.

Harper matched strides with him. "I don't know," he said with a shrug.

"For what it's worth," Lance offered, "she didn't reach out to me either. Not sure if she spoke to the kids."

"Probably. Auntie J is usually on the case."

"Yeah, you right. Y'all cool?" Lance stopped walking to face Harper and wait for an answer. Harper stopped too.

"Me and Jordan? Far as I know, yeah? Why?"

"She may have some insight for you on your dating escapades. She always has." Lance's words were an understatement. Jordan Armstrong had made a mark on every aspect of Harper's dating and married life, all the way since college at Westmore. From the time she friend-zoned him back in the day, Jordan could always be counted on to give him insight into himself and the women he desired. All the women, except for Jordan herself. As long as they had been friends and flirted with the possibility of being more, they never could get in perfect sync. There was always some barrier, some obstacle that kept them from consummating their relationship. Even when things got hot and heavy between them, cooler heads prevailed.

Well, *her* cooler head. It was always Jordan who corralled him back whenever Harper deigned to escape their platonic status. Unlike Harper, Jordan knew how to set boundaries. Jordan was about Jordan. And handling her B.I., Jordan rarely involved her heart. She was always measured. Harper knew she liked having him as a friend. At least that's what she seemed to value from him. He was mostly happy to be there if for nothing else but to be close to her. They were as intimate a pair as could be, just not physically. Crossing the line was likely never going to happen given their respective and similar ambitions. Equally yoked, but destined to stay in their respective corners.

That was, until he wrote *Unfinished Business* and fictionalized their relationship into a fantasy of what they might have become had they taken the leap. Had they had their night. The handful of times they had time and opportunity, the serial monogamist was dating, then married to the woman that Jordan had declared was "the one" for him. That union lasted over twenty years, produced a thriving career and a beautiful young spirit named Mia. So presumably she knew what she was talking about. And when that relationship ended, what did the even-keeled Jordan say? *I can't be your safe place to land, Harper.* So there he was, back in the friend zone. Seemingly where he belonged. He should at least repair that. Yeah, Jordan *would* have an opinion about getting back into his own life. Harper could hear her now remarking on the Bailey situation: *You're fuck-boy adjacent, Harper.* Harper smiled and shook his head.

Harper and Lance resumed their pace and quickly reached Jasmine, Murch, and the birthday girl.

"Good to see you again, Hoppa." Jasmine lifted her arms out to Harper who returned her hug and a cheek kiss.

"Same here, Jasmine. Y'all be safe going back to Jersey."

"Oh no. We staying in the city tanight. Lance doesn't like driving at night. Sometime I think he forget where we live."

"Stop," Lance declared.

But Jasmine continued. "And working fa a hotel chain has its perk. You need a room tanight?"

"Nah, I'ma get a ride back." Harper gestured to Murch and Candace. "Y'all wanna ride back to BK?"

"Oh no. Jasmine got us a suite," Murch said. "So we're staying in Manhattan too. The girls'll be good. You wanna join us for a drink? Little nightcap?"

"Ahhhh . . ." Harper mused.

"Have a quick one, Harper," Candace offered. "It won't be long because I'm trying to see what's up with that ass play I heard about tonight." The group laughed as Murch rolled his eyes, smiled, and shook his head.

"Fucking Quentin . . ." Murch sounded off in faux frustration.

Harper weighed Candace's offer. "Thanks for the invite,

Candace," he responded. "But I should call it a night and get back. I gotta deadline. Need to get some work done." He leaned in to kiss her goodbye. "Happy birthday again. And I can return the salt lamp if it's lame or you don't want it."

"Stop it, Harper," Candace reassured him. "I'm going to put it to great use. Thank you for the gift. And more than that, thanks for coming. I know you're busy."

Harper nodded as he contemplated the statement that had always been his default. *Just busy.* His MO. His excuse. But that wasn't working anymore. And it was time to make a change.

"Night, y'all." Harper turned to head down the street, away from his friends, focused once again on what awaited him back at home.

# CHAPTER SEVEN

## Harper

From the windows of Harper's living room, even at 2:00 a.m., the lower Manhattan skyline was still dotted with many lights in windows, and a snake of traffic moved steadily uptown across the river. And he was up to see it. He'd been working for a solid couple of hours, freshly fortified by the high vibrations of his time with the crew. But in his work, he still grappled with the one question that had been haunting him since it was first posed by his agent.

*What's the big idea?? The big idea* . . . Stan had challenged him to dazzle the studio executives with a so-called big idea. All Harper had so far was a story, *his* story, a meaningful one that held the lives and dreams of him and his closest friends.

"How the hell am I supposed to know what the *big idea* is?" Harper mused aloud in frustration. He'd been glad to see his friends that evening. They were his encouragement, his inspiration, and now, especially for this project, his motivation. Nonetheless, the time had cost him a late-night return to his project to meet his deadline. Still, with the focus on the big idea, he was able to push the distractions of the evening out of his mind: unexpected news . . . about Robyn . . . and Jordan.

*What's the big idea?*

*Okay . . . What if we all stayed around the same city when we graduated? Johnson gets drafted by the DC team—they were the Bullets then . . .*

"When did the Bullets change to the Wizards?" Harper said aloud as he typed the line into his search engine.

*Okay, the year is 1997. Johnson gets drafted. Then he and Casey get married and all the college friends come to town for their wedding. . . . No. Too close to home. Make something up. Use your imagination, asshole.* Harper's inner voice was often harsh when his muse was being elusive.

*What's the big idea?* Harper took a seat at his desk and tapped a pen on the surface.

His living room was littered with diagrams, outlines, corkboards with index cards with small ideas, scene descriptions, and pieces of dialogue, but nothing that really coalesced.

*What's the big idea?* he asked himself again.

Harper had tried many incarnations of a story that followed up on this group of college friends. *Unfinished Business* ended at graduation. How was he going to continue this story as some Black post-graduate *St. Elmo's Fire*–type of narrative? The studio often referenced the iconic Brat Pack movie of the eighties with then-teen-heartthrobs Rob Lowe, Emilio Estevez, and Demi Moore.

What could Harper say about his characters in a sequel that honored his original work but gave the studio the hook they expected? And delivered the moviegoing audience the story they wanted to see? It seemed like an impossible task.

*What's the big idea?* "I don't know!" Harper yelled. These were the frustrations of being a writer. The long nights of solitude. In these invisible times, aside from the public moments of accolades and star treatment as a bestselling author, it wasn't always easy to pry brilliance from his overactive mind. *Stop thinking. Stop. Just write. It doesn't matter what. Just write.* Harper placed his hands on the keyboard and began to type.

> Jackson and Kendall have had sex. They crossed the line, but do they make it as a couple? Casey and Johnson did. Cleavon went to law school and Darby stuck by him. Or does she? Do they break up? What about Flave?

Would that mess with Shelby (Darby) and Quentin (Flave) now?

*Shit. This is so difficult.* Harper stopped typing. Quentin and Shelby were okay with everything he'd crafted to date. Murch, though, he hated Cleavon. *I hated Cleavon too,* Harper thought. *But now I can fix that . . .*

Jordan seemed fine with Kendall. *Jordan . . . how could she not call me . . . ? Stop thinking, Harper. Just write.*

The studio wanted these characters to remain the same and to catch up to them a year or two later. But people evolve, people change. People don't remain the same or go backward. . . . Nobody. Goes. Backward. *Goes Backward? Wait. Go back . . . What were these characters' original plans?* And suddenly an idea sparked.

> It's five years after graduation. JACKSON is now a sports personality, covering Johnson's basketball career with the Wizards.
>
> Okay . . .
>
> Jackson's a sportscaster making his living in FRONT of the camera.

When Harper arrived on Westmore's campus he was aiming to be part of the school's prestigious broadcast journalism program and felt he was destined for a career in front of the camera. But it turned out that his skill with the spoken word wasn't as honed as he believed. In fact, he was a disaster. The cool, collected, and polished author, who only forty-eight hours ago recommended must reads to a nationwide audience with charm and wit, had been a quivering mess when it came time to audition for the competitive program. He was soundly rejected and summarily excused because he didn't have "It." But that's what happened to Harper. After graduation, *Jackson* could have decided to make a shift back to his true passion. Harper began frantically typing again, trying to make his fingers move fast enough to capture the idea rapidly taking shape.

> Jackson thought he was destined to be a journalist, but a career altering twist of fate shifted his chosen path. While interning at the local newsroom a ~~beautiful~~ no, ~~sexy,~~ no, HOT female producer took a liking to Jackson's chiseled physique and ~~handsome face~~ striking facial features.
>
> She declared, "You belong in front of the camera." Jackson agreed and after a short, but torrid love affair with her, a make-over and personal trainer, he became a local celebrity being wooed by the National News outlets. Jackson had never given up on his desire to be a news personality. Bryant Gumbel started in sports, so did Robin Roberts. Al Roker was a weatherman—still is, but also an invaluable part of the morning team.

"Jackson could have gone that route," Harper said out loud as he typed the words. "Hell, I could have." *Bullshit.* There was that negative inner voice. Harper pushed it away and kept flowing . . .

Then, after a five-year stint filled with money, notoriety, LOTS of GLORY PUSSY and on the precipice of true stardom as the host of the local morning show, JACKSON is full of himself and KENDALL is the news producer brought in from ~~Chicago,~~ no, ~~New York,~~ no Los Angeles to revamp the broadcast!

*This is good,* Harper thought . . . And every one of the crew could still be part of the narrative.

Of course, this hiring takes Jackson by surprise. Just when he finally gets a promotion and his own way of doing things, here comes Kendall with her own agenda to upend his entire world. She's made quite a name for herself on the West Coast. Moving and shaking with the biggest names behind the scenes in the broadcast space. Of course, there's friction because they haven't spoken or been in touch in quite some time. They left—or rather—SHE left on weird terms. She kind of disappeared. . . .

*Just like Jordan . . .*

She's powerful. She's beautiful. She's a ballbuster. She hasn't spoken to Jackson in five years and she's MARRIED!

*Married?! How could she be? She was never on that. Maybe she had a moment of weakness. Maybe the dude swept her off her feet. Maybe he's a white dude . . .*

Married, but not happily. Turns out she should have stayed the course because the chemistry between Kendall and Jackson is as palpable as it ever was.

*Best sex either of them ever had.*

The news program goes through twists and turns. Kendall and Jackson feud over the show's direction, have late-night meetings, have hot office sex and that tension spills over into the workplace. At first, it's detrimental to the ratings, Jackson blames her, Kendall blames him.

*. . . lots of sexual tension. This is gonna work. . . .*

Harper's fingers began blazing across the keyboard. He let himself get lost in the story's potential and the freedom of the late hour fueled by his own creativity and alkaline water. Coffee, Red Bull, and caffeinated colas couldn't match the internal burning fire when Harper's muse took over. Only when his fingers started aching and the cacophony of ideas trickled to a halt was when the *real* Kendall entered his consciousness again.

Jordan.

*How's she gonna come to town and not call me? I thought we were in a good place. . . .*

The whole crew went to his Pulitzer ceremony a year ago for *Pieces Of Us.* Robyn even sent Mia to celebrate with her father. They all had a lot of laughs. It was then that Harper discovered Jordan had moved to Malibu. He'd been hermitting and leaning into the pain he was feeling while he wrote that epic love story. She said it was brilliant. She said it made her cry. And cheer. "The best thing you've ever written, Harp. Full stop," she said. The world agreed. But she was back in his life. It was beginning to feel like it had in college. Besties, but more mature . . . with more experience and gray hair. Homies again . . . until late December when she backed out of attending Lance's New Year's Eve party. The break was abrupt. Maybe it was too much of a painful reminder during the holidays that they'd lost Mia Morgan, Lance's first wife and Jordan's best friend, and Jordan was trying to "protect her peace." Whatever it was, there was a shift. He felt it.

*Maybe she's busy?* Sure. And Harper was feeling lonely—maybe extra lonely these days. Still, he wondered. And wanted to see her. He missed her. But . . . *she came to town and didn't reach out?*

"What's up with that?" Harper asked out loud. "Fuck it." Enough wondering. *Call her.* Call her and call her out. They had that kind of rapport. Didn't they? They did. Was that still the case? Why not now? Why was it weird? *Call her ass right now.* Harper willed himself to action. The time stamp on his computer read 2:57 a.m. Almost midnight in Malibu. She could still be up.

*No need to overthink . . .*

Harper was scheduled to go to LA for a book signing for the paperback release of *Pieces Of Us*. And the studio meeting about the *Unfinished Business* sequel that was suddenly looking promising. Now that he had an idea, he was getting amped about it. The studio's requested face-to-face had been fucking scary at the beginning of the night, but now he was empowered. Face-to-face is always better. Body language, eye contact, pauses, etc. He liked that. A genuine connection is what Harper preferred. . . . Wait, was he thinking about the studio or Jordan? *Both, I guess. Fuck it.* He picked up his phone to craft a text to Jordan.

I'm coming to town for some meetings and ~~I want to . . . I'd like to . . . I'd love to~~ . . . if you're free, let's get drinks or dinner . . .

*Yeah.*

Send.

Jordan didn't respond. No response, no text bubbles.

*She'll respond tomorrow,* Harper told himself. *Even if she doesn't, don't sweat it. The text went through and when you get to LA, text her again. Call her. No way I'm going to her neck of the woods and not call. Be the bigger man, Harp.*

12:04 a.m. in Malibu. Harper twisted the corner of his mouth, let out a tiny teeth suck and shook off the non-response. 3:04 a.m. 8:04 a.m. in Accra. Time to call Mia before school. He was usually up writing anyway and would often check in at this time. He wanted his daughter to see his face and hear his voice as much as possible. Based on the disclosures at dinner, he had plenty to check in on. *Robyn.* He wished her well, genuinely. Though he never agreed with her decision to move to Ghana, especially since that decision meant taking their daughter, Mia, with her. *What's so wrong with living here?* Robyn always had a way of moving to the next thing, as if it held a better future for her, maybe just because it was . . . new. And now, a new person. *Seeing someone, right? But, who?*

## CHAPTER EIGHT

# Robyn

Robyn Stewart gritted her teeth just a bit as she opened the passenger-side doors of the mini SUV for her daughter, Mia, as they went about their set morning routine. The back seat was to place her school bag, and then the front was to place herself—a uniform-clad eleven-year-old, the preteen combination of Robyn and Harper, from her neat cornrow braids to her gangly cocoa-colored legs shining with shea butter. "Do you have your assignments?" Robyn asked. "Did you remember the lunch I packed?"

"Uh-huh," Mia's little face beamed with big-girl pride. Her bright smile was only outshone by the sun above Accra, bathing them in a blanketing heat that Robyn still found more intense than what she'd ever experienced in the States, even in the South. The sun felt closer here somehow, a welcoming presence, but also, it was one more new thing to get used to over the years. It hadn't been easy. Not *at all.*

"Belt yourself," Robyn said as she climbed into the driver's seat. Just as she'd secured her own belt and started the vehicle, Robyn's phone rang from her purse in the back seat. She could hear it, but she wasn't pressed.

"Mommy, it's your phone."

"I know. I hear it."

"You gotta answer it before it goes away," Mia protested as if the urgency was life or death.

"The voicemail will get it, Mia."

"It might be important. I'll find it," Mia contorted her body toward the source of the ringing.

"Do not undo your seatbelt, young lady . . ." Robyn admonished, alternating her gaze between the road and her daughter, who had managed to do a complete one-eighty in her seat and was now rummaging through her momma's stuff, causing several items to rain onto the floor.

"Mia . . ." Robyn said, annoyed. "Come on, baby. You're making a mess . . ."

"It's Daddy!" Mia announced with a smile. The light glimmered in her eyes. Her hand emerged with the cellphone like a trophy. Sure enough, Robyn glanced to see Harper's face illuminating the screen. She released a small sigh of relief. Better that it was Harper than Aboagye again, whom she'd been avoiding.

"Answer it," Robyn said, exhaling as she maneuvered the vehicle out of the driveway.

"Good morning, Mimi," Harper's voice boomed through the car speakers.

"Hi, Daddy."

"Hey, Mom.

"Hi." Robyn responded pleasantly, although she wasn't really in the mood to chat. *Why is he calling on my phone?* she wondered. Mia had her own, and Harper had made sure his little girl had one that was top of the line. Overcompensating as usual. So he should've used it. Though as soon as Harper spoke, she remembered why he hadn't.

"Yeah, I tried Mia's phone but it went straight to voicemail." Mia looked at Robyn with childlike guilt. Robyn didn't flinch.

"Tell him."

Mia looked away from her mom and out the window.

"Tell me what?"

"Well, when Ms. Mia came back from her *extended* trip with you, it was quite the back-and-forth we had about phone screen time."

"Oh. I see," Harper responded flatly.

"So, your daughter had her phone taken away from her for the next few days."

Mia sighed audibly.

"When is she getting it back?"

"When her mom thinks it's appropriate."

"She's not going to have it at school?"

"No, Harper. They don't allow that here."

"What if there's an emergency?"

"Then the school will call and let me know what's happening. Remember like when you and I were growing up?"

"Robyn, come on, it's not the same—"

Robyn cut him off. "Mia knows the rules, don't you, Mia?"

"Yes," Mia said under her breath.

"I'm sorry, I didn't hear you. And I'm sure your dad didn't either."

"Yes. I know," Mia responded with extra spice and sauce.

"It's okay, baby." Harper's reassurance rang out through the car's speakers. "I know that phone is tempting but try to do what Mommy says, okay?"

*Try?* Robyn thought. *Thanks for the support, Dad.* Since Mia had gotten that phone Robyn made sure her daughter's screen time was limited to an hour a day (including FaceTiming her dad). Two hours on the weekend. "The world isn't in your phone, baby. It's all around you," Robyn would remind her daughter often. It was her dad's gift, but Mom's rules would be enforced.

And Harper unexpectedly extending Mia's last trip to New York hadn't helped. It certainly made Mia happy (and likely Harper as well), but it didn't make her return easier. Robyn *thought* she and Harper had established a good rhythm and a healthy respect, but of course Harper's lack of structure had introduced a lack of structure to Mia that simply continued even now, well past the time to get back to business.

Mia loved her dad and missed him. She was no longer a little girl who worshipped her momma. She was a precocious eleven-year-old with her own thoughts and ideas and the often accompanying three letter word "why." It was exhausting explaining parenting decisions to a mini-me. Robyn didn't employ the "because I said so" reason very often, but oh had she been tempted.

While Mia chatted with Harper, Robyn navigated the dense Accra rush-hour traffic through the affluent Cantonments neighborhood of the British International School, regarded as the best school in the city, where Mia was enrolled in the sixth grade. Harper's money was good for many things and Robyn was thankful.

Mia filled her dad in about school, classes, her homework, and what she was excited about for the day. Art class for sure. She always loved to use her creativity. "Et je parle français," Mia said in her little girl version of a French accent.

"Très bien!" Harper replied through the speakers. Robyn had to smile at that. Surely, those were the only French words he knew. And Mia's laughter was contagious. Their rapport was pure joy to witness, despite the distance. A world away, as it needed to be. She was so happy that Mia was learning, expanding her horizons. She was going to be a true citizen of the world, with dual citizenship and *options.* The number of expats—more lovingly known as "returnees"—was growing rapidly in Accra. They were returning from all over the world: the United Kingdom, the Caribbean, and just like them, America. It was simultaneously an escape from the toxicity of white supremacy and a return to home. America, that place . . . just wasn't for them anymore. Robyn loved that her little girl would get to grow up never knowing some of the cruelties she'd otherwise face. Robyn saw the writing on the wall long before the results of the last United States presidential election. She had no more interest in fighting in a land that didn't want her. She didn't even watch much of the news other than the BBC and what came on her social media feed. It was a relief to be away from the constant barrage of conflict and discord. *What a mess.* No, instead, Robyn relished the ability to keep her spirit clean and her mind focused on Mia, on her business, and her healing.

The drive passed quickly enough, even with the traffic, and by the time they arrived, there were still a considerable number of other brown-skinned children in their identical uniforms milling about at the school façade, making their way through the entrance.

"Don't forget your lunch," Robyn reminded Mia, satisfied to see her daughter scramble for her bag, and instantly felt that familiar pang of imminent separation, of missing her even before she was gone. The ache of love and the relief too, of having fulfilled her biggest responsibility of the day, both flowed through Robyn. Now it was her time to take on the rest of her own concerns that she'd been holding at bay. "Have a great day, Mimi." Robyn kissed her before she exited the car. "I love you."

"I love you too, Mommy. Bye, Daddy. I love you." Mia looked into her mom's phone.

"Love you too, baby," Harper's gravelly voice responded.

"Call me if you need me. That is, when your mom gives your phone back."

"K. Here you go, Mommy." Mia handed Robyn's phone back to her before running off to catch up with her good friend, Mawusi. Mawusi was the daughter of Haniah, Robyn's de facto sous chef, guide, partner in business, sister in crisis. They'd met during Robyn's initial visit to Accra, when the Mindinu Organization recruited her for the Nomadic Dining Experience that essentially changed her life. Now their daughters were besties. Robyn dropped the phone in the passenger seat before putting the vehicle in drive and taking off.

"Was that last part necessary?" Robyn declared.

"What? I just wanted her to know she can call me anytime."

"The dig wasn't necessary, but okay." It wasn't worth an argument. After a pause, Robyn decided to reset the energy between them. "Well . . . how's it going, Harper?" she asked. Small talk really wasn't her thing in the mornings, particularly with her ex-husband, but she wanted their call to end quickly and on a positive note. This was supposed to be the start of Robyn's "me time" and every second was valuable, especially today. She had . . . plans.

"Fine," Harper swore. "I'm a little behind on my deadline, but . . ."

"You'll get it done. You always do."

"Yeah, I guess. It's just this new form of writing screenplays is a little restrictive. . . ."

"Well, structure is good, right? Maybe it'll help to be more succinct, efficient—" Robyn cut herself off. She was doing it again: helping Harper problem-solve, giving encouragement. *Not this, Robyn,* she counseled herself. *It's not your job to solve Harper's problems. Not anymore. Just listen.*

"You're up late," she said, glancing over to see a vague outline of Harper in one of the rooms of his new expensive place, in the pitch-dark of the nighttime there. A stark contrast to the brilliance of the day that had already fully erupted in Ghana.

"Hey, can you move the phone so I can see you? The Ghanaian sky is nice, but I would rather see your face." Harper sounded kind and sincere.

*Why?* Robyn thought. *He's not your responsibility anymore, Robyn.* She grabbed the phone and put it in the cradle anyway. "That better?"

"Much. You alright?"

"I'm fine, Harper."

"Good. You look pretty." Robyn tried not to react. *What does he want?* Just as she began to wonder, he continued. "Sorry about the dig earlier. It just came out. I was only teasing."

"I get it, but it'd be nice to not paint me as the *mean* parent who's doing her best to set limits for our child."

"I think you're overstating it a bit . . ."

"That's fine. You can think that. It's my opinion and I'm sharing. Okay?" Robyn knew she was being short. She wasn't in the mood to debate or argue.

"Look, I was just saying good morning to you guys." Harper had a touch of impatience in his voice.

Robyn stayed even-keeled, but with growing curiosity. This wasn't an ordinary call. She knew that now. But she hoped that with civility, she'd bring him quickly to his point. "And Mia appreciates it. You've been good about being present. But next time you decide to extend her stay, we should discuss it and not have you just spring it on me. It's not fair." Robyn swore she heard a huff from Harper's end of the line. "What was that?" Robyn expected him to take her concerns seriously.

"Nothing. My bad." Harper replied with fatigue scraping through his voice. "She was having a good time. And had an opportunity to hang at Keisha's birthday party. She felt like a big girl being asked to stay over with Uncle Murch. And you said it was cool."

"I did . . . but I just think at this age, we need to give her the rules that we expect her to follow. She's already taking leeway where she can. I don't want this to start getting worse."

Harper sighed. *Give him grace, Robyn,* her mind implored. That was her nature anyway, not this version of her that was short and terse. She allowed a deep breath for herself.

"Listen, Harper, do you need anything else?" She hated the way the mobile device made her available at all hours of the day. Harper knew that. "I have to get my day started," she reminded him.

"I get it. I'll let you go . . . I just . . . uhhh . . . Oh. Candace's party was fun."

"Good." Robyn couldn't help smiling. "Did you get her the soy candle?"

"Wellll . . . by the time I got your suggestion . . ."

"By the time you got it? Well, *maybe* you should have asked me sooner," Robyn said flatly.

"I should've . . . just been . . . busy . . . you know . . ." He trailed off.

"Yup, I know." *All too well.* "What'd you end up getting?"

"Himalayan salt lamp. From Pakistan." Harper's response sounded tentative.

Robyn let loose a sardonic chuckle. "What saleslady convinced you that was the right thing?"

"It was fine . . ."

*Why am I engaging with him?* Robyn asked herself.

"The food was good," Harper continued. "I think you would have liked it. Nice atmosphere too. Very New York. Very Black . . ."

Robyn didn't respond other than with a barely audible and disinterested "uh-huh." She'd already tried disengaging twice; cordial didn't seem to be working.

"You were missed," Harper said finally. The tenor in his voice implied he'd thought about saying it before he did. There was something there. *He **definitely** wants something. He needs something. He needs a lot of things. . . .* Robyn didn't have the time or patience to probe.

"That's nice. Candace sounded like she felt celebrated," Robyn noted.

"She did. She was. Murch did it up. Yup." Harper lingered.

After an unnecessarily awkward few seconds, Robyn exhaled loudly. "Okay, sounds like you should get some sleep. I'll talk to you later—"

"Are you seeing somebody?" Harper lobbed the question quickly.

For the first time Robyn looked at the phone for more than a beat. *That's what? No, he didn't take this roundabout path to get in my business.*

"What?" Robyn said aloud. Maybe she'd misheard. *He wouldn't dare repeat that.*

"Uhhhh, I said, are you seeing somebody?"

"Why are you asking me that?" Robyn tried to be gracious, but that question? Coming from Harper now, it was out of line. Audacious even.

"One, I'm curious," he said casually, as if that had been a perfectly normal inquiry.

*Did this man just say he's curious? About who I'm dating? There's no way that Harper would have the nerve to . . .*

"And two," he added, "you're the mother of my child."

"And? What does that mean?" Harper was setting himself on thin ice.

"It just means that . . ." Harper paused. He looked away from the screen. "I mean, if you're seeing someone, I just want to know what man . . . or men . . . are around my daughter, that's all."

Robyn shook her head in disbelief. "Oh really, Harper? All of a sudden, you're so very interested in what's going on here?"

"Is that so strange?"

Robyn released a heavy sigh and searched for the right response. "You have got to be kidding me," she said softly as her head shook in slow disbelief. And then her disbelief became louder. "I'm living *my* life, Harper. And Mia is safe. My life may or may not involve dating someone, but that is none of your concern."

"Well, has Mia met this someone you may or may not be dating? Hypothetically, I guess," Harper pressed.

"Harper, we can talk straight. You aren't worried about Mia. You heard from somebody, Candace, I imagine, that I'm seeing someone and you're just being nosy. In *my* business."

"No, really, Robyn, that's not it . . . it's just—"

By now, Robyn had lost all patience with him and this conversation. She decided to end it and quickly, for real this time. "Okay, Harper, let's say I take you at your word. That this is about Mia. So then, are you seeing someone? What women have you had around? Are you seeing somebody—or some*bodies?* Out there having fun, right?"

Harper exhaled deeply and rolled his eyes dramatically. "Robyn," he pleaded.

But she wasn't about to let up now. "What's the matter? You don't like me asking you about your personal business? Who are you fu—"

"You know what?" By now Harper was waving his hand in the air, as if to clear things up between them. Robyn made sure to stifle her smile to let him continue. "It's not that serious. I was just checking in. I didn't mean to pry. I know we're not together and we have our separate lives, but I do still care about you and what's going on in your life. What affects you affects Mia. And after all, we're still a family, even if it's an unconventional one. So forgive me for being . . . *nosy.*"

Harper's words rang a bell in Robyn's gut. She had called him nosy. Maybe she was being too sensitive? She closed her eyes and allowed herself another deep breath. *Grace, Robyn. Give him grace.*

She returned to the conversation with a much lighter demeanor. "Like you said," she replied as breezily as she could manage, "it's not that serious. But I do have to go. The day has started, and I need to get to the restaurant." She felt relieved to see Harper smile and nod. "Goodbye, Harper." She reached toward the screen to end the call. And saw his head bob forward.

"So, just to be clear," he said quickly, "you're *not* seeing somebody, then?"

Robyn laughed. It was all there was left to do. "*Goodbye,* Harper," she said, and ended the call before another word could pass between the two of them.

By the end of the call, Robyn was renavigating Accra's rush-hour traffic, headed east, making decent progress toward her destination. Despite this morning's bumpy exchange, she was glad for the evolution of their relationship, which was more cordial now, friendly even, with each other's supposed best interests at heart. Maybe Harper even meant well by questioning her about who she was dating—though it was doubtful that was his motivation. Was Harper Stewart actually jealous that his ex might be keeping the company of another someone? She smiled at the notion that Harper felt some kind of way. Still, it was her business and her business alone that yes, there *was* someone.

*Kwesi*... just the thought of his name brought a smile to Robyn's lips first and then to her entire face. He had already left his usual good morning text during her call with Harper. Kwesi would be back in two days, this Thursday, from another one of his regular work trips. Robyn had already been contemplating how she'd show him in more ways than one how much she'd missed him while he was gone. She was in need of some attention, some desire, some passion beyond just being needed for care and survival.

The call with Harper was an uneasy reminder of how much Robyn had poured into her marriage. And it seemed like her ex-husband was growing, but slowly, like a stubborn shrub. He still wanted what he wanted when he wanted it and wasn't trying to take her needs into account. But that was no longer her concern. *I'm not his comforter or counselor,* she reminded herself. Even that small adjustment had taken a long time. Now it was her opportunity to decide where to next, not just in her life, but for the day ahead. She was free, temporarily, to be Robyn the person and not just the mother. No longer the wife—instead she was a healing version of herself who could and was willing to meet her own needs. Right now Robyn needed Robyn and Labadi Beach called to her.

It was only eight kilometers to the beach, but the traffic and aggression of the Accra drivers rivaled those of New York City. There were so many vehicles—mopeds, motorcycles, bicycles, trotros (their version of dollar vans), Sprinter vans, and SUVs transporting workers from their villages to their city jobs—alongside Robyn's RAV4 and jockeying for space on the road.

Seeing Black people everywhere and Blackness being the

default was an adjustment. One that Robyn embraced the hell out of. She marveled at the grace and determination with which the Ghanaians walked and moved through life. Children heading to school; street vendors opening their shops; the women and the men who could balance massive, wide baskets of supplies, produce, and fabrics on their heads. They moved like the statue of the great former president Kwame Nkrumah at Memorial Park come to life: erect and pointing forward with purpose. She drove past the large digital billboards hawking everything from soft drinks to makeup and haircare products to politicians looking for their vote. Accra was a city in transition: brand-new hotels, restaurants, fashion boutiques, and art galleries neighbored buildings that were in various stages of deconstruction and reconstruction. Accra was also adjusting, blossoming, and the energy of the people reflected that. Closer to the beach, the buildings were spaced farther apart, giving way to larger individual homes and beachside hotels. At Labadi, Robyn quickly reached the small clearing where she liked to park.

Despite the beach's many hustlers trying to get the *obruni* to buy artwork, horse rides, sightseeing tours, jewelry, or souvenir T-shirts, they mainly left Robyn alone. When she first arrived, she too was obruni but now they greeted her with a smile and wave of recognition and familiarity. When she'd arrived in Accra, Robyn promised herself that being this close to the ocean she would make an effort to meet its shores often and commune with the ancestors. Come here to Labadi, to think and reflect, especially in the early times of their move, when the sting of the divorce from Harper was still especially fresh. Twenty-one years of marriage, ended. Twenty-one. That's a child in college, a whole lifetime of experience with a person, and *as* the person she *used to* be. Married to a great American novelist. The consummate supportive wife and partner. Sure, Harper was an inspiration. His creativity and drive were fuel for their family in many ways, and particularly financially. His hard work made it possible for them to have wonderful experiences and a lifestyle many would envy. But that hadn't ever been what Robyn wanted, not really.

True, Harper had supported the exploration of her different interests, paid for culinary school even. They'd had good sex; he was an attentive lover and, damn, could he wear the hell out of a nice suit. Robyn had to smirk a bit at the thought. Especially remembering how she felt in the good times, before the passion had evaporated. Before the sex became perfunctory at best and then sporadic and then virtually nonexistent. Every marriage goes through its phases, but theirs just seemed to take a turn they couldn't come back from. Not even with Robyn's gestures, suggestions—that they find new experiences together, have more date nights, hell, she'd even suggested they buy property in San Pierre. But what do you do and how do you fix it when someone else is simply happy to take what you're giving? And giving, and giving, and giving. That was Harper—he took everything Robyn gave and still seemed to want more.

*Now I want more,* Robyn thought as she looked out at the white sand, clear ocean, and cumulus clouds. The shores that had once been a backdrop of terror for her ancestors gave Robyn fortifying energy. The rich breeze filled her with a sense of wonder, of power. Harper was on the other side of that ocean, five thousand miles and a world away, and it was up to Robyn to keep sight of that and chart her own path. She would follow her heart now, like she did then, when she made the difficult decision to move. It was in moments like this one, when she stood at the edge of the ocean, almost like she could fly, when her spirit was ready to soar, that she knew she'd made the right decision.

Robyn pulled her shoes off to let her feet sink into the sand.

She walked toward the water's edge, deciding on a whim to let the whitewash lap up to her ankles as she strolled along the shoreline. She began to quietly repeat her affirmations, spoken daily, sometimes here, sometimes in the mirror. They were what she needed to remember. What she needed to be true.

"I deserve happiness," she said. "I deserve healing . . . I deserve wholeness . . . I deserve peace . . . I deserve rest . . ." And then thinking of Kwesi for the first time, she added, "I deserve . . . to be . . . *desired.* I deserve passion. I want to be wanted." And in reply, the sea roared back and the breeze blew its way under her clothes.

Later, just a few miles from the beach, Robyn wove her way through the bustling central Makola Market. Robyn had many vendors there she was loyal to for her restaurant's vital ingredients, but she was always down to explore, to feel the crackling energy of the crowded streets and browse the open-air stalls. The noises and smells were loud, commanding her attention. All around her were offerings of artfully arranged peppers in the reds, greens, and yellows of the Ghanaian flag, and metal bowls filled to the brim with orange and brown spices. Robyn quickly found Adjua, her shopper/helper in the market.

"Maakye, Robyn!" The tall industrious teen balanced a huge metal bowl full of produce on her head and greeted her with a bright impish grin.

"Maakye, Adjua." Robyn returned her good morning in native Twi with a smile. Adjua pulled the massive bowl from her head to reveal ripe red tomatoes, bright green cucumbers, pale yellow garden eggs (Ghanaian eggplant), firm green plantain, magenta petals of dried hibiscus flowers, lush green taro leaves, and silver and yellow salted eel. Robyn smiled and sifted through the items nodding and adding, "Yesss, okay. You found the velvet tamarind! Nice job, Adjua . . ." Adjua was pleased to know she had done well by her boss. "Did you find the palm wine?" Robyn asked as she inhaled the spicy aroma of a scotch bonnet pepper she held to her nostrils.

"No, miss, not yet," Adjua answered bashfully. "I couldn't find, but . . ." She dug farther in the bowl to show Robyn a healthy bunch of bright red palm nuts and some freshly pressed palm nut oil. "The vendor said these mixed with the oil could maybe be strained to make the wine . . ?"

Robyn shook her head no. "We need the wine. Come . . ." Robyn offered to help Adjua lift the bowl back over her shoulders and to the top of her head so she and Adjua could complete the mission. "Can I help?"

Adjua turned away from Robyn's reach respectfully. "No, miss. I have," she responded and waited for Robyn to lead the way.

Robyn didn't love the idea of the hierarchy that existed in Ghana. In Robyn's eyes, Adjua was part of her team, not a servant, but traditionally, like any other society, there were the haves and the have-nots, no matter how much kinship Robyn may have felt. It took getting used to. Again, she adjusted.

"Akwaaba, miss!" the vendors called out to Robyn with smiles on their weathered obsidian faces. "Bra, bra." They summoned her to approach their stalls hawking cassava flour and mackerel. Robyn returned a smile and wave with a "Maakye, maakye," and strode through the market with a confidence that she hadn't previously possessed. Her early experiences with Makola Market had been intimidating to say the least—she had little familiarity with the language and as much as she had wanted to feel at home right away in the culture, there was still so much for her to learn.

Eighteen months ago, she'd decided on having her own restaurant to showcase her culinary approach and honor the beauty of her new home. That meant fresh ingredients and produce, the flavors of the land—starting in the market. There, no-nonsense female vendors took their produce—and their worth—very seriously. Their mixture of Twi, Ga, and English was overwhelming.

"Bo-ko, mepawokyew" Robyn would plead, attempting *"Slowly, please"* as politely as she could. These women wanted her business, but they didn't appreciate her unfamiliarity with their modes of communication. They had little patience for the obruni, the foreigner. Colloquially, the word meant "white person." *What? Me? White?* From the time she'd first arrived, Robyn was so hurt to have that term applied to her. Not only was Robyn obruni but a single, American, female obruni. These women were native to the land and had seen plenty of interlopers coming in to *see* the culture but not *be* the culture.

Robyn was an intruder—and one without a man? Why should she have a better chance at a better life in their homeland? They would sell to her . . . for a price in cedis that was often double what it would cost back home. At first, they'd just wanted her obruni money, so they hustled her. If Robyn had questions about texture, taste, or "smoking point," they by and large seemed annoyed, kissing their teeth with impatience. If she asked, "Do taro leaves cook down like collard greens?" the vendors rolled their eyes and just repeated the price again, scrunching up their faces in bewilderment and looking away. Meanwhile Robyn tried to learn, squeezing and smelling plump red tomatoes, massaging bags of anise seed or whole black peppercorns, and tasting bitter turkey berries and sweet tiger nuts.

Today that rejection no longer occurred. The vendors knew Robyn now by face and name and they greeted her with smiles as they clamored for her business.

"Akwaaba, Robyn! Etisen?"

"Me ho ye." Robyn replied she was fine in their native tongue.

"Maakye, Robyn. Fresh okra over here for you. For your stews . . . !"

"Daabi, mepa wo kyew," Robyn responded with a smile, saying no thank you, but assuring her she'd be back. She was on a mission for palm wine; she needed it for something . . . special, very special. Robyn kept moving and swiveling her head, searching for the vendor that she heard sold it in small batches.

"If you blink you'll miss it," Robyn recalled one of her favorite people saying. Robyn found the vendor sandwiched between a stall selling cornmeal and another selling to-go bottles of bright red sobolo. Though Robyn loved the familiar taste of this refreshing elixir that reminded her of Jamaican sorrel, she stayed focused on securing the palm wine she wanted. As she traded her Ghanaian currency—the cedi—for the bottle of the milky, sweet, and effervescent liquid, she heard a warm, booming, and familiar voice behind her.

"Aaaah, you found it!" Robyn turned with a smile. It was Thema. "Maakye, Robyn!"

"Maakye, Thema," Robyn returned, arms outstretched as she embraced the older towering Ghanaian woman with a youthful spirit that was so full of wisdom. "What are you doing here?"

"Grabbing a few items. The velvet tamarind is about to be in season and I want to plant some."

"Yesss, I started working with it too," Robyn was happy to report. "That was the last thing we needed."

Thema gestured with her head to follow her. "Come, let's catch up."

Robyn couldn't help but smile at Thema as they made their way toward the market's exit. It had been a few weeks since she'd been to see Thema, her usual visit to this miracle worker of a woman who had been the key to Robyn's salvation on this continent, when she'd most needed saving.

Robyn first met Thema during her time being hazed in Makola Market. In her early days of starting Robyn's Nest, Robyn had also tried her hand at negotiating with the fisherman down at Osu Beach. They peddled red snapper, grouper, and lobster for a fair and decent price, but it was still a shock to see the conditions these industrious folks lived under. Osu Beach was full of colorful fishing boats that painted a beautiful picture against the sapphire sky and azure water, but it was littered with abandoned "donated" clothing, plastic bottles, bags, and rubbish. The stench of sewage and waste invaded her nostrils depending on which way the wind blew. After a few frustrating attempts, Robyn was overwhelmed. She sat down on the sand with her just-purchased fish and cried. The poverty, the living conditions, the disparities—it didn't feel right, or fair. Nor was it what she'd expected. And as hard as she tried, she didn't feel like she understood her new home. Had she failed? Had she made a terrible mistake? Was moving halfway across the world . . . impulsive? Silly, even? Admitting that to herself, or anyone (especially Harper), would have been devastating. Thankfully, at least Mia seemed to be adjusting okay. But Robyn had been feeling out of place like the fish that sat by her side on the sand. She wasn't suffocating but she was looking for air.

And then she saw her.

An older Black woman dressed in flowing white fabrics standing on the rocky outcrops close to the ocean. Her copper arms were outstretched toward the sea as if to say, *"I am here and I dare you to move me."* She stood fierce and erect, communing with the powerful sea, immovable. She was performing some kind of spiritual ritual that Robyn couldn't understand, but she commanded Robyn's gaze. Robyn envied her calm, her confidence, her majesty.

As the woman retreated from the rocks, Robyn watched, trying her best not to stare. Unexpectedly, the woman turned to Robyn and approached, introducing herself. Thema (Tema) was her name. Rather than treating Robyn like a stranger, she offered a comforting touch. "Are you okay, my dear?" she asked in a raspy yet soothing voice.

"No. But I will be, thank you." Robyn had been honest even if she didn't fully believe it. Her glass-half-full posture demanded it. Thema examined Robyn head to toe and told Robyn to come visit her at her place because she "looked in need."

Robyn shook her head. "No," she said. "That would be selfish of me to think *I'm* in need." She gestured to her surroundings.

"There are different levels, Robyn," Thema replied. "You can't give your best unless you are your best. *You* are the work. To be good for yourself, your business, and your children."

Robyn smiled and nodded. "You're right, but I only have one child. My daughter, Mia."

"You have a son," Thema said declaratively. *What?* Robyn instinctively leaned away.

"N-No I don't," she said, but her mind whispered, *Solomon.*

"Yes, you do. He's right next to you." Thema gestured to the air at Robyn's right side. Robyn cautiously looked in that direction, saw nothing, and was rendered speechless. The way Thema looked at her, she knew what she was talking about. She didn't guess. *She knows about Solomon,* Robyn thought. "Come see me," Thema said and squeezed Robyn's hand before she even knew she was holding it.

Robyn showed up at Thema's Healing Compound. It was a sprawling green beachside campus, an oasis of interdisciplinary learning that focused on culture, sustainability, and most of all, healing. The land was home to a garden of fresh vegetables, robust farm animals, a neem healing tree, and a yoga studio. There, Thema specialized in spiritual, ancestral, and emotional healing. Robyn had practiced many of Thema's modalities before, so her spirit was open and drawn to these earthy, bohemian vibes.

On Thema's healing table, Robyn was an open wound. Thema laid her hands with care, clearing energy, working with Robyn on unlocking her healing. And after a number of sessions, the next miraculous thing Thema said was an answer to a question Robyn hadn't asked out loud.

"You belong here," Thema declared.

She didn't just mean "here" with her, but here in Accra, here in Africa. Robyn was right to be *here,* to have followed her heart.

"You have so much to offer and being here will produce your offerings in abundance." Warm tears released from Robyn's eyes immediately. Thema gently wiped her cheeks, radiating energy that was powerful yet peaceful. She possessed great strength and had helped many other returnees find their rightful place in their new world.

"Give it time," Thema assured her. "Let go of what you've known. Start anew. You will discover your life's purpose. You've always been searching for you. You're finding her. She's here." Robyn felt a rush of tension release and convulsed with a full-body weeping. Thema continued to run her hands over Robyn's face and scalp, down her neck and shoulders.

"You're home, Robyn. Your daughter is home. Your son is home."

As Thema gently held the space, Robyn mourned her and Harper's loss in a way that she hadn't at the time of the miscarriage. And then when the mourning was complete, Thema helped Robyn create a pathway toward healing—breathing, meditation, intuition, acknowledgment. Over time, bit by bit, she untethered herself from the trauma of her short time with Solomon. She could say his name. She knew where he was, his place in her life, in the Universe, comforted that his spirit had never been lost after all.

Over the next year Robyn's confidence grew. She visited Thema every week to continue her journey. Her Twi and Gaa got stronger. She made allies, sisters, and community. With an expanded mind, everything fell into place, including the space in East Legon for Robyn's Nest. Perfect for an up-and-coming enclave of upwardly mobile Ghanaians who wanted the pioneering culinary experiences Robyn was offering.

Now, exiting the marketing with Thema, Robyn walked arm in arm with her to Robyn's RAV4. Adjua followed with the bowl of goods still expertly balanced on her head. Thema smiled generously. "Your new friend. When does he return?"

Now it was Robyn's turn to show her own happiness. She couldn't help it, smiling so big, her eyelashes touched her cheeks. She looked around to see if Adjua could hear and stepped Thema away from the rear of the vehicle like a high school girl bursting to share gossip. "*Kwesi.* He comes back Thursday,"

Robyn answered. Just thinking of him, speaking his name, she felt giddy.

"We're going to meet at his place. He wants to cook together." Robyn's smile grew wider. Thema's face showed excitement with a dose of her usual restraint.

"Aaah, and what are you making?"

"Oh, just some waakye." Robyn threw out the name of a local street food made of rice, black-eyed peas, and chicken. "He's been raving about his grandmother's. And I think I can best it." Robyn nodded with confidence. Thema looked at her blankly.

"You're kidding me, right?" Thema said.

Robyn's voice rose to a defensive pitch. "I'm going to make it great. Put my own spin on it. Some rosemary. Some scotch bonnet."

"I don't understand. You want him to think of his grandmother?" Thema asked earnestly.

Robyn laughed. "I just wanted him to think of *home.*"

"You could be his home. Make him think of *you.*"

Robyn smiled, exhaled, and looked away in thought.

"What is that . . . look of doubt in your face?" Robyn began an explanation but couldn't quite find the words. "Uh-uh. Speak," Thema encouraged her. "Express your feelings."

"I don't know, it's just . . . should I be doing that? I mean, should I be . . . 'catering' to him?"

"You are a caterer, are you not?"

"Thema . . ."

"You act like that's a bad thing."

Robyn frowned. "It can be. What if he doesn't really appreciate my efforts?"

"Kwesi is not your ex-husband," Thema stated simply. Robyn

nodded and blinked slowly, pressing her lips together. *Thema's right.*

"Robyn, don't let your past relationship or someone else's definitions and agenda dictate what's in your heart to do. Be true to *yourself.*" Thema stepped closer to hold Robyn's face in her hands. "You are a gift to the world. As a master chef, you stimulate and excite all the senses, the nose, the palate, the heart, the soul." Hearing Thema describe her like this made Robyn feel like a superhero. "Show him who you are through your food and in any other way you choose. This is your love language. Use it."

Robyn could only smile and nod in recognition. *I'm still healing* . . . she realized.

"It's a process, my dear," Thema said as if she'd read her mind.

Robyn sighed. "Yes, it is." Just then, the sound of the pattering of raindrops started to fill the air around them, dropping onto the muddy gravel of the parking clearing. Thema looked around expectantly.

"We had better go. I'll stop in later this week for dinner."

"I look forward to it. Medaase." Robyn thanked her with a hug. Adjua shut the hatchback door as Thema retreated down the street, seemingly unbothered by the thought of getting soaked. Robyn marveled at her. *She is one with nature. . . .* Robyn and Adjua ducked into the mini SUV and shut the doors, leaving Robyn to think of what dish would be her *own* version of home.

# CHAPTER NINE

## Robyn

As Aduja and the rest of the staff helped unload the RAV4, Robyn rushed through the downpour across the restaurant courtyard to pull open the wrought iron and glass door of Robyn's Nest. Stepping inside, to get away from the rain that was flooding her pergola-capped patio, she splashed into at least two inches of water inside the entrance.

"What the hell?" Robyn said. Her staff was using big push brooms to sweep the water away as fast as they could. Her heart sank to see the buckets strewn about between the lovely coffee brown wooden tables she'd so carefully picked out. Now water was everywhere—drowning the usually spotless dark gray floor tiles, dripping into buckets, splashed on the bar counter in the back. The only place that seemed somewhat dry was the kitchen, where Robyn could see the team scrambling to try to prepare for a lunch service despite the inconveniences. At least the power was on.

Haniah, her restaurant manager, chief of staff, and all-around Ghanaian superstar, rushed over to meet her, a concerned look crossing her usually resplendent hazelnut face. "Welcome to Atlantis," she said. Haniah's wry sense of humor wasn't amusing Robyn now. Haniah pointed toward the bar where the water had breached. "The rain came swiftly and through the side wall. We're grabbing sandbags." East Legon's streets were not the best built for drainage when large downpours hit the neighborhood. The water gathered and went where it could. Another development thanks to global warming.

"Didn't the city say they were coming to fix the street?" Robyn placed her market items on the nearest dry surface. Haniah looked at Robyn with a thin smile and pointed glance.

Robyn recognized her error right away. "You're right. I'm sorry. 'This is not America.'" She echoed what Haniah had said about the many challenges of having a business in a developing area.

Robyn looked toward the spots in her ceiling that dripped. "And the roof . . . ugh . . ."

"We'll deal with it," Haniah reassured her.

"Thank you."

"Because we have bigger fish to fry. And I don't mean tilapia."

"What now?"

"Well, the refrigerator wasn't working this morning—again—but it seems they were able to fix it before all of the perishables spoiled. We only need to remake the chicken stock." Robyn closed her eyes to release an involuntary exhale. *Breathe deep, Robyn,* she reminded herself. Haniah ran her hand through her dark asymmetrical locs as she continued her updates. "*And* Aboagye. Aboagye came by again, saying that he needs to speak with you most urgently about the rent. And he brought a visitor! Someone he said wanted to see the location. But I told him he would have to either start a tab or leave! Of course, he left." Haniah looked particularly satisfied with herself.

"Thank you." Robyn made a point to look into Haniah's eyes and then grabbed a rag to attempt to wipe down the tabletops.

The thanks was as futile as Robyn's attempt to dry the dining room. The more days that passed, and the more calamities that mounted, the harder it became to keep a brave face amid this level of chaos. Haniah needed a raise. Rent for the year was a full sixty thousand American dollars, and in Accra it was due in advance for the year. It was already hard enough to manage the regular expenses, but the additional burden of coming up with a lump sum of that magnitude was crushing. Robyn's Nest was just barely making enough to break even every month. "Did Aboagye say anything about when they would fix these holes?" Robyn pointed to her ceiling.

"I asked him about that. And he said that he would fix the roof when you fix the hole in his bank account where the rent should be."

Robyn shook her head and released another sigh. Robyn had been paying month to month—which was difficult enough—and holding the remainder hostage until Aboagye agreed to fix what was broken, including some faulty appliances and a jalopy of a food truck. They were playing a game of chicken and Robyn was certainly stalling until she could generate more events, pop-ups, and marketing opportunities for her restaurant. Sixty thousand would not completely deplete her savings, but it would hurt. And she was already hurting enough. Robyn had so many challenges—with suppliers, a tenuous line of credit in Ghana, and the expenses of having to maintain her own water supply and a backup generator in case the power went out—that there was little room for error.

There wasn't much that could be done today other than to strategically place a few more buckets and sandbags until the storm cleared. They would clean what could be cleaned, and prepare for a lunch service for whichever patrons were willing to brave the rain for a good meal. On a typical day, this would be disheartening. But on this day, even the calamity of the rain, and the leak, and the rent, and the potential shortfall on the lunch service, none of it was going to ruin Robyn's plans. In fact, the lighter lunch rush meant that she could do just as Thema said and create something from her culinary heart for Kwesi that would light him up with flavor and communicate through a special dish just how she felt about him.

"Okay," she said with resignation and put down the rag.

"Okay?" Haniah looked puzzled.

"There's nothing we can do about it now, Haniah. We'll make do for lunch service. And, honestly, I need a little brainstorm about my dinner in a few days."

"It's chicken waakye, Robyn. You can make that in your sleep."

"I'm going a different direction." Robyn revealed the palm wine with a small flair. "And I'm going to feature this."

Instantly, Haniah's face brightened. It was almost as if the sun had come out within the restaurant. "Whaaaat? Ohhhh, I like the sound of this." Haniah began to pick up the handles of the bags of produce that Robyn had set on the bar top. "Come, come," Haniah said as she took off toward the kitchen. "We have work to do."

Moments later, the kitchen was filled with rich and deep smells of peanut curry and roasting meat as the chef de cuisine and his two sous chefs bustled about preparing the lunch menu selections. Robyn dipped a tasting spoon into the nearest pot as she passed.

"That needs to be thicker," she instructed. Her chefs were still learning, but Robyn's refined palate was the marker that kept diners coming back. And she'd use it with focus now, for her one special guest—the man who kept making her smile. Haniah spread the fresh ingredients from the market across the stainless steel prep surface, inspecting them.

"Pull out the shallots and garlic, please," Robyn said as she headed to the temperamental refrigerator to retrieve a pound of mussels. Haniah took notice.

"The jewels of the sea, huh?" she said of the sleek, ebony shells. Robyn dumped them into a rinsing pot. "What are you doing with these?"

"After I clean them, I'll steam them and make a rich broth using the palm wine." Robyn was beginning to feel confident in her plan. "Ooh, where did I put that lemongrass . . . ?" Robyn said to the air.

"Here you go." Haniah presented the narrow and fragrant yellow-green stalks to Robyn, who was adding flour to her mussels to remove excess sand.

Robyn looked at what Haniah held in her hand and quickly shook her head. "Oh, thank you, but no. Not that one," she said, recognizing the bunch she'd bought earlier at the market. "I brought some in from my garden the other day . . ." Robyn went off in search for the ingredient.

"Mmmmm, I'm liking the sound of this, chef," Haniah said behind her.

"Me too." Robyn smiled, returning with the precise herb she was seeking. She held it to her nose. *Mmmmm. That's it.* She was going to give Kwesi something that he could love, something of her. This was a new start, a fresh page, and a new twist on known flavors. Thema was right. The dish that she'd create would be for him and he would only think of her. No sense in competing with Grandma.

"He's not going to know what hit him." Haniah gave Robyn

a playful nudge with her shoulder. Robyn laughed with her. Somehow, they always managed to find the joy in the challenges they faced together, those now and past—over the last year building Robyn's Nest. There never was enough of anything other than creativity and faith along this journey. Robyn had already exhausted the money she'd earned selling her food subscription business, and the bulk of Harper's alimony money was dedicated to Mia and her costs for school. After securing their modest home, she hadn't touched another dime of it. Something in her needed to know that she was capable of succeeding on her own.

While Haniah continued the counter prep—chopping onions, mincing garlic, and crushing the fresh lemongrass—Robyn remembered the moment that Kwesi first walked into the restaurant, between the lunch and dinner service, trying to nab a meal even though they had none of their usual items to serve. With thin margins, the restaurant didn't have many days when the specials for lunch and dinner weren't sold out by the end.

And so, when this tall and handsome man, with Ghanaian features and a notable British accent walked through her doors, Robyn was taken aback. As harried as she was, she could still recognize beauty when she saw it. She wanted to ask him to come back later, but she also didn't want him to leave. Not with that smile—she did not want to see those broad shoulders sauntering out. She wanted to feed him, to nourish him with what she'd created. He apologized when he learned he was both late for lunch and early for dinner. He'd lost track of time on a string of business calls but had made it a point to come specifically to *her* restaurant—he'd heard so many good things from friends, he'd been meaning to stop by and taste a sample.

Robyn couldn't resist. She threw together what was available:

a little leftover seafood stew that had some heat in its aftertaste, some roasted plantain and peanuts, homemade cassava bread, and roasted root vegetables. Oh, how that man devoured what she'd provided him. He moaned with delight, left a generous "donation," and, most important, promised to be back. That was six months ago. And he kept his promise. He returned to Robyn's restaurant at least twice a week. After a month, it became clear that he was no longer returning just for a plate. And then he made it undeniable.

"Could I take you out on a date sometime?" He'd asked so tentatively, on his way out the door, as if he'd just slip out and away if she said no. It was a sweet and charming gesture from a masculine man with a kind spirit. In her mind she was ready to leap into his arms at the invitation. But the practical part of her paused—running a business, raising her daughter—when would she have time for a date? Preemptively, Kwesi made it easier—or harder—for her.

"You seem like a busy lady, so we can work around your schedule." A number of early morning coffees morphed into attending a yoga class, some visits to the beach, and even a trip to Kwame Nkrumah Memorial Park with Mia. Robyn found it exhilarating to be courted. She didn't think it would happen in this way. And certainly not by a man who was too beautiful to be spending so much time with one woman. He too kept a busy schedule as a real-estate developer and entrepreneur with ties to his ex and the teenage boys they shared. They hadn't so much as kissed until four weeks ago. It wasn't from lack of desire or attraction. She didn't want to go there without having the time and space "to go there." She enjoyed her time with him; it was a delight, and in two nights, they would cook together at his Cantonments apartment. That's why this needed to be special. She wanted to share more than just her cooking with him.

They'd waited to make love. *Thursday, the wait will be over,* she thought.

The scent of fragrant garlic and shallots brought Robyn's attention back into the kitchen as Haniah stirred the translucent aromatics in olive oil. Robyn snapped out of her past and future thoughts of Kwesi to add thyme, parsley, minced lemongrass, and green lemon slices to the pot. The citrus essence supercharged Robyn's senses. Her mouth watered and she smiled. She poured a quarter cup of the milky palm wine into the pan and it sizzled.

Robyn took the rinsed mussels and poured them into the developing elixir with a clatter. The taste would come from more discreet decisions—how long to simmer, how much of the turn of the wrist in stirring—Robyn was aware of each of her choices. She knew when these mollusks opened their delicate flesh, they would take on the aromatic essence of what she created, transforming them into a culinary treasure. Ten minutes later, by the time the lunch service was almost over, they were. Robyn removed the pot cover, and the opened mussels were bursting with flavor that you could almost taste in the billowing steam. They looked perfectly cooked and delicious, making them as alluring to the eye as they would be irresistible to the palate. Robyn dipped her wooden spoon into the pan, scraping the bottom and pulling up a bit of the pale milky broth to cool and then to taste. She rolled her tongue around the broth in her mouth. Haniah slid her face next to Robyn's to take in the sight and smell.

"That looks and smells incredible," she said. "How is it?"

"Can you plate the cassava?" Haniah knew her well enough to interpret her response. If she was moving forward, it was already perfect. Robyn gestured with both hands to make a circle. "Large shallow soup bowl."

"That means it must be *delicious,*" Haniah said, returning with steaming chunks of cassava. Robyn spooned out a handful of mussels with a deep ladle of the rich palm wine broth, being careful to drench the cubes of the starchy root. It was a work of art to the eyes and an olfactory symphony to the nose. Robyn handed over a metal spoon to Haniah, who used it to pop a fleshy mussel out of its shell, and then scoop it, a bite-sized piece of cassava, and a generous helping of the broth toward her mouth.

Robyn studied Haniah's face as she tasted, releasing her breath only when she saw her eyes nearly roll to the back of her head in delight.

"Robyn, this man is going to marry you," Haniah said, licking the last of the juice from the spoon. "And if he doesn't, I will." Robyn laughed. "That palm wine broth is heavenly."

"He said he was making bread." Robyn began to assemble her own sample of mussel, cassava, and broth. "That bread is going to sop up the broth and take it on."

"I don't know what else you have planned for the cocoa butter and the tamarind but if they taste anything like this, Mia may need to stay at my place for the weekend!" Haniah smiled with delight. "What time is the date on Thursday?"

"I was thinking that maybe she should go with you from here, after school? Then I'll have time to get ready and—"

"Uh-uh." Haniah cut Robyn off. "Let her see you beautiful." Haniah gave Robyn a look of concern. "She should see her mother as a goddess, when you are in the fullness of who you are. Don't hide that from her. Let her see you. Bring her on your way to your date."

Mia was not quite blossoming, but showing Robyn enough of a challenge at eleven that perhaps it would be good for her to see a different side of her mother other than just the disciplinarian, just the hard worker, just the cook, school chauffeur, and cleanup crew for their home. What she showed Mia would set the stage for what Mia would expect for herself as she grew. *Yes,* Robyn thought, *yes, this might be just what my little girl needs to see.*

# CHAPTER TEN

## Harper

Something about the New York City mornings brought an invigoration to Harper, even when he worked all through the night. Since Candace's birthday party and the breakthrough he'd reached even after hearing rather disturbing news, he managed to push both Robyn's dating life and Jordan's life without him out of his mind, to refocus intently, *alone* for two straight days. He'd taken that time to perfect and refine his big idea and was now feeling very bullish about his movie pitch—evidently so was his agent. Harper stepped out of his spa shower into the steam of his bathroom feeling refreshed. And he continued to replay the feedback he'd gotten from Stan in his mind as he toweled off. "*That sounds great, Harper,*" Stan said excitedly after hearing the highlights of this new direction. "*It sounds just like what those Hollywood muckety-mucks are looking for. Great job!*" Their conversation had gone perfectly. Stan was planning on meeting him in LA, and he'd also be at the book signing that Cassidy set up.

Later in the afternoon, Cassidy called him to review the final details for his trip. "You all set?" she wanted to know. The question was mostly rhetorical because Cassidy always made sure Harper had everything he needed for his appearances. *Cassidy gets shit done,* Harper thought. "How's your kitchen today?" she deadpanned through the phone receiver. To the untrained ear, it'd be difficult to decipher whether she was joking, but Harper knew better.

"Ha ha" was his sarcastic response. In return, Cassidy delivered a low "heheheh." She didn't judge, but she also didn't want anything to interfere with his burgeoning public image.

"You could still stand to post a little more on social media," she nudged. "I know that's not your thing, but it helps, you having a presence out there. The national morning hit was good and the authors that you shouted out are appreciative. But let's give folks a little more access to you . . . *online.*" Cassidy pushed gently, but was definitely about business.

"I agree" was Harper's response. "On all."

"How's Mia?" Cassidy asked, as she normally did. Mia was always Harper's primary concern when he traveled, especially when time-zone changes disrupted his schedule of speaking to her.

"She's good. We had a great visit last month."

"And Robyn?"

"Living her best life far as I can tell."

"Good for her."

Harper paused. "Yeah . . . I guess so."

"And what's that pause about?" she asked. She always caught everything.

"Nothing."

"Harper . . ."

"She's seeing somebody. Apparently." Harper tried to feign casual disinterest.

"Oh. Good for her."

"You're right," he said.

"You jealous?" Cassidy asked flatly.

"No. Not . . . jealous . . ." Harper mused. "Just, I don't know. I'm processing it, I guess?"

As usual, Cassidy was all business. "What's to process? She's seeing somebody. You're seeing many bodies. You're both adults, you're both responsible. You live half a world apart and co-parent a beautiful daughter."

"I know. I got it."

"Just saying . . ."

"I heard you. I still gotta pack."

"You haven't packed yet . . . ?"

"It's only three days."

"Okay, wear something handsome. Take pictures. Post them. Let your fans know you're coming."

"Bye, Cass."

Harper, now dried and groomed, stood in his closet in just his underwear picking out clothes for his LA trip. He was packing late as usual. His flight was at six p.m. and it was already three in the afternoon. He'd be gone for only three days, so he needed just enough to fit in one carry-on. He hated waiting for checked baggage. But he'd also put a hold on a villa on Maui. If the studio liked his pitch he planned to head to Hawaii to do some writing on the screenplay—with no distractions. He had thought about inviting someone to go there with him: Tracy, Michelle, Jessica, even Bailey, but if he was really going to get work done, he'd have to be by himself. He worked best solo, but something in him hated being alone. Best to head somewhere he could be soothed by the calm of nature and focus on nothing but his work.

As much as he liked his routine, the loneliness that came

could tempt him to deviate from his task of writing. As disciplined as Harper normally was when it came to work, he was vulnerable right now to wanting company. The right text at the wrong time was often a combination that led to poor decisions he (and his work) would pay for later. And it never seemed to end well. If there was distance between him and New York, he'd be much less tempted. But maybe . . . if he allowed one of these paramours seeking girlfriend-status to be more integral to his process, if he allowed them in, then maybe they could be of support. Maybe they could be a partner. Maybe they could be . . . like Robyn. . . .

Not by replacing her, no, but by helping him like she used to, to shape an idea, build concepts, bounce thoughts back and forth. Someone to be his partner. That would be an ideal mate. Then his life might fit again. Maybe he should be more open. . . .

Or maybe that's a crutch. Harper produced his finest work by hunkering down and getting shit done. He didn't have time for distractions, worrying about someone else's schedule and what they wanted for breakfast. But being honest about that made him an asshole. He wanted to have his freedom, but he also wanted someone there for him. It was very much a "have the cake and eat it too" scenario. *Harp, you're a mess. . . .* Jordan would have held him accountable, told him to "pick a lane." Make a decision and stick to it. Hopefully she'd respond to his text before much longer. He could really use her counsel. It'd be great to see her again. She'd help him figure his shit out. *Fuck.* He missed her.

Whether he got the chance to see Jordan or not, still, this trip would allow Harper to have some much-needed introspection. Do some deep meditations, be present. Yes, get this script written, but more important, reflect on this station in his life, and where he wanted . . . no, *needed* to go. Everyone else in his life seemed to know what they wanted and were getting it, living it. *What do I want?* Harper pondered. The answer sounded so simple: happiness, love, fulfillment, friendship, companionship, financial success. He'd had all those things at one point, mostly with Robyn. But he also hadn't always considered Robyn. He remembered her saying in their marriage counseling sessions, "*I think of you, I* consider *you.*" He listened but he didn't *hear* her. Not always. Too caught up in his own self-worth and career. Too preoccupied to be reciprocal because she always picked up the slack. The next woman he chose to be with had to bring a lot to the table, but what was he going to give or sacrifice? How could he *do the work*? That part he had to figure out.

Time was getting short; he needed to make some quick decisions. He opened the drawer and pulled out tees, shorts, underwear, and socks, then grabbed his toiletry bag from the bathroom. He zipped up his monogrammed carry-on. With that done, his matching knapsack for his computer, noise-canceling headphones, notepads and pens were all he needed. He was ready to go.

Packing made him think of the reality of his trip. After LA, the change of scenery would be good. He could keep a low profile, take some hikes, have some poke bowls, and figure out his next steps. His next chapter. The only drawback was that he'd be even farther from his good mornings with Mia. She'd be more than half a day ahead with him in Maui. He'd have to be very mindful and set alarms for himself. He'd never want to disappoint her or not keep his promises to call. He pulled out his phone and noticed, *Hmm . . . Still nothing from Jordan.* He tisked his teeth and released his frustration into the emptiness. "Come on, J. Leave me hanging . . . ?"

It was already 3:30 p.m. The driver would be arriving soon. That time in New York translated to 8:30 p.m. in Accra. Mia was likely getting ready for bed. Even if it was late, Harper wanted to touch base with her and not take any risk missing their usual call. *Has Robyn given her back her phone yet?* he wondered. Even though the last conversation with his ex had *ended* cordially, he didn't want the likelihood of his own awkwardness to set the vibe of another exchange. He'd try Mia's phone. Maybe Mommy had relented.

Two rings in Mia's sweet smiling face appeared. "Hi, Daddy."

"Hey, baby. Looks like you got your phone back. Yayyy!"

"Yup" was her response.

"Somebody must have been a good girl. How was school today?"

"Fine."

"What Mommy make for dinner tonight?"

"Jollof rice and chicken waakye from the restaurant. Ms. Haniah brought it for me and Mawusi."

"Ohh," Harper said in faint recognition. Haniah was Robyn's right hand. They had met when Harper first visited Accra, and he'd heard the name Mawusi before associated with Mia's school and playdates. They were buddies. "Good, all right. I'm sure it was yummy." Then slowly, Harper began to realize that Mia was in a background he didn't recognize.

"Wait where are you, Mimi?"

"Mawusi's apartment," she stated matter-of-factly with an "of course" intonation.

"Oh. It's bedtime soon. What time is Mommy coming to get you?"

"She's not. I'm staying here. She said I could. And we're going to bed soon. . . ."

"Where's Mommy?" Harper wanted to know instinctively.

Mia shrugged. "Mm-hmm. She said she'll get me from school tomorrow."

It was a Thursday night and maybe Robyn was still at the restaurant. . . . It's a parent's right to grant their children sleepovers and playdates for whatever reason they sought fit. *But on a school night?* he wondered. *Where is Robyn? What's she doing? And who's she with . . . ?* Harper reminded himself of Robyn's reprimand. *None of your business, Harp. None of your business . . .*

"Hmmmph. Okay. You guys doing alright, though?" Harper struggled to bring himself back from more spiraling thoughts of none-of-his-business kinds of things.

"Uh-huh. We're looking at this funny thing on TikTok."

"Okay, but don't spend too much time on that device. You got it back so respect Mommy's rules, even if she's not there."

"Okay," Mia responded with a sigh.

"Okay, Mimi. I'm going to California in a few hours for some meetings."

"Really?"

"Yup. I'll probably be in the air when you're sleeping. When you wake I'll be there. Will you call me in the morning?"

"Mmm. Maybe."

"Maybe?" Harper playfully feigned disbelief. "What?!" Mia laughed. He lived for that laughter.

"I'll think about it," she said.

"Well, good. You can call me anytime. You know that, right?"

"Yup."

"If you ever need me for anything, do not hesitate to call or FaceTime me, okay?"

"K. Bye, Daddy."

"I love you."

"Love you too."

Harper hung up after Mia did. He stood there for a full sixty seconds before he managed to shake off what he felt. *Stop.* He shouldn't care. It wasn't his business. But Harper was a little concerned and definitely curious. Was Robyn on a date? With that guy? Harper didn't want to seem pressed, but *Who knows about this guy?* he thought. *Murch.* He seemed like he wanted to say more the other night, but Candace had stopped him. It was Robyn's news to tell, but she wasn't telling and Harper was curious. So he'd find out from Murch. Harper pulled out his phone to send a quick text. Hey, man, give me a call. Something I wanted to run by you. No rush. Harper was not *supposed* to want to know, but he couldn't resist adding: What do you know about this guy Robyn's dating?

# CHAPTER ELEVEN

## Jordan

Facing Dr. Clark, Jordan took her usual seat by the window. The sheers were drawn, keeping out the heat of the Southern California sun but leaving downtown Santa Monica in view from her therapist's second story office. A scented white candle sat on the coffee table, nestled between the two of them, Jordan on one side and Dr. Clark on the other, seated in her cushiony cream-colored oversized chair. As usual, the latter woman's posture was erect, and she was attentive, her face largely expressionless behind glasses so stylish it made Jordan wish for readers even though she didn't need them (or bigger fonts . . . yet). Dr. Clark's dark hair was evenly streaked with gray and strategically short. The precise lines of her haircut complimented her high cheekbones and caramel skin. She dressed like her office looked—in neutral colors—grays, blacks, whites, and creams—and today was no exception. She wore an off-white sleeveless cashmere sweater and looked pretty, flawless, calm, and professional.

Jordan always assumed Dr. Clark was ten to twelve years her senior. The kind of woman that Jordan hoped to morph into when she got north of sixty or seventy. That's probably why she chose her. In this sea of white male and female therapists, Dr. Clark was like an oasis in the desert. A Black woman who had lived some life. Jordan felt comfortable with her. At least, as comfortable as Jordan Armstrong could feel in such a situation.

*Therapy? Me?* she'd thought when she first contemplated it. *Therapy isn't for me.* Shelby, on the other hand? Yeah. HELLO. The woman ran through therapists like she ran through husbands. Not Jordan, though. Jordan was a "strong Black woman." The very idea that she'd need to speak to a stranger about her so-called mental health had been a foreign concept to Jordan Motherfucking Armstrong. It was a miracle she'd found Dr. Clark and even more so that she kept coming.

"Strong Black women don't need therapy?" Dr. Clark had posed the question early in their sessions. Answering that in the affirmative made Jordan feel really stupid. Particularly the way Dr. Clark had posed it—confidently, rhetorically. Softly challenging Jordan's notions. It was particularly jarring because Jordan *was* a strong Black woman who'd left a high-paying, powerful job at the height of her career because she was *feeling* anything but that. However, she'd since been reconciling the notion that she'd needed help processing all the thoughts and feelings she'd been having, not just in the past two and a half years since she quit, but perhaps for her entire adult, professional life.

At the start of every session, Dr. Clark had Jordan light a white scented candle of her choosing. Neroli calmed her and relieved the anxiety she felt with being untethered from a job *and* arising from telling a stranger her innermost thoughts. When each session was over, Jordan blew out the candle and felt better. It served as a ritual to close the open wound they'd just explored. In fact, every time she saw Dr. Clark, she enjoyed working on herself, like going to the gym. It was hard to get there, but she was always happy she went. Soon enough, being vulnerable in a safe space became freeing. So, *yes,* Jordan concluded. *Strong Black women do need therapy.*

In this session, her neroli candle burned slowly. The wick was strong and unwavering. *That's an expensive candle,* Jordan thought. Probably why her prices were so high. Plus, the rent in the area was astronomical. But, Jordan concluded, her mental health was worth it.

"Do you think she was being rhetorical?" Dr. Clark asked of Evelyn's response to Jordan's pitch during her New York trip's final meeting. She inquired flatly, without blinking.

"No . . . not completely," Jordan said after a moment of consideration. "She has to find a way to sell it to the top floor. I get it. I did the job. Evelyn is doing the same thing I would have done. Like, 'Come on, sis. Give me a little more ammo for the white boys.'" Jordan looked away. *Why should we care?* she remembered hearing. She recalled the moment perfectly. It had been on constant replay in her mind since she'd returned.

"Why do you want them to care, Jordan?"

Jordan's face scrunched up involuntarily. "Are *you* being rhetorical?"

"No. I'm asking you to articulate why you want them to care."

"Because . . . I know how it feels—the stress, the anxiety, the taking on of others' expectations of what they know or think a strong Black woman is. And having this feeling that you have to overachieve, you have to represent, you have to live up to a standard that *no other women* in society have to contend with. We get questioned by *everyone,* not only from other women, white women, white men, Black men. But *nobody* cares?" She paused to recalibrate; she hadn't expected to get so emotional. "When I went temporarily blind three years ago, I brushed it off," Jordan said with a sniffle. "I didn't prioritize my health because I had to be the one. I could not fail. If I did, someone else would take my place and I'd be out and labeled weak. Weak . . . is the antithesis of a strong Black woman. So, who is asking what this costs us?" After months of experiencing debilitating migraines in her last job, at the peak of her career, Jordan's eyesight had slowly begun to dwindle over the course of the scariest weeks of her life. She knew then she'd needed a change.

"And when you left?"

"When I left, I was still a strong Black woman. Who put herself first," Jordan said with the confidence of reciting an affirmation.

"And?"

"*Learn, earn, return,* as Denzel Washington said. I've done the first two, and now I want to share—with other high-achieving Black women. Every aspect of wellness. I need to reach people who feel what I'm feeling. Or at least what I felt. I want to let other Black women know how to get some balance in their life. As Black women go, so goes the world. When we're at our best everyone else is, everyone benefits, everyone wins. That's facts. Why should anyone care? Well, I just said it, *that's* why."

"Did you tell your friend this?"

"Ev? No. It's kind of coming to me right now. You can't do off the cuff in a meeting unless you've already got the answers for everything."

"Have you thought about inserting yourself into this process?"

Jordan was puzzled by the question. "What do you mean? I already have. I wrote the copy, designed the PowerPoint—"

Dr. Clark delivered a rare interruption. "I mean the show. It sounds to me like you are the show. It's so deeply personal to you." Jordan still looked puzzled. "Have you considered hosting?"

Jordan sincerely laughed. She finally felt Dr. Clark was out of her depth—she'd been waiting for that temporary comfort. Jordan was always the smartest person in the room, except *this* room. "Why is that funny?" Dr. Clark asked.

"Because that's a bad idea. I'm not a host. I've never done that," Jordan said.

"But why couldn't you? You're beautiful, charming, tell it like it is. Why wouldn't the public trust you?"

"They also have to like me. And I can be a bitch. Plus, with me out front as the face of the show, who would run it?" Dr. Clark cocked her head slightly as Jordan pointed to herself with both thumbs. "This bitch right here. That's my comfort zone. That's my expertise."

Dr. Clark took a beat and then looked down at her pad to jot down a note. "Okay," she said flatly. Jordan took a swig of water from her bottle. There was too much silence.

"Soooo . . ." She extended the word, filling the void between them.

Dr. Clark looked up from her writing pad. "Why did you forgo an opportunity to see your friends? Your godchildren?"

Jordan felt a slight pang of regret. "It wasn't the purpose of the trip," she explained. "I wanted to get in and get out." Jordan took a look at Dr. Clark, examining her face for judgment. "And we had an appointment." She gestured to Dr. Clark. "You charge whether I'm here or not. And you know I don't play with my money." Jordan laughed.

Dr. Clark nodded with a small smile in return before countering. "Strictly business," Dr. Clark said.

"Yup."

"Uh-huh." Dr. Clark jotted something again. "And were you satisfied with the results?"

*Not totally satisfied,* Jordan thought. "Jury's still out. I have some things to work out, some questions that need to be answered. Plus, Evelyn left me with an interesting challenge. I'll find it."

"Okay, then. And Harper?"

"Harper? What about Harper?"

"You said you received a text from him."

"I did." Jordan tried her best to sound nonchalant, but her body had become alert.

"Have you responded to him saying he'd be in town? Are you going to his book signing?"

Jordan frowned. "No, I haven't responded. And no, I'm not going to his book signing?" She knew she sounded defensive.

"Why not?"

"It's over at the Grove and I'm not fighting that traffic to and from the west side so I can be on Harper's time."

"You don't want to see him," Dr. Clark summarized declaratively.

Jordan searched herself for the truth of the answer. "No. I want to see him," she corrected. "I mean, I don't want to *not* see him. I want to. Yes, I want to. I just don't want to be available . . ." Jordan tried to explain.

"Did you tell him this?"

"How would I . . . I mean, no, that would be . . . I don't know . . . poor form?"

"So you're ignoring him?"

*Ignoring him?* "I'm going to . . . I'm gonna respond. When I'm ready." Jordan straightened up and adjusted her seated position.

"But you're friends, right? Are you in a fight? Is there tension in your relationship?" Her rapid-fire questions were direct enough to put Jordan fully on the defensive. She *hated* playing defense.

"I—I—I guess. . . ." *Shit.* "I mean, look, we had reconnected last fall and it was nice awhile back, like college again. We could talk about any and everything. And we did. Even about our dating lives—well, his *busy* one and my sporadic one."

"Mm-hmm," mused Dr. Clark. *Mm-hmm? Fuck does that mean? This lady* . . . Jordan's patience was wearing thin. Somehow, they'd found themselves on an emotionally charged topic. And she wasn't prepared for the confusing swirl of feelings.

"Look, I'm fine with his sexcapades. He should be doing that—sow his oats. I don't care." Jordan folded her arms around herself.

"Then what is it?"

"I just didn't want to hear about him being serious with somebody else. Stop with being boo'ed up all the time. Taking them to events, New Year's Eve parties and such."

Dr. Clark seemed to register something that she'd said. Jordan felt caught, swirling down the drain.

"New Year's Eve. That bothered you. So, you're avoiding him." Again, it was a statement question that Jordan would have to defend.

"I wasn't traveling across the country to just hang with the crew," Jordan countered.

"You mean your college friends and your godchildren." Dr. Clark didn't let up. "And Harper."

"And his girlfriend du jour."

"You don't like his girlfriend?"

"I never met her. Them. Anybody," Jordan said.

"Is there something wrong with Harper having a girlfriend?" She paused with her pen hovering over her pad in her lap. "He's your friend, isn't he? You want him to be happy. You said yourself his divorce was a painful time for him. Maybe this is his way to heal. Maybe he feels complete with a partner. . . ."

"That's *exactly* who he is," Jordan shot back. "And that partner should be me." She looked directly at Dr. Clark as she threw out the words. "Why isn't it me?" For a moment Jordan was temporarily stunned. *Did I just say that?* Maybe the feeling had been there, but hearing the words . . . in her own voice? She'd said it. The truth. She'd been intentionally putting distance between herself and Harper since the clock turned to a new year. It wasn't jealousy Jordan felt when hearing about those random chicks Harper was reportedly bringing around the college crew. It was incredulity. "Why hasn't he chosen me?" Jordan heard herself say, sounding . . . *angry?* Angry. Her voice had even cracked a little. But she regained her composure and cleared her throat.

"You want to be chosen." Another declarative statement. *Duh.*

"What woman doesn't want to be chosen?"

"People want to be chosen," Dr. Clark countered. "He *did* choose you, Jordan," Dr. Clark reminded her. "And you said no."

Jordan remembered the moments leading up to her walk with Harper on the Brooklyn Heights Promenade three years back. He'd intimated that maybe it was finally their opportunity to make a go of it. Take their friendship to the next level. But Jordan's response was "I can't be your soft place to land." And she meant it. As much as she might have wanted to explore, she knew that he had to work some things out, personally and creatively. Jordan had no regrets. Days later at Ginny's Supper Club, Shelby yelled across their banquet table, "You told him what?!" Jordan shook her head as she sipped on her cocktail. Shelby was far less resigned. "Who falls on the sword when they can fall on a dick?" she'd said in classic fashion. "When did you become so altruistic?"

"I've always been that way, Shelby," Jordan had said. That she was. Altruistic, practical, and cautious.

Bringing herself back to the present, Jordan explained with more clarity to Dr. Clark. "That wasn't a choice. It doesn't count. He had just gotten divorced. He was rebounding. Looking for a free option, a distraction from what he really needed to do—write that book. Not use me as a cushion. He didn't need to be involved with *anyone.* And look what happened—he wrote his great American novel AND won the Pulitzer."

"You feel responsible for his victory?"

"Partially, yes. I do. I'm happy for him. And proud of him." Jordan felt herself sit a little taller. "*And* I left the door open," she added.

Dr. Clark looked up again from her writing. "You did, but it had a lot of conditions. A lot of 'ifs' as I recall."

"That's self-preservation. But I was also being *selfless.* It wasn't about me then, or what I wanted. He *was* really hurting and me being there wouldn't have helped him. Or me. I wanted him to succeed."

"In order for him to be ready for you." *How did Dr. Clark surmise that from what I said?* Jordan wondered. She hated the way this woman put words in her mouth—even if they fit. But did these words fit?

"Nooo," Jordan protested. "For himself. First and foremost, Harper and I are friends. We've been friends all of our adult lives. I love him and I want what's best for him," she professed.

"Even if what's best for him isn't you?" Dr. Clark made direct eye contact. "Is that truly what you want?"

The words caught in Jordan's throat.

"What do you want, Jordan?" Dr. Clark pressed. The question was overwhelming. Jordan didn't know what to say.

"Jordan?"

"Everything," Jordan said finally, throwing her hands up in the air. "I used to want everything—a high-paying job, to be a boss, have the fly-girl car, get married, maybe have kids . . ."

"And now?"

"I want to be fulfilled in all the ways. I want to be happy. Settled. I want shit to be easier. I have and I've done those things I thought I wanted. And now . . ."

"Now?"

"Now I want to be chosen."

For a moment, there was a silence between them. A silence that Jordan hoped wouldn't be filled by the most obvious question. But true to form, Dr. Clarke asked, "By Harper?"

"I don't know" was what came out of Jordan's mouth.

"Okay," Dr. Clark said. "Let me ask you this—why haven't you responded to his text message?"

*I'm scared. I'm scared of getting my heart broken.* Jordan followed Dr. Clark's eyes as they gave her a once-over assessment, and then traveled back to meet her squarely, unwaveringly, for an extended beat of the silence she hated. She needed to answer, to be honest with her therapist, but all that she could manage as a reply to Dr. Clark was, "It's not worth discussing."

Dr. Clark's usually stoic brow crinkled. "Are you sure?" she asked. The question sounded earnest—not a summary, really an opportunity. *Hell no, I'm not sure. Of course I'm not sure,* Jordan thought. But she wasn't ready. Not yet.

Jordan met Dr. Clark's gaze and waited out the clock, soldiering through the silence. *Ding,* sounded the chime. Jordan didn't even wait until she said "Well, that's our time . . ." before she blew out her candle, sending a dark plume of neroli smoke into the air. Standing to gather her things, Jordan said a quick "See you next week" as she beelined for the door.

Jordan closed her eyes to take in the warmth of the Southern California springtime sun. She'd picked a choice seat at Urth Caffé's patio, in midday competition with a handful of tourists, ladies of leisure with their designer dogs, and what looked like students hard at work on their computers. She too had her computer open, as she'd been crafting follow-up emails to the execs she'd met with in New York. Or, rather, she was stuck trying to craft an email, given that the meetings hadn't gone as she'd expected them to. The show was her passion project, something to call her own and an exciting new direction. It wasn't that she didn't have options. She'd received near-weekly offers trying to woo her back to a high-powered, high-paying desk job, but she had so far kept them at bay or flat-out said no. "But I'll consult" she'd always let her headhunter know. It felt good to be wanted, to be needed and respected, at least professionally. The consultancy jobs kept her engaged and busy, but there was no *ownership* in them.

After two years of consulting, Jordan wanted something to call her own, like her father had encouraged. Daddy always said "Don't just stay working for the man." Sure, *From the Culture* was her baby, among other shows she helped green-light that she believed in, but that wasn't true ownership. Jordan never did have ownership in the many shows she created for the network. True ownership meant equity, a stake, and a piece of the profits that could last forever. As the creator and producer of her wellness journey show—she'd have ownership or at least be in partnership with a buyer and the network when it got to syndication. And, *baby,* when that syndication money came in, she wouldn't have to work ever again.

Jordan took a slow sip of her pistachio latte, savoring the warm nutty flavor as she considered the words of her note. *Thank you for your time this week and your interest. If I can answer anything else that can help you make your decision I'm on the other end of the phone. . . .* She typed out each of the words knowing she'd delete them later. Her mind wasn't as focused as usual; her appointments with Dr. Clark were always provocative, but this last one had opened a door she couldn't seem to shut. She still felt raw and exposed and unfinished. *Don't sound desperate or needy, Jordan,* she thought as she deleted each of the words she'd just entered into the white body of an email. *You hated seeing emails like that unless there was a true connection.* These days, she was avoiding feeling like she had to be busy. And she really needed to think through her next steps on this show idea before she sent any kind of follow-ups. Evelyn had given her the strongest feedback she'd received out of all her meetings—that she needed to find on-camera talent with a story in order to package the show. Who else had her story and was still in front of the camera? She'd been the one to walk away, to leave it all behind in the name of self-care. Who was available who'd both maintained their brand in front of the camera and *also* walked away? Wasn't that a contradiction?

Taking another sip of her drink, she decided to shift focus to her bread-and-butter clients, the projects that were easy for her, consulting work that she'd accepted just because they'd practically begged her to give a few hours out of her schedule. She weighed in on what Horizon Pictures needed for their marketing rollout. She sent her notes on KTLA's new midmorning format and their new anchor. She also scheduled her panel appearance at the Aspen Institute. They were paying for all arrangements and offering a ten-thousand-dollar honorarium. Ten grand for a forty-five-minute panel and an opportunity to ski? Hell yeah. *Way to use other people's money, J,* she thought. *It* ***would*** *be nice to take a trip like that with somebody.* The girls' trips had been fun, a good silly time in the Caribbean and Mediterranean. A group of good-looking, successful Black women always turned heads on vacation. Lots of photos in expensive sunglasses and thirst trap social media posts. Ass shaking and twerking under a waterfall or against a railing over the ocean somewhere. That female love and energy was great, but sometimes a sistah needed some consistent *male* companionship, something *real.* Some good dick with good credit *and* emotional intelligence.

It was exactly that kind of male companionship that was in short supply in Los Angeles. Especially the Black kind. Jordan had met men online leading to a couple dates, and met a few dudes in yoga class and at the gym, but they were mostly full of shit. She kept her options open, and needed to. And the sex? The sex she'd been having ran the gamut from great to terrible. None warranted an encore. Thank goodness for toys and online porn. Those would have to suffice until she found someone in flesh and blood who stimulated her mind and spirit as well as her clitoris. Who even knew to stimulate her clitoris. *Sigh.* Today's discussion with Dr. Clark was forcing her to think about companionship. Was that her answer to *What do you want?* It'd be nice to travel with someone, hold hands, snuggle, laugh, wake up with coffee and morning sex. Was that too much to ask? Jordan stretched. The combination of the direct sunlight and the caffeine was having canceling effects on her productivity, so it was time to stand and head into the next part of her day. And just as Jordan was pulling out some tip money, a nice-looking brother passed by with a smile and a "Morning, sis" greeting.

"Hey," Jordan returned succinctly with a measured smile of her own behind her sunglasses. She'd spotted him walking up from a distance when he parked his Lexus coupe at a meter on Main Street. He was probably in his forties, easily six foot four, dark chocolate with a head of curly hair that was tapered on the sides and back. He was definitely cute. Eligible brothers were a rarity in LA so Jordan took a beat to scrutinize him further. There was no ring on his finger, and his tall and athletic frame was dressed nicely in some close-fitting joggers and a half-zip top. *Probably coming from working out,* Jordan thought, peeping him over the top of her shades.

*Does he live out here in Santa Monica? Is he in the entertainment space? Does he work for the Rams? Or the Dodgers? Clippers? Maybe he's in tech . . . It's possible.* It was automatic, trying to figure out who this Black man was, trying to place him, just like white folks did to her and her girlfriends. *It's different when we do it,* Jordan rationalized. But how different was it? Blackness in white spaces did conjure up thoughts of "Who are they?" and "They must be exceptional Negroes." Sigh. *I hate that about us. Why can't we be normal AND exceptional and not the exception,* Jordan wondered.

Jordan decided to extend her stay a little longer and adjusted her seat to subtly get a better look at dude. *Nice ass,* she thought, starting to imagine how they might strike up a conversation when he returned to the table he'd scoped out. He stepped inside to the order line, snaked his way toward the front, right behind a white girl with a fake ass. She turned around, thrilled to see him, as he pinched the sides of her waist. And as the woman preened and swayed her dark flowing hair with all the privilege it conveyed along the pronounced ridge of her ballooned backside, Jordan's hope deflated.

"Aww hell," Jordan said loud enough that her neighbors looked up at her with concern. "Nothing, I—nothing . . ." Jordan shook her head quickly to assuage any fear. It would take another Black woman to understand that shit, and these people weren't that, not sitting midday in Santa Monica. She added one folded dollar to the three singles under her coffee cup and raised herself up from the wrought iron metal seat. She took a final look at the brotha, who by then had turned his girl into a mess of giggles in cute cuddle mode. And she was eating it up. With twisted lips and a head shake, Jordan did a one-eighty and headed down Main Street. *Niggas . . .*

Jordan shook her head as she approached her BMW. *They can have them bitches.* In fairness Jordan had no clue whether the white woman the brother chose was cool or not. *Hell, she might be. And?! Fuck that. Fuck her. Fuck him.* She let the top of her convertible down and pressed start on the ignition.

Jordan pulled onto Ocean Avenue and rode down to merge with the flow of traffic emptying onto the coastline-hugging Pacific Coast Highway. Eager beachgoers and sightseers sped up the coast trying to take advantage of the picturesque stretch of road. The view was beautiful and would always be, even now with the scars on the land serving as a constant reminder of how fortunate she'd been. All Jordan wanted to do was get back to Malibu, to her place. She checked her reflection from behind her designer sunglasses in the rearview. She was still looking good—hair flowing in the wind, great skin, no lines. And how could she not? She hiked three days a week, did Pilates, strength training with a personal trainer, drank nearly a gallon of water daily, and got regular massages—everything was paying dividends. Her skin was clear, she slept well, and she was in the best shape of her life. *Self-care* . . . Jordan shook her head. "Bitch, you have come a long way," she said into the wind.

But who was Jordan fooling? This life of self-care and leisure was nice, but her industry still owed her. And if she wanted to move her show forward, she'd need to figure out the missing puzzle piece, a host . . . someone to sell *her* story. Dr. Clark intimated that she'd possibly be the right fit, as if she'd even *considered* hosting . . . with no experience? "Hah!" Jordan exclaimed as Kendrick Lamar's "Not Like Us" cranked through her Beemer's sound system. "I can't do that shit. That's not for me." But neither was therapy or self-care or edibles the one time she tried them. At the end of a gorgeous twenty-minute drive, Jordan approached her fabulous beachfront Malibu home. If Jordan Armstrong was going to do LA, she was for sure going to do it right. She had earned it (and a whole lot more). She pulled into her side of the two-car garage, leaving the other side unoccupied, as it always was. She put her car in park, grabbed her phone, and looked again at Harper's "carefully crafted" text message. Still unanswered. If you're free . . . it said. *Really?* Still nope. Jordan looked at her reflection again in the rearview. She wanted to be chosen, just like she'd said to Dr. Clark.

# CHAPTER TWELVE

## Robyn

Robyn drove to Kwesi's home, in Accra's Cantonments, where the chicest high-rises could be found, housing many of the diplomats and especially the jetsetters who criss-crossed the globe servicing their successful businesses. Kwesi was one of the latter, who as a real-estate developer actually had a hand in building his ritzy Diamond In City complex. He was often in London, but also other parts of the world. This time, he'd just returned from Madagascar.

Robyn pulled her small and dusty SUV into the valet circle, making her suddenly a bit self-conscious of the differential in his standard of living versus her own. It wasn't like she was looking for a repeat of old patterns. In a tote bag she carried the palm wine broth, velvet tamarind dipping sauce, and cocoa butter risotto, all made by her hands. She knew the melding of flavors was just right, even better than before. And with this, she was assuredly carrying her own treasure.

As Robyn entered the spacious lobby, the uniformed attendant at the desk looked up at her right away. "Mr. Emmanuel is expecting you Ms. Stewart. The elevator is straight ahead to your right—penthouse."

Robyn took in the impressive surroundings as she crossed the veined marble floor. The entire lobby was sparkling, immaculate, and modern, with the sound of cascading water echoing throughout from a nearby fountain. And despite all the grandeur, there was still a distinct grounded-ness to the entrance, with its foliage and greenery, moss and a certain aliveness that brought an earthy feel to the place. *Yes . . . this is very Kwesi,* Robyn thought. He was at once elegant and yet understated. She approached the elevator and pushed the illuminated PH circle as she was instructed.

Robyn left the elevator and Kwesi's doors opened into a greeting of sound—trumpets and alto saxophones in the melodic combination that she instantly recognized as Hugh Masekela's classic "Grazing in the Grass." She walked slowly as the room and its décor revealed itself to her with exposed concrete and dark wooden shelves filled with rows and rows of vinyl album covers. Hmm . . . *Fela Kuti, Aretha Franklin, Angelique Kidjo, Miriam Makeba,* Robyn read, as she walked past the record collection and toward the running faucet sound in the kitchen.

"Kwesi?" Robyn called out ahead of her and heard the running water abruptly stop.

"Hello, Robyn! One second, I'm coming!" And sooner than she expected, Kwesi's frame entered her view. He wore a form-fitting dark eggplant button-down shirt, with short sleeves exposing his sinewy arms and well-toned biceps. At the neck, a triangle of his chest showcased a modest silver necklace lying flat against his oiled mahogany skin. His matching tailored slacks draped his footballer physique, maintained in part by the pickup games of soccer he still played recreationally. His broad shoulders moved as if in rhythm to the music as he quickly crossed the distance between them, wiping his hands against his thighs. A smile illuminated his face and made Robyn's breath catch in her throat. He was gorgeous, as usual.

*Stop looking at his lips,* Robyn repeated to herself. But as he hugged her, and while still holding a tote bag of her carefully curated culinary experience, all she could think of was kissing him, and what she anticipated for the night they would hopefully share. He seemed preoccupied also . . . with her. He stepped back to take her in.

"You look incredible," he marveled. "Are you getting more beautiful?" He spoke straight to her, looked her in the eyes. Robyn could not hold his gaze as she smiled.

"Thank you. You look very handsome yourself."

"I think Accra agrees with you. Very much." He quickly maneuvered to relieve her of the tote and take her shoulder bag as well, directing them into the kitchen, while the sounds of Hugh Masekela continued to follow them into the room.

"Did you get the mussels?" Robyn asked.

Kwesi flexed his bicep with the tote in hand. "Yeah, I hit the gym this morning," he teased. "Can't you tell?"

Robyn gave a smirk that did little to hide her thoughts. *Boy, do not play with me. Dinner might get skipped if you keep that up.* "I guess I walked into that one. But I can tell."

"Yes, they were delivered fresh less than twenty minutes before you walked in the door." Kwesi laughed and gestured to the mollusks in a colander in the kitchen sink. Robyn began heading toward them.

"That's a really impressive collection of vinyl you have," she said. "It's not common to see . . . or hear."

Kwesi smiled even bigger, setting Robyn's tote on the counter. "I'm a music head. It's a collection that needs a lot of care and space, and the sound quality is unmatched. The tone can really expand to what it was intended to be. The only way to experience the greats. Is there something you'd like to hear?"

Robyn shook her head no. The harmonic choruses of highlife rhythms, the horns, the sound of the bass guitar keeping the drive of the music, were enough. She was happy with this groove. "This is perfect, Kwesi. I wouldn't change anything about it."

"I'm glad." Kwesi smiled, slow and sexy. "Shall we unpack this?" He gestured for Robyn to take the lead in arranging her items along the generous counter space. "I'm working on some fresh bread for us. But I have to say I'm a bit intimidated to be sharing a kitchen with you."

Robyn grabbed an awaiting apron, grazing him with her arm.

"I hope you brought your A game," she teased. Kwesi was gleefully slack-jawed for a beat before launching a deep, boisterous, full-throated laugh. It made Robyn chuckle as she donned an apron.

Over the next hour the bottle of wine between them dwindled as they worked seamlessly with one another to prepare the meal they'd share. Robyn was thankful to have the distraction of her own dishes to keep her from sneaking extended glances at Kwesi working that mound of rubbery dough on the flour-dusted counter next to her. As his hands kneaded the dough, flattened and smoothed the surface, and rolled it into shape, she imagined his hands doing the same to her and her soft parts. She envisioned her skin between his thumbs, encircled by his strong hands, and lost herself in the thought.

It did not take long to finish his flatbread, or bring her warm dishes to the table. Robyn's reward arrived in a glorious moment sitting across from Kwesi, at the table lit by candles, in his loft filled now with the Afrobeats jazz of Fela Kuti. She watched with rapt attention as he dipped a square of spongy bread into the palm wine broth. As the food met his mouth, Robyn held her breath.

First his eyes closed as his mouth wrapped around his fingers. Time slowed as she carefully observed his mouth move, chewing in lazy circles, as his head started to move back and forth.

"Mmmm . . . Robyn. This . . . is so, so good." His eyes opened slowly just as Robyn let out an extended breath, only partially of relief. The truth was she was turned on, *right now.* The sounds of his enjoyment stimulated her. She loved to see someone enjoy her food. Especially someone she cared for, who happened to be as fine as Kwesi, who seemed to not only care for her but desire her as well.

"Try the mussels," Robyn encouraged. Kwesi cut his sexy eyes at her.

"Yes, ma'am." He nodded dreamily before searching his bowl for the perfect morsel. He easily found it with his spoon and used his fingers to gently pry the mussel open farther. Then taking the shell to his lips, darted his tongue inside to snatch the succulent meat inside. Robyn was mesmerized by his technique and couldn't help imagining herself on the other end of his mouth. He slurped the inside of the shell and chewed slowly with delight. "Wow," he said finally, in between bites. "Robyn, that is delicious. It's like, like a sea breeze captured to eat. And that's only the tip of the iceberg."

Robyn smiled tacitly. *Just the tip huh?*

"I'm glad you like it."

"I don't like it. I love it." Kwesi dipped into his plate for more.

"Thank you." Robyn took a flirtatious sip of the wine he'd poured her from the bottle of red blend they'd been sharing. The taste of it was incredible, almost like jam. The minerally finish made it seem exotic, like it had come from a paradise somewhere with rare soil, unlike anything she'd ever tasted in the States. "And this wine, it's delicious." Kwesi's smile in response made Robyn curious. "Where's it from? The taste is so . . . unique."

"This is a special wine. I brought it back just for tonight from my trip."

"From Madagascar?"

"Yes, from my vineyard."

For a moment, Robyn was at a loss. "You mean, you *sell* this? All around the world?"

Kwesi laughed. "No, not all around the world. The vineyard is very small, very select. It started as one person's labor of love in their backyard. Just one varietal, only the most delicious wine. They did one thing well, and that was enough. My partners and I, we decided not to change a good thing when we bought it. We've kept it just the way it was at the beginning. This is the first year that we've offered a blend, though. I'm glad you like it."

Robyn took another sip. "That's so nice to be able to focus only on one thing. To make it the best—"

"You could do that too," Kwesi interjected. Robyn raised her eyebrow. "This dish is incredible." He took her hand from across the table. "If you just made this one dish, you'd have a line of people from miles around. It's absolutely delicious. It's so . . . *you.*" Looking into his eyes, Robyn melted.

"Thank you," she said. "I have a lot to offer, Kwesi." It was Kwesi's turn to raise his eyebrow.

"Is that right?" Kwesi replied.

Robyn nodded and leaned forward toward Kwesi. The food was delicious, but she didn't want to eat much more. She wanted to feel light and relaxed, no need for extra calories poking out in unwanted places. She moved closer now, so close that she could smell the light fragrance emanating from the top of his shirt. He smelled warm, like tobacco and spice.

"I can think of only one thing more delicious than my plate," Kwesi said, wrapping his arms around her, pulling her closer to him. He dipped his lashes low and brought his face closer to hers. Robyn sipped at the air between them, feeling herself drawing closer to him. When their lips met it was electric, the touch of sensitive skin to skin. Robyn was happy that he took his time with it, with her, drawing back to make another slow approach to her mouth with his, teasing a bit, just a brush at first. She felt the warm flush on her cheeks, yet she still felt fully comfortable in his arms, next to him in the delicious halo of his scent. It was hard to keep herself from leaning too far into his kisses. He brushed her lips once . . . and then twice . . . and then a third time, lingering just a bit longer with each one. Waiting, she bit her bottom lip with anticipation of his mouth returning to hers. His lips were so soft, lush pillows to get lost in.

Kissing Kwesi was so innocent at first, so slow and lovely, just the two of them still sitting at the table, leaning toward each other in chairs, taking the time to explore just this version of intimacy. He pulled her closer, bringing his lips to her ear. Robyn let her eyes drop closed and softly released the breath she'd been holding.

"Shall we move to the living room?" His accent was enticing and elegant, and the way he delivered his words—on a tickling breeze at her ear, it all started to bring the heat to rise between her legs. She wasn't sure how much longer she'd last in this seat anyway.

Robyn nodded eagerly. "Uh-huh," she managed to say with a smile.

Kwesi stood up, pulled Robyn to standing, and ushered them

both to the sofa in a room with a wall of shelved albums and books. It was even more enticing to be surrounded by the energies of art and ideas, of music and brilliance. The paintings on the walls were gorgeous as well, filling the space with sumptuous patterns of color. The sofa in front of her was brown suede leather. When she sat down, she felt welcomed by its comforting buttery feel. Kwesi allowed her to settle while he dimmed the overhead lights, leaving only two flickering candles on the coffee table, bathing the room in soft illumination.

Kwesi approached again, looking handsome and perfect, like his skin tone was made to come alive in candlelight. "There," he said, settling next to her. "Is that better?" He smiled at her in a way that must have been illegal somewhere. The curve of his lips, the slight slant of his eyes, the way Robyn could see him searching her face for a response, she breathed him in, wanting to savor every moment. Something about this was special, and Robyn felt it.

She sighed and leaned closer to him, allowing their bodies to touch in more places.

"Would you mind if I made you a bit more comfortable?" Kwesi placed his hand on Robyn's leg as he asked.

*Do I mind?* "I don't mind at all," Robyn said softly.

Instantly, he shifted his long frame down to kneeling beside her on the floor. When he reached for her foot, Robyn said a quiet thanks for having gotten a fresh pedicure. Slowly, sumptuously, he pulled her leg toward him and slid her shoe inch by inch from her foot. He did the same thing with her other foot, spreading her legs a bit in the process and allowing the cooler air to tickle the warm wetness that had begun to build between her legs.

With his hands, he began kneading the bare skin of her foot, like she saw him work earlier, crafting the dough for the bread.

This time, it was the arch of her foot he kneaded, rolling a loose fist against it, releasing tension there as his thumbs worked the center. Robyn loved that he anticipated her desires. "That . . . feels . . . so good," she breathed out, leaning her head back and savoring the sensation. She allowed her legs to spread farther, to the edges of her skirt. It was the fabric now that was the only thing holding them together. He'd made her feel so relaxed. Kwesi reached her toes then, rubbing up the length of her foot, through the center, and lacing each toe with the tips of each of his fingers. Kneading them and stretching them. Pulling them toward him . . . even as he . . .

Robyn gasped with surprise. The sensation of warm moisture hit her suddenly, then she opened her eyes and found her toes wrapped by Kwesi's mouth. *Is this man sucking my . . .* Robyn's thoughts were interrupted by the moan that escaped her lips. Kwesi kept his eyes trained on her, meeting her curious gaze with his own full of intensity. When his tongue flicked between her toes and entwined its way to caress each one, she couldn't help herself. She moaned again and felt surprised to hear herself express pleasure so loudly. *But it feels so good,* she thought. She hoped he wouldn't stop and he didn't. At least, not until he finished with her feet and began to make a warm trail of kisses up her leg.

She leaned forward momentarily, wondering what she could do to deliver her own gifts of pleasure when he was so far away from her hands and mouth. She started to move closer to him, but he laid his large hand at the base of her belly.

"Just relax, Robyn, I've got this." Her breath caught in her throat, but she obeyed, mesmerized by his smile in the candlelight. He returned to his work of inching his lips and tongue along the inside of her leg toward her now pulsating center.

Robyn's pulse quickened with anticipation; her breath became heavier as the warm, tingling flush of arousal started to build in her body. Kwesi's lips on her skin, brushing, sucking on her inner thigh, made her want to moan, to growl, to use her hands to grab his head and hold it there. She wanted to rip her own clothes open. He was making her wild, edging toward her limits of control, inch by inch into a wonderful swirl of desire. And she loved it.

"I . . . I . . . want this," Robyn whispered. She was sure she meant everything that was happening physically, but also, more of this, of him, of Kwesi. She wanted his mouth on her neck, her breasts, her nipples, the small of her back. She wanted to feel him suck her, bite her, be on top of her, inside her, she wanted . . . *more.*

It seemed to be all the permission he needed. Kwesi looked up at her briefly, processing her desire. Then, directly, he pushed her skirt all the away up and spread her legs wide enough to accommodate him sliding between her thighs. His tongue grazed the side of her panties, just before she felt the moist heat of his mouth and pointed pressure laded directly on her where it was most sensitive, using slow, dragging flicks to set a fire in the rest of her body. Robyn whispered his name, "Kwesi." And kept saying, "yes . . . yesss," moaning her permission, her approval, and her pleasure, particularly when he slid her panties down past her thighs and pulled them off to drop on the floor. It became easier and easier to lose herself in the deft swirls of his slippery kisses, his consistent touch, and the tease of his two fingers. This was exactly what she needed to release, to let herself succumb to waves of pleasure overtaking her, like the tides of the beach until one after another the jolts of ecstasy crashed through her body, convulsing her over and over and over again.

## CHAPTER THIRTEEN

### Jordan

"Why the hell not?" Shelby's voice floated through Jordan's phone speaker in typical animated fashion. The late afternoon sun was setting over the Pacific and Jordan slowly paced her deck trying to enjoy her glass of Malbec. She reached down to throw on her oversized gray cashmere wrap, perfect for Malibu evenings just like this. The scenery was pretty but it got cool out there, particularly in March. Also, she was stalling. Shelby's question hung for a few seconds in the air before Jordan could find the right response.

"Because I'm not *you,* Shelby," she said finally.

"Well, obviously."

Jordan rolled her eyes playfully. *How did I even come to commiserate with Shelby?* They had NOT been cool in undergrad. In fact, they couldn't stand one another. But their common denominator was Mia Morgan. Jordan had been her resident assistant back in the day, and Mia became the sweetest little sister she never had. Mia and Shelby were sorors, so also sisters of another kind of bond. Neither Jordan nor Shelby saw the appeal in the other, but Mia saw something in both. When she died, Shelby and Jordan found themselves in conversation about their dear friend and vying for auntie time with the Sullivan children. Forced to communicate and coordinate schedules, they eventually found common ground, knowing their angel sister played a vital part every day. Including this one.

"What I mean is I'm not an 'in front of the camera' person," Jordan responded.

"Oh, please. Do you really think any of those housewives were 'front of the camera' people before a camera was put on them? It's all smoke and mirrors. And *you* have substance, J," Shelby argued, fully employing her undergraduate debate team skills. "They don't care because there's not enough of *you* in it. The essence of this show is *your* story."

"My fingerprints are all over this, Shelby. . . ." Jordan briefly recalled the six repetitions of what she'd thought was her perfect show pitch.

"That's not what I'm talking about. People should get to know the *real* you. People love Oprah because she gave us her vulnerabilities. She wasn't just reporting the news; she told us about *her.* She let us in. You need to do the same, fly-ass Black woman." Jordan could feel Shelby's targeted energy. However, what was good for good TV wasn't always good for the folks providing it. Jordan valued her privacy.

"That's not going to happen, Shelby." Jordan took another sip of her red.

"Look, I know you're risk averse, but when are you going to take the big swing?"

"I've taken plenty of big swings in my life. *Calculated* big swings and ninety percent of the time it's paid off." Jordan sat in her favorite patio chair triumphantly.

"You've also been gun-shy, and it's been to your detriment. You have to go for what you want. And if being in front of the camera is what it takes, then do it." So said the woman who infamously broke up a wedding in pursuit of her now-husband, Quentin. "I know it can be scary, but you'll be happier in the long run that you took the chance." Something about Shelby's intonation made Jordan pause.

"Wait, are we still talking about my show?"

"Oh, I'm past that. I've already started talking about Harper," Shelby quipped.

"Oh God, Shelby—"

"Are you going to see him?"

"What are you talking about?"

"Don't play me. Play Powerball," Shelby said sharply. *Only Shelby.* "He's coming out there for a book signing and meetings and asked to see you." *How'd she . . .* Jordan didn't have much time to wonder. "I overheard him and Quentin talking," Shelby added. *Ah, of course.*

"So you *eavesdropped* on your husband's convo?"

"Call it what you want, but I got the info." Shelby remained smug and casually unbothered.

"You better be careful. You might hear shit you don't want to hear. Some secrets need to be kept from spouses."

"Fuck that. Give it to me raw, bitch. It's gonna come out anyway. We will deal with it regardless of what it is. Better to know and go through it together. This life is finite, so be open." Shelby was all drama and emotions, no matter how high or low. Jordan wasn't built to revel in all the feels. *What do I have to gain by seeing Harper?* She imagined Shelby would counter, *What do you have to lose?* Instead she heard Shelby say, "Stop hiding from him."

Jordan took the last swig of her wine and placed the empty glass on a coaster atop her patio coffee table. She pulled her cashmere wrap around her like a shield. "Who's hiding? He knows where I am."

"Does he?"

"He knows I'm out here. He knows how to get in contact with me." Jordan curled up deeper in her wrap, pulling her feet up under it. The breeze was getting cooler.

"He *did* get in contact with you, and you've been ghosting him." *Damn this woman's eavesdropping.* "And, hell, you moved out there to get away from him anyway." Jordan wouldn't let on, but Shelby had struck a nerve. There was something about the prodding that she appreciated. A testing of her resolve.

"I *moved* out here to get a new start, Shelby. To take care of *me.* This LA lifestyle suits me. I'm making my own schedule, eating right, exercising. I get to wake up and go to sleep with this majestic Pacific Ocean every day and night. It's working for me."

"Oh really? No dick is working for you? Trifling ass Black men chasing BBL white and Indian chicks is working for you?" Shelby was dramatic and raw, pulling no punches. Jordan felt like she was on the defensive, again.

"Who says I'm getting no dick? I do fine. And I got toys." Jordan quietly recalled that she did in part move to Malibu to take herself out of the Harper and Robyn divorce equation. She had to leave New York—otherwise she'd want to see him, check in on him, have him to herself . . . finally. And that was not going to help him, his writing, or her. She couldn't be waiting for him to get his shit together. But her large ego had no patience for something that may or may not happen. "What's for me is for me, Shelby," Jordan continued, ready to pounce.

"You're right. *Harper* is for you." *Shit.* Jordan's shoulders slumped back. "This is stupid," Shelby continued. "You two have been circling each other for-EVER. Stop with the hesitation and dumb excuses."

"He was married. I wouldn't call that a dumb excuse."

"He's divorced."

"He needed to process and heal."

"He's healed, he's processed."

"Really, Shelby?"

"Well, he's *continuing* to process. A lot of random pussy," Shelby admitted.

"He's not processing *this* pussy."

"How can he from the friend zone? That *you* put him in. Again! You didn't even tell him what you wanted." Shelby was right about that. But who was Jordan to have to tell a grown man to pursue her?

"He should know."

"Arrghh! When are you going to understand? Men are stupid! Hello?! You have to tell them what you want *and* what they want. They don't fucking know." ***He** should already know,* Jordan thought. *He knows me. Doesn't he . . . ? Shouldn't he?* As Jordan considered Shelby's words, she had no idea Shelby was gearing up for her closer, her strongest point. "Don't . . . push him toward another Robyn. You should at least see him. And fuck him."

"*Fuck him*?!"

"Yes! *Who cares*?! Just fuck him. We're too old to play games."

"I can't just . . . *fuck* Harper."

"Why not?" Shelby demanded. Jordan released a slow exhale.

"I just . . . there's too much history; it's too complicated—"

"It's *not* complicated. You've waited your entire adult life for this man. Sample the goods. If the fantasy doesn't meet the reality, then bam! Banish his ass back to the friend zone." Shelby made it sound so simple. "But to be honest I don't think the fantasy will disappoint. You love him and you may as well find out why. For real."

"I have to go, Shelby." Jordan had finally reached her limit. Shelby had overloaded her circuits.

"Jordan, stop. It's not a big deal," Shelby quickly interjected. "Just go to dinner. He's not seeing anybody—or at least he's not letting anybody he's seeing be seen. He was solo at Candace's party." Jordan sighed at the welcomed news. Finally, something in this conversation brought relief. The serial monogamist was alone. "I told him 'No random bitches.'" Shelby laughed. "But I think he came to that conclusion on his own. That nigga is *struggling*." It was amusing hearing bougie-ass Shelby be so free with "nigga." It seemed unnatural yet so perfect coming out of her mouth. "He's not happy, Jordan. *And* he was hurt when he heard you were in town and didn't reach out."

"I don't have to tell him all my moves."

"Okay, boss bitch. We know. But put that shit on pause for one second, please? Stop acting like you don't want him. And that you don't want him to want you. Stop making yourself unavailable because you want to be on top. Be open, Jordan." Jordan loudly sighed her objection. "And you can still be on top when you ride that dick. Eeeyyyooww!" Jordan couldn't help but smile and shake her head. *This bitch . . .*

"Okay, I'mma let you go." Shelby sounded like she meant it. "But stop with the bullshit. Call him, text him, DM him. Reach out. Go see him, let him see you. And lead with your pussy. Okay?"

"'Lead with my pussy'? What is wrong with you?"

"So many things. But I said what I said."

"Goodbye, Shelby." Jordan was starting to shiver at the chilly air blowing in off the Pacific.

"Love you."

"I love you too." Jordan pressed the end button on her phone.

In the distance, the sun was dropping behind the ocean's horizon. She watched with her heart beating fast despite her glass of vino, realizing she did have *real* feelings for Harper. But Jordan didn't do feelings. She replayed Shelby's pointed dig in her mind: *Don't drive him to another Robyn.* Fuck, that hit. Hard. Shelby was right, though. *Take control. If not now, when?*

She stood, grabbed her glass and walked to her patio door to let herself inside. *Fine. Fuck it.*

*Lead with my pussy?* "Girrrrl . . ." Jordan was going to do it on her terms, in her way. *Do not meet him for his book signing. Find out where he is staying . . . no fuck that. Make him come to me.*

She stepped over to her couch and turned on her sixty-inch flat-screen. She sat and pulled her phone up to her face, searching for Harper's text. He was probably still in the air or just landing. *So, I'm going to text him.* Jordan finally decided. *Tomorrow . . . but my pussy will be in panties . . .*

# CHAPTER FOURTEEN

## Robyn

Robyn awoke with the sun on her face, lying in Kwesi's bed, still in his embrace. His arm was warm and solid under her neck, comfortable. It had been a long time since she last had that kind of pillow when sleeping. She turned to look at him and then observe their tangled bodies, an intermingling of her bronze and his mahogany limbs. Her body was still relaxed from climaxing, from the two times they'd made love in the night, plus the one gift he gave her on the sofa. The memory of it was still . . . *delicious.* Robyn smiled at the thought. It was certainly something to bask in.

She kissed him gently on his cheek and then felt a slight pang of guilt when he began to stir. He turned toward her with a slow blinking of his eyes. After focusing on her face, he smiled.

"Good morning, beautiful," he said softly. Even this early, his words sounded like he was singing a song.

Robyn smiled back at him and traced the contours of muscle along his chest. "It *is* a good morning." Everything was perfect—Kwesi was more than she imagined he'd be, and she'd done a lot of imagining. He was the type of guy who could make you start to envision a future, a *long* future together. And Robyn felt ready for that. It was time for this new beginning also, the budding of love and all its possibilities. She sighed as she reached her arms upward, stretching.

"Did you sleep well?" Kwesi asked.

"Did we sleep much at all?" Robyn teased.

"I'm not sure, but I feel incredible." He smiled at her again.

"'Incredible' . . . that's a word." Robyn pondered how she felt, really. What was the word for it? "I feel . . . *hopeful*," she said finally.

Kwesi turned to look at her, propping himself up on an elbow. "And what might you be hoping for?" His tone was teasing, but his eyes were sincere. There were so many ways to answer his question, but right now, Robyn just wanted more, more of him, of this, of last night.

"I was just thinking that this feels nice, you know? Everything. Being with you, cooking with you . . ."

"I feel the same." Kwesi picked up her hand and brought it to his lips. "I'm going to London in a few days to tend to family matters, but I would really like to see you again when I return . . . like this." His eyes flickered across her naked body. Robyn felt turned on instantly, like she could make love to him all over again *right* now. She started to reach her hand down toward his belly button, and around the hard cleft of muscle at his hip, and the ripples in his abdomen flexed as he responded to her touch.

As she touched him, Robyn casually continued the conversation. "Your family is in London? Your parents? Do you have siblings?'

"My parents are here, in Accra. As are my brother and sister," he said.

Robyn continued to trail her fingers along his leg, looking

for morning wood. "Ahh, so which of your family is in London? The boys? You have a business there?"

Kwesi reached down for her hand and brought it up between them, holding it while he searched to meet her eyes. "My wife and children are in London," he said. *What?* "At our family home." Robyn was sure she heard wrong.

"Your ex?" Robyn shot up like a firecracker and snatched her hand back, then pulled the sheet up to cover her body. "Did you just say—?" she spat out with a stutter. "Did you just say . . . 'wife'?"

Strangely, other than a bit of surprise, Kwesi did not change his countenance. "Yeah," he replied calmly. "My wife. My ex. We are separated but still married. We live separate lives. Hers is in London, where our children are in school and it's what they know as home. I am based here for business. We're an unconventional family, sure, but there are no secrets between us, if that's what you're wondering. And no secrets between you and I."

"Well, this feels like a secret that I am just hearing about. . . ." Robyn said, running through her mental Rolodex of conversations about Kwesi having older kids and an "ex." She naturally assumed *ex*-wife. Not *wife.*

"Wife?" Robyn found herself repeating. For a moment, it seemed to be the only word she had access to. She searched the room for the hidden camera, the one that would tell her that this was all just a joke, an unwelcome one, but at least not real. *This can't be happening,* she thought, shaking her head to try to dismiss the unfolding circumstances.

Kwesi reached for her hand again. By instinct, she pulled it farther away. "Robyn, there's nothing to be worried about. This is not the conventional way that you might be thinking in America. There is nothing wrong."

"Oh, there's a whole lot wrong, Kwesi," Robyn began, trying to control her mounting anger. "This is some bullshit." She was sitting up in the bed now. "You never said *wife* before. Was I supposed to interrogate you? Ask you, 'did you actually get divorced?' Aren't we adults?"

"I wasn't trying to deceive you, Robyn. I don't think of her that way. She is my ex. But she is also still my wife . . . on paper. Most people I would say that to would understand."

"But you could have said it a million times before, just like that. In any of our other conversations. In fact, that should have been the first thing you said. Not after . . . after we . . ."

"Made love?" Kwesi offered.

"Oh, is *that* what happened? Because now I just feel fucked." Robyn got up to look for her clothes.

"Robyn, last night was magical, beautiful, everything I could have wanted. And I want to have more of that with you. There's nothing to stop it."

"Except your wife!" Robyn found her bra and pulled the sides around her back to fasten the clasp. She wasn't about to get caught up in this kind of madness. There was no role for her as the other woman in someone else's fractured family. She'd already had enough of that. She started to stuff her breasts in the bra cups.

"Robyn, Robyn, wait, please." Kwesi stood up with her, not bothering to even attempt to replace any of his clothing. Even under the circumstances, his body looked amazing. Robyn was disappointed that she was still moved by it. With his hands and arms now, he continued, gesturing passionately. "My *wife* would love you. She'd love to meet you." He smiled his contagious smile. *Meet me?* Robyn did not respond, although the corners of her mouth threatened to rise. "Come on, Robyn. Please, please listen to me. This is not what you're thinking. I assure you. You have no reason to be upset."

"Oh no? Just because you entered my body doesn't tell you how I feel, Kwesi!" Robyn shouted at him, without meaning to.

Kwesi approached her and placed his hands on her shoulders. So close to sliding those bra straps down and starting all over again. He leaned down to look at her. She didn't slap his hands away like she wanted to. "Tell me why. Why are you upset?" he said, craning his neck down. Robyn scrunched up her face in incredulity. *Negro, are you kidding me . . . ?*

"Are you serious right now? Because . . . you're married. And I feel stupid. And used. Why didn't you just tell me, Kwesi? So you could have sex with me and just leave . . . to go back to your *wife*?" Robyn felt like she was going crazy. The moment was too overwhelming to fight.

Kwesi wrapped himself around her, pressing her folded arms into her chest between them. He hugged her tightly and as much as she wanted to, she didn't resist.

"Robyn. That is not what is happening, I promise you. The opposite is happening. I want to spend every day with you. That is what I am feeling." He stepped back and looked her in her eyes. "Come to London with me." He said it as if he'd just had the most wonderful idea. "Would you like to come?" He held her eyes with his and waited for her response. The invitation was disarming.

"I . . . I can't. I have Mia and the restaurant. I . . ."

"Then I will call you every day when I am gone. I will do whatever will make you comfortable. But in the meantime"—he stepped closer to her, wrapped his arms around her again, and spoke with his lips to her ear—"over these next days before I leave . . . will you let me show you what you mean to me?"

Robyn could have said no. She felt she should have. *How could I have been so stupid? So trusting?* she wondered. *What have I gotten myself into?* But there, in his arms, wrapped in that way, she felt something for him beyond the doubt. And that was something she wasn't quite ready to let go of. Not just now.

# CHAPTER FIFTEEN

## Harper

Harper and Stan sat opposite the two studio executives in a modern conference room that looked out onto a sprawling production campus. Harper wet his dry throat with an expensive gulp of glass-bottled mineral water. He had just laid out his new direction for the *Unfinished Business* sequel as "a Black *St. Elmo's Fire* meets *Broadcast News* movie with the *Unfinished Business* characters." Mark, the lead studio exec, nodded as he looked up to the ceiling, presumably running the concept through in his head. After taking another sip to calm his nerves, Harper sat in awkwardness, waiting for his answer. Mark was an executive vice president of production or something like that. White, thin, great hair. Probably could have been an actor himself. The personification of "a suit." His colleague Cynthia waited for his response, as was appropriate for their hierarchy. "That sounds fantastic," he said finally, returning his focus to the room. "You're right, another college story does feel passé. What else can we really say about these characters in college?" he asked rhetorically.

"This generation doesn't have a *St. Elmo's* or a *Breakfast Club,*" Stan added. "I loved those movies."

"Who didn't?" Cynthia chimed in. Harper didn't remember her title, but it was clear she was doing the heavy lifting with this project. She was unremarkable looking. Tall, thin, and blond. Clearly smart and leading with it.

"So what are we talking? Five or six years removed from the *Unfinished* movie?" Mark asked.

"Yeah, I think so," Harper replied, encouraged by the follow-up. "We'll set it in DC. Johnson plays for the Bullets. He and Casey are married with kids and Jackson covers sports for the local television affiliate. Flave is spending his dad's money. . . ."

"Right, right. So it's still period. Nineties," Mark said with a tinge of surprise (*or was it apprehension?*). "Mmmm." Harper noted his response. Had he forgotten the movie—and more importantly the book—took place in the nineties? Harper soldiered on.

"Well, it could be the early 2000s, turn of the century, I suppose. They'd be the Wizards by then, but the Prince George's County area in Maryland is one of the most affluent areas in America for Black people —"

"I'm asking because, you know, nostalgia is one thing—" Mark said, cutting him off.

"And we love it," Cynthia added.

"But we also need for people to be able to relate. Period pieces don't always work. We got lucky with the last one," Mark argued.

"Big hit though," Stan reminded them.

"Huge. But to be completely transparent, one of our leads hasn't really taken off since the movie," Mark continued. "He's been in a couple of flops. And he's been in the tabloids getting some unwanted attention."

"Yeah, he's kind of polarizing," Cynthia seconded. Harper had heard about the young man who played Flave in the movie.

He had been caught by TMZ saying some questionable things, something to do with pink cocaine, a gun, and some sex workers. Hollywood shit. It was fitting that he embodied the character Quentin was modeled after. Life was sometimes stranger than fiction. . . .

"Do you know who we love? Damson Idris," Mark continued.

"*Love,*" Cynthia declared.

"Do you know him?" Mark turned to Harper directly. *Does he think that all Black people know one another?* He briefly contemplated dropping a joke, but they don't know him like that. Plus, doubtful that's the context in which he was asking. Instead, Harper shook his head while answering plainly.

"I don't know him personally. He's a Brit, right? He wrote me a nice note through a rep or a manager or something about *Pieces Of Us*. That was kind."

"Riiiiight. And what's going on with that? Has someone optioned that?" Cynthia perked up, interjecting excitedly. "Phenomenal book. Phenomenal."

"Thank you. Thanks. That's nice to hear. Ummm . . ." Harper wasn't sure how much to reveal to them about his latest book.

"We're considering a number of offers right now," Stan said, saving him. The truth of the matter was that Harper had had several meetings and offers to option his Pulitzer Prize–winning novel, but he was feeling particularly overprotective of it. He had always been an artist, but he really didn't want *that* work that had been so hard to birth put in someone else's hands again. *Sometimes a book should just be a book,* he'd said to Stan more than once. *Does Hollywood have no new ideas? Where's the integrity?* he wondered. But he already knew the answer to that, even sitting in the studio offices on this day: lost with the promise of a big-ass check, that's where.

It was another reason Harper wanted his crack at this

Hollywood thing. If he could prove he could do it himself, he could cut out the middleman and protect his work. And his fans echoed that. "Please don't let Hollywood fuck this one up @harperstewartwriter." ". . . they don't know what #Blacklove is . . ." Whether online, in the blogosphere or the day before at his book signing, Harper Stewart's fans always appreciated his artistry.

So Harper wasn't going to let Hollywood co-opt his shit if he could help it. Not this time around. *Pieces Of Us* was not going to the highest bidder. At least not yet.

"Well, keep us in mind." Cynthia smiled from Stan to Harper, Harper to Stan.

"Of course," Harper assured her, offering his own tepid smile.

"Anyway," Cynthia continued. "We love Damson and perhaps it could be set closer to now?"

"Or even now." Mark's suggestion sounded like more of a request or maybe even . . . a demand?

"Yeaaah, but isn't he younger than they would be now . . . ?" Harper countered.

"We could always adjust," Mark said. *Adjust?*

"For sure," Cynthia added. "What you're proposing can still be called *Unfinished Business.* Makes it really juicy . . ."

"Juicy . . . sure, I guess . . ." Harper tried his best to sound open-minded.

"We don't want to have to deal with period cars and costumes and such. Your characters are so rich and sophisticated," Mark offered.

"Grown and sexy," Cynthia echoed Mark. Again.

"Exactly. So, let's embrace that. You know? Get some great music, stylish clothes. Can you imagine Damson Idris and like, Coco Jones?" Mark offered.

A gasp came from Cynthia's direction. "Oh my God. *Love,*" she gushed.

"Well," Harper said, "I suppose. . . ."

"Look, I know we're hitting you with a lot, but we love your direction and it's generating thoughts for us."

"Right. Exciting thoughts. But just thoughts. If you hate them, we can do something else. Stick to what you feel. . . ." Cynthia said.

"No, no I'm open . . ." Harper shifted in his seat, unsure of what that would mean.

"Very open," Stan volleyed. They were beginning to sound like the suits.

"Great." Cynthia was enthusiastic. "You can set it in New York. Very sexy."

"But we'd shoot it in Toronto. Or Atlanta," Mark informed them as he looked at Cynthia before returning to Harper and Stan. "Tax incentive."

"We get it," Stan said. *Do we?* Harper wondered. He'd opened the door to the liberties the studio could take, so all he was able to do was buckle in for the rest of the meeting.

"Listen, it could be the same cast, could be older. And we certainly could recast the Flave actor." Cynthia turned to Mark for his passive approval. They'd started a back-and-forth volley, continually spinning their version of Harper's story.

"Yep. Fans loved him, but we can find somebody great in the recast. No matter what, we gotta keep that Cleavon character." Mark laughed and was quickly joined by Cynthia, as if what he'd just said was hysterical. Stan did so to be polite. Harper didn't. He wasn't laughing at all. All he could see was Murch's face, irate and betrayed. Cleavon . . . *That's the character that started all this bullshit.*

"Well, you know, that character is different now." Harper

interrupted the raucous laughter with a note of gravity. "He's much more mature, not nearly as henpecked . . . and he's a lawyer and didn't marry Darby . . ." Harper was on a roll and starting to feel good about the redirect, just as Mark's assistant entered the room to hand him a note.

"Oh really? Noooo," Cynthia said. "Darby! Oh, well we *have* to keep *her*. Perfect casting. She has *blown up*." Cynthia emphasized the words with her hands.

"Could Jackson hook up with her?" Mark inquired as he communicated to his assistant something in some secret telepathic language they clearly both understood. Judging by his body language, Mark wasn't long for this meeting.

Cynthia was right there with an enthusiastic volley to Mark's suggestion. "Oh my God. Darby and Jackson? Hot! And could be *hilarious*. He's so uptight, right? And so is she." The blurred lines between the characters onscreen and the ones from his original novel, contrasted with who he and his friends were then versus now, were starting to give Harper a headache. Picturing himself kissing Shelby turned his stomach into a knot and his face into a grimace. He could feel the eyes in the room on him, but there was no poker face for this.

"He hates it," Mark commented with a half laugh, sounding just slightly disappointed. Harper immediately downshifted into shaking his head with a reassuring "of course not" coupled with a very forced, but pleasant smile. He even mustered up a chuckle as he rubbed his temple. Thankfully, Stan intervened.

"Nooo, he doesn't hate it. It's just that Harper has a vision about the movie, that you seemed to respond to." *Good job, Stan.*

"Oh, absolutely," Cynthia said.

Stan continued, "And no one knows these characters like he does."

"Hey. No question," Mark reassured them. "We just get so

excited about this title. Everyone does. Your fans, the film's fans. The cast's fans. Go on with what you're thinking, Harper. Please."

Harper wanted to be in control of the material. It was a risk, but he'd demand it and not cede control. Not this time. He gathered his gumption. "I—I—I guess it *could* be modern. . . ." Harper hesitantly said.

"Great. So Jackson and Kendall. It'll be a great will-they-won't-they scenario," Mark replied. Harper nodded with a barely audible "yeah."

"And they'll have sex again. Will *they* get married?" Cynthia asked.

Harper laughed with a scoff. "Well, maybe, if that's where the narrative takes us. Then sure."

"So wait." Cynthia turned to Harper, fully engaged now. "Why didn't they end up together after college? They seemed so suited for each other. Soulmates, right?" She caught Harper a bit off-kilter. It must have shown in his face. "Your words, not mine. . . ." Cynthia threw her hands in the air.

Harper scrambled for a response. "Right . . . I haven't written it yet . . . but I can explore it. . . ."

"Did something happen between them? Is there a scandal? I mean other than Casey and Johnson . . ." Cynthia clearly wanted to know.

"'The Ebony Humper'—I love that name," Mark said with a chuckle.

"He was such a dog." Cynthia was giddy. "I know so many girls who would have gone for his game in a second."

"But he loved Casey and that's what made it so great," Mark added. "All his struggles with his toxic masculinity and his faith. Ohhh, so good."

"Right. They seemed destined to be together. Did those two ever get married?"

"Kendall and Jackson?"

"No. Casey and Johnson." *In real life? Or fiction, like I pitched?*

Harper struggled to answer the questions, trying to maintain the separation of the characters from the lives of his friends. "It can all be explained," he said. "The main thing I want is to be true and authentic to the characters and the story."

"Of course. Listen, you had me at 'Black *St. Elmo's Fire* in the sports world.'" Mark stood up suddenly, signaling the end of the meeting. "I have a thing," he said by way of explanation. "But just think about the possibility of setting it modern day. So much easier on production and let's get folks back in the movies. Really think about Damson for Jackson. . . ."

"You should have seen all the assistants when we walked him through our offices. . . ." Cynthia was now standing too.

"Some of these execs too." Mark gave her a sideways look. Cynthia raised her hand.

"Guilty. The man is sex personified. So, Harper, how fast do you think you can turn that concept around?"

"Ummm, well, I think a solid outline in maybe . . . three weeks?"

"Oh my God. Great. Great. We will lose Damson if we don't get this solved quickly," Cynthia said.

"He's got a lot of people who want to work with him. But he wants to be a romantic leading man. And what you're pitching is the right ticket."

Once again, Mark attempted to shore up Harper's confidence. Now that Harper's deal was secured, the studio couldn't risk overwhelming their writer. "Look, follow your vision. Don't think about setting it modern or back in the early aughts." *Then what do you want me to do?* Harper wondered. So many conflicting points of view, suggestions, pieces to reconcile. At this point, everything was just a blur. "Just write the story from your heart and give us those rich characters. We'll figure out the rest down the road. Sound like a plan?"

Harper turned to Stan with a shrug and a nod, and then back to Mark. "Yeah. Sounds good."

"Great." Mark reached out to shake Harper's hand. "Harper, it was such a pleasure to meet you in person finally. I'm so glad we did this face-to-face."

"Me too." Harper returned the firm handshake with one of his own.

Seconds later, Stan and Harper made their escape from the conference room. Heading back toward the lobby elevator, they walked by the studios' film posters past and present affixed to the hallway walls, including the original one for *Unfinished Business.*

"That went really well," Stan remarked.

"You think?" Harper was dubious.

"Oh, for sure. You just have to be open to their suggestions."

Harper nodded. "Hmmm," he quipped, deep in thought. Those suggestions had been overwhelming. Stan seemed more enthusiastic.

"How about Damson Idris, huh? Dude's a star. And a stud."

The doors of the elevator opened. The ride continued in silence as Stan whipped out his phone. Harper thought about the actor who played Flave and how much of a drug fame could be. *Hollywood shit.*

"Can't believe they can just replace an actor like that," he remarked. Stan looked at Harper as if he didn't know what he meant.

"The one caught on TMZ . . . ? Pink cocaine?" Harper reminded him.

"Oh yeah," Stan replied. "Hey, they replaced Aunt Viv and Lionel Jefferson. Remember that?" Harper nodded in recognition.

"It's not like they're replacing Denzel or Tom Hanks," Stan continued. They rode down for a few beats watching the digital display of descending numbers.

"Tough business," they said simultaneously. The coincidence brought a laugh as they reached the bottom floor and exited into the sun-splashed studio lot.

"You really think you can get it done in three weeks?" Stan asked as they made their way to the studio's valet stand.

"I think so. I'm headed to Maui tomorrow afternoon. Locking myself away in that villa and drilling down. I feel good. It's just an outline."

"True, but they really want to see something special. Make sure to drill down on that Jackson and Kendall storyline. Fans really want to know what's going on with them."

"Hmmph. Yeah. Me too," Harper mumbled.

"What's that?" Stan inquired as he looked up from his texting.

"Nothing. I'm good."

He looked at his phone for any sign from Jordan. Still nothing.

"You're about to do the hermit thing for three weeks. I know how you get."

"I'm just hoping I can keep it going. The muse is always slippery." The valet pulled Stan's car forward.

"Well, don't let her get away," Stan said. *Too late,* Harper thought. What if Jordan really was his muse? In many ways she was. So was Robyn to an extent. But clearly now, when he had to make something up about Kendall, he could do so unchecked. Was that a good thing? Harper wasn't sure. He really didn't like the thought of delving into Kendall's inspiration without being in some kind of contact with Jordan. Heading to Hawaii without at least touching base with Jordan felt like doing shit behind her back. There was a balance he didn't feel without her, caused by some kind of schism that Harper still failed to put his finger on. He'd stressed authenticity in his meeting, but how authentic could he be right now?

He didn't need Jordan's approval for his creative process, but he's always *wanted* it. Her acceptance. As bad as he felt about their distance, he felt worse that he didn't know what had caused it. In the process, he'd lost touch with what was going on with Jackson and Kendall for real.

Stan interrupted Harper's thoughts. "Look, I have to meet a client for a drink but I'm open for dinner tonight. I can get us a place. Just let me know."

"I will," Harper said, and extended his hand.

Stan gave him a handshake and a hug. "Great job, buddy. You always come through."

"See ya, Stan. Thanks for coming," Harper said as Stan jumped in his ride and started a call. Harper's rental car pulled up and he exchanged a five-dollar tip with the valet for his keys. He sat down, plugged in his phone, and continued to contemplate. Jordan hadn't said anything in like a day and a half since Harper reached out. His options were dwindling to see her, as was his hope. *Fuck it,* he decided. *Can't worry about it.*

But he *was* worried about it. And what about Murch? He hadn't responded to his questions about Robyn's new dude either. It seemed like the women who used to care for him, despite his flaws, were moving along without him, in their own orbits. *Not everyone revolves around your schedule, Harp.* He shook his head at his thoughts. People are people, not characters. *Tap-tap-tap.* Harper was startled when he heard the rapping on his rental's driver's side window. He must have been sitting for longer than he realized. The valet nonverbally wondered if Harper needed anything else. Harper raised his hand with a "my bad" gesture and shook his head. Then he cranked up the car and drove off the lot. The problem was he just didn't know where to go. Have dinner with Stan or head back to his hotel in Santa Monica. It was too early to eat and it didn't make sense to brave the traffic toward the west side now. Harper shrugged and sighed, feeling like he should have better options, but then he got a text, a flash on the screen from Jordan Armstrong.

Nobu, Malibu 8p.

The message spun Harper into a double take. Did Jordan just finally respond? He felt the quivers of butterflies, but a smile came over his face. "All right. 'Bout time." Now with a purpose, Harper approached the entrance to the 101 freeway. He punched in the Nobu address. It was going to take ninety minutes to get there. Mostly due to rush-hour traffic. "Mmmm," he mused. "Fuck it." Harper wanted to see her and wasn't even about to risk being late. He'd brave the traffic tonight heading west into the shifting sunset. *Why'd Jordan take so long to respond? Busy? Nah. There's something else going on.* But he'd worry about that later. Hell, in person, he could ask. If he was lucky with the traffic, there'd be time to freshen up at his hotel beforehand. He should. Even if it wasn't exactly on the way, more important, he wanted to look his best. He merged onto the freeway with the swiftly moving traffic that his map app said would slow to a crawl in about eight minutes. No matter. Nothing else mattered. He was going to see his friend. He touched the car screen to respond to her text and said out loud:

See you then.

# CHAPTER SIXTEEN

## Jordan

Jordan took a deep breath as she swapped places with the parking lot valet, stepping out of her car and tugging down her dress so it once again grazed her knees. Nobu always looked stunning at night, even from here—the carefully placed lights illuminated the beige stone building like a modern palace set right on the Malibu coastline. She walked quickly. The breeze off the ocean was full of moisture and nothing about her appearance was up for compromise. Jordan knew she looked great and confirmed it in her own reflection in the glass pane of the large wooden door. Cleavage sitting high, saying *hello* but not too much, figure and frame set, all curves and shoulders. Her hair was cascading waves of glossy ebony strands, opening elegantly to reveal her subtly accentuated features. She was ready.

"Armstrong, party of two," she said to the slightly distracted hostess. The restaurant was full, bustling both inside and on the generous outside balcony. She'd beat the reservation time by a full twenty minutes and was going to need a drink, at least to settle the fluttering in her belly. *Why am I nervous? It's just*

*Harper,* she thought. But *just* Harper? Was there any such thing? "Lead with your pussy," Shelby had told her. Every time she thought about it, she had to laugh. *I'll lead with my pussy when I'm good and damn ready.* It felt good to be in control, with her vagina tightly wrapped up in satin fabric and willpower.

Jordan followed the hostess's directions to the adjacent bar, walking with enough intention to notice the various sets of eyes that followed her. The attention was confirmation she'd come dressed to slay, on the outside at least. *This damn panty line,* she remembered; the only hitch in an otherwise flawless appearance, but the insurance she needed to not get carried away. It was the parking brake to keep her pussy from rolling down the hill and crashing right into disaster dick.

At the bar, Jordan stood for only a split second, inhaling the salt air in the open room, appreciating the colorful décor and the ultra-premium bar with elaborate tequila bottles that looked like a row of blown-glass sculptures and probably cost just as much.

"My table is ready. Would you like my seat?" Jordan's attention was brought to a once-occupied barstool and the gentleman now standing in front of it, all typical Malibu casual. His arm was placed gently on the waist of a silent waiflike blonde, in high heels and enough makeup to signal who was in charge. *Tonight, I'm in charge,* Jordan thought. She decided to take the seat and promptly a handsome bartender appeared with flirtatious eyes and a warm welcoming smile.

"What can I make for you?" he asked. *He's extra,* Jordan thought, but appreciated the attention.

"I'll have a sidecar."

"Hennessy?"

*Hell no,* Jordan thought. *Not tonight.* "I'll take the Rémy."

"Sugared rim?" By now the bartender was smiling at her slyly, like he was offering her more than a drink.

"I'll pass on that, just straight up."

"You got it . . . gorgeous." He winked and busied himself with making her cocktail. Jordan stiffened at the compliment, a sure sign that she was still far too uptight for what the night called for. The bartender was cute. Not her usual type, as she'd mainly been focused on the brothas lately, but he was brown. *Asian,* she thought. *Maybe Filipino.* Interesting. *Loosen up, Jordan,* she reminded herself and made an extra effort at smiling when her drink arrived. She'd need a big swig of it if she was going to keep herself cool, calm, and under control while waiting for Harper.

"Cheers," she offered, tipping her glass to the bartender.

"Enjoy," he returned, with that same smile. Sexy, for sure. And the first sip confirmed he knew what he was doing. "Let me know how you like it," he said.

That first sip was delicious. The burn of the cognac met her nose even before the first wave of sweet citrus hit her palate. He'd balanced it just right, the way she loved it, and her eyes closed in enjoyment and delight. "Mmmmm . . . it's . . . delicious," she granted.

"Damn, I'd like to be that drink."

Jordan froze. She'd know that voice anywhere. And all at once, time stood still. No more buzzing din of the bar patrons all around her in their empty conversations. No more sound of the ocean outside. No more clinking glasses. Just the sound of her heartbeat in her ears, the woosh of her breathing deep, and the long exhale leaving her body. And . . . Harper. *He's here.*

Jordan took her time turning slowly on the stool, smiling now, because at her very core she was happy to see him, to have him close. And too happy perhaps, because . . . *damn. Damn,* this man looked good. For a moment, all familiarity was lost as Jordan took in the sight of him, standing there in his dark turtleneck and buttery brown skin, just a hint of low scruff on his face, smiling at her with those midnight eyes and perfect teeth. Yes, this was her friend, and still, this man was *fine,* undeniably so.

"Heyyyy." Jordan opened her arms to take him in. And of course, Harper came in at a strange angle and made the embrace awkward and slightly sideways. The side of her face wound up on his chest, or rather, against the muscles of his chest, and as she gripped his arms, she felt how solid he was, how carved. As she pulled herself away, reluctantly for sure, he came toward her and laid his lips softly on her cheek. *He smells good as hell,* she thought as his sandalwood scent wafted toward her in the wake of his movement.

"What's up, stranger?" Harper teased with an extra glint in his eye. He stood back while still grasping her shoulder to take her in. "You look . . . *fantastic.* California is treating you well."

Jordan's first reply was a reflexive look of side-eye at the "stranger" comment, but then she remembered the mission. *Lead with your pussy* was starting to take on new meaning, and she had no intention of friend-zoning this experience. *Hell no.* And the way he was taking her in, his lingering glances she caught, made her swallow the sarcasm and respond with flirtation. "You think so?" she said, and capped it off with a sexy smile. "Thanks."

"You look amazing." His eyes definitely ran across her cleavage and back to her face before gesturing to her cocktail. "What you drinkin'? Wait, sidecar, right?"

"You know that's my shit, Harper." Jordan turned to retrieve her drink from the bar. "Want one?"

"Nah," he replied casually, signaling the bartender. "Sable on the rocks, one cherry please?" he ordered.

Jordan leaned her back against the bar then and looked at Harper seductively over the rim of her glass. She sipped her drink again, looking for a recharge of liquid courage against her suddenly active nerves. *What the fuck?* she wondered. *Why in the hell am I nervous? It's just Harper. Keep it business for now, Jordan,* she reminded herself so she could at least try.

"So, what brings you to LA?" she asked. "Book signing?"

"Yep." Harper retrieved his drink from the bartender. "Cheers." He positioned his glass to clink against her own. "Paperback release of *Pieces of Us.* It was a good crowd over at the Grove." He looked directly at her.

"Yeah, sorry I couldn't make it."

"I understand." Harper shifted, leaning on the bar next to her despite the open seat. The proximity was unnerving. She felt herself watching too closely every time he brought the glass to meet his mouth. Every time the caramel liquid passed between his lips. Seeing the moistening of his skin . . . the hint of his teeth, she wondered what it would be like to kiss him . . . "I'm just glad I'm seeing you now," Harper said, penetrating her thoughts.

"Oh . . . yeah . . . of course. I'm glad too . . . that we were able to make this work. And you had a studio meeting too, right? For the *Unfinished Business* sequel?"

Harper sighed and wet his lips again with a sip of his Sable. Jordan focused on every drop of glistening moisture as his mouth moved to reply. "Yeah, that was good. I had been struggling with that pitch, trying to find the right direction for it. But they liked what I had to say, so I feel a lot better about it."

"That's exciting."

"Yeah, I guess . . . Yeah, it is exciting."

Jordan perked up. "What's that pause?"

Harper seemed surprised that she noticed. But of course, she noticed. After thirty years, she had him memorized. "Oh, I, um, I just wanted to think about how I really feel, rather than just give a stock answer," he said. "I've been doing that a lot lately. It feels good to just be real with someone . . . with you."

*With me?* Jordan wondered. *You want to be real with me?*

"Ms. Armstrong?" From nowhere, the hostess appeared holding two menus. "May I take you to your table?" It was a moment of relief for Jordan. An invitation to stop analyzing. Except, *these damn granny panties* . . . she thought, as she started to follow the hostess. That panty line was not sexy, not in the way that she felt now, how she wanted to be. It wasn't what she wanted Harper to see as her ass swayed while she walked ahead of him. She wanted him to see her ass *work* in that dress. Her perfect curves swaying from side to side as she walked. *Dammit.* Jordan knew that her ass was NOT ass-ing. She'd done this on purpose, she had to recall. *And why again?* She could just imagine what Shelby would say: *Why would you do that? I should have drawn you a diagram,* she'd chastise. Jordan wanted . . . no, she'd *needed* some amount of control. She already knew that her grip on temperance was slipping quickly.

The walk to the table felt long, especially with a stark panty line that she hadn't anticipated wishing would disappear. She had tens of thousands of dollars' worth of gorgeous lingerie. Much of it for a night such as this one. She had thongs and lace and demi cups that allowed her nipples to pop perfectly and her ass to sit like a shelf. Hell, the salespeople at La Perla knew her by name. But it was too late to escape now, to dip back and slow down to walk next to Harper instead of ahead of him. They were already at the table. When she turned around to take her seat, just as she thought, his eyes were focused right where her hips had been.

Seated next to the window, across from one another at a quaint table for two, Jordan sighed, relaxing finally into the chair. Harper, for his part, seemed completely oblivious to the crisis of her underwear, and the current conundrum Jordan faced in wanting to be free of the constraints she'd imposed upon herself—*all* of them. *What in the hell was I thinking?* she questioned herself.

"Really gorgeous view," Harper said with his head turned toward the cherry-wood-framed bay window. "I bet it's spectacular during the day."

"I'll bet," Jordan said, distracted. She already knew what the view was like during the day. It was spectacular, just like her ass looked in its regular shape. *Fuck.* It was not going down like this. Hell no. "Hey, Harper," Jordan called. He turned his head back to her. No way was she going to lose his attention to the view of the ocean or any other view. "Could you order me another sidecar? I'm just going to run to the restroom." Jordan gestured behind her, but she was already up and standing, bag dropped into the seat, and turning to make a quick dash.

In the bathroom stall, Jordan shimmied the hem of her dress all the way up to her hips and pulled those gotdamn big draws down to her knees and stepped out of them one foot at a time. She contemplated flushing the loose carcass of fabric down the toilet, but she wanted to throw them all the way away, forever. She pulled open the metal trashcan cover, the final resting place of so many other unmentionables, and dropped the wadded-up mound of cloth on the top of the tissue-wrapped tampons. *Good fucking riddance,* she thought. In the mirror, even in front of the sets of curious eyes beside her, she pulled her breasts up and set them at the top of her bra, so that her nipples were perked and protruding obviously, outlined underneath the material of her bustline. Satisfied, she puckered her lips in the mirror and reset her lipstick before heading back out the door to handle that shit like the boss she was and how it should have been handled from jump.

Back at the table, Harper was fidgety. As she approached, Jordan saw how he'd been apparently biding his time while waiting for her. He even stood to pull out her chair. So formal, so gentlemanlike. *At least he's not looking at his phone,* she thought. She'd set the night off on the wrong foot. But as she sat down once again in her seat, this time feeling the chill of nighttime air tickle between her thighs, she knew what she needed to do.

A fresh version of her drink sat on the table, and Harper, with his attention fixed on her now, was looking like a snack. *This is happening,* she decided. *Tonight.* She grabbed the glass and took a big swig, pulling half the liquid into her mouth at once.

"Everything okay?" Harper looked concerned.

Jordan forced her swallow down. "Uh-huh." She needed the liquid courage immediately. She looked at Harper directly, met his eyes, softened her voice and asked, "So, how are you doing, sir?"

His face showed the relaxed lines of sincerity as he replied, "I'm good. Really good." And then he asked, "So, how's that show you've been working on? The idea you were kicking around a while ago. The Black woman wellness thing?"

"Oh, that?" *Let's not talk about work, Harper.* Jordan shrugged and moved to dismiss the topic as quickly as she could. "Still kickin' it around. Not much to report."

Harper leaned forward. "It's a good idea, I mean, from what I remember. It's been . . . a while." *Oh yeah, 'cause I wasn't fucking with you,* Jordan recalled. Harper took a sip of his Sable and cherry and seemed like he had his own hesitations. "I . . . um . . . you know . . . speaking of a while, I was just . . . wondering . . . if . . . everything is all right?"

By now, Jordan was leaning forward, already irritated with his halting words. "All right with what?" she countered, confused.

Looking troubled, Harper continued, "All right . . . between you and me?"

*Oh, hell no. What is he doing?* Now wasn't the time for some sentimental deep conversation to undergird their friendship. She and Harper could go for years and not speak and still be solid. They were solid. But tonight wasn't about being friends. It was about the rapidly drying walls of her pussy that should have been leading the way from the GATE. But in the midst of her silence, Harper continued, "Look, I know you were just in New York and the past couple of months . . . our correspondence . . . it just hasn't been the same. And I—"

"Harper, I—" Jordan tried to cut him off.

But still he continued. "Look, I don't mean to put you on the spot . . ."

*Then don't—*

But Harper was undeterred. ". . . but we've been friends for so long, and been through too much just to . . ."

Jordan took another sip of her drink. There wasn't much left. But thankfully, it allowed her to watch Harper's lips moving in his seemingly endless soliloquy, and at the same time tune him out. There had to be some way to get them out of this soapy drama of friendship woes. So *what* they hadn't talked in a while? They were going to fix that, *tonight.* For damn sure. And nothing was in the way, especially not those panties, and certainly not anyone or anything ruining the mood. Not even Harper himself. Mercifully, the waiter appeared and introduced himself, stopping Harper in the middle of his sappy flow.

"I see you two already have drinks. How do you feel about food? Are you ready to order?"

Harper pulled up the menu and after a few seconds of looking at it gazed back at her. He had his readers on, looking sexy. Jordan bit her lip and squeezed her legs together. It was hard staying in the seat. It was hard looking at him. It was . . .

"You want to split a couple, J?" *Was he talking to her? About food?*

"Yeah, uhh, sure," Jordan managed to reply.

"This is your spot. . . ." *My spot?* "So, I'll leave myself in your capable hands. . . ." Harper set the menu down and looked at her expectantly. *Oh, he wants me to order,* she realized. *Naked beef. How about that . . . ?*

"How about I tell you guys about the specials tonight? Give you a bit more time to decide." Harper nodded. And the waiter began listing a litany of food items that would have sounded delicious on any other night. *Come on, J, you gotta make a move,* Jordan's inner voice urged. ". . . Crispy okra with ponzu sauce, garlic prawns with sesame noodles . . . and a crab fried rice . . ." the waiter continued.

Jordan took a deep breath. ***Now**, Jordan.* It was urgent. She set the menu down with a snap on the table. "Um, sorry, can you give us a minute?" The waiter looked surprised but stopped his recitation and then promised to circle back.

"I definitely want to try that truffle salmon," Harper began. "Wanna split it . . . ?"

"Yep," Jordan replied without hesitation. "Let's split."

"Cool. Anything else you want to order . . . ?"

"No, I mean, let's go. Let's get out of here."

"Now?" Harper looked startled, but Jordan was already pushing her chair back.

"Now."

"Everything all right?" Harper said, standing up now, dropping his folded napkin on the tabletop.

"Yep. I . . . need some air," Jordan said, but she was already walking toward the door, ass swerving right to left, just like it was supposed to.

## CHAPTER SEVENTEEN

# Harper

*Man, that was weird,* Harper thought as he drove his rented Audi coupe up the PCH trying to keep up with Jordan's speed. By the time he reached valet, Jordan had already gotten the keys to her royal-blue Beemer. "Did you rent or Uber?" she asked.

"Rental . . ."

"Follow me," she said simply before ducking into the soft top convertible. *What the hell is going on with her?* Harper had been looking forward to an evening of reconnection and food. He hadn't eaten since breakfast and saved his appetite for some five-star cuisine with his bestie. He'd really been missing Jordan and was genuinely glad to see her. Relieved, even. She looked beautiful—no shocker there, but her energy got strange when they sat down for dinner. *Maybe she was feeling sick?* he wondered. *Some female trouble?* Jordan was usually a trouper and muscled through whatever. But maybe this was *"self-care Jordan."* Self-care Jordan had been taking her health seriously and maybe registering more of how she was feeling. *Makes sense.* Harper nodded to himself. Whatever Jordan needed, he was down to support, even though self-care Jordan had rejected him (again) three years ago on the Brooklyn promenade. It felt shitty, but she'd been right (again).

Jordan and Harper had always been great as friends and to make that murky with blurred lines, especially right after getting divorced, would have been a disaster for their friendship. Still, what had been happening over the past four months wasn't quite their friendship either. And that's why he wanted to see her, clear the air. They had entirely too much history to be anything other than honest. Though at the restaurant, she seemed disinterested, even offended, when Harper brought up their decades-long bond. "Maybe she didn't want to discuss it in public or . . ?" Harper mused, attempting to rationalize with himself. "But we gotta be honest with each other. Right?" These were all questions that needed answers. But for the moment, Harper had to focus to keep up with Jordan along the winding curves of the PCH.

Jordan put her left signal on between traffic lights in front of the open gates of a driveway at a beachfront house. "Must be the crib," Harper said softly. He was already impressed. A garage door lifted until it was parallel to the ground, revealing space for two cars. The house, illuminated by the moonlit sky and landscape lights, had a modernist structure that boasted clean lines and glass panels, all shimmering with the golden glow of understated luxury. It was both untouchable and inviting. Kind of like Jordan. "Nice."

Oncoming traffic prevented her from making her turn just yet. As the headlights zoomed by in the opposite lane, Harper could see Jordan was in conversation with someone, moving her silhouetted head as if she was on a speakerphone, gesturing with her hand. She was animated about something; self-care Jordan was still probably bossing someone around. The traffic let up enough to let her turn into her space. At first, she didn't quite make room for his car, but then the Beemer backed up and negotiated a snugger fit to the left to accommodate Harper's vehicle. Even after waiting for oncoming traffic to pass, as he pulled in, he saw that Jordan was still engrossed in her conversation. She glanced over at him as he put the car in park. *Hmmm, not smiling,* he noticed. She wasn't mad, but she was serious. He shut off his engine.

Harper opened his door and stepped out just in time to hear a woman's voice on Jordan's line shout the muffled words "Get it done!" To which Jordan replied, "Goodbye," while keeping her eyes on Harper. *Business call?* Who knows. Maybe it had something to do with the quick bolt out of Nobu. Even though she didn't have a steady job, Jordan was always working. She exited her ride, seemingly unbothered, and walked around to the trunk area where Harper stood admiring her car.

"Nice ride. I always liked the Beemer."

"Thanks. Come. I'll give you the nickel tour." Jordan gestured with her head for Harper to follow her toward the front of the house.

"Everything cool?" Harper inquired as he walked alongside her.

"Everything's fine." Jordan's tone was nonchalant, but definitive as she hit the alarm on her car and moved toward her home's grand entrance.

"Aight . . ." Harper responded. Something about Jordan was different.

Did she put on lip gloss or something? And those breastesses were on display differently than at dinner. *Maybe I didn't notice,* Harper thought as Jordan punched her garage door code and the door folded down silently. *I would've noticed though . . . right?* They walked along a gravelly path to the sound of ocean waves crashing on the nearby shore, feeling the crisp air wrap around them, cooler than it had been at Nobu. Jordan punched the code to her outside door to let them both in. She walked ahead as Harper closed the heavy white wooden door behind him.

He followed her as he watched Jordan ascend the illuminated steps of her lush-ass place. Also lush AF were Jordan's legs and the sway of that dress that was flowing but hugging the curve of her ass. *Whew. She's still fine.* But they were friends . . . and in some weird place that he couldn't quite put his finger on. Other than Robyn and his mom, Jordan had been the most important woman in his life. His life . . . that he felt kicked out of and out of sync with. He wanted—no, he *needed*—to right the ship with her. His homie. The one who kept it real with him from way back.

The blues guitar lick of Tony! Toni! Toné!'s "(Lay Your Head on My) Pillow" kicked off, echoing its unforgettable rhythmic riff throughout the foyer. Jordan dropped her car key on the wooden table that looked like it was carved straight out of a big-ass tree. Harper was already bopping his head to Raphael's groove.

"This is my shit," he said, his neck hugging the beat.

"I know," Jordan responded. At least that's what it sounded like. It was hard to tell because the ceiling speakers were dominating the space, filling it with music. It wasn't obtrusive. In fact, it was perfectly calibrated to the acoustics of the room and the scenery, and it made the moment breathtaking. Everything in here had its place. A designer clearly took their time and definitely listened to Jordan (as if they had a choice). She had a gorgeous home. Each detail a testament to the life of a woman who had conquered worlds and carved her own space on the edge of the sea. Again, no surprise. Harper whistled.

Jordan smiled as she sauntered into her living room. "You like?"

"Ummm, yeah," Harper said, stating the obvious. "What's not to like?"

Jordan had always wanted nice things, the good life. And she got them. She'd earned them. This place—just like her old spot in DUMBO—suited her. But this was another level. It was grown and sexy. The sexiest. Just like Jordan. "This is dope," Harper said as he took a moment to explore. Jordan sat on the back of her couch, her left thigh lifted to rest on the edge. Harper stepped over to the windows that fronted the beach and stared at the darkness. The whispers of the ocean kissed the shore with a soothing rhythm, as if serenading the brilliance of this house's owner—a sister whose success radiated through every meticulously chosen detail inside. It was more than a home; it was a statement, a sanctuary, a dream realized, shimmering in the Malibu moonlight like poetry in glass and stone. Harper shook his head and smiled. *She did it again.*

"This must be incredible during the day."

"It is," Jordan replied. "You should see it."

Harper threw a brief look to her over his shoulder, and said, half joking, "Well, if I'm invited back I'm sure I would love it." And then returned his gaze to the wonder outside.

After a beat, he heard, "You don't ever need an invitation, Harper." Jordan's voice floated over his shoulder. The tenor in her voice had dropped an octave. Harper knew he heard it. He furrowed his brow and turned around to look at her. Her glossy lips parted, her eyes unblinking and staring directly at him. Her legs were open, and she was half sitting, half standing, striking a model's pose that accentuated her entire figure. *Damn,* Harper thought. *She looks sexy as hell.* But when hadn't she to him? It was taking more effort than usual to maintain his restraint. Why did they *always* have to be friends? Because that's the way this relationship has worked. *Be cool, Harp.* Raphael Saadiq echoed that same sentiment: *And just reeelax, reeeelax, reeelax.*

*Chill, Harp. Friend zone.* He unfurrowed his brow and responded, "Well, that's good to know." Harper then gave her a warm smile, trying to remain even-keeled. This was good, Jordan opening the door back up to their friendship. Had it ever really been closed? Hard to decipher. The last few months had been odd. But now even more oddly, Jordan was just looking at him. It was confusing, but there was a vibe. A vibe that Harper has been familiar with since they met as freshmen. When they were just overachieving teenagers. When they were seniors in the newsroom dancing and making out to Stevie Wonder's "As." The same vibe had been present at Lance and Mia's wedding on the cusp of his debut novel being introduced to the world. It's the same vibe that engulfed them on the night of the movie premiere of *Unfinished Business.* Harper had always liked Jordan. He grew to love her deeply. Their friendship helped him be the man he became. The author he became. Wouldn't sex have changed that? Undoubtedly. But he wasn't seventeen anymore. He wasn't burdened with "making it" anymore. He wasn't married anymore either. Still . . .

Harper swallowed and parted his lips, looking back at her as the haunting harmonics of Coco Jones's "ICU" began to play. Jordan broke the silence.

"Harper?"

"Yeah?" he responded.

"Come here." There was nothing ambiguous in her voice, look, or stance. Nothing ambiguous at all. Harper moved toward Jordan, and this time, as he headed toward her and the space between her open legs on the back of the sofa, it sure didn't feel like he was reentering the friend zone.

## CHAPTER EIGHTEEN

# Jordan

Jordan knew very well what she was saying, and the reality of what it meant. Even though Harper stood just a few feet away in the living room, his approach took an eternity in Jordan's mind of swirling thoughts. Right away she understood what it had taken for Shelby to go after Quentin, even to break up a wedding. To find the courage and put it all on the line. *Right here, right now, Jordan.* Because even as Harper walked toward her, step by step by step, Jordan knew that one way or another, that night everything was going to change.

*He understands now,* she thought. There was nothing to say, just the music playing its haunting melody, the gravelly voice singing *I see you,* and Harper's procession toward her. His eyes were as dark as the ocean outside now, intent and looking right at her. She studied him, his face, his shoulders, his body. Her breath was faint, much quieter than her heartbeat, which was pounding loud enough to hear outside her chest. In three of those shallow breaths, he was there, right in front of her—all body heat and fragrance. She lifted her chin toward his descending face and without hesitation, his lips were on hers—warm, soft, and wet. Gently at first and then his mouth pressed into her own more forcefully, just like the hunger that had been building between them for decades. This was dangerous, frightening. Consuming. Here, there were no barriers or guardrails. Only desire. Maybe it was a bad idea, maybe this was the end of the world, but Jordan's body had reached a place of no turning back.

Harper's tongue slipped between her lips just as she felt his fingers in her hair, pulling her into him. She gripped him back. Under her hands on his torso, ripples of taut muscle contracted with each of his movements. She pulled him closer, between her legs so she could enwrap him with her thighs. His tongue danced around in her mouth, making it feel all at once like he was swirling it within the space of her entire body, tickling inside her, causing her to squirm and writhe. Between her legs, Jordan felt herself getting much wetter than she had ever been; her gap was warm inside and pulsing with its own type of heartbeat. She pushed against him with her mouth, back in the game of give-and-take, and she answered each of his movements: a lick inside his mouth against the soft underbelly of his upper lip, or a tiny bite and tug of his lower one, just to keep things unexpected. But there was no rush; they could explore all night, every crevice of mouth, crook of arm, space of cleavage, with clothes or without, they were only each other's now.

With their mouths connected, tongues in play, Harper's hands began to explore her, tracing the sides of her body, his thumbs tripping over the protrusion of her nipples. The stimulation sent a shock of concentrated pleasure through her and Jordan reached her arms up to pull him even closer, letting his tongue fill more of her mouth. *More . . . more* was all she could manage to think, curious about how long he would explore her, loving it, and wanting him to simply consume her all at once. In response, Harper's hands traveled down to grip the cheeks of her ass. The fabric of her dress rubbed against her skin, a conduit of the warmth of his palms as he squeezed, spreading her more open than she already was, and making her start to think about him filling her in even more places. She slid herself forward toward him, to pull down his soft wool suit jacket. It fit him so well, and peeled down his arms like an expensive rind, revealing the contours and curves of the well-hewn muscles in his arms.

*Harper* . . . she whispered to herself, a reminder that it was really him, really them, really now.

And as his jacket came down, the hem of her skirt went up, pushed by Harper's hands sliding against the smooth skin of her glistening legs, until it sat scrunched at her waist. The couch fabric beneath her bare ass awoke new sensations in her body, in anticipation of what would come next. How and where she would be touched, what to explore next on Harper, but she didn't get the chance to decide. Harper's warm mouth on her nipple brought her attention exactly there, to the delicious sensation and then even more alluring, to meet his eyes. *Yes,* it was . . . him . . . *Harper* who she'd been wanting. It was him making her feel this way, exciting her, pleasuring her, taking slow claim over each part of her body, enjoying it, enjoying her. Slowly his eyes closed as he sucked, pulling her breast into his mouth with gentle tugs. And then he slid his fingers into her mouth, twirling them there too. The added stimulation made Jordan lean her head back and widen the opening of her legs, leaving her warm center exposed and vulnerable to the flow of cool air in the room. It was only a matter of time before Harper would touch her there, but too much was happening now to consider it. There was no time to think. He was already everywhere. His fingers dipped into her mouth again and she sucked on them until he pulled them out. He brought his moistened fingertips to twist around her left nipple, doubling the stimulation at her chest and the rapture she felt. "It feels so good." She sighed out the words, releasing the breath she'd been holding on to. *Yes, Harper . . .* And she squirmed as the heat in her body threatened to explode its way out of her. "Yes . . ." she exhaled.

When her nipples were swollen and hard, darkened with arousal and slick with moisture, Harper captured her gaze again, and kept his eyes on hers as he trailed down past her torso to lift her dress higher. She was fully exposed now and didn't care, not even minding the friction of Harper's sweater against her thigh as he lowered himself down past her hips until he was eye level with her carefully groomed panty-free pussy. Her body tensed with anticipation, not knowing at all what to expect. Then, the touch of his finger, right at the tip of so many nerve endings, was electrifying, and she moaned into his mouth as he brought himself up to kiss her again while his fingers fondled her deeper into arousal, just teasing at her opening but not yet inside. Her body was freed now; she was too turned on to think clearly or to be uptight. Everything was a haze of want and desire and building lust. Yes, it was Harper. *Harper, yes, it's so good . . . I need to know . . . to feel it,* she thought as she brought her hands down to rapidly unbuckle his belt.

She dove downward into his pants while his fingers teased, making their way through her slit without any resistance. She was so wet already, dripping, so wanting. When her hands maneuvered past the band of his boxer briefs, and she wrapped her fingers around his thick erection, feeling the weighty girth she'd never expected throbbing in her palm, it elicited a quiet gasp of imagined pleasure as she stroked it with approval. His fingers entered her now, but she wanted more. She was going to need all of him, *this* . . . the hardness of Harper's erection in her hand, to feel his full manhood instead. *Yes, Harper . . . let's make it real.*

Harper's breath became heavy while kissing her. "Jordan . . ." he whispered. So she stroked him more, liking the feeling of controlling him with her hands. He was hers. She pulled him toward her, closer and closer to see if his bulbous tip could reach the opening of her lower lips. She couldn't help herself; her body was in control and begging for this . . . *come closer to me, Harper . . . closer.* His hand cupped her breast, the flesh squeezed to point her nipple at him, only briefly, before his mouth covered it again, leaving her to breathe out a long and slow throaty moan of "ahhhhh . . . and ummmm . . . Harperrrr." Harper sucked and bit her. His fingers twirled down below, one hand still inside her making room, a place for the rest of him. Jordan had to steady herself. She let go of Harper to put both hands behind her, gripping the edge of the sofa she was leaning on. Her head fell back, letting her body rock, making her legs spread wider, opening farther. Harper began to lower himself down the front of her body again, seeming to change angles with his fingers, until he was low enough to lift Jordan's leg to rest over his shoulder. Jordan easily adjusted her balance with her heel on his back, loving Harper's adventurousness. She let herself go with her mouth open to the ceiling, gasping with the waves of rapturous pleasure.

And then, wrapping his hands around her buttocks and squeezing, he pulled her to him quickly, delivering a sudden shock of warmth, between her legs, right on her most sensitive point. Jordan snapped her head forward to look down at Harper, to watch him looking up at her with his mouth on her now. *Oh my God . . .* She let her head roll back to rest on her shoulders, shaking slightly with the effort of holding on to the back of the sofa. She loved the flicking of his tongue, its texture and muscular dexterity, the hot moist air of his breath on her as he tickled her so lightly and sucked so gently it made her wonder how he'd figured this out about her body so quickly. It was exactly right and it drove her crazy, sending waves of pleasure all the way up into her jaw. She wanted to be taken, now, *now Harper* . . . but she was no longer in control and he let her know. He pulled away, looking at her with sly intensity, with mischief, examining where he'd been. Taking his time to look at it, then meet her eyes, to tease her slowly with his fingers again. "Wh-what . . . are you . . . do—" she barely managed to whisper, just before he returned his face to burrow between her legs and continued his warm stimulation and circular motions.

Another moan escaped her, and forgetting about her balance, with one hand she laid her fingers on the back of his head. Too tentatively, because he grabbed her wrist and pulled her hand to wrap firmly around the back of his neck, signaling, *Push me in deeper, Jordan. Hold me in place.* He wanted to be there. He let her know. He wanted to taste her. He wanted her to lose control. The orgasm began to build within her. The intensity of Harper's stimulation, the excitement of *finally,* the smells of her own musk, coupled with the sounds of suction and her own moans of desire at Harper's intense application of those lips that she'd finally kissed as deeply as she wanted, she let her hips rock toward him, her ass against the hard edge of the sofa, sliding back and forth, back and forth, digging her heel into the contours of his back.

The intensity of his movements grew, the sliding in and out of his fingers, the swirls and suction of his warm mouth against her, the grazing of his teeth, the tip of his tongue in places she thought he wouldn't go. "Oh my Gaa—Harpe—It feels so good, please don't stop," she managed to whisper with what breath she could spare. Her orgasm was mounting, steadily, steadily, taking her higher and higher, her body opening, rolling and rocking forward into him, and higher until she had no choice but to let go and release it all, her hips thrust into the air with violence and convulsions one wave after another, after another, and again. "Yes . . ." she managed to say. "Yes!" she cried out. "Thank you, thank you, thank you," she prayed, asking for even more. *Please don't let this ever be over . . .*

When he stood up again, and their eyes met, it seemed only inevitable that they would start all over, kissing, slowly again, lazily, with lust and exploration. And it occurred to Jordan that Harper, breathing heavily, was still very hard, very erect, and pressed against her, set right against her still-wet opening. Exploring him, his smooth ebony skin, much more muscular and filled out now than she'd ever known him to be—a full-on man—she realized that she did not know him at all, not this way. This way, aroused like this, delivering pleasure like this, she could not take anything that she'd ever learned about him for granted. She did not know *this* version of him. He was new to her, different and unpredictable. She was in the arms of a stranger now, with no idea what he'd do to her or with her next.

The realization made her even wetter, turned on by the idea of being so far out of control, of being turned loose in this place of the unknown, of fucking a stranger who loved her and who she loved, of being lost in kissing and everything physical that wasn't taking place at all in her head, not at all. "I want it . . . Harper, I want . . ." was all she managed to say. She felt her legs being lifted, the penetration of her lower lips as Harper entered her, picking her body up with ease from the edge of the sofa and sliding her onto him, and then slowly back and forth as he made room for himself inside her. "So . . . good . . ." she managed to say, carried on one of her moans. It felt so perfect, so tight, so much of a stretch, Harper made a custom fit. *Shit . . . shit . . . shit,* she'd forgotten to mention protection. But, truthfully, she didn't want it. Not with Harper, not now. She wanted to feel every part of him, to make it matter, to put everything on the line. Because that's what it was now. It was everything. She was going to give him *everything.*

His manhood continued to fill her as he rocked his way inside her, thrusting, pumping, deeper and deeper. She held on to his sinewy shoulders as her fingers slipped across the sweat gathering on his skin. She loved hearing her name between his heavy breaths. As the thick air of passion swirled, Harper's voice penetrated her moaning. "Where's the bedroom?" He tightened his grip on her, holding under her knees, which were tightly set against him. They were fully connected and she started to bring her legs down to show the way. But he pulled her in tighter and met her eyes directly. "Just point." His voice was masculine and firm, deliberate. Primal, not the erudite intellectual. A man, a lover, *her lover.* Jordan raised an arm to point, sliding wet strands of her hair off her glistening shoulder. He swung them around as directed and carried her with careful measured steps all the way across the threshold. The bedroom was illuminated by only moonlight and a sprinkle of lights from the Malibu mountains through the large window. Harper and Jordan, Jordan and Harper, connected as one entity, him inside her, her wrapped around him, moved to the bed in the center of the room. He laid her down on the soft comforter. For just one second, he left her, and she felt empty at the separation. As he stood up, she saw the moonlight reflect off the ridges and contours of his body, the defined muscles of his arms, the taut curves of his ass, his thighs and the power they seemed capable of delivering. He was carnal, and so was Jordan. There was no need for thinking, no need for conversation. She just wanted him back.

"Put it back in," she said. And his face responded as if he'd found his true purpose. As quickly as a moment, he was back, the warmth of him on top of her, the hardness of him against her, pressing against her opening, pushing forward and making a way into her. He was taking his time again, but she didn't need that, not now. She was already open. She brought her hands down around his ass and pushed him in, pulling him close to her, closer and closer, and he began to move again, in and out. "Har . . . perrr . . ." She whispered his name into his ear again and again, losing herself in the perfection of it, the feeling as he filled her, leaving no room for anything but love, overwhelming love.

"Oh my God, Harper. I love it," Jordan declared.

"I want you to love it," Harper said between breaths.

"Yes, yes. I love it. I love it. I love it." Jordan lost herself in being able to express everything, to show everything, to feel everything. She couldn't stop. "I love . . . I love . . . I love *you.* I love you, Harper. *I love you.*" Jordan felt sweat dripping down her face and could barely hold back what felt like a scream in her chest. She'd said it, she'd actually said what had been built up for so long.

Right away, Harper responded, voice deep in his chest. "Jordan . . . I love you, baby," he declared breathlessly. "I love you so much, Jordan. I love you sooo much." His words were without hesitation, pouring out of him, sounding pure and as care-fucking-free as hers were. Jordan felt every word, every thrust, every kiss, every element of intonation Harper expressed. Harper heaved harder, his hips swirled deeper and longer. Jordan's pelvis met his rhythmically. This level of intimacy, the built-up anticipation that had led to it, and the love wrapped into the ribbons of pleasure between them had reached a peak, overwhelming in its magic and meaning for Jordan. It was too much, more than she'd ever hoped for.

And then, as the convulsions started to build within her, she felt another orgasm mounting, this time deeper in her core. She knew it would rip her to shreds and send her into pieces. She was going to have to let go, to let her hips rock and buck against him as his pacing began to increase. The deepening of his thrusting, the quickened pacing, the thickening of his shaft, she felt the signs that he was close also. She knew that he would release soon, and there would be no barrier between them, that she would receive all of him. After so long, after so *so* long, and so *so* much that had kept them apart, she wanted it all.

"Jordan, I'm coming, baby . . ." Harper managed to say through heavy breaths. He was close—if she wanted him to pull out she would have to tell him. *It would need to be now, Jordan,* her mind warned.

"Do it," her mouth whispered. "Come for me, baby . . . please . . . come . . . come for me . . ." she pleaded. She did want it. She wanted all of it. She wanted all of him. As her body began its own convulsions, she squeezed around him, moaning, gasping, calling to him. It didn't matter what happened next. He could do anything he wanted; she was prepared for anything. Harper yanked his hips back, leaned back on crouched knees, and released with an extended staccato growl.

"Yes, baby, yes, let it all go," Jordan encouraged him, sitting up. He was stiff and breathless. She grabbed his waist and pulled him closer, grasping him tightly to quickly close the gap between them. She guided his still convulsing body to her bed. Their bodies came together, hot, breathless, sticky. And perfect. Behind Jordan's closed eyes, the room opened to the sky and the stars and the moon and the ocean outside. All at once was she floating, floating high above them, seeing them together, on the bed, two brown bodies holding each other tightly, so tightly, as if they'd never let go.

And it was then that Jordan took her last breath as herself. And breathed the next as someone different, someone who wasn't just her own anymore, but now more of Harper's and from that she knew there'd be no going back.

# CHAPTER NINETEEN

## Harper

Harper tried to catch his breath as he mopped his face with his hand. He lay side by side, face-to-face with Jordan. They breathed in each other's exhales and stared at one another, knowing but still discovering each other. There was no looking away, no shame, no awkwardness. Until Harper felt a chill in the air, an awakening to the little bit of self-consciousness he felt about how free he'd been.

"Let me get us a towel or something," he said.

"Lay down, Harper," Jordan replied in a soft and feminine voice he'd never heard her use. "I got you." Relief washed through him, easing the sense of shame and self-awareness that maybe he'd gone too far. He was still excited, still catching his breath. Resetting. Harper looked at Jordan, wondering *Do you mean that?* but not wanting to ask. Not needing to, when she kissed his lips before lifting herself up to retreat to her en suite bathroom. Harper watched her go. He didn't want to close his eyes and miss any moment of her spectacular form. He had been so busy exploring her body with his mouth, his hands, and his manhood that his eyes had missed the delight. Her body now was more perfect than he had imagined, ever, even when he'd wondered what was under those baggy clothes she often wore back at Westmore. He was in a dream that he didn't want to awaken from, floating on Jordan's bed, looking toward the bathroom door, waiting to see her again. Was he really in Malibu at Jordan Armstrong's house? Was what just happened real? Did he really just *finally* make love to his best friend? The woman who'd been his inspiration? His infatuation? He sat up on his elbow, hearing water running in the bathroom, but then it shut off. *What is she doing? Taking a shower?* he wondered, hoping she wasn't a room away from him holding any regrets. Neither of them should have any regrets. What they'd just shared was beautiful. Before he could wonder any further, Jordan reentered the carpeted bedroom as naked as she had left it save for holding a large white towel.

"Lay back," she commanded with gentle energy. Harper did as he was told, lowering himself to rest on her plush blanket. Harper felt the warm, moist towel wiping him down. Jordan lovingly cleaned him with slow soft strokes. Not used to seeing her like this, Harper reached toward her to try to help. Jordan pulled the towel away.

"I got it, Harp," Jordan said softly, and met his eyes with hers. Harper relented as she continued carefully, adoringly wiping him down. *She loves me?* he thought. She'd said it when they . . . when he'd said it too. But now, her gentle touch across his body answered his question. She climbed up to straddle him as she used a clean corner to wipe his neck and his forehead, which were still beaded with sweat. Their eyes met again.

"Hi," Jordan whispered.

"Hi," Harper returned and smiled at Jordan.

Her smile broke into a chuckle. It was contagious, and they both began to laugh.

"What?" Jordan asked, playfully.

"I—I can't believe we just did that," Harper confessed. He was far too open now to try to play it cool.

"We did," Jordan said, smiling. "It happened. Believe it."

"I hope . . . it was okay."

"It was *magical* Harper."

"It really was . . ." Harper pulled her down on top of him, her breasts collapsing on his chest. *So you felt it too,* he thought. He looked into her eyes and moved forward to kiss her deeply. Harper wrapped his arms around her, pulling her to him with all the love he could channel in his body. She squeezed her arms around him tightly.

"I'm not letting you go," Harper found himself saying and meaning.

"You better not," Jordan answered, her head resting on his chest. She looked up at him with sincerity in her eyes. They held each other closely, tightly, exchanging gentle kisses as the ocean smashed against the shore. For this moment at least, they had all they needed, deeply satisfied and content. And then, between them, Harper's stomach rumbled. A loud physical growl of emptiness. Jordan pulled up to look at him.

"Hey," she said with a teasing smile.

"Yeah?"

"You hungry?"

At 10:37 p.m. the doorbell rang. The Postmates delivery came right on time. "Thanks, man," a bare-chested Harper greeted the casually dressed driver holding a giant Nobu-branded paper bag. Harper anchored the door with his bare foot against the cold ground and reached forward to grab the bag. He had no casual shoes, no extra clothes. He'd brought only what he wore to dinner and just dashed out of Jordan's bedroom in dress slacks and bare feet, skipping her offer of some of her flip-flops . . . *as if I'd fit them shits.* Bridging the painful divide of gravel and sand that made up Jordan's exterior landscape, he handed off a handful of crumpled bills from his pocket and took the bag while trying to keep his balance against the door.

He bound up the entry steps and headed to find Jordan in the kitchen. She had the counter bar top illuminated, and had already surfaced two plates, some utensils, a bottle of wine, and two wineglasses neatly set out for them. Against an ethereal background of woodwind chords and rhythmic bassline riff, Sade told them what they both knew, that this was "No Ordinary Love," and the song resonated, permeating the atmosphere as Harper set down the bags.

"I'll plate us. Can you open that?" Jordan handed him a fancy corkscrew.

"Yup." Harper grabbed it, using the opportunity to take Jordan in with a long glance. She'd changed into a silk kimono in blue print, and was looking relaxed, alluring, and, as Harper could see clearly . . . *happy.* Her smooth brown legs moved effortlessly, her breasts, those of a fully blossomed grown woman, were full and moving pendulously. Remembering the task at hand, Harper managed to pull his eyes away and set to work on opening the bottle. Jordan unearthed the contents of the bag. The aroma hit the room, of crispy rice with tuna, miso black cod and garlic noodles, an assortment of everything they would have ordered if they'd stayed at Nobu. But better as takeout, because . . . *I wouldn't have changed one thing,* Harper thought. Jordan plated evenly for her and Harper; he uncorked and poured, handed her a glass and lifted his own. Jordan turned to Harper and took her glass with a raised eyebrow and a smile, meeting him for a toast.

"Cheers, Harper Stewart," Jordan said sweetly.

Harper couldn't help but smile back. "Cheers, Jordan Armstrong."

"Preference?" Jordan offered Harper a fork and chopsticks. Harper selected the latter to pinch a piece of spicy-tuna-topped crispy rice and lift it to his mouth, taking it in whole. The cavalcade of flavors exploded in his mouth with a crunch. "Mmmmm." He closed his eyes briefly and moaned.

"Dang. Is it that good?" Jordan poked his arm.

Harper smiled. "We've come a long way since Jefferson Hall and lemon pepper wings."

"Freshman year. And you weren't even fucking with lemon pepper until I put you on," Jordan reminded him.

"Hey, I had a limited palate back then." Harper moved to sample the cod with buttery miso, the umami striking all corners of his mouth. "Barbecue and buffalo were it. Those Jasper's lemon pepper wings used to hit though."

"For real." Jordan took a long swig of wine, looking at him. Harper jerked his head toward her as he examined her, trying to read her mind. "You've come a long way, homie."

"No doubt. We both have."

"Well, I was a bit more polished than you," Jordan teased.

"That's not saying much." Harper winked.

"Say that." Jordan smiled. "Those boat shoes, those big-ass owl glasses, and them rugby shirts, bruh?"

Harper nearly spit out his garlic noodles, laughing.

"Hey, those striped joints were official!"

"Jesus, help. What the hell did we know?" Jordan shook her head and laughed as she dug into the salad between them.

"You always had a plan," Harper said.

"We both did. Regimented, self-important," Jordan reminded him.

"We were kids."

*"Young adults."*

"We did what we thought we had to do. Our parents gave us an opportunity and we had to live up to the sacrifices they made and their expectations."

"It was good pressure," Jordan added.

"Yup," Harper agreed as he sipped. Jordan's smile waned. Harper noticed her pensive gaze and brief silence. She looked away.

"So, when are you headed back to New York?" she asked.

"Why? You trying to get rid of me?" Harper teased with a smile.

"No. I'm just seeing how many more times I can have you in my bed before you go."

"Well . . . I was headed to Maui tomorrow."

"Maui?"

"Yeah, I was going to chain myself to my computer, rent a villa, see the Pacific when I want, dive into this rewrite."

"Sounds exciting."

"It is." Harper studied Jordan, put his chopsticks down, and walked around the island to approach her. He cornered her against the counter. "But I don't need to go to Maui." He looked directly into Jordan's eyes, watching for her reaction. *Does she want me to stay?* He wondered. *To go?* "I didn't pack a lot and I'd probably grab some more underwear and things. . . ." She looked up at him. He held his breath awaiting her response.

"I have a washing machine. And a dryer," Jordan said. Harper exhaled.

"A dryer too. Hmmmm." He leaned in to kiss her. "I do have to get some progress on this script."

"You'll do it." Jordan kissed him back. "I'll make sure of it. I'll keep you on task. You know I'm good with deadlines."

"I remember." Harper lifted her onto the kitchen counter before negotiating his torso between her legs. They were eye to eye.

"We never missed one at the *Westmore Review*." Jordan smiled, looking almost exactly like her younger self who used to share the newsroom with him. "Even if we had to stay up all night."

"All night, huh?" Harper kissed her again.

"If necessary." Jordan's sultry voice was dripping with impossible-to-resist sexual smolder. She brought her lips to meet Harper's again.

"We do what we have to do . . ." Harper echoed.

"We can discuss it in the morning." With a kiss, Jordan gently pulled his bottom lip into her mouth and released it.

"That sounds really good," Harper whispered into her ear."I'd really like to see that view in the sunlight."

"Good. I want you to experience it, over"—she kissed him—"and over"—another kiss—"and over again."

This time, when they looked into each other's eyes, Harper understood finally that they were both really here, together, in this moment on the same page. His insecurities melted.

"It's settled, then. I'm staying," Harper declared with certainty and sincerity.

"Good. I want you to stay."

*Jordan Armstrong wants me to stay* . . . Harper smiled, then pressed his lips to hers and put his all into a deep, slow, sensual kiss. Jordan wrapped her arms around him, giving him the room to tug on the tie of her kimono, letting it fall open loosely. Harper brought his hands up the sides of her torso, slowly brushing past her supple breasts to her shoulders, caressing her softly, feeling her, reminding himself, *this* . . . *is* . . . *real* . . . He spread his hands across her shoulders, sliding the silky fabric down Jordan's arms and wrapping his fingers around the small of her back. He pulled himself closer and kissed her deeply again. She rested her arms on his shoulders, and her hand wrapped around the back of his head, guiding Harper into a tighter embrace and urgent kiss. Harper felt the draw, the urgency, the desire to make up for lost time, the keen understanding that even if they had an eternity, there'd still be a yearning for each other. Time was fleeting. Harper's slacks dropped to the floor. He stepped out of them and lifted Jordan off the counter. Her legs wrapped around him as they got lost in one another again, serenaded by the music of longing—Sade crooning echoes of promises suspended in the air like a lover's gentle caress. "Cherish the Day" floated through the speakers with its wah wah guitar and deep syncopated bass . . . *you only can rescue me . . .*

*You only, indeed,* Harper thought.

# CHAPTER TWENTY

## Jordan

Three days later, Jordan was floating on air. That's the only way to explain why, despite the smallest bit of trepidation, she told Shelby about the turn of events with Harper. There was something oddly satisfying about seeing Shelby's face frozen on the screen, mouth agape and yet silent. Shelby's mouth was never both open *and* silent. Jordan held the phone in front of her in amused patience, until she started to wonder if the call had frozen. But finally Shelby moved and screamed. "Aaaaahhhhh!" It was so loud Jordan winced.

"How do you wait *this* long to tell me!" Shelby reanimated in a frenzy, clearly pacing now. Her free hand was flailing wildly in the air behind her. "*You* and Harper?"

Jordan felt her face stretch into a smile. *Yes, me and Harper,* she thought and let out a sigh without meaning to. It felt so right, so natural, so as it was supposed to be. So long overdue, but so normal now. Still, even after three days, she needed to pinch herself just to make sure it was real. It had to be real, *had* to be. She was way too far gone for any other possibility. "I obviously couldn't call you in front of him, Shelby," Jordan protested.

And plus, they'd been far too busy with each other to be preoccupied with anyone else.

"Right. I mean, how could you talk with a dick in your mouth? Takes special skill . . . but that's enough about me." Shelby muttered the last words, but quickly continued with, "Jordan, you've been *fucking* Harper Stewart for *three straight days*?!"

Jordan smiled again at the thought of it. "We have. Anywhere and everywhere."

"Where are you now?"

"I'm sitting in my car. We just picked up his stuff from Shutters."

"Damn. You were fucking in Shutters too?"

"*Everywhere,* Shelby."

"On the balcony?"

"Yep."

"In the bathroom?"

"In the tub, the shower, on the floor."

"I mean the public bathroom."

"Ladies room, last stall in the back."

"Jordan! You're a freak. And where is Harper? Balled up in a corner?"

Jordan laughed. "He's dropping off his rental and then we're going to get some brunch."

"Well, clearly he needs to replenish his electrolytes."

Jordan just continued right past Shelby's snark. "He's also saying good night to his daughter. Eight-hour time difference to Accra," Jordan informed.

"Amaaazing. Well . . ." Shelby paused with a deep breath to adjust her flowing layers of hair to again perfectly frame her face—a sure sign that she'd moved past her initial shock. "How long is he staying?"

*Forever,* Jordan's mind replied. It was her wish. She could live like this with Harper forever, and she wanted to. To just shut the world out and stay focused only on each other. Well, each other and work. "He doesn't know. I don't know either. We're taking it one day at a time. He has a project to work on and so do I."

"So, you're just living in a bubble of bliss."

"It's real life, Shelby. We wake up together. He does his work, I do mine. Day-to-day stuff—we go shopping. He journals. We're headed to the Hollywood Bowl next week. Isley Brothers. We eat—"

"And fuck. Don't forget the fucking."

"Yes," Jordan said with a chuckle. "And we are fuuuuuckkkkkiiinggg," she said, savoring the articulation of every letter in the word.

"Agggghhhhh! I can't take it!" Shelby was screaming again on her end of the phone so loudly Jordan had to pull it away from her. When she brought it back, Shelby looked as happy as Jordan had ever seen her. "I'm so happy for you Jordan, really! I love it. I mean, I really love it. I can see it in your face . . . you're really happy. And . . . oh, wow, I might actually fucking cry. This is the most amazing news."

The quick sound of knuckles rapping on the window brought Jordan's attention back to her surroundings. She turned to see Harper at the passenger-side window, bags and all. Jordan quickly straightened herself and hesitated before reaching for the door lock. She popped her trunk instead, indicating to Harper to drop his bags back there. "Hey, Shelby, gotta go," she said.

"Aww, let me talk to him! Say congratulations." Shelby was clearly lingering.

"No, Shelby. Gotta go." Harper nodded and went to drop his suitcase in her trunk, buying her a bit more time.

"What? Why?"

"Look, let us just live for a second. It's—" Jordan was interrupted by Harper opening the door and taking his place in the passenger seat.

"I can't even tell Quentin?" Just then, out of the corner of her eye, Jordan saw Harper perk up and turn his attention to the phone. Shelby's voice was unmistakable and audible enough. He heard it, for sure. This Jordan knew. What she didn't know was how he'd react. This new version of them had been a world of only two. Who knew how fragile it was? What it could withstand?

"Hi, Shelby," Harper said, seemingly unfazed. And even though she felt slightly guilty, his smile and wink gave Jordan comfort that maybe it was all good, just as it seemed.

Shelby wasted no time engaging with him. Her voice rang out over the phone's speaker. "Hiiiiii, Harrrrper," she sang. "How's Cal-ih-for-ny-ay treating you?" Jordan looked at him for his response. The easy smile on her face belied even just that tiny bit of concern she had, her own whispering wonder of *Is this real? Can things really be this good?*

But Harper was steadfast, relaxed even. And when he met Jordan's eyes, he declared confidently, "I've never been happier in my life."

Shelby's screech of pure elation echoed through the car and caused them both to wince—Jordan from embarrassment, but Harper just chuckled. "Goodbye, Shelby," Jordan said firmly, relieved to hear Shelby's reply.

"Call Quentin, Harper, so we can talk about y'all. Okay Byee!" And finally, she hung up. Jordan breathed a sigh of relief and looked at Harper.

"Everything okay?" she asked. Sure, she was asking about his hotel checkout, his good night with Mia, if he had everything he needed. But it was also a check-in. The moment with Shelby had been a reality check, that there were layers to this. That this was so sure and so fragile all at the same time. Harper looked at her for a full three seconds before leaning in to kiss her lips softly yet assuredly. He pulled back, eyes still locked in on hers.

"Everything is great," Harper responded. It was a relief that he sounded so sincere.

Jordan's shoulders relaxed. "So, then, where to now, Mr. Stewart?"

Harper leaned his head against the seat back. It was a glorious day. Even in the parking circle of Shutters, the salty air blew in through the windows from the ocean-facing side of the quaint hotel. People moved leisurely about, hopping in and out of cars pulled up by the uniformed valet. And they were just two lovers, sharing the sunshine. Harper reached for Jordan's hand resting on the gearshift.

"Let's see where the day takes us."

"Are you sure?" Jordan wasn't used to this version of the usual workaholic Harper. "I don't want to get in the way of whatever work you need to do."

He smiled and squeezed her hand. "You won't. You're not. I'm flowing on this project like I haven't in a long time. I'm . . . inspired." He leaned in to kiss her again. She closed her eyes and met his lips with a lingering soft touch that surged through the rest of her body, tingling through her center and all the way to her toes. She could do *this,* stay like *this . . . forever.* And they could. The day was ahead, and they had all the time in the world.

# CHAPTER TWENTY-ONE

## Harper

Journal entry 3/16/25

Malibu is beautiful. Waking every morning to the ocean and the sun, I see why folks move here. What a spectacular view of natural vastness. Having Jordan's naked body next to mine is unreal. We actually sleep well together! The only reason I'm up is because I'm still kind of on New York time. I <u>love</u> waking up next to her. She's so beautiful and as long as i've known her, I've never been this close to her. Just being able to look at her, rub her, feel her curves. I love waking her up with the dick. She loves it too. She be sleep but she ain't that sleep. And I haven't needed any Viagra! My joint just be ready. The newness and the familiarity is all its own aphrodisiac. It is exciting, mind-blowing sex. but it's also been incredible just <u>being</u> with her. Spooning, fucking, making love, talking, watching the morning news, bathing each other. Having coffee at this spot in Santa Monica. We are never more than one room apart at all times, and yet we both still have enough space. We eat meals together without pretending I don't want to kiss her. I can't get enough. In the mornings I get out on her balcony and not only do my brain dump, but I'm making real progress on this Unfinished Business outline. I'm no longer in a creative rut. jordan's presence is an additive not a deterrent. She respects the process. I am locked in on Kendall and Jackson. I wonder why. hah! No duh. i know where kendall and Jackson are now! That shit is unlocked and I'm getting the hang of this movie pace. maybe it's the California air. Hah!

I facetimed Mia at the end of her day again. I think she's okay with our end of the day calls. She's definitely more of a morning person. I'll try to do a midnight call one of these days . . . that's if I'm not FUCKING . . . !

We been taking walks on the beach, hiking up in the mountains, we did Solstice canyon loop twice. We been holding hands, window shopping, grocery shopping. farmer's market. Did I mention the sex was incredible? it just all feels so natural. But also surreal. I mean everything is <u>easy.</u> Can it really be this good? Can it last? STOP. just settle in it, Harp. go with the flow. Everyone should feel this good.

I still can't believe it. Where are we going with this? i don't know but it's not stressing me. I don't have to move. LA is nice but that new york energy fuels my creativity. FUELS <u>ME</u>! Plus, most of the publishing houses are there. but the movie studios are here . . . still, i couldn't do this year-round. ocean, mountains, sun all the time. i like that change of seasons. I'd miss it. Plus, getting to Accra and Mia would be <u>a lot</u> tougher in LA. But I do like it here.

Jordan would be the only reason i'd be here so probably. i don't see me committing to screenwriting and tv writing like that. But maybe . . . ? Why even consider it? I wouldn't have to move. Neither would she. We could do that bi-coastal thing.

"hey j, i have a meeting, i'm just going to stay in the brooklyn spot. i'll catch the last flight. oh you're coming out. oh cool. you have a few meetings too? yeah, quentin is throwing a party. we gotta go. hang with the crew . . ."

holy shit. why not? I wonder what she'd be like to live with? We'd need two homes to hold all of her wardrobe. Ha! she doesn't cook. but she likes good food . . .

stop, harp. enjoy this.

this is Jordan and this is you.

if there's a problem we can work it out. open and honest communication is the key. why wouldn't we be anything else with one another? We have no expectations of one another other than friendship. and love. I love jordan. and she loves me. it's not all about love, but what a start.

Quentin hit me up yesterday. Undoubtedly Shelby let him know what was happening with me and j. he wants details. I sent him a selfie of us walking in the Canyon we look like a bougie-ass black California couple. we look happy. fuck it, we are happy. I know i am. and she seems happy.

"good shit, joe." he texted. Shelby said it's giving #couplegoals. it's not a secret, right?

Harper stopped writing, his pen hovering over the page. He looked up and above, contemplating his last written question. *Is it?* Sade's "Mermaid" could be heard crisply through Jordan's outdoor speakers. They'd been playing *Love Deluxe* on repeat since their first night together, living the lyrics. It just seemed like such a fitting soundtrack. The closing song's mysterious open melody, simple, with no words, left to interpretation was very much the road ahead for Harper and Jordan. Open, a mystery, a deep love filled with yearning and hope, deep like the ocean beyond with its crashing morning waves. Harper set the journal on the side table and placed the pen on top. He pulled up his phone and looked at the selfie he snapped of himself and Jordan. Harper inhaled with a small smile and exhaled deeply. They looked good together. Suddenly Murch's face appeared on his phone with an incoming call.

"Ayyy, man," Harper answered.

"Hey, Harp. Sorry for the delay," Murch said, still sounding busy. Harper was momentarily confused by the apology. *What was I calling him about?*

"No problem, Murch. How's everything? You alright?" Harper asked, trying to buy time to jog his memory.

"I'm good. I'm good. Busy week. You know how it is. Where are you? Still LA? Weren't you headed to Hawaii?"

"I'm still in LA. Yeah . . ." Harper considered how much information to reveal.

"I can hear the ocean. Where you staying?"

"Umm . . . I was at a spot in Santa Monica. Really nice. Been getting some work done. It's been good. I see the appeal."

"Oh boy. We already lost Jordan to the West Coast. Are you becoming a convert too?" Murch laughed. Harper forced a laugh from his side as well.

"Haaaaa. Hahaha ha ha. Nahhh. Not yet . . ."

"Not yet? Oh no. Say it isn't so, Harper Stewart. The man's going Hollywood," Murch declared. *What the hell did I ring him about?* Harper stood up and began pacing Jordan's deck. He really wanted to steer the conversation the way he wanted and something about Murch knowing where he was made Harper a little nervous.

Then the patio door opened revealing Jordan in her flowing blue kimono. She and Harper made eye contact. She smiled and mouthed, "Coffee?" Harper nodded quickly in response. Jordan jerked her chin toward Harper's call. Harper mouthed, "Murch," as subtly as he could.

For a moment Jordan stood with furrowed brow.

After a beat, she mouthed, "Who?"

Harper repeated, "Murch," with more silent enunciation. Jordan shrugged again, shaking her head. Harper sighed and decided to make it clear by turning the phone to show Murch's image on the screen.

"Ahhh," Jordan said quietly, getting it instantly. "Ohh, tell him I said hi."

Harper nodded quickly and barely whispered, "Okay," before quickly bringing the phone back to his ear. Jordan slipped back inside, sliding the patio door closed behind her. And then he felt the slightest bit of panic. He wasn't prepared if Murch asked . . .

"Who's that?" *Shit.* Harper ran many scenarios through his head during a longer than necessary pause for a response to Murch's question. *It's not a secret, right?* He'd never reached an answer to the question from his journal. *Is it?*

"It's um . . . it's . . . it's Jordan," Harper finally eked out.

"Oh, you guys connected. That's great. You meeting up for breakfast?" Murch asked, sounding excited.

"Ummm, we haven't decided yet" was the best close-to-truth that Harper managed to muster.

"Cool. Well, please tell her hello from me and Candace. Those flowers she sent for her birthday lasted for a while. I need to know who her florist is."

"Yeah, I'll let her know."

"Anyway, you had asked me about Kwesi," Murch said. Harper cocked his head, crinkled his brow, and thought, *Kwesi? Who's Kwesi?* But all that came out was "Uh-huh . . ."

"So, I hear he's an entrepreneur of some sort. Mostly in real-estate development—it's big there—chocolate too and something about a vineyard, I think. Anyway, he's successful, speaks multiple languages, is about six foot four, and Robyn's happy," Murch reported. *Vineyard . . . ? Multiple languages . . . ? Six foot . . . ? Ohhhhh, the dude Robyn's dating. . . . Jesus, I'm getting old. What the fuck?* Now, finally remembering the purpose of the call that had set this in motion, Harper began to process what Murch had just said.

"Oh, oh, oh. Right. Right. Yeah . . ." Harper intonated an escalating understanding of what Murch had told him, which was . . . *a lot.*

"Yeah. That's what I know," Murch said. Through the patio doors Harper watched Jordan use her built-in very fancy coffee system, grinding fresh beans to make Harper's cup of morning brew. The lustrous rhythms in Sade's "Mermaid" aided his dream-like daze, reminding him of the depths of his own good fortune.

"So, she's happy, huh?"

"Seems to be," Murch responded. Harper nodded while looking at Jordan in that kimono as she pulled creamer from her Sub-Zero.

*Nah,* Harper thought. *It's not a secret.* He filled with a swell of confidence. "That's great," he said to Murch. "You know what? I'm happy too." Harper switched Murch to speakerphone.

"That's great," Murch said congenially. "And it's very mature, Harp." As Murch kept speaking, Harper immediately found what he was looking for. "Wishing Robyn well is good growth," Murch continued. "You said yourself you guys were in a good place as co-parents and maybe even—"

"Where are you right now?" Harper inquired, cutting him off.

"I'm home."

"You alone?"

"Yup. Why do you think I'm calling you? Candace and the girls are out shopping or something. It is sometimes nice to be the king of the castle . . ." As Murch droned on, Harper crafted a message and hit send.

"Check your texts. I just sent you something." Abruptly Murch stopped talking.

"Oh, okay. Hold on . . ." he said, sounding farther away.

Harper looked at his phone at the photo of himself and Jordan that he just shot through the text-o-sphere and did a silent countdown: *five . . . four . . . three . . . two . . .*

"Holy shit," Murch said. Harper smiled. "Is this for real?" Murch sounded genuinely surprised.

"Yup."

"This is amazing!" Murch's enthusiasm brought a welcome laugh to Harper and made him feel much more comfortable sharing a recap of the past few days with Murch, who quickly became as giddy as a schoolgirl.

"Congratulations. I can't wait to see you guys!"

"Thanks, Murch. I'll be in touch. Thanks for the call back," Harper responded as he closed his journal and grabbed his pen to head inside through the patio doors.

"Oh, no problem. Oh my God. I'm so happy for you guys. This is great," Murch continued to effuse loudly through Harper's speakerphone as he approached the kitchen. Jordan suddenly lurched forward over her coffee mug, pursing her lips with wide eyes toward Harper. She swallowed hard and mouthed, "What?" dramatically. Harper was all smiles as he reached her and placed his hand on her waist. "Please tell Jordan I said hello and give her my love." Murch's voice was warm and full of palpable affection. Jordan looked at Harper as if to say *Should I respond?* Harper smiled and half shrugged; he'd leave it up to her.

"Thanks, Julian," Jordan said into the phone. Harper pulled her closer into an embrace.

"Oh, Jordan. I am so happy that you guys *finally* made this happen," Murch's excitement poured through the speaker. Jordan gave Harper a look of combined skepticism and curiosity.

"Well, we're having a good time." Harper gave her a wink.

"Well, let the good times roll. You guys enjoy yourselves."

"All right, Murch. Peace," Harper said before disconnecting the call. The final notes of "Mermaid" trickled out as Jordan looked at him and he back at her, in a bit of stunned silence. It was clear they'd both just realized what had happened.

"So, you told Murch." From Jordan, this sounded like only half a question, mostly a declaration.

"Yup." Harper poured creamer into his coffee cup. "Sent him our pic too."

"Our pic . . ." Jordan's face scrunched up. "What pic?"

"Same one I sent Q of us on the trail at Solstice Canyon." Harper handed his phone over to Jordan so she could see for herself. Jordan studied it as the distinctive bassline of Dennis Edwards and Siedah Garrett's "Don't Look Any Further" started playing over the surrounds.

"That's cute," Jordan acknowledges. "But Murch, huh?"

*Too cool to be careless,* the song leads sang in the background.

"Yeah. Problem?" Harper said and sipped his coffee.

"Well, I just think we should be sure what we're doing before letting others know what we're doing."

"What are we doing?" Harper asked as he put down his coffee and pulled Jordan into another embrace. He looked into her eyes awaiting an answer.

*Oh baby, don't look any further* . . . the song continued.

"I don't know," Jordan said, meeting Harper squarely in the eyes. "But I like it."

"Good. Because I love it." Jordan smiled and looked away, taking in a small breath.

"Yeah?" she responded, much more timidly than usual.

"Yeah," Harper said definitively.

"Okay." Jordan nodded, with a deep exhale. "Cool. Just slow down on the pics."

"Too late. I already posted to IG and Twitter," Harper joked.

"You mean X?"

"Aww, damn it. That's right. Guess it's a post and delete." He winked at her.

"Good. That just leaves our own personal Black tweeter," Jordan warned, the look of amusement dropping from her face. Harper returned a look of curiosity.

"You know he's going to show Candace and she won't keep that to herself."

"You think?"

"Harper, don't be messy. You just sent a loaded gun," Jordan remarked, giving him "the look." Harper considered what she said and delivered a nod of understanding. He took her chin between his thumb and forefinger and gently tipped her gaze toward his.

"Don't worry," he said gently. "We're fine." He felt sure about that. Did Jordan? She studied him, her eyes moving across his face.

"Okay, Mr. Stewart," Jordan finally responded, with only a hint of skepticism. "I'm showering and getting dressed." With that, she made an about-face toward her bedroom, leaving Harper to watch the sway of her kimono as she retreated.

"Can I help you wash your back?" he offered.

She dropped her kimono, exposing her glorious backside, and kept moving toward the bedroom. Understanding the assignment, Harper took his last sips of coffee and left a trail of his discarded clothes behind him on his way to do his duty.

Along the way, only very briefly did he even think about that photo he sent to Murch. Harper knows he sent a loaded gun. *But if it goes off . . . so be it . . .*

# CHAPTER TWENTY-TWO

## Robyn

Robyn sat up in an easy position on her yoga mat after her restorative Savasana pose. Along with the other class attendees, with her hands at prayer over her heart center, she saluted Thema, who'd concluded the class with namaste—peace onto you. Robyn had had to forgo Labadi Beach this morning, so this was her time of recentering. After a weekend of poring over details at Robyn's Nest, of Ghanaian-Caribbean and Black American fusion cooking that included four shifts, *and* yesterday's Sunday brunch, she needed some restorative energy. Robyn also needed to not taste any "elevated" food for at least a day. Instead, she had a taste for simplicity and would have killed for a basic PB&J. She settled for a Ghanaian staple instead, kofi brokeman—a roasted plantain and peanut street food that a local vendor wrapped up for Robyn to snack on en route to Thema's Kokrobite beachside compound.

Robyn was fairly well settled into Ghanaian life, but life was still lifing for sure. Since the restaurant was closed this and every Monday, today was her day to regroup and recalculate, to try to find enough mental footing to keep her head above water. The bills kept coming—Mia's school, the mortgage, the water supply, the staff, the fresh food, and of course the rent. Besides the steady stream of bill collectors, coming one after another with their hands out, threatening to take some other essential away, the interest rates were astronomically high for a returnee. *Welcome home* . . . but you still gotta pay (and pay much more). Nothing was as easy as it had seemed on the other side of the ocean when she'd first decided to come to Ghana. Robyn sighed as she returned her consciousness to her present moment—the complexities and tarnish on her silver linings.

"He's married," Robyn said to Thema. They sat side by side in the beachside café sharing a pot of chamomile tea in cups with lemon and honey sourced from the compound. Thema cocked her head in a fleeting look of confusion. "Technically," she corrected. "He and his wife are separated. So, they're *not together*."

"I see. So why does this concern you?" Thema looked squarely at Robyn as she sipped her tea.

"Look, I know I'm coming to this with my Western glasses on, but Ghanaian men do have a reputation." Robyn referred to the rampant rumor that the men of Ghana juggled, even flaunted, multiple girlfriends, even the married ones. "The more successful the man, the more women."

"American women have a reputation too," Thema returned. "Does that mean we should believe them all?"

"No, but I don't want to be played, Thema. I don't want to share," Robyn admitted. "I did enough of that in my last marriage."

"Your last husband had another woman?" Thema inquired. Jordan's face popped into Robyn's mind and she exhaled.

"I don't know that anything physical happened, but there was definitely an affair of the heart that was outside of my marriage," Robyn said. "And I made space for it. I don't think that was good for me."

"What do you see in Kwesi?" Thema asked. "Why spend time with him?"

Robyn couldn't help but smile when she thought of him, even despite her misgivings. "He's beautiful, he's kind, he's thoughtful. He seems to care about me, about Mia. He makes me feel special." Thema nodded. Robyn rolled her eyes as her face flushed. "I sound stupid."

"You sound like you're in love." Thema said it as if it were the most obvious thing in the world.

Robyn mused, "I might be, but my eyes are open this time."

"And what do they see?"

"Possible heartbreak. I don't want that. I can't afford it." Robyn shook her head. "Not now." *Especially not now,* Robyn thought, remembering the weight of the other obligations she carried. There wasn't enough of her to go around, and definitely not as the walking wounded.

"Robyn, what is it that you want from this man?"

"How about somebody else meet me halfway for a change? Maybe just a little reciprocity? And at the same time, I don't want to have to rely on anybody. I'm strong enough to make it on my own. I have to be. I'm responsible for me. And Mia."

"I understand, Robyn. I believe you will find love again. The way that serves you best."

"Serves *me* best. That would be good for a change."

"Men will always do what they want. So will women. We cannot be all things for our partners. Do you really think he will satisfy your every need? Your every whim? Your passion? Can you fulfill his?" Thema asked. "What you want is respect, Robyn."

Robyn considered her words and shrugged in agreement, although she was still doubtful. Thema seemed to know it.

"Hopefully you find the man who wants what you want.

This man sounds like he's got a lot of responsibilities to handle," Thema opined.

Those words grated Robyn slightly. She bristled. "So do I." Her tone was defiant.

"Yes. And you're both coming to this relationship with more than just yourselves—your business, your family, your home, you . . . *most important*, you." She waited until Robyn's eyes met hers. "He's got the same, yet he's making time for you. Why is that?"

"I don't know."

"Yes, you do. You're not ordinary, Robyn. There are plenty of women, but who is he making time for? You. Why? So he can sleep with you? So he can get a taste of your special stuff? To put another notch in his belt? I don't think so. He wants you. He knows who you are and what you want. But do you know?"

"Do I know what?"

"Do you know what you want?"

Robyn paused for a moment to consider the question. She looked around at her surroundings—the lush greenery, the peaceful salt water crashing on the shore in the distance, and the air of serenity—and that made Robyn feel settled and grounded. This was the Ghana she wanted. This was what she'd imagined. But this peace was fleeting because soon she would have to pick up Mia, prepare for tomorrow's menu, and pray for the rain to stay away. Being settled and grounded unfortunately wasn't going to pay bills. "I know what I don't want," she declared. It was all she could muster as an answer. Time was short. She rose, thanked Thema for the tea and the talk, and left to battle the impending Accra traffic.

# CHAPTER TWENTY-THREE

## Jordan

Days later, sitting across the table at 1212 Santa Monica for brunch, Harper repeated Jordan's words to her: "Hosting a show?" Their food had already arrived, and Jordan decided to float her very nascent idea past Harper over his meal of chicken-topped endive salad.

"Stupid, right? Jordan broke the yolky egg atop her salmon benedict with her fork and brought the bite to her mouth. *Delicious.* She was prepared for Harper's response, expecting an echoing of her own self-ridicule, but instead, he seemed relatively unfazed, like he was really considering it.

"I wouldn't say stupid," he said. "I think it's an interesting thought. Do you want to?"

*Do I want to?* "No. I don't see that for myself." She shook her head as punctuation. *No, definitely not.*

"Tell me why." Harper looked at her sincerely.

Jordan crinkled her face. "It's not my thing. Hosts are beautiful, charming, 'on' all the time. I have rough edges. I give it to you straight."

"First of all, you're beautiful and charming. Your edges are not rough. You're just real. As for being on all the time versus giving it to you straight, in my opinion we need more of the real." Harper took another stab at his salad. "Jordan, you have a lot to offer women and men—*period.* I know working behind the scenes is what you're used to, but I think you may be underestimating yourself. And that's not something I'm used to from you."

Jordan felt challenged. As the millennials would say, she "felt some kind of way." *A sistah can't have doubts? Maybe . . . he's only seen me at my best?* Jordan wondered. Had she only shown Harper her strongest side—when she was most confident? Hadn't she been showing some of her vulnerability by now?

"Believe it or not, I do doubt myself sometimes, Harper."

"That's okay. That's healthy. You're not Superwoman." Harper smiled.

"Is that your way of convincing me to do it?" Jordan immediately regretted the slight bite of sarcasm.

"You really want a recycled old biddie representing your show?" Jordan smiled at Harper's old-school reference to cute women. "Seriously, who reads more than you? Every day I see you scouring *The New York Times, TheGrio, The Atlantic,* NPR, *The Wall Street Journal, Financial Times, The Washington Post,* and *USA Today.*"

"Don't forget the BBC, *The Economist,* and Al-Jazeera," Jordan teased.

"Exactly my point! You can discuss any topic at any time, and we need to see a Black woman like you do it." Harper was animated, like he really believed in the idea. *Really?* Jordan wondered. What Harper was saying, she wanted to believe, but she wasn't at all convinced. There really wasn't anyone more qualified than her to speak on a wide range of topics. But is that what the network execs, and more important, Evelyn, had really been saying? Were Dr. Clark, Shelby, and now Harper right about this? The people who knew her best? Especially Harper now that he'd seen *all* of her?

"Harper, there's the whole thing about being on social media and always having something to say, making snappy videos and all that. That sounds exhausting and I don't want to be a sound bite."

"I definitely get that . . ." Harper said, his thinking face showing.

"Hell," Jordan said, hoping he wasn't seriously proposing she become some kind of *influencer*. "That might stress me out more. And I'm trying to talk about wellness and how to help Black women achieve well-being. You know, from a place of real substance. With experts and quality content—writers and producers. The show is a way I can bring forth my story week after week. Get others on their journey—"

"Why not just give them your story?" Harper interjected, as if making the most obvious point.

"What do you mean?"

"Well, the show is your story, so why not tell it for real? You know, books were the original social media." Harper smiled. "Why not write your memoir?"

"Me? *A memoir?* Harper, I'm not a writer."

"Of course you are. Everyone has a story and yours is a good one, a great one. One that many women, and not just Black women, need right now." *Interesting, but no,* Jordan thought, unconvinced.

Harper continued. "Look, the key to any kind of writing is to pour *yourself* into it. Maybe that's what Shelby and your therapist are talking about."

"Right now, the network wants to know why anyone should care. Why would they care about this? About me? I don't have a platform, Harper. I'm a behind-the-scenes person."

"Because you're the one and only Jordan Motherfucking Armstrong. You've been through it and only you can tell everyone else what it's like from the other side, that's why," Harper declared.

Jordan heard him and smiled, but her head was still shaking no. *Maybe he doesn't understand,* she thought. But it was amazing that he believed in her so much. He did though, that much was clear.

Hand on the table now, he continued. "Start with a couple of articles, some think pieces, maybe even a podcast with a couple of guests that you could easily book. Get your perspective out there, build an audience. Have fun with it. You'd ease into a host role naturally."

"You sound like Shelby." Jordan dismissed his suggestions with a wave of her hand.

"That's scary, but she's not wrong, J." Harper smiled at her reassuringly. "Let the people know you. You have so much to give."

Harper took a bite of blackened chicken from his nearly forgotten salad, and then seemed to remember an important point.

"But it's got to come from you. You have to be raw. And vulnerable. Your story can be inspirational to people. They'll listen. You just have to be the one to shepherd it and birth it and mother it and . . . fight for it, to slay all the dragons so that it can survive. Because everybody tries to kill your dream when you have one. That's the nature of dreaming, Jordan."

"I'm not . . . a dreamer like you, Harper."

Harper looked deflated for a moment, but then seemed to regain his conviction. His belief in her was always contagious. And now it was no different. Jordan wasn't dreaming, but she had started to wonder. To his credit, Harper wasn't giving up.

"It's in you though . . ." he said, reanimated. "You just haven't had the support to do it. Yeah, you been dogged in your pursuit of reaching that corporate mountaintop. And that was a dream and you achieved it."

"And it nearly killed me."

"Then whose dream was it? Yours? Your parents'? The Black community's?" Harper asked. "Who'd you do it for?" Jordan shifted in her seat and looked west toward the horizon. It was a big question; one she had no answer for at the ready.

Harper contined. "Remember in undergrad, I was determined to become the next Bryant Gumbel? I wanted to be a broadcast TV star? And when it came time to step up, I didn't have the 'it' factor. You helped me come to terms with that. It was all I thought I wanted and tough to have to figure out another way, but it forced me to find my voice."

Jordan remembered that time well. Harper had been heartbroken when his dream was shattered. But that had just been his first dream. Tough love taught him and brought him around to becoming the voice of a generation. Jordan not only had the right advice for Harper once, but several times.

Jordan took a deep inhale, let it all out, and then turned back to him. "Just because you became a world-renowned novelist doesn't mean that formula works for everyone."

"Okay, have you ever journaled, kept a diary?"

Jordan chuckled. "*No.*" Harper looked surprised. "My therapist has encouraged it . . . But it's not really for me. I'm not even good at having a *verbal* discussion of my inner thoughts. Now you want me to keep a record that someone else can discover? No thank you." Jordan's shoulders slumped. The conversation was leaving her feeling vulnerable and defeated. She sighed with resignation. "I don't know. Maybe I should forget about the show for a while . . . just keep consulting. I'm making money; I have a good, virtually stress-free life. Maybe the show thing just isn't for me anymore."

"Bullshit!" Harper's eyes burned, lit from within. "You want something of your own. Not just working to make other people's ventures better. You want fulfillment. I know what that's like. You're just afraid."

*Afraid?* "I'm no punk," Jordan corrected him. "I'm just not a writer."

"More bullshit. Try."

"Try what?"

"Write down the thing you've never shared with anyone. A childhood memory. A memory that scares you."

"I'm not doing that," Jordan said. *No way.*

"Take a chance," Harper encouraged her. He handed her a pen. Meanwhile, her food was getting cold. This conversation had consumed them. *Why is he doing this?* Jordan wondered. *Why can't we just finish eating, take a walk, go back to my place, and . . . Sigh.* But she knew Harper wouldn't let this go. This was their dynamic. They always pushed each other. *Always.* She gestured to her phone.

"Fine. I'll just do it on my phone."

"No. The brain-to-hand-to-paper is more powerful and emotional. You'll get something great."

*I can't stand it when he makes logical sense . . .* Jordan sighed.

"I don't have anything to write on, Harper." Harper patted down his pockets, surfacing with only a receipt and half-folded napkin. Then he ripped a long piece off the paper tablecloth and handed it all to her.

"Here, it's paper," he said. "You don't have to share it with me. It's just for you. Take five minutes and just write. Don't think." *Don't think?* Jordan's heart started racing. Her leg bounced under the table, making the water glasses jostle. Harper noticed. A look of concern crossed his face.

"You don't like this, right?"

"No."

"Good. You should be uncomfortable. Growth doesn't come from doing easy things."

"Okay, Confucius."

"Do you trust me?" Jordan studied him through her sunglasses. "Not the twisted lips," Harper teased with a charming smile.

*He's lucky he's cute.* Jordan dropped her shoulders, smiled back, and let a deep breath release, shaking her head as she relented. "All right." Harper was never going to let it go. She wasn't thrilled with being pushed to do something she wasn't fully on board with. As much as Jordan hated playing defense, she hated being cornered even more. But it was Harper, so . . . *fine.* She snatched the pen from his extended hand. With a deep breath, she closed her eyes, cleared her mind, and hovered her hand over the paper tablecloth, willing a memory to come forward that she could write quickly and get this over with.

"Do you have the memory?" Harper prodded.

There was . . . *something* . . .

"Yes," she responded finally, with a slight bite of her lower lip. The swell of emotion she felt pointed to a memory taking sharper focus in her mind.

"Okay. Now write," Harper encouraged. She brought the pen down to the paper slowly . . . "Don't think. Just write . . ."

Jordan began to free flow:

*I was sixteen. I had come home from SAT prep and walked in on my parents in the kitchen. Daddy's powerful voice—I still feel it in my* bones when I think about this. So powerful. I wasn't afraid of him until that day. They didn't hear me come in at first. The big dutch oven was on the stove warming up some oil. Mom was chopping onions, garlic and potatoes for daddy's favorite beef stew. She used a lot of different spices. She tried to get me to pay attention whenever she would make it, but I didn't know marjoram from thyme from paprika. Didn't care either. I was all about making the dean's list and scoring 1500 on the SAT. Daddy's influence. He was mad about something. I didn't even know what. His voice demanded you be on point if he summoned you. It wasn't military but commanding. For whatever reason mom wasn't on point that night.

All that came out of his mouth was pure disdain. Said she was "just a pretty face and a beautiful body." He could have chosen anyone, and she was **lucky** he chose her. I couldn't believe he said that. And mom didn't argue. she just took it. She kept chopping, but looked defeated. On some level she must have believed it was true though. Fight back mom. Fight back. don't let him talk to you that way. Don't cry, Don't be a weak woman. "Dinner will be ready soon," she said as if that was going to make him stop belittling her. Bullying her.

Mom never finished school. She was a pageant queen at North Carolina A&T where she met and ultimately just…followed dad. This wasn't the first time he'd made some off-hand remark about how lucky she was. But prior times it was wrapped up in a joke. It felt like marital banter. Because she would laugh and say "you're so silly." I didn't like it. Even then. It was mean but I loved daddy. He was strong and powerful and I wanted to be him. More than I wanted to be mom. I wanted him to love me. Not because I was pretty—even though he told me I was—all the time. though not as much as mom. I didn't want to hear that from her. As if that was my worth. "Good looks will only get you a husband," he'd say. "And better to BE by yourself than with any no-good niggas." "Be better than the boys. Smarter, compete. Don't rely on your looks." He never once said "don't be like your mother" but I swear I heard it. He claimed mom and propped her up as his prize. He used to fucking weigh her. Why did he do that? Mom was always the epitome of a trophy wife. <u>Look pretty, make him look good at the expense of yourself and your own self-worth.</u> Daddy talked at her something terrible that day—like she was beneath him. Like she was property. Like he **<u>owned</u>** her. Mom had no retort. All she did was cater to him, make sure he had his dinner and his scotch. I was frozen until I found the courage to make my presence known by dropping my bookbag on the ground and said "HEY!!" As loudly and as naturally as I could. I think I startled them.

They instantly and completely changed their respective demeanors. "OHH Hi baby. How was your day?" TOTAL BULLSHIT! SHE pulled me into *an extra big warm hug that I didn't want. She blamed the onions for her tears. I looked at daddy and he smiled and asked how test prep went that day. Prep he paid for, prep that was investment for me. I stared at him a long time, hating that he talked to mom that way but knowing he held all the cards. He was in charge and therefore I said what I usually did. "Fine." That was enough for him. "Stay on track, be better than the boys" and don't be your mother. He took a sip of his scotch, grabbed his Chicago Tribune and covered his face with it. Left the cigarette burning in the ashtray. I couldn't look mom in the eye when she asked me if I could help her with dinner. Fuck no! was all i thought. I'm not about to sear beef for a man who expected it. But all I said was I couldn't. "I had to catch up on work." It just came out. I wanted to help her, I wanted to help her stop him from berating her. He wouldn't do it if I was in the same room, but what about when i wasn't there? I couldn't stay there knowing what I knew. And that made me hate her for being weak. Why was she so weak...?*

Tears blurred the writing before her, stained the ink on the paper, but Jordan had more to write, almost as if it was pouring out of her, the stopper of a bottle removed.

"Breathe," she heard Harper say. His voice was soothing, calm. It reminded Jordan to take a breath, to exhale. To close her eyes, take a moment. But she kept seeing the past, feeling it. And now that it was there, the only release was through her hand, on the paper, written down, like the release of a pressure valve. At the table, with little privacy, the tears continued to stream down her face. It was all so uncomfortable, unfamiliar. Jordan didn't do feelings, especially not in public.

"Oh God," she sobbed quietly. Harper's hand, full of care and comfort, covered her non-writing hand.

"It's okay, there's nothing to be embarrassed about." He handed her some paper napkins to wipe her face. She took them but kept writing. She needed to finish. Harper scooted his seat closer, rubbing her back, holding her free hand. Even from the corner of her eye, it was clear he wasn't trying to read what she wrote. She didn't want him to. The exercise was for her only, that's what he'd said. Finally, with the last word written, Jordan let the pen drop onto the tabletop. She looked at Harper, feeling the still-wet tracks of tears on her cheeks. Her heart beating hard, her breath short. He wiped her face and she reached for him, wrapping her arms tightly around his neck. She needed to feel something solid and real and comforting, to bring her back to now. He held her tightly, standing them both up so their entire bodies could make full contact. Jordan sobbed into his chest. She wanted to fall into him completely, relieved to disappear into his comfort and safety. Into *Harper* . . . *Harper* . . . He received all of her, finally now, *all* of her.

# CHAPTER TWENTY-FOUR

## Harper

Holding Jordan in the restaurant, Harper knew whatever she wrote was likely going to bring up some emotions, but he hadn't really expected it to be so visceral. He didn't ask her what the memory was, and wasn't going to, but her intense reaction warranted his immediate concern. He certainly wasn't going to judge one way or another.

"It wasn't the unthinkable, Harper . . ." Jordan assured him as she patted wads of balled-up napkins against her face. She folded the paper she'd written on, tucked it away in her purse. A clear sign to him that it was time for a change of scenery.

They took a walk down to Santa Monica's shops on the Third Street Promenade, but Jordan was distracted, preoccupied. Harper kept asking if she was okay. "Mm-hmm," she'd respond, and quietly get back into her head again. When Harper suggested they head back to her place, Jordan didn't hesitate. She handed him the valet ticket to have him drive them back.

At Jordan's place, Harper noticed her early disengagement with the movie they chose. Their plan to Netflix and chill began in her living room, but when he asked if she wanted to watch something else she assured him she didn't. Instead, she wanted to "do some reading and lie down." She rose from the couch, gave Harper a loving kiss, and walked to her bedroom. Harper watched her stroll through the doorway before she closed it. Maybe she needed some space. After all, they had been spending a lot of time together. And both were used to being by themselves. *Give her space and enjoy this flick by yourself,* he told himself, settling into the couch.

An hour later, when she still hadn't returned, he decided to check on her and walked over to the closed bedroom door, opening it a crack. He found Jordan inside, on the bed. She lay on her side, her back to the door, stock-still save for the deep rise and fall of her breath as she slept. There, she looked so small, so vulnerable, so . . . alone. Harper gently climbed in next to her, spooning her and wrapping his arm around the front of her waist, pulling himself to her, to cover her. She pressed her backside into the warmth of his torso. Then he knew. *She wants me here. . . .* With that permission, he kissed her shoulder and held her close. He knew that he'd pushed her, perhaps too far without realizing it. She pulled him closer to her and he tightened his arms around her, *his* Jordan . . . his . . . *love.* It was his job to give her shelter, safety, and bring her back.

When Harper woke up on the bed, the afternoon sun had already set for the evening. Lamps illuminated Jordan's bedroom, creating a warm glow. A song he recognized from Erykah Badu's *Mama's Gun* album was softly playing overhead. No longer next to him, Jordan moved about the room, already looking refreshed in her sexy undergarments and a fully beat face. As he continued to blink his eyes open, she leaned over him on the bed and placed a gentle kiss on his head.

"Come on, sleepyhead," she said playfully. "We need to get going. Hollywood Bowl traffic is *insane,* and you know I don't want to walk in late for the Isleys." She was back-to-normal

Jordan, moving with purpose and energy. Harper was grateful to see her back in a state he recognized, but he still wondered about what he'd witnessed. There was something deep there, a place he'd never seen her go. They'd talk about it again someday. But not tonight. They had plenty of time. *Forever* . . . She interrupted his thoughts, holding up two nearly identical black dresses. "Which one?" Harper pointed to the one in her left hand. Jordan took another look at it. "Really?"

"Yeah. Other one looks nice too." They both looked the same. She held the first dress up against her body and looked at her reflection in her walk-in closet mirror.

"You think?"

"Mm-hmm."

She held up the other dress and said, "Okay. Get up. Get dressed." With that, Jordan ducked inside her closet. *Yup. She's back.*

After battling traffic and paying for valet parking to avoid the long walk up the hill, Harper and Jordan arrived at the Hollywood Bowl's plaza of restaurants and refreshment bars. Jordan looked stunning in what was the fifth dress option, and Harper felt good in a fitted gray sweater, jeans, and a black suede jacket he'd purchased earlier. Jordan insisted he get it. She was right—it fit as though it was made for him. He didn't need more convincing after that, despite the $2,500 price tag. They walked in holding hands, blending seamlessly with the rest of the grown-and-sexy crowd of couples who came to hear some old-school R&B. Harper offered to grab them a couple of cocktails while Jordan made a run to the ladies' room.

"I'll get you a sidecar or something similar," Harper said as he gestured toward a bar with a winding queue. Grown-and-sexy folks liked grown-and-sexy "dranks."

"Perfect." She kissed him before she left, mashing her

painted lips against his. She pulled back to look at her handiwork and rubbed her smeared mark off him with a thumb. Harper smiled back at her. "I love you," she said. Her words made Harper's smile even broader.

"I love you too." He kissed her again.

She smiled back and pointed at his lips. "You get it this time. I'm going to reapply. See you in a minute." Jordan turned and headed to the restroom. Harper carefully wiped the remnants of lipstick off as he watched her disappear into the crowd. He sighed at the long line ahead and resolved to decipher the menu offerings. The buzz of his phone captured his attention. He wasn't expecting any calls but always kept his phone on him for Mia. Frowning, he reached into his jacket's inside pocket and saw an image of Murch on his screen.

"Sup, Murch!" Harper answered with a smile. "It's a little loud where I am. We're at a concert."

"Okay, cool. I won't keep you long. Just wanted to ask you something." Murch's tone had an uncharacteristic seriousness, out of sync with the festive nature of the concert venue.

"Shoot," Harper responded.

Murch exhaled, the sound was loud and audible through the phone's earpiece. "Did you send that picture of you and Jordan knowing I'd likely share with Candace and *knowing* she'd share with Robyn?" His question poured out, direct and accusatory. Harper was silent for a few beats trying to process it. *What?* He searched for an answer, realizing slowly that Murch's question might have been its own fairly accurate summation. Murch had started his career as a lawyer, and his juris doctor was certainly being put to use on Harper at the moment. "I started thinking about it later," Murch continued. "Our conversation about Robyn's boyfriend and how she was happy and then you were like, 'Bam me too!' Was that just a coincidence?" The question sat out there for a few beats as Harper had been surprised into silence. Despite the accusatory nature of the inquiry, he was trying to find the most honest response.

"Well . . . I can't say that it was the *main* reason, Murch, no," Harper said tentatively. "I did want to share what was happening with Jordan and me with you. And . . . um . . . I guess . . . if you ended up sharing it . . . then I don't know . . . it'd be like . . . whatever . . . ?"

"Uh-huh . . ." Murch said after a beat. "Right. Because I can't keep anything to myself. I'm the town crier."

Suddenly, Harper felt a knot in his stomach. *Fuck.*

"It's . . . It's not like that, Murch . . ." Harper stammered out. "I mean if you shared it with Candace that would have been fine. You know?" Murch didn't respond. "Hello? Murch? You still there?" Harper asked. Over the din of the crowd, the ladies in line cackling, and the band starting to warm up it was getting hard to hear if Murch let out another audible sigh or not. "Murch, can you hear—?"

"I'm here," Murch responded. Then more silence. Harper had almost forgotten about this new Murch who was no longer letting bullshit go. He was holding any and everyone accountable. *Every time you have the opportunity to choose yourself over doing the right thing, you always choose* ***yourself!*** Those unfortunate words were ringing true right now. It was a sharp contrast to earlier when Murch had expressed such exuberant joy. *Me and Jordan . . . that's happy news, right?*

"What can I get you, sir?" the bartender asked expectantly. With Murch still silent on the line, Harper searched for the word "sidecar" on the cocktail standee, but didn't see it. He had not figured out what a sidecar substitute could be and he felt awkward asking with Murch still silent.

"Ummm . . ." Harper uttered as he read but didn't quite

comprehend the cocktail menu. His head was swimming as he tried to formulate his words into comprehensive sentences. "Uhhhh . . ." The ladies behind him were restless and getting impatient.

"Is this nigga serious, not knowing what he wants . . . ? For real . . ." went the gaggle of women. Harper began to sweat under his armpits. He looked back at the ladies who were surprised he was making eye contact but looked like they were ready to return whatever he was coming with.

"Sorry. Y'all can go ahead of me. Still figuring it out." Harper gave an awkward smile.

"Thank you," one of the women responded with an air of triumph. Harper stepped behind them to buy himself some more time. He put his free finger to his ear to better hear what Murch was saying, and more important, what he was *not* saying.

"Sorry about that," Harper said into the still-quiet phone. "You there?"

"Yup."

"Hey. Is . . . ummm? I mean, did you share the photo with Candace?"

"No. I didn't, Harper," Murch said. Harper felt a tinge of anxiety and an equal one of relief. Murch continued, "And here's why: When *you* heard about Robyn's boyfriend you felt fucked up hearing about it from *us* rather than *her*." Harper swallowed and glanced around the lobby. "When you heard about Robyn being happy you doubled down with this Jordan thing, which is *very immature*," Murch declared, "but human."

"Okayyyy." Harper scrunched his forehead in confusion.

"You should let Robyn know *yourself* about you and Jordan. It's the adult thing to do. I am not doing your dirty work for you."

*Really?* "Dirty work, Murch?" Harper said with a chuckle.

"Yeah. It's messy. And you should do better. Especially at

this point." Murch wasn't letting up. He had always been the moral police, but he was also an unconditional friend. Always. Now he'd become the friend that wouldn't let you slide, even if it made for easier conversation. Harper's mouth started to dry up, his chest hot and damp.

"Have you decided, sir?" the bartender asked again. *Shit.* Harper waved on the next couple in line to go ahead of him.

Murch continued, "Look, you're my brother and I love you. When I tell you how happy I am for you and Jordan to have finally connected I don't even have the words. You two deserve each other in the best way. But you should come clean with Robyn about it."

"What do you mean 'come *clean*'?" Harper spit the words out. "I'm not sneaking around here, Murch. There's nothing to 'come clean' about. Nothing happened during our marriage that needs to be confessed to."

"I'm not saying there was, Harp—" Murch started.

"Then what are you saying?" Harper snapped back. His words hung in the air as the Hollywood Bowl atmosphere flooded with the howl of the guitar solo opening to "Choosey Lover."

"I think I'm being clear. Don't let Robyn find out about this without you telling her," Murch said matter-of-factly. "It's not a good look. And you owe her that respect."

*"Owe her?"* Harper's jaw tightened as he swallowed.

"I said what I said, Harp."

Looking off in the distance, Harper's eyes landed on Jordan returning, with a look of confusion on her face and a shrug like, *where are the drinks?*

Harper gave her the "one minute" hand signal. He needed to handle business, and quickly. He turned back to the bartender and addressed Murch through the phone.

"Yo, Murch," Harper said. "Thanks. I hear you. I gotta go." Then Harper pressed end. Thoughts of Robyn had no place here tonight, not between him and Jordan. Maybe he'd fucked up, but he'd have to think about Murch's warning later. Jordan was only steps away. Noticing that, he turned to the impatient-looking bartender with eyebrows raised ready for his order and leaned in over the bar. "Hey, can y'all make a sidecar?"

# CHAPTER TWENTY-FIVE

## Robyn

At Robyn's Nest, Robyn carefully counted out the cloves of garlic on the prep counter for Friday's special. Mia was doing her schoolwork on a stool at the long family-style table and Haniah was moving quickly from chore to chore, cleaning and arranging all the place settings for the restaurant's dinner service. Lately, everything felt much more critical, to get the flavors balanced and the ambiance just right for the patrons. There wasn't much financial wiggle room now, with the leak in the roof and the shoddy refrigerator. It all added pressure to maintain and, better, grow the existing base of customers. But still, there was no straight-line route to finding a year's worth of rent anytime soon. And sure enough, at just about the same time as his regular visit, the landlord, Aboagye, sauntered through the door with his round belly leading the way, followed closely by his bellowing voice echoing through the still empty dining room.

"Hello dere, sweetness," he called out. Robyn hated that pejorative name. There was nothing sweet about Aboagye or the way he treated her as a tenant. Instead of fixing the issues with the place, he'd opted to hold the repairs over her head. To his greeting, Robyn barely responded.

"How can we help you today, Aboagye?" Haniah swept in from one of the corners to meet Aboagye before he passed the first set of tables. Her tone was pleasant but all business. Robyn perked up one ear to hear the exchange.

"Ah, just checking on my prime real estate today. I understand this past weekend this place was full of high-paying customers with great appetites," he bellowed. "Business must be good, eh? So you must have something for me, then."

"Now, Mr. Aboagye," Haniah said gently, "would you rather come here to fill your pockets, or your belly today? Because we are preparing a delicious rasta pasta, and it demands all our attention."

Aboagye's big laugh reverberated throughout the space. "A meal well-earned by fixing the leak in the roof. And my pockets? My pockets are crying, they are so hungry. Right, little one?" Aboagye directed his voice in Mia's direction. Robyn watched Mia turn to look at him, clearly unsure of who he was or what he wanted. Robyn set the knife down hard on the counter and pulled off her cooking apron. All the better that her hands were covered in garlic—she'd see if it worked as it was supposed to on *vampires.* Swiftly, from the kitchen, she marched into the dining room and took her place next to Haniah.

"Aboagye. This is not a negotiation. You said you'd work with me as long as I showed good faith. I've paid through the month. And you know that," Robyn reminded him.

"I am losing faith, sweetness," he said. "And I can no longer make exceptions because you make great jollof or smile pretty. This is not America."

"I know where I am, Aboagye, and you can't go reneging on

your word because you feel like it. Not to mention I'm still paying for repairs on the food truck you sold me and the roof—if it rains God forbid—it might as well be open. As the landlord, it's your duty to make the repairs. You know that and we know it too."

He leaned in just as she finished speaking. Close enough that his large belly almost grazed her hand. "Perhaps, Ms. Robyn, the repairs could be made for a *paying* tenant. You"—he pointed a thick finger—"may be moving out very soon. Perhaps even before the next rain." Robyn averted her eyes and head away from his finger to compose herself, and she caught a glimpse of Mia's little head perked up and watching the exchange with concern. Robyn turned back to Aboagye with resolve.

"Are you threatening me?" Robyn leaned in, unsure of what she was inviting as a reply. Over Aboagye's shoulder, she saw the unmistakable tall frame of Kwesi walking in, holding a bouquet of flowers, his third of the week, smiling as if all was well with the world. Aboagye turned quickly, as it was hard to miss Kwesi's enthusiastic greeting.

"Well, hello there! Am I interrupting anything?" Kwesi walked over to Robyn's side and offered her the large assortment of flowers that he was holding.

"I'll take those," Haniah said, sweeping the flowers into her arms and heading back toward the kitchen. Aboagye sized Kwesi up quickly with a visible swallow and change of demeanor as Kwesi towered over him and looked him in the eye.

"What say, bruv?" Kwesi extended his hand. "Kwesi Emmanuel."

Robyn breathed a release of tension from her body.

"Kwesi, this is Aboagye," Robyn said. "He rents us this space for Robyn's Nest."

Kwesi's face lit up with instant recognition. "Ahhh, the man with the plan for fixing the roof, amongst other things I presume. Pleasure."

Aboagye's face scrunched up. Robyn had to stifle a laugh. Haniah had been advocating for Kwesi ever since Robyn told her of his "day after" disclosure following the first night they spent together. Haniah, like Thema, seemed unfazed to learn about his family life. "Give him a chance, Robyn," she'd said. "It's very helpful to have a good man in your life. And his situation is not as uncommon as you might believe." And true to his word, he'd made it a point to show up daily at Robyn's Nest, always with a gift for Mia—a book or musical playlist or her favorite, chocolate!—and most times with flowers for Robyn, plus two helpful hands and listening ears. Robyn had been enjoying the attention, but in this moment, his presence was appreciated far beyond the visceral attraction she still felt.

Aboagye, obviously uncomfortable, reached out to shake Kwesi's hand. "The pleasure is mine, brudda," he said tersely. "Well, sweet— Err— Rob— Ms. Stewart, I must be going. I have many other properties to tend to today." He reached into his pocket to pull out his cellphone, although no one heard it ringing before.

"Oh. So soon? I was hoping we could have a little chat." Kwesi leaned in, putting his hand firmly on Aboagye's shoulder. "I'll walk you out, bruv," Kwesi said and extended his arm toward the door. He looked Robyn in the eye, "Excuse me for a second, would you, Ms. Stewart? Hello, Mia! Fancy seeing you here," Kwesi called out. "Enjoy that chocolate! But make sure you ask your mum when you can have it, alright?" Mia smiled and nodded back as Kwesi walked ahead of a much tamer Aboagye to grab the door and escort him outside.

It wasn't until he was fully gone that Robyn remembered to turn to Mia, who was sitting attentively at the family-style table, attentively examining her chocolate bar. Aware now that she'd witnessed the whole exchange, Robyn quickly walked over to her daughter, calling out to her. "Mia, honey, wait until after dinner to eat your chocolate. How is your homework going?"

Mia barely looked up, but put the chocolate bar on the table in front of her. "Fine," she said, kicking her legs underneath the high stool.

"Do you . . . want to go into my office and study?" she asked. She wanted to give Mia agency, to not alarm her if she wasn't alarmed. Lately, however, her daughter had become more of a mystery—much less straightforward than the little girl she used to be. No longer could Robyn assume that her tight-lipped response was all innocence. No telling how much she saw or what it meant to her when Aboagye addressed her directly. *He had no right.* She just hoped that she gave enough openings for communication if Mia needed it.

"Nope," Mia said, craning her neck toward the window. She seemed more interested in what was happening between Kwesi and Aboagye outside. Robyn stepped over, obscuring her daughter's view.

"Good. Make sure you check everything twice. And finish up." Robyn made sure to make eye contact. Mia put her face back in her studies, seeming to find focus in her homework papers again.

"Okay." Robyn gave Mia a lingering look, but when she began to scribble on her paper in front of her, she felt satisfied enough to turn and walk away. She'd check on her later. As she walked, Robyn did her best to hide her close attention to the two men outside the window by wiping imaginary dust off the table. She could see Kwesi gesturing a lot with his hands, calmly but firmly, looking like a man who was accustomed to tough negotiations. He cut Aboagye off several times, so mostly the other man listened and nodded quickly. The exchange lasted no more than ninety seconds but spoke volumes.

Kwesi had shown up at the right time, and had been consistent thus far, just as he said he would be. The moment softened Robyn's resolve, allowing her to take it as a sign that maybe she should give him a chance, to stop writing the future from her own *American* mind or what was left of that part of her, and to let things unfold as they would, here in her new home. After all, she had come here for a new life and the new experiences that came along with it.

Aboagye and Kwesi shook hands and Aboagye swiftly moved along. Kwesi watched him go. Quickly, Robyn retreated to the bar and busied herself. As Kwesi returned inside the restaurant, she made eye contact and summoned him over. Kwesi headed toward her, passing Mia's table with a smile, and settled in at the bar. Robyn poured him a beer and leaned over the counter to speak to him intimately.

"Well, I'd ask you how's your day, but—" he began.

"It's better now," Robyn interrupted him. "I'm glad you came by." She smiled at him, heart warm and open. "So . . . what did you say to him?"

"I just told him that I thought he was taking advantage where he didn't need to. And if he didn't know a person to fix the problem, that I do. I also told him that I'm a real-estate developer and we will certainly cross paths again when I'm looking for building managers. He should do the right thing."

"What'd he say?"

"He was noncommittal, but I told him he should come back when he has a plan and not before. That's all."

Robyn smiled at the sound of that.

Kwesi's smile got just a bit sexier as his mouth turned up slyly at the corners. "I don't like the idea of anybody trying to take advantage of you. And so I wanted to do what I can to make sure that doesn't happen. I'm here for you. And my offer still stands to help you with the rent."

Robyn drew in a sharp breath.

"You know the answer to that," she reminded him.

"I do." He nodded resignedly.

Robyn smiled a tired smile at Kwesi. His words and actions were appreciated, and she wanted all that he was offering, just . . . "I'm . . . scared, Kwesi," she said, not quite meaning to be so blunt. "I . . . just can't afford to make any big mistakes. I don't want to be played for a fool." She looked him in his eyes. His expression softened and he reached for her hand, taking her fingers in his.

"I know that where you're coming from, everything about me probably all sounds very complicated. But it's not. I've dated many women, Robyn. But no one has been in my home, not like you have. Nor has anyone been invited to share in my world, to meet my family. You have an open invitation. Anywhere I go, you are welcome."

"What is it . . . about me, specifically?" she asked him. What he'd said and done for her, it was all enticing, but she was *grown* and had the scars to prove it. She *needed* to know.

He took a pause, then a deep breath. With his thumb he caressed the top of her hand. And his eyes held hers for a beat before he spoke. "Robyn, you are nurturing and loving and *selfless.* You give to everyone around you. You raise and uplift your daughter; you teach her to be kind. You are feminine and beautiful. And you're smart, but still vulnerable. Like a sunflower. Even the sunflower—with its strong stalk and plentiful seeds—it still needs to be watered and cared for or it will wilt under the weight of everything that everyone else needs from it, trying to reach for the sun."

"That's . . . what you see?" she asked with a tone of disbelief. It was an infrequent delicacy to feel seen. He smiled and nodded. His words had made her breathless. Like he'd reached into the core of her and touched upon some buried truth that needed air. She felt weary, but here, with him, she had a sense of ease and peace that she experienced nowhere else. It was easy to feel hopeful. Was this what she wanted? Robyn let her fingers wrap around his. When their eyes met this time, her lips parted, just slightly. And slowly, the distance between them shrank. They were drawn by gravity until they were so close to each other that she could feel the heat of his lips next to hers. There was almost no distance left between them, then the moment their lips touched, she let herself be swept away in the kiss.

"And so . . . you have another week . . . before you leave?" Robyn asked when they finally parted.

Kwesi smiled. "Yes, another week . . . and we'll make the most of it."

Robyn smiled. *Yes, yes . . . we will,* she thought. And then, seeing a motion over Kwesi's shoulder at the back of the room, she focused in time to see the quick swivel of Mia's head, back toward the tabletop with the scattered papers of her assignments as if she'd been looking down there all the while.

## CHAPTER TWENTY-SIX

# Jordan

*Fifteen days plus thirty years . . . That's how long Harper and I have been together. . . .*

The clock read 2:12 a.m. and Jordan lay awake watching her lover sleep. *Harper* . . . asleep in her bed. Soundly. Peacefully. They'd just made love *again.* Jordan looked at him, shaking her head to clear the disbelief. They'd shared a bed before, but not like this. Not with her body exhausted *and* exhilarated from experiencing his. *This man can fuck* . . . she thought. He could also make love. *He stimulates so many parts of me . . . I can't believe I waited so long* . . . But of course, she'd waited. That's who she was. Jordan Motherfucking Armstrong—always guarded, not doing feelings, not getting caught up in anything, but always standing on business. *And now Harper Stewart got me all in my feelings* . . . Jordan released a deep sigh, the sigh of being open . . . wide open.

Two days ago had Jordan thoroughly shaking her ass and swaying with Harper and the rest of the crowd to the sensual grooves at the Hollywood Bowl. The Isleys sounded just as amazing as they did when she listened to them on vinyl back in the day, encouraging all to *do what you wanna do* because "It's Your Thing." The night had been perfect—a celebration of "their thing," hers and Harper's. Sharing with the college crew was fine, but no one was going to define "it" but them. And right now it was really special. Shelby was constantly checking in: "How's it going?" "Is he still there?" "Are you guys sick of each other yet?" "Where else have you done it?" Was she waiting for the other shoe to drop? Wasn't everyone always waiting for that shoe to drop when things are just too perfect? Jordan didn't need any help with healthy skepticism. She was built to keep her guard up. But that was almost impossible now with Harper, who'd said this was the happiest he'd been in years. Maybe even decades. How could that be an exaggeration when Jordan knew herself, she hadn't been this full . . . *ever.* Never allowed it. At least not since college. She was crazy once about Demetrius Mercer—that pedigreed, privileged Kappa pretty boy. But when she got caught up with him, lost herself, and he stomped on her heart, who was there to nurse her back? Her best friend, Harper. She wasn't about to lose herself again . . . And now here she was. But this time the well was Harper, and who knew how deep she could fall. He was different though, stable now, he was her person.

*It's been fifteen days and thirty years. . . .*

Jordan didn't want this feeling to end, *ever.* Her heart was so full. Not only because Harper was the man she thought he was, but he had truly inspired her the other day at 1212. They were supposed to be having brunch but he'd pushed her to write. She'd gotten to see him as a true artist—her best friend, her lover. Harper had opened a door for her. And when she walked through it, Jordan felt a breakthrough like never before, even in therapy. What she wrote at that table, it led her to emotions she'd locked away for so long. An overwhelming release. And that night, Harper had wrapped his arms around her and laid with her. And he was still here, lying with her now.

That memory she hadn't thought of in decades was an experience that had shaped her. What she wrote on that tablecloth all made sense. Lying in bed, she felt the tears pricking her eyes again. *I'll never be my mother . . .* she reminded herself. She would never be just a pretty face and a beautiful body to some man, *never.* Jordan followed her dad's example: strong, demanding, outworking everyone, especially the men, and *most* especially the white men. Only employing her mother's femininity when necessary. Disarm them with a smile and a soft voice to gain the advantage she needed. Use what you have to get what you want. No pussy was promised and none was given. *I don't fuck for free or if you pay me.* Jordan could easily have been a trophy wife for the right dude, but after that day . . . with her folks . . . she vowed *no man* would ever own her, ruin her, diminish her. *Ever. Fuck that.* Was that love? Was that marriage? Was her mom the first woman she'd seen dick-matized? *No thanks.* She'd be the alpha *and* the omega if necessary.

What else had she buried in favor of self-preservation? Maybe her sessions with Dr. Clark had laid the groundwork for such a breakthrough, but Harper had pushed her down the runway. Their intimacy was already present, as was the trust, but now there was safety. Unlocking herself could lead self-care Jordan further into her own healing. Isn't that what she was striving for? Isn't that what she'd centered her show on? We're all a product of what we've struggled through. And that's something to celebrate and continue to evolve. That's growth. And even in her advanced years, she acknowledged she was still growing. What is the point otherwise? How can you be an expert in wellness and healing if you don't go through the process? In her next session with Dr. Clark, she'd bring up Harper and this latest idea for a memoir. Maybe that was something worth exploring. It was, after all, her story to tell. And now, she'd found the beginning.

*Memoir.* She hadn't thought about it before, but she was starting to see a vision for it now. It did feel daunting. But it made sense. Not writing the whole thing, but she could and should commit to writing more. Journaling, just like Dr. Clark had suggested, what Harper got her to do. Little by little she could uncover a multitude of aspects of herself. There were no deadlines. There was no rush for the show, no rush to build a platform. She was financially independent. She had Harper now. It could develop organically, slowly, beautifully. Right now, everything was better. *I want that,* she thought. *More of this life with Harper.* And bit by bit, she'd write under the supervision of her best friend and lover, who just happened to hold a Pulitzer. *"Harper, you're the voice of a generation,"* her twenty-year-old-self had declared to him. And he turned out to be just that. Jordan didn't have his voice. She only had hers, but Harper made her feel like it was just as valuable.

She snuggled closer to Harper and settled into a spoon. *I'm going to write a memoir . . .* she thought dreamily, aligning her body with his. The energy coursing through her body now was its own orgasm of excitement, making her toes curl. She could live in this forever.

*This is the beginning of the rest of our lives. . . .*

*Wait, Jordan, what the fuck are you doing?*

Wasn't she getting ahead of herself?

Jordan shifted down the bed and laid her head on her pillow. The crashing waves served as an aural melatonin that flushed away her bubbling thoughts, lulling her into slumber. She yawned and involuntarily closed her eyes. The waves continued to caress her ears and paint a picture. The whitecaps receded as another wave painted the sand gray. Jordan exhaled deeply and settled into bed.

At the shoreline, Jordan and Harper walk barefoot on the wet sand, holding hands. The air is windy but warm and it's so sunny outside you need to squint—the perfect Southern California day. Together they run from the rushing water. She squeals and giggles, his throaty baritone laughs back at her faux fear. He snatches her up in his arms and swings her to avoid the rush of seawater engulfing their feet and the bottom of their rolled-up jeans. Her hair cascades in her eyes and mouth as she voices her delight. Harper sets her down on the drier part of the beach, smiles at her, takes her hand, and leads her farther inland.

"Come on. We're gonna be late," Harper says.

Jordan doesn't know what they're late for, but she gladly lets her man lead. They walk up her patio stairs still holding hands to discover, among others, her parents awaiting them with proud smiles.

"Hey, champ," Daddy says to her before engulfing her in a big bear hug. He smells like old English cologne and cigar smoke, warm and familiar. Mom kisses Harper, then holds him at arm's length to look at him. Jordan can't decipher what she's saying to him, but she's all smiles and approval. Mom looks as beautiful as ever. She looks like she did when Jordan was a teenager: the epitome of elegance and grace. She turns to her daughter with the warmest smile. Jordan smiles back and approaches Mom without hesitation. Her embrace is filled with enchanting scents of orange, jasmine, rose, and patchouli. Mom always smells so sweet.

"I *love* him, Jordan," Mom declares. She pulls back to look her daughter in her eyes. "*Love.* Oh, I'm so proud of you. You deserve it." Jordan's heart is so full hearing her mom speak those words. Her cheeks nearly burst from smiling. Jordan rests in the crook of Mom's armpit. Even though they never discussed it, Jordan knew her mom was disappointed she never got married. That changes today. Harper and Daddy share some E&J brandy. Jordan can feel it burning in her own throat, but Harper muscles through. Her dad laughs and backslaps her man. Harper seems to enjoy it. The sun dips behind some clouds outside. The wind starts to pick up and the ocean seems to be churning louder. Jordan sees the tide moving closer to the patio.

"When are you two going to have kids?" Mom whispers to her daughter.

"Mom, please . . ." Jordan says. Didn't she know that moment had already passed?

Shelby comes out of nowhere to say, "Fuck that. You're never too old to have a baby." *Ummmm, that's not true, Shelby.*

Daddy and Harper laugh as Quentin and Murch join them in a toast. Jordan makes eye contact with Harper who smiles, shrugs, and makes a silly face that cracks her up. Lance sits off to the side with Jasmine. She's not Mia, but she takes care of him and Jordan likes that for Lance. The wind picks up again and suddenly the skies turn gray. It's Jasmine who suggests they get inside Jordan's house. Everyone seems to move inside at once. *Wait,* Jordan thinks, *I'm not ready for all these folks in my space. How'd they all get here anyway? Where'd everybody park . . . ?*

Harper approaches her. "I love you," he says. He kisses her and disappears into the party forming in her living room. She watches him go as the sound of the waves crashing gets louder and more present. It suddenly feels dangerously close and loud. Jordan looks back toward the ocean and the waves are very high now and threatening to overtake her deck. Jordan is breathing heavy, panicking . . . looking for . . . Harper. Then . . .

Jordan's eyes popped open as she stirred awake from the dream. After a moment of reorienting herself she fully awakened to the dawn. The gentle sounds of the ocean crashing on the shore coupled with Harper's voice floated their way to her. It was gray and looked cold outside as the near-daily marine layer obscured the morning sun. Her bed felt a bit too cold without Harper in it. She'd gotten used to his warmth. She could hear his muffled voice in the distance, but didn't see him outside, as she scanned the misty horizon through her bedroom sheers. Then she found him, shirtless on the patio off her bedroom, talking and looking delicious. She squinted to focus in on him—he was looking at his phone. *FaceTime?* Is he FaceTiming? As she came to this realization, she heard his frantic and panicked voice. His speech stopped and started as if listening and trying to understand what was being said.

"Honey, tell me what . . ." he faltered. The voice on the other side was hard to decipher with the double-paned windows and the ocean waves crashing against the shore. But it was definitely female. . . .

"Okay," Harper said. "I'll be there. Don't worry."

Jordan heard *that* clearly. She saw Harper hang up. She saw him look out at the ocean and his shoulders drop. Then his head dropped too, looking at the phone in his hand as if it carried all the weight in the world. *Something's wrong.* . . . But Jordan could help, she was equipped. His problem was *their* problem. Whatever it was, they'd figure it out together. Like they always had. *Together.* Harper carefully pulled back the patio door, ever so quietly.

"Hi."

He looked up surprised to find Jordan awake, looking right at him.

"Hey," Harper said back. His voice sounded heavy, troubled.

"Everything okay?"

Harper didn't answer right away, only looked down at the phone in his hand.

"Yeah," he said finally. It didn't sound convincing.

"What's wrong?" Harper sighed loudly.

"I gotta go, Jordan. It's Mia."

# CHAPTER TWENTY-SEVEN

## Jordan

*It's Mia* . . . Jordan was grinding her espresso beans, which was drowning out the sound of Harper on the phone with his assistant, but not the words on replay in her mind: "Gotta go." He'd said that *to her.*

"I don't care what it costs, just *book* it. Use miles, my Visa, whatever . . . yeah, I always travel with my passport . . . okay . . ." The act of making coffee was a useful distraction, an attempt to quell the anxiety in Jordan's stomach. She watched Harper's continuous pacing; it was frenetic even. A complete departure from his cool, calm, and collected lover-boy self that had just moments ago shared the bed with her. Following his footsteps down the hall, she peeked through the cracked door of her bedroom to find him sorting through his clothes, suitcase splayed open on the ground. He didn't even notice her. That same suitcase that had been carefully put away in the closet because . . . *he was supposed to be staying . . . forever,* Jordan thought.

Amid Harper's frenzy, Jordan managed to maintain her calm and rational demeanor, taking deep breaths and using her learned self-soothing skills. But inside, the unease was stirring her inner beast, which she was desperately trying to keep at bay, holding back the anger that was quietly bubbling. *Stay open, Jordan,* she reminded herself. There was a rational solution to this.

She returned to the kitchen and pulled out the WESTMORE U–labeled mug Harper liked drinking out of since he'd been spending mornings here in Malibu. She put it on the counter and walked over to take out the creamer he liked and began pouring his cup of coffee. He emerged from the bedroom still shirtless and in his sweatpants, his eyes darting around the room.

"Harper . . ." she began. He looked at her but headed toward her door that housed her stackable washer and dryer.

"I can't find my zip down jacket that goes with these . . ." he said as he opened the dryer and dug through it.

"Harper. Slow down. Just take a second here," Jordan tried again. "What exactly did Mia say?"

Harper yanked the clothes out of the dryer and just kept shaking his head as if he was trying to remove the memory from his mind. "I already told you." This impatient tone was definitely *not* the Harper of the past days. "She . . . she just asked me to come, Jordan. I can't *not* go. I told her that if she ever needed me that I'd be there."

"Well, did you talk to Robyn? Maybe she can shed some light on this—"

"No!" Harper snapped. "I don't need to—" Harper cut himself off. Jordan knew her face said clearly what she was thinking, *What in the hell?* She was jarred, shocked. Looking at Harper but momentarily seeing a stranger, a *real* stranger. She suppressed her immediate response and with a *very* deep breath, gave him grace. He closed his eyes and rubbed his temples, exhaling and holding out his hands in semi-surrender. "Sorry," he said, his tone reset to a modicum of calm. "No, I haven't spoken to Robyn. She didn't call me. Mia did. . . ."

"So how do you know if this is even real?" Jordan returned. "She's ten years old—"

"Eleven," Harper corrected her. "She's eleven, Jordan." Harper balled up the clothes in his hands and headed back to the bedroom. His abs rippled in a way that would have been enticing under different circumstances, how they could have been spending their morning. *Should have been.* Harper turned back to address Jordan again. "Besides, what the hell is Robyn gonna do? She's out there boo'ed up with some Mandingo-assed nigga not even paying full attention. If she was, my daughter wouldn't be calling me in a panic."

*This . . . this is how it all goes wrong. . . .* The thought arrived in Jordan's mind even as she fought it, determined to stay hopeful, optimistic even. The past two weeks had been blissful, perfect, worth holding on to. Surely, this was just a misunderstanding, and one that could be rectified with reason and logic, and a little creative problem-solving. She'd managed much more challenging problems running a ten-figure division of a major media conglomerate. This was what she did—Jordan Armstrong was a champion of solving difficult problems.

"Harper, listen to yourself. That doesn't even sound like Robyn. She's a responsible person. And an adult . . ." Jordan argued. For a moment his face flashed a look of receptivity and openness. Jordan took the opportunity. "You need to relax. Let's take a beat. I made us some coffee, let's figure this out together." Harper seemed to take in her words and exhaled some of his tension. *That's my guy,* she thought. *Come on back.* Jordan reached for his strong arms, attempting to soothe him, and herself. If they could just get back to—

Then Harper closed his eyes and shook his head.

"Look, I don't know what the fuck is going on, but I gotta go and find out. What kind of father would I be if I just said 'Oh, go to your mother. Let her handle it.' That's bullshit. I'm not that guy. I gotta be there for her; I promised that I would. I gotta go."

*Dammit, he's saying it again.* It was always something, wasn't it? Some kind of excuse that gave him a reason to run? She'd seen it before, many times. But all those times were with other women, *not . . . me,* Jordan thought.

"Hey, I'm not questioning your love for Mia—" Jordan tried again, calmly.

"Then what are you doing, Jordan?" There was a quaver and vulnerability to his voice, but the words were detached, harsh. His vulnerability wasn't about her or toward her. They'd come to a place where she wasn't his concern any longer . . . at all . . . "Because I don't have time for this." Harper headed back into the bedroom with an armful of clean laundry. Jordan's legs carried her in behind him.

"Harper, you don't just 'have to go' to Ghana. It's an entire day of flying. It's literally two continents away." Jordan could hear the words coming out of her own mouth and still it sounded like someone else was speaking them. She could feel herself getting more intense. That same apprehension she'd felt in her dream. Something ruining a good thing. Jordan wasn't sure what was worse: being engulfed by a tidal wave or Harper threatening to fly away. Jordan's breath staggered as she saw Harper shoving loose pieces of paper into his knapsack, clearly preoccupied.

"Where did I put my journal . . . ?"

All Jordan kept hearing in her mind was *Don't go.* She disguised that desperation with rational questions and thoughts appealing to his logic. *This is my boy. My homie. We have always figured shit out together.*

"Let's think this through, Harper," she said. "Look, maybe I could go with you."

"No."

Wow. His no was so definitive. So final. So, *I don't need you.*

"Well, why not?"

"Because I don't need to be clouding things up by having Auntie Jordan by my side," Harper snapped back.

*Clouding things . . . ?*

"I don't know what this divorce has done to my little girl, but I know it's hurt her. I'm not going to further damage her with confusion over whoever this Prince Akeem nigga is Robyn's shacking up with. And then me bringing you in the mix inexplicably? Switching up what she knows. How am I gonna explain that? This ain't the time or the place for that, J." Harper spoke at her as if she was a clueless child. "Can't you understand that?"

Despite Harper's condescension, his holier-than-thou explanation, despite his intractability, inside her head, all Jordan heard was *Please don't go,* speaking for her heart. The voice, the feeling wouldn't go away. *Stop it, Jordan. Get a hold of yourself.*

Before waiting for her reply, Harper seemed to answer his own question.

"You're not a parent. You don't understand . . ." Harper said dismissively.

Jordan's heart dropped into her stomach. And inside, the rumbling began. He'd struck a nerve with his callousness. She could feel her guard coming up, the involuntary defense system. The beast was awakening.

"What the *hell* does that mean?" Jordan said in a flash of anger. *Stay open, Jordan,* she told herself.

"What do you mean, 'what does that mean?'" Harper looked at her incredulously as he loaded his folded laundry into his suitcase. "I don't have a choice here. This is my daughter we're talking about. That's *my* daughter. *My* flesh and blood. And make no mistake, it is killing me to have to leave—"

"You don't have to leave," Jordan cut him off. *Please don't leave,* the voice inside her pleaded.

Harper approached her and held her shoulders with his hands. He exhaled and looked her straight in her eyes. "Jordan, you know I love you. And I really don't *want* to leave . . ." Harper said.

"Then don't," Jordan said softly, and immediately her eyes welled. "Don't go." She couldn't swallow back the lump forming in her throat. She shook her head at him. "You can't leave," she heard herself saying. She saw herself looking weak and pitiful. She heard herself, begging and pathetic. *Stop it, Jordan. STOP.*

But she couldn't stop . . .

*Please don't go,* the voice inside her said. *I can't handle this. I don't have control of myself. You're gonna leave and I'm not going to be able to hold it together and . . . I don't trust myself. I can't trust myself right now. I don't even know . . . who I am right now . . .*

*I don't know who I am without you . . .*

*Stop it, Jordan! Don't do this.*

*Don't be Mom.*

*Don't be weak.*

But it was too late. The look of sadness and . . . *pity* on Harper's face *infuriated* her. He was looking at her like she was *one of them.* The other girls, the women, the chicks that Harper would love bomb and withdraw from when they got too close and began to move him out of his comfort zone. She knew them—and how he treated them—all too well. And now *I'm one of them,* she realized.

*No . . . no . . . no . . . no . . . no no no no!*

And then he said the most terrible thing. "Jordan, baby, I really need you to be my friend right now." He caressed her shoulders.

*Your . . . friend?* That was it, the last kiss on the forehead. *Friend?* The beast was *woke.*

"Your friend?!" Jordan growled. *What about me? What about us?* her heart screamed silently.

"Yeah . . . the fuck, Jordan? I don't have a choice here," Harper only repeated himself.

"Your *friend*?! What the fuck else am I *being,* Harper? Do you not hear yourself?" Jordan felt her eyebrows arch and her nostrils flaring.

Harper's forehead and eyes crinkled in confusion. "Hey, look, Jordan, I'm coming back. I just have to see what's going on and I'll—"

"No," she said loudly, plainly, definitively.

"What?"

"No! Leave, Harper. Get going. Go." Her inner voice was quiet now. There was only anger. Now she wanted him to leave. To hurry up and get on with it. Just go ahead and do what he always did . . . to everyone . . . including her. "I don't care. I don't need you. Get out."

"Jordan, please don't do this—

"Do WHAT?!" She was ferocious now.

Suddenly Harper was silent. Doing nothing other than a hunch of his shoulders and a flip of his hands, giving up.

"Oh, you got nothing to say now?" Jordan wanted to know. She wanted him to be plain.

No, she didn't.

She just wanted him out of her sight.

"I . . . I . . ." Harper continued to fumble.

"Say it," Jordan said again, growling in frustration. "What

don't you want me to do?" But he just stood there, frozen. Stuck, stuck in time like he had never changed at all. He couldn't even be honest. He was going to leave anyway. He was always going to leave. And if he couldn't say it, then Jordan Motherfucking Armstrong would have the balls to do it herself. "You don't want me to be angry? Be emotional? Be clapping back against your selfish ass?! You think I don't know anything about this so-called real-life moment you're having because I don't have children? Fuck you. And take your ass on. Right the fuck now!"

"Jordan." He walked over with his hands out toward her. She recoiled before he even got close.

"Don't fucking touch me!" she said, not knowing that she felt that way, but hearing the words involuntarily leaving her mouth. "I knew your ass was going to do this, Harper!"

"Do what? I'm just going to go see what Mia needs and I'll be back." Harper kept walking toward her and Jordan felt herself inching backward with each one of his steps. The distance between them felt like the miles he was preparing to travel. And she was losing all hope of them ever being able to bridge it again. To come back here, to finally be in the same place and at the same time together, to find that right fit between them ever, ever again. *It was never real, was it?*

"Get out," Jordan heard herself say, low enough to be its own rumble of thunder.

"You can't mean . . ." Harper looked as if he'd been shot. *Good,* Jordan thought. *Now both of us are hurting.*

"GET. THE FUCK. OUT! Get out!"

Harper stood frozen in the middle of the floor, still only in sweats, a chiseled onyx statue. One that Jordan never wanted to see again.

"NOW!" she roared. And she turned to leave him standing there before he saw the first tear fall from her face.

# ACT II

# CHAPTER TWENTY-EIGHT

## Harper

Matching the number on the airplane storage bin above his head to that on his boarding pass, Harper flopped into his business class seat with mental and physical fatigue. He'd grabbed the almost impossibly expensive first flight he could because Mia had made it seem so urgent. But the real cost, he hadn't even yet processed. *What the fuck had that been about?* Thanks to frequent flier miles and disposable income, the first nine hours of a full day of travel would be on a flight with a spacious workstation, catered meals, a lie-flat bed, and unlimited alcohol. Sure, he'd be a zombie changing planes in Amsterdam, but this was the quickest available way to Accra.

The affable male flight attendant stepped over to him with a neatly arranged tray of drinks.

"Can I interest you in water, champagne, or mimosa?"

"Thanks," Harper said, reached for a water, and downed it in one gulp. He checked his phone again. He had sent several "check-in" texts to Jordan. But he received no return messages. *Fuck.* He shook his head in frustration. *I thought she might have cooled off by now* . . . She hadn't. And nothing from Murch either.

He'd made sure to text Julian on his way to the airport. All the drama that he'd been through with Jordan this morning had crystallized for him the unpredictability of the female mind. Because of that, and his tense conversation with Murch last Sunday, Harper didn't want to leave anything to chance. He reread the message he'd sent to Murch at the airport.

> Yo, delete that photo. Delete it. U were right. On my way to Accra now. Too much to explain. I'll hit you. Delete the photo!

It wasn't his most elegant text, but that message needed to be sent right away. He hoped it had arrived on time. Murch was right; blindsiding Robyn was wrong and he couldn't run the risk of that photo being shared, innocently or otherwise. She'd be irate hearing about this new chapter with Jordan from anyone else but him.

"Can I take your jacket, Mr. Stewart?"

Harper handed over his new jacket, the one that had witnessed his incredible night with Jordan at the Hollywood Bowl, and opened up his journal. The writing he'd do today would be robust for sure. "What the fuck, man?" he whispered again. He took a deep breath to settle down and start writing but succeeded only in jotting the date.

Harper couldn't get the sound of his daughter's voice out of his mind. "Mommy needs you," Mia said this morning. She intimated that Robyn was being threatened by a "bad man." When Harper pushed for more details, Mia was vague, like she didn't have the words for it or maybe the right words would have gotten her in trouble. She spoke about the restaurant having a "broken roof" and "stinky food." But she was mostly talking about a "bad man."

"Is it that Kwesi guy, Mia?" Harper asked. She didn't answer directly. She just looked around over her shoulder over FaceTime as if someone might be listening.

"There's bad men here, Daddy" was her response. The sound of her voice was unmistakable. His daughter was scared. It was Harper's job to make her feel safe.

*Daddy loves you and will always be there for you,* Harper had promised.

He wished he understood exactly what was going on so that maybe he didn't have to just pick up and leave. He wanted to stay right where he was. With Jordan. But that was selfish. *Wasn't it?* He was a parent. A divorced parent who hated hearing his daughter feeling alone and helpless halfway across the world. He couldn't do nothing. And if he'd called Robyn? Sure, she's the adult, the co-parent. He could hear her say, *Oh, you're too busy in your life to be there for your daughter in her time of need?* Fuck no. He wasn't going to be "that dad." But Harper had asked Mia to put Mommy on the phone.

"Noooo, Daddy. Please. Don't tell Mommy." Tears were bubbling at the corners of her big eyes, each one pricking at Harper's heart. He could be there quick enough to speak to Robyn in person. And so he decided to do what his little girl asked of him. He had to go; Mia had asked him to and he had promised. And she'd asked him not to tell Robyn.

"Why not?" Harper inquired of his daughter. There was a noticeable pause as Mia looked down and away.

"She told me not to tell." Mia had sounded scared. While under normal circumstances he would have questioned this, lately Robyn *had* been less than transparent. *What secret is Robyn keeping?* This gave Harper nothing but anxiety deep in the pit of his stomach.

"Daddy's coming." But his promise to Mia meant leaving Jordan . . . and now, when she'd asked him to stay? He'd never heard Jordan sound like that.

Maybe he'd have decided differently if Mia hadn't told him Robyn was keeping secrets. Why would Robyn do that? Was she in over her head? Was this new boyfriend . . . *hurting her*? He and Robyn had formed a good co-parenting situation, and they were friends. At least friendly. So why hadn't she told him about this? Then again, she hadn't told him about this tall-ass African dude she was dating . . . and he hadn't told her about his paramours. Why would he? Why would she? That's their respective business. Still, he cared about Robyn. He still loved Robyn. And didn't want anything to happen to her. But he had a bad feeling about Africa. And finally, he had unraveled enough of his jumbled thoughts to write.

> Stop it, Harp. Don't let western propaganda dictate what you feel about an entire fucking continent. Western education and white supremacy have done a number on all of us. Hell, what I've experienced in Accra was pretty nice . . .
>
> I hate being so far away from Mia in times like this. A problem that only daddy could fix. Or at least she thinks only daddy can fix. <u>And fuck yeah, I can fix it. I'm still her hero. And i will be that. damn it . . .</u>
>
> Robyn has always had a lot of pride and even when we were married.
>
> Even if she needed help now she'd try to figure it out herself. She was resilient in that way . . .
>
> <u>Man, I've never seen Jordan so upset like that.</u> The way she said

"don't go." That got me. She was—I don't know—not like the Jordan I've ever seen. It was irrational, crazy. She was so . . . Broken . . . so sad . . . it was all I could do to say no. I tried to reassure her I'd be right back. And when I asked her to be my friend. MY FRIEND, she fucking lost it . . . She acted like I told her to kiss my ass. This is my DAUGHTER we're talking about. She takes precedence over ANYBODY. Even Jordan, my best friend . . . wow. She's so much more than that now. But still that's our foundation. That's history, That's my girl, my peeps. How does she not understand that? Shit, she knows how I feel about her. Doesn't she? Wasn't that evident in the last two weeks? I know I felt it. How could she not?

I need to handle this—whatever "this" is—myself. I don't know what is happening yet and I don't need to bring anyone else into it. I love Jordan and we had an amazing time but that would have been messy. Messier than I've already been . . .

Harper was more tired than he realized. His eyes got heavier and his handwriting trailed off the page. He fell asleep upon takeoff and woke up over Nevada. He immediately checked his phone for any sign from Jordan.

Nothing.

*Shit. So we're back here again . . . ?*

Murch? No. Nothing other than an email from Stan. His way of checking in was to tell him how excited the studio was about the new direction Harper proposed, closing with his real message—with a week to go, "stay focused" and "bring it home." Harper sent a quick reply about how excited he was as well and how great the process had been going. At least, it had been going well . . . when he was with Jordan.

Hours later, long after a snack of nuts and black coffee,

Harper had purged his thoughts once again. When he checked his phone for what felt like the hundredth time for any messages, there was still nothing. Nothing from Murch, nothing from Jordan, nothing at all. *How could that be?* He sipped the last of his coffee and flagged the flight attendant.

"Yes, Mr. Stewart." The uniformed attendant arrived almost immediately. Harper gestured with his coffee cup.

"Yeah, is the Wi-Fi working? And could I get a refill?"

"It should be. I'll go check." He took Harper's coffee cup and napkin before dashing away. Harper stuck his head back into his computer and phone to check the signal again. Minutes later the flight attendant returned with Harper's hot coffee and news.

"Looks like the Wi-Fi was down, but I just rebooted it. Should be on soon."

*No Wi-Fi?* What if Jordan had responded? What if there was something he could say, anything now, to get them back on the right track? It killed him to be stuck with no connection to her, sentenced to his own thoughts and ruminations on ruining the best time of his life. For now, he'd just be haunted by the last words he'd heard her say to him.

*"Just go!"* Jordan had screamed. *"Get the FUCK. OUT!"*

Harper couldn't get her voice and the look on her face out of his head. She may as well have said "Get the fuck out, fuck boy." She didn't even come out of the room to say goodbye. Silence was the feminine death knell of relationships. When a woman's fed up, you are fucked—left on read.

Before leaving Malibu, he heard Jordan on the other side of her bedroom door talking to somebody about her television project and setting up a meeting. He made out the name "Evelyn." Jordan said that she had the "answer" to her question. Somehow, with "Evelyn," she was just as cheery and engaging as ever. A complete contrast to how she'd been coming at Harper just minutes before.

*Jordan Armstrong could turn it on, boy. Maybe she* ***should*** *be a host . . .*

*What is up with this Wi-Fi? Is this shit working or not . . . ?*

"Excuse me?" Harper got the flight attendant's attention as he was serving lunch entrées. "The Wi-Fi? It's still not working."

"Oh. Let me check again. Some of our seats are fine. I'll try another reboot. More coffee? Or are you ready for your lunch?"

"Lunch is fine. Sure. Thanks." Harper wasn't hungry at all and huffed his frustration. He had always been able to compartmentalize. But every time Harper tried to engage with *Unfinished Business,* Jordan's face miraged in front of him in a distracting and unproductive way.

*"You haven't changed one bit!"*

Her words made his head hurt and his heart ache. The flight was only over Utah and there were at least twenty hours of travel left to relive every word.

*"Your selfish ass!"*

*She was hurt, Harp.* He began retracing the steps of the morning. Jordan wouldn't even let him touch her. He was trying to be a good father, keeping a promise. He shook it off and wrote a text to Mia in anticipation of the Wi-Fi working.

Daddy will be there when you get out of school tomorrow. I promise.

The flight attendant returned with Harper's unappetizing lunch. Before Harper could inquire again about the Wi-Fi he saw another flight attendant behind him approaching with a sympathetic smile and a pamphlet and pen between her hands. This was not good.

"Mr. Stewart. I understand you're having trouble logging on to our Wi-Fi?" she said with rhetorical sympathy. *Not good at all.*

"That's correct."

"Right. We're so sorry, but the internet is down for the flight," she said. "We've tried to reboot it several times but we've had no luck—"

"What?" Harper was incredulous. "This is a eight-hour-plus flight. And I don't even know if I'll be able to connect on my layover. I have some urgent matters—"

"—Yes, sir," the flight attendant cut him off with clearly practiced kindness. "We know and we know how loyal customers like you rely on us to provide you with all the services and amenities you're used to."

"And pay for," Harper added while trying to remain calm but factual.

"Of course, sir."

"Fuck," Harper mouthed and jerked his head down and away from the eyes of the flight attendants.

"So, there's *nothing* that can be done?" Harper pleaded. They both shook their heads with as much sincerity and empathy as possible.

"We are so sorry, Mr. Stewart. You are a valued customer, and we really appreciate your business. And by way of apology, we would like to award you with ten thousand miles. . . ."

"What am I gonna do?" Harper asked, as if the attendant had any more answers than he did. "I have some really important emails and texts to send . . . my daughter, and my . . . I just—"

He didn't know how to describe Jordan. His friend? His girlfriend? His lover? His soulmate? All he was given was an airline pamphlet with credit for miles.

*Fuck.*

"And if you need coffee, tea, or something stronger, we got you, sir," the flight attendant said with a wink before leaving. "And you can keep the pen."

Thirty minutes and a sidecar later, now over South Dakota, Harper did his best to shake off the feeling of not knowing anything from the outside world for the next several hours. He tried to make progress on Jackson and Kendall's story, but he found it incredibly hard to concentrate. Somehow what had been smooth about their relationship over the last two weeks now felt inauthentic on the page. Harper had a tough time separating Jordan from Kendall and Jackson from himself. Everything was so . . . *raw.* He really wanted to—no, he *needed* to talk to Jordan.

He tried watching movies, reading a book, listening to music, but he couldn't get his mind right. Sliding back into his seat, Harper reclined to meditate and calm his nerves. With deep breathing he counted down: ten . . . nine . . . eight . . . eyes closed until he reached one. Maybe he could fall asleep and wake up in Amsterdam. . . .

His heart would not settle, his mind would not stop firing. All he could see was Jordan hurt, angry, pleading. After a few beats Harper's eyes snapped open and he lifted his laptop lid. He addressed an email to Jordan. He wanted it to be the most carefully crafted and heartfelt love letter he could manage. If he couldn't reach her, he would write until he made it undeniable. He just wanted to be clear and sincere. He wanted Jordan to feel what he was feeling. When the Wi-Fi returned, it would be ready, perfect.

From: Harper Stewart

To: Jordan Armstrong

Subject: US

Jordan, I'm stuck on this airplane, with no Wi-Fi, going crazy because I haven't heard anything from you. I have no idea how you're feeling other than how we left each other this morning. I hated leaving you like that. I am sorry I made you so upset. Leaving was a painful decision. Please know and understand that I did not want to leave. I am devastated that you were hurt by it.

But I want to be clear, I'm never choosing anyone over my daughter. Mia will always have her father's attention. I'm sorry if that is unacceptable to you and if it is, as painful as it is to say, then we can't have a future.

Jesus. Even writing those words is causing me an ulcer, Jordan. A pain in my heart because I can't see a future without you. Now that we've gotten here, Jordan, how can we go back? Or worse, how can we NOT move forward? Together. We can work this out. I know we can. I love you. I've loved you since we were teenagers. I've never stopped loving you. The past two weeks weren't just a new love discovery. It is us. It is our destiny. And it should be fulfilled. You are what I've been waiting for, what I've been missing in my life. I want to do so much with you and <u>for</u> you. We belong together, Jordan. You can't tell me that you don't feel it too.

I need you, Jordan. I mean it. I know you felt it these past few weeks. These have been some of the most incredible times of my life. Now that we've crossed this barrier I can't turn back. Can you? Can you really say you don't need me too? That you don't love me? I can't. I need you, Jordan. I have so many things that a person could want: money, success, loyal friends, a great career, but I don't have you.

I've been kicked out of my life since Robyn divorced me. Nothing fits anymore. You are my missing piece of the puzzle. I can't guarantee it, but if you're back in my life in the way we've been in each other's lives the past 2 weeks I KNOW we could be in this for the rest of our lives. The rest of our lives is NOW Jordan. Whatever happened this morning isn't insurmountable. We can work this out. Say your piece and whip me into shape like you always have. Maybe I'm not supposed to have it all, but damn it I want to try, Jordan. I hope that you do too.

I love you with all my heart, body, and soul,
Harper

# CHAPTER TWENTY-NINE

## Robyn

Robyn hustled to the school building, her mind on the red red stew she'd left simmering. It smelled so fragrant with aromatics of ginger and scotch bonnet pepper filling the kitchen. With the extra cooking time, it would be thick and hearty to pair with the fufu she had the staff prepare. She was in her own head and moving so fast that she didn't hear someone call out to her.

"Robyn?" Robyn looked around but didn't slow down. She had to get to Mia's classroom, scoop her up, and get back to Robyn's Nest in time for the dinner rush. "Robyn!" the voice bellowed again. Robyn finally stopped and turned around. She spotted Ms. Ekuwa, her daughter's teacher, tending to another one of her students reuniting with her parents, a white couple. Robyn sighed at the reminder, the irony that even in a country run and buoyed by Black people, there was still the presence of whiteness looking for privilege. Perhaps the times had changed and these white ones would do better than what others had done in the not-so-distant past. . . .

"Hey, Ms. Ekuwa," Robyn said as the teacher approached

with a smile and slight look of bewilderment on her face. "Sorry, I didn't hear you. Always on the go. How'd Mia do today?"

"She was great as always," Ms. Ekuwa said. "But . . . did you forget something?" *What?* Robyn's skin between her eyes crinkled.

"Forget something? I'm here to pick up Mia as usual."

"Mia has already left," Ms. Ekuwa replied, looking confused now.

Robyn was sure she hadn't heard her correctly. She cocked her head, frowned, and pursed her lips before responding.

"Already left? With whom?" Robyn had a lot going on, but she was positive she hadn't told anyone to pick up Mia today. Haniah was out running errands at Makola and maybe she picked up Mia? She wouldn't have asked Kwesi.

"Her dad," Ms. Ekuwa responded with a bit less assurance in her tone.

"Her *dad*? Her dad is five thousand miles away in New York," Robyn shot back, now feeling the start of a cold sweat of panic.

"Yes, her dad. He was here," Ms. Ekuwa said matter-of-factly.

"Ms. Ekuwa, that's impossible. Are you sure?" Ms. Ekuwa nodded assuredly.

"Yes. I've seen your husband before. The author. It was him. He looked tired."

"*Ex*-husband," Robyn corrected her.

"Right. My apologies. Mia had talked about his visit all day and rushed into his arms when she saw him," Ms. Ekuwa reported.

"What?" Robyn's head was spinning. *Mia spoke about it?* Her mind raced back to drop-off this morning. Mia had been unusually quiet, but Robyn didn't think anything of it, chalking it up to moody preteen stuff. Ms. Ekuwa interrupted her thoughts politely.

"I'm sorry, Robyn, I didn't know that you were unaware. He *is* authorized to pick her up—"

"With *my permission,*" Robyn snapped back. Ms. Ekuwa looked taken aback, making Robyn quickly realize her tone hadn't matched Ms. Ekuwa's own polite one. Yet she remained courteous and firm.

"Robyn, with all due respect, that is not true." Robyn shifted her stance, squaring off with her daughter's teacher, expecting but not getting an acceptable explanation. Ms. Ekuwa continued, "Listen, I am sorry about this. I feel terrible if there's been some kind of miscommunication between you—" She paused without judgment, kind. Robyn took a breath. Ever since she placed Mia in this school's care Ms. Ekuwa was one of many welcoming, nurturing teachers that Robyn felt a strong rapport with. She was part of Robyn's extended village and had always been supportive. But now, this moment . . . when she should have been on her side, she wasn't. But it wasn't Ms. Ekuwa's fault, Robyn reminded herself. It was . . . *Harper*. That's who her issue was with. And that was who she was about to deal with. *Right now.*

Robyn exhaled as she spun on her heels and headed back to the school parking lot with determination and urgency. "Robyn, I'm sorry—!" Robyn heard Ms. Ekuwa's words behind her back as she whipped out her phone to call Harper. She wanted fucking answers. *Now.* She pulled open her car door, dropped in the driver's seat as her call went straight to voicemail.

"Harper, what are you doing here in Accra? Call me when you get this. As *soon* as you get this." Her voice was neither measured nor calm. Robyn was agitated as she cranked up her RAV4 and pulled out of the school parking lot, drawing up dust under her wheels. Some parents grabbed their children closer to them as Robyn sped past. In the rearview, she stared back at her own tense face—a deadly serious Black momma. Robyn's countenance wouldn't change at all, all the way back to Robyn's Nest. She wanted her daughter—***and*** her goddamn father—to see it. And if by any chance it wasn't Harper, then God help whoever it was. But somehow, Robyn already knew. She let out an audible sigh as her RAV4 rumbled down the road at least ten kilometers over the posted speed limit.

Speeding down the street she almost missed the voicemail notification on her phone's display. She never paid attention to her smartphone most days, instead preferring the restaurant's landline where the people who needed to reach her did. She was already a slave to the restaurant, there was no room left to be a slave to her device. Needing to check her voicemail now only added to her agitation. Because as she'd both hoped and suspected, the voicemail was from Harper. "What the fuck?" she said aloud. She pressed play on Harper's message, telling her he just got off the plane and was picking up Mia. *Got off the plane? What plane?*

"Why the hell are you here, Harper?" Robyn mused out loud. As the dots were connecting, her nerves began to calm, but not her anger and certainly not her confusion. She was confused as hell. And angry. No, she was pissed! *What is so urgent that Mr. Harper Stewart would take time out of his busy schedule to fly halfway around the world to Ghana and then pick Mia up from school? And Mia had known about it? This little girl is keeping secrets from her momma?!* Robyn tried to grasp the entire situation. How dare he *and* she keep this from her? *What is this about?*

"Call Robyn's Nest," Robyn commanded her phone. After a few rings, Haniah picked up.

"Robyn?" Haniah said through the din of kitchen noise.

"Yes, Haniah. What's going on? Is Mia there?" Robyn asked with the tone of a woman not to be fucked with.

With a mischievous note in her voice, Haniah responded, "Yes, she is. She is here having a snack with her daddy . . . And Kwesi is here as well."

Robyn's teeth and lips folded back into her mouth as she took a full five seconds before speaking. "I'm less than ten minutes out," she said and pushed the pedal to the floor of her RAV4.

Robyn's heartbeat was pounding in her ears by the time she stepped across the threshold into Robyn's Nest. The scene unfolding in the center of the restaurant was impossible to believe. There, in front of her, standing on the far side of the room was . . . *Harper? Harper Stewart, in Ghana. In Ghana? And Kwesi?* That was surely Kwesi, with his broad shoulders and tall frame, facing away from her but closest to the door. And Harper was pointing a finger right in Kwesi's direction.

"No, you don't talk to her, you talk to me," Harper said loudly, pushing Mia defensively behind him. Robyn's mouth dropped open.

"Listen, bruv," Kwesi said, thankfully sounding much calmer, especially relative to a strangely hostile Harper. "I'm not sure you've got the right guy. Everything is cool, everyone knows me. . . ."

"Just what is going on?" Robyn called out, finally snapped out of shock and walking with quickened pace to stand between the two men. "Harper, what are you doing here?"

Both Kwesi and Harper seemed stunned to see her approaching. Surprising to Robyn, given that she was who they'd been talking about and it was her damn restaurant. But Harper turned to her and spoke first, just as hostile as he'd been earlier, defiant, like he was ready to defend some square of territory. Of which he had absolutely none in East Legon. He was here, on her turf. In her space. *Uninvited.*

"I'm here, Robyn, because our daughter asked me to be here," he said. "Because there is clearly some kind of problem with . . . *him.*" Harper gestured toward Kwesi, who, thankfully for Robyn, didn't seem to be taking much offense to the rapidly escalating insanity. Whatever *this* was, whatever was going on, and whoever started it, Robyn resolved to get to the bottom of it, and quickly.

"Harper, there is no problem with *him.* This is Kwesi, and he's . . . a friend. I'm sure Mia wouldn't call you about *Kwesi,* so there must be some kind of mistake."

"Oh no, the mistake here is not mine, Robyn." Harper did not seem to be backing down at all. Behind him, Mia cowered silently. Robyn narrowed her eyes in a moment of rapid assessment. *If Mia called Harper . . . about . . . Kwesi?* But Harper interrupted her thoughts. "And Mia said that there was a man who came around causing a problem here. And evidently the roof is leaking, there have been floods, and you're delinquent on rent so, your *friend* here doesn't seem like much help to me."

Robyn felt a sharp stab of horror at Harper's words. First, the nerve! And second, there were the obvious issues that Kwesi had helped with and offered more help beyond that, but Robyn wanted to fix her own mess. She hadn't come to Accra to create the same situation she'd left back home. But Kwesi wasn't to blame. And Mia? Why would Mia call Harper and tell him anything about Kwesi? *Unless . . .* Robyn thought back to the day Mia sat at her usual spot at the family-style table doing her homework, when Aboagye made a bit of a scene, Kwesi took him outside . . . him coming back in . . . *Oh God. She saw.* Behind those big brown eyes of Mia's was a quick mind. Robyn was constantly surprised by her daughter, and some surprises were better than others.

Robyn turned to look at Mia, ignoring Harper's comments about Kwesi for the moment. Mia gazed back at her mother with obvious trepidation. "Did you call your father about Mr. Kwesi?" Robyn asked her directly. If she was old enough to make big-girl phone calls, Mia was old enough to answer for herself.

Mia looked down and shuffled her toe into the ground.

"Mimi. Tell me what is going on here." Still, silence from Mia.

Robyn felt a warm hand on her arm and then heard Kwesi's voice. Calm and soothing. "Look, Robyn, it seems like you've got a bit of a family thing happening here and you could use some . . . privacy." Kwesi's eyes subtly gestured to the staff that was paying attention to this center-stage fracas. "I'm going to get going. And . . . umm, see you later?" *Later?* Robyn almost forgot their date that evening. They were meant to spend what time they could together before Kwesi left for his latest trip. There was no way Harper was changing that. She turned to Kwesi.

"Yes, Kwesi. Absolutely. Later is good. I'll have gotten to the bottom of this by then. And figured out exactly *who* owes you an apology." She turned the heat of her gaze back to Harper and Mia. "You two, in my office. *Now.*"

As Robyn ushered her ex-husband and her daughter through to the back of the restaurant, she turned only briefly to look back at Kwesi. She hated to see him leave, especially like this. But this situation needed explanation and resolution right away. She gave a weak, tired smile to Kwesi, who waved as he exited, then turned back to follow behind Harper and Mia as they entered her office next to the kitchen that was just starting to smell like dinner preparations.

# CHAPTER THIRTY

## Harper

The march across Robyn's Nest, through the kitchen and into Robyn's office, felt to Harper like a long walk to the principal's office after he'd gotten into a schoolyard fight. Except, while his body was still bristled for confrontation, there hadn't actually been a fight. Not to say there wouldn't be. Nonetheless, how could this Kwesi character, all six foot four and chiseled, already feel so comfortable around his family?

Passing through the kitchen, the wafting food smells were unfamiliar yet intoxicating and immediately set off an embarrassing rumble of hunger in his stomach. Since those in-flight short ribs, he hadn't eaten, nor had he stopped to think or reflect at all on what circumstance he was actually in. Mia had called, said there was trouble, and he'd reacted. *That was enough,* Harper reminded himself. Yet, by the time his hand touched the doorframe of Robyn's office and his foot went through the entry, he started to feel the slightest weakening of his resolve. Clearly, there was more to this story.

"Mia," Robyn said, arms folded, "it's time to explain yourself, young lady. What's this about you calling your father? And why didn't you speak to me first?"

Harper's eyes traveled to Mia. Instinctually, he wanted to protect her, even here and now. She was so small, so vulnerable. His heart ached about having her here, so far away from him. He should be the one to look after her, not some new dude, Kwesi, or whatever his name was. Mia looked at him, tears brimming in her eyes. It took every bit of restraint not to pull her into his arms and comfort her, to shield her.

"Mia?" Robyn repeated.

Harper forced himself to let go of Mia's hand. He kneeled to meet her eyes. "Mia, I'm here now. You're safe. Mommy's safe. You can say what happened." Still, Mia was quiet, looking like a small animal in headlights. Harper decided he'd support her in telling her story. "Didn't you say, there was a dangerous man, and that Mommy was in trouble?"

"Trouble? What man?" Robyn interrupted. She was angry and that didn't seem to be helping Mia along.

"Well, Robyn, *who* could she be talking about? Clearly, she's not as comfortable as you are with whoever it is you have coming around."

"Harper, you need to back down." Robyn's face was clouded over now, tight. It'd been so long since he'd seen her like this, or since they'd even come to a place of real confrontation. But the results didn't lie. He'd seen with his own eyes the run-down refrigerator, the buckets in the corner, the look of a place that wasn't anywhere near the spit shine of a New York establishment, even to Robyn's standards. Something here was off and he knew it.

"Kwesi is not causing any trouble." Robyn said firmly. She turned to Mia again. "Is he, Mimi?"

"Hey, take it easy on her—" Harper tried to intervene.

"Uh-uh." Robyn held a halting pointer finger up toward Harper. "*Your daughter* is going to answer." Robyn turned to Mia again. “What did you see, Mia? Why did you call your father and tell him to come here?”

“She doesn’t need a reason to call me, Robyn!” Harper regretted his tone, but anger was getting the best of him. He didn’t approve of anyone jumping bad with his daughter.

“Harper, this isn’t about you. You shouldn’t be here.”

He felt his own voice rumble in his chest. “You can’t tell me where I belong—”

“You heard correctly!” Robyn retorted. “The audacity of you traveling *five thousand* miles—” she shouted over him.

“Daddy! I’m sorry!” Mia’s voice cried out into the room, startling Harper, who by now was braced in his core for an argument. He drew his gaze away from Robyn to right down at his side. “Don’t fight, please?” Mia blubbered and tears streaked down her cheeks. In a confusing whirlwind of emotion, Harper’s instinct to protect won easily. He dropped to a crouch on the floor and took her into his arms immediately. He was all reaction, all love, all anger, all sadness, wrapped together with his arms around his child. Only then could he look at Robyn, who seemed equally stunned, suspended in time.

“What is going on, baby?” He wiped tears from her face. “Why are you sorry? You don’t have to be sorry, ever. You called and Daddy came. I told you I would always come. You know that, right?”

Mia nodded slowly and pushed her next tears away with a small fist.

“Then what is it? What can’t you say?” Harper looked at Robyn, who seemed to be waiting just as he was for an answer.

Mia sniffled once again, shuddering her whole body. And time seemed to stand still, pregnant with all the possibilities of what she might say, or that she might still say nothing at all. But finally, she did begin to speak.

"Daddy, I'm . . . sorry." *Sorry?* "I . . . called you because . . . I thought Mommy was in trouble and I thought you could help." She spilled out all the words in her little-girl mumble and punctuated them with another sniffle.

Robyn's face crinkled with concern. "In trouble with whom, Mia?" She approached, joining them in a crouch, four eyes now focused directly on Mia.

"There . . . there was a man . . ."

"Was it Kwesi?" Harper asked.

"Stop it, okay?" Robyn answered.

"Let Mia answer that," he replied sharply. No reason for Robyn to keep defending this man who obviously made their daughter uncomfortable.

"No, it wasn't Kwesi," Mia said. Harper cocked his head and parted his lips to form a question. *Wasn't Kwesi?* The disclosure was short-circuiting Harper's mind.

"It was another man . . . with a round tummy and sunglasses. He wanted money from Mommy."

"Aboagye . . ." Robyn said quietly. *Robyn needs money? Hasn't she been getting the alimony checks? Ohh boy, Robyn . . . And who the hell is Aboagye?* "Mia, did you call your father because you saw me talking to Aboagye? That's the only reason?" Mia shook her head no. "Did you see me with Mr. Kwesi?" Mia nodded yes. And Robyn took a deep, long breath. Harper could see the fatigue in her, on her face, and the look of instant recognition. Now he was on the outside of the moment.

"What is going on, Robyn?" Harper asked.

Robyn's eyes never left Mia's face. "It seems," she said slowly, "that our daughter hasn't been completely honest with either of us. Isn't that right, Mia?"

Harper swiveled to look at Mia. And with disbelief, he watched as she nodded, *yes.*

*Yes? My Mia? Dishonest?* It was impossible for Harper to process. After all, he was here, in Accra. And not to even imagine what he'd left, or *who* he'd left. Or *how* he'd left. He pushed Jordan's voice from his mind, and the seared image of her telling him to go when he'd insisted he needed to be here. *He did need to be here, right?* He prayed silently for Mia's response, one that wouldn't make him out to be a fool.

"Mia," Robin repeated, insistently. "Did you call your father because you saw me kiss Mr. Kwesi?"

"Kiss?" It was already reaching the limits of what Harper could process. He looked from Mia to Robyn. Robyn cut her eyes at her ex-husband before standing up and looking down at her daughter.

"I see," Robyn said, standing now, arms folded again in her momma stance.

"Mia, you owe your father—and me—and Mr. Kwesi an apology."

"You don't owe me an apology, baby," Harper reassured Mia. "And you do not have to apologize to that dude."

"Oh yes, she does. And so do you." Robyn looked right at Harper. Then she got very close in Mia's face and pointed at her. "What you did was extremely selfish and irresponsible, young lady. You scared Mommy and Daddy half to death. How dare you." Mia lowered her eyes and the teardrops fell to the floor.

Harper couldn't allow another second of this. "Hey, hey," he intervened.

Without looking at her ex-husband, Robyn fired back.

"I am the parent here, in Accra, with our child. My entire afternoon was upended because Mia was dishonest. And sneaky." Robyn looked back at Mia. "I am very disappointed in you." Harper had heard those words before and they still hurt him to hear as an adult, even directed toward Mia. For her, hearing it from her own mother looked like she'd received a gut punch.

"Robyn, you see she's—"

"No. No." Robyn shut him down. "You're supposed to be an adult. I have enough going on here without you inserting yourself in my parenting and my personal life." *Inserting?* Robyn turned to Mia. "Go to the bathroom and clean yourself up."

"Yes, Mommy," Mia's quavering voice responded, and she rushed herself toward the staff bathroom. Harper watched her go, feeling for her, wanting to comfort her, but was frozen still, overwhelmed with the feeling that he had made a *very* big blunder.

"Robyn, don't you think —?" Harper tried to say.

"I don't have time to think, thank you very much." Robyn grabbed her chef's apron and called out to her staff from her open office door. "Okay, let's fire those prawns . . . !"

At that moment it was clear to Harper that a whole world—Robyn's world—was functioning without him. How well, he wasn't exactly sure.

## CHAPTER THIRTY-ONE

# Jordan

Even before Harper's plane took off for Ghana, Jordan had already scheduled a follow-up meeting with Evelyn. As he was saying the words that she'd heard him say so many other times, that he's "gotta go"—words he'd said to and about the other women he'd left when things got too intimate—she already knew she'd need something on the other side of the fathomless gulf of his absence. He'd been in her bed, in her mind, in her skin, in her heart. She'd foolishly allowed him to have all of her, *all of her,* and still, she'd passed through his heart like an open net. Harper didn't want to be in love. He wanted to be admired. She'd made it too easy for him, broken her rules, and that was her mistake.

Mistakes could be corrected, however, and while she had given Harper her heart, he had given her one thing in return that he couldn't take back. Not his love or his devotion. She didn't need that. Harper had helped her understand that she had a story. And with that story, she had a voice. She was supposed to be the host of her show. That's how it would sell. And so, the piece of Harper that she had remaining, the piece of *herself* that he'd given her, the key to her next chapter, she was going to hold on to that, because she'd never be able to hold on to him.

So who had time to cry, to think, to wallow when she had a new pitch to finalize? Evelyn fortuitously had Los Angeles on her travel calendar, giving Jordan just forty-eight hours to prepare, to turn her focus entirely on herself and make the worker bee she'd been into the queen.

Today, the honeybees were abuzz in the bedroom suite of Jordan's Malibu home. Typically by midmorning, her resting quarters and dressing space were a place of relaxation, offering a perfect view out of a wall of glass onto the glory of the ocean's undulations in the distance. But today was not a day for rest because Jordan Motherfucking Armstrong was back. In just hours she would dazzle Evelyn during an otherwise impossible-to-get face-to-face television network meeting. Over crudités and spinach dip, she'd unlock the door that had been blocking her future. She was clear on it. Her show idea was brilliant. She just needed a new way to bring it to life—not behind the camera this time, but in front of it. That realization was the eureka! moment, from a flood of insight that had crystallized all at once, and Jordan wasted no time in acting upon it.

"How about this option, Jordan?" Reese, her stylist, was holding up a hanging concoction of a draped silk color-block dress and suede boots with a dose of fringe on the side.

"Who's the designer?" Jordan inquired.

Without hesitation, or looking at a single tag, Reese flipped her ponytail of locs and replied in rapid staccato, "Dress is Gucci, boots Ferragamo. Bag for this look . . . I'm thinking the Bottega."

"Hmm . . ." Jordan contemplated. "I like the dress, but we need something different for the accessories. No boots. Something higher on the heel, sexy. I want all eyes on me, Reese."

"Ummm, okaaayyy, Miss Jordan," Kai, Jordan's hairstylist, purred from behind her. A tendril of hair was in Kai's hand, ready to meet the flat iron for a perfect ribbon curl. That hair was going to walk its own runway when Jordan entered her meeting. Kai knew exactly how to make sure of that. And Jordan knew how to command attention, to hit the exact right professional note. She was suited for this, the queen bee amid a flurry of attention. She had no time to think, which was perfect, given Harper's many half-assed attempts to contact her. *A waste of time,* she thought, remembering the text messages and the email she'd received. *Or maybe it was emails?* She saw them all come in, but read none of them, even though, at moments it was tempting. But Harper was a man of many words, convincing words, words he shared with the world. What she wanted was the part of him that was hers and hers alone. The part of him she didn't have to share because he wouldn't leave her when she most needed him to stay. When she'd *asked. Pathetic.* She pushed the memory out of her mind.

Jordan felt hands patting around the top of her hair, finger styling the silky curls as they turned into flowing waves almost magically in Kai's hands. "You betta be going out with somebody's son after this," Kai said. "You look like a million dollars, Miss Hunty."

"A *billion* dollars, boo," Tanisha corrected, approaching with a feathered eyelash pinched between tweezers. "And once I put on this three-comma-red lip, Ms. Jordan Armstrong is going to be in full effect. Watch out, Oprah!" The room broke out in easy laughter, and Jordan let herself relax into the expert finishing touches on her look for the day. This was comfortable, a foreshadowing of what life would be like, her new life, as a television host of her *own* show. So many times she'd created platforms for others, propulsion systems for stars to form and shine, and left behind a legacy of brilliant choices and tastemaking storytelling. Only now, the story she'd tell would be her own. And with it, she'd tell the story of millions of other women, millions of her sisters in culture, Black women who needed to *truly* have it all, and not just by counting their net worth. She'd usher in a new era of happiness, of health and wholeness, with new definitions. And she'd start right here, with moving on in epic leveling-up fashion.

"You know I saw you at the Bowl for the Isley Brothers with a bald-headed zaddy who looked *expensive,* gurl. Tell me you didn't throw that catch back, because he was foine foine."

Jordan tried not to move her head, even though it threatened to move on its own, to physically shake the thought of Harper out of her mind. *No, hell, no,* she thought.

"That . . . was . . . just . . . a friend. A friend from college," she said very matter-of-factly.

"If you say so, hunty!" Kai shrieked, and the room broke out again in laughs. Jordan remained tight-lipped and thankful for the makeup application. She didn't want to miss a single comma of that so-called three-comma-red lip Tanisha was applying. And it was good cover. She didn't want her face to show a thing, especially not letting on to her moment of atypical foolishness, thinking stupidly that an old dog, a *fifty-year-old* dog, could learn new tricks. And so what about those calls, and voicemails, and whatever long assed email that was sitting in her inbox? *Distractions,* she thought and forced herself to refocus. *That's right, Jordan, keep your mind clear and centered on the one thing that matters.* This meeting with Evelyn was her *real* second chance. *Harper's doing his thing . . . cool. No hard feelings because I'm gonna do mine. Not on some silly memoir shit, a book that nobody wants to read. Think pieces and podcasts are for amateurs. Shelby was right: I can be a household name overnight. It's not hard.*

Her modest social media presence was deliberate. Once she ignited the right team, people would know Jordan Motherfucking Armstrong and all her accomplishments in an instant. *I'm going straight to broadcast. My message in millions of homes, my face, my words, my voice. I'll leave the books to Harper and leave Harper . . . alone.*

"That's it, babe. You're all set." Tanisha's voice was Jordan's cue to open her eyes. All the hands around her had stopped their flurry. She looked in the mirror and blinked, seeing the image of perfectly laid ebony beach waves against her shoulders. Immaculate contouring on flawless brown skin. The perfect slant to eyes set under a careful fringe of lashes. And yes, Tanisha had applied a money-making boss-bitch pouty red on her mouth with showstopping expertise.

"Perfect," Jordan said, pushing herself out of her chair to slip on the dress waiting for her. All Jordan could see was her name on the show marquee while her stomach roiled with an equal mix of excitement and fear.

# CHAPTER THIRTY-TWO

## Harper

Harper fumbled his way through Robyn's kitchen as a guest in her home. It was a modern contemporary, spacious and open, but still modest. Very . . . *Robyn.* Each time he'd been there, it was strange to observe the purity of her choices, a home as a true extension of just her. And he felt like he learned more about her every time. The square gray tiles on the floor were a nice complement to the earth-toned walls adorned with boldly colored Ghanaian artwork that Robyn had chosen, made by local painters and sculptors. There were massive portraits of Black women with full lips, bold hairstyles, and curvy shapes presiding over the living room, while expansive landscapes bursting with bright greens, oranges, yellows, and reds took up the remaining space. Plants decorated the floors, windows, and her backyard, which was complete with a patio and a hammock. Even her small garden was flourishing, in sharp contrast to the one she had built back in the day at their Upper West Side brownstone. Her neighborhood of Airport Hills was gated and quiet, a few minutes and a world away from Accra's bustling city center. It was a nice place to settle and maybe even grow up.

After searching through the refrigerator and cabinets, Harper managed to assemble all the ingredients for lamb kebabs and started to prepare the dish from memory. Whether Harper liked it or not, Robyn had made it clear before they'd left the restaurant that she had a date and was keeping it. She'd been planning on letting Mia sleep over at Haniah's apartment. But Harper didn't want to leave Mia that night, so he "inserted" himself. He was in Accra for her after all, so why not spend the time with his daughter? He warmed some pita and got a salad together with some fresh tomatoes, local greens, and mint from Robyn's garden as he took a sip from a red blend he'd opened. Setting the vibe was music that he didn't know by name, but was some female Afrobeats artist named Efya that Robyn had put on. It certainly felt very Robyn: old school, sonically acoustic, and soothing.

Harper sipped his wine, waiting for the lamb kebabs in the oven to sizzle their way to a perfectly timed tenderness. During a moment of stillness—Robyn was getting ready and Mia was in her own room—he reflected on how in the hell he'd found himself in Ghana. *What had Mia been thinking causing that kind of panic?* Harper wondered. He was still in disbelief over her admission at Robyn's Nest. Clearly, her call was about something deeper—it had to be. Maybe Mia had still not fully accepted her mom and dad's divorce. But she hadn't acted out before.

Harper thought back to his own childhood. He grew up a happy kid in Montclair, New Jersey, with both parents under one roof his entire life. His parents had conflict and arguments and the like, but they always seemed to work it out. Of course, Harper and Robyn grew up when divorce was in the zeitgeist in the eighties. Women had autonomy like never before in history and decided what *they* wanted from love and marriage. Husbands would have to adjust or the wives were choosing self-determination. At that time, it seemed like divorce was everywhere, leaving men like Dustin Hoffman's characters stuffing bread into a glass of egg yolk trying to make French toast "like Mommy." Even through spats, Harper's folks laughed off the notion of separating. His dad let him know divorce was "expensive" and it was "cheaper to keep her." His mom let him know marriage was hard sometimes and folks had disagreements, but you work through them, look at the bigger picture, and try to be good partners to one another.

*Had I been a good partner to Robyn?* Harper wondered. Had he looked at the bigger picture? Maybe and maybe not. Mia was in distress and yes, she needed to mature and grow up, but had they been fair to her? Was this somehow their fault? Mia had gotten caught in the middle of their midlife crises—three years ago Harper had been so busy feeling sorry for himself and Robyn had been unflinching in her decision to uproot herself from America. Especially now, he couldn't help but wonder how these life changes were actually affecting her. Harper had muffled his doubts with FaceTime, expensive gifts and gadgets, elaborate trips, and taking transatlantic trips like a commuter just to be with her. Clearly now, he saw that none of that was the same as being in her life day-to-day.

At the timer ding, Harper pulled the lamb kebabs out of the oven and put the dish on the counter, admiring his handiwork with a deep inhale of the savory aromas he'd created. Before Harper could take another sip of wine from his glass, the doorbell rang.

"Grab that, please!" Robyn bellowed from her bedroom. Harper looked toward the home's entrance, took a small breath, crossed to it, and opened the heavy wooden doors. The open entryway revealed a tall, dark, well-built brother with a bouquet of flowers. Kwesi in his very sharp African-inspired ensemble. An outfit Harper didn't think he could pull off, but this dude was like a model.

"Hey, man. Those for me?" Harper remarked at the sight of begonias, trying to keep things light between them given their inauspicious first meeting. Kwesi didn't really seem to get it. Or simply was not amused. He certainly looked surprised to see Harper opening the door.

"Ummm, no. They're for Robyn," he responded with that damn elegant accent, sounding cooler than cool, with charm in his faint smile, clearly waiting to be invited in. *This dude . . .*

"I'm just joking, bro." Harper made sure his tone was jovial. "Come on in. Robyn's still getting ready. You know how it is . . ." He gestured for Kwesi to enter with a sweep of his arm. "I'll take those." Harper pointed at the flowers. Kwesi hesitated, looking at Harper before he handed them over as he walked in.

"Sure." Kwesi walked past Harper into the foyer. His size was imposing. Harper found himself looking up at the dude, with his expensive outfit and cologne on.

Harper offered to put the bouquet in water. "I'm sure there's a vase around here somewhere. She used to collect them back home." He headed to the kitchen, trying to play the hospitable host. It was far easier than a straightforward apology. "Can I get you something to drink?" Harper said as he retreated into Robyn's kitchen.

"Oh no, I'm fine," Kwesi said as he stood awkwardly in the doorway by the patio.

"It's no trouble, man. I already got this red blend poured that I'm sipping on. It's pretty tasty." Harper gestured toward the open bottle on the counter as he searched Robyn's cabinets for a vase.

"Ahh," Kwesi said with an air of recognition. "That's from my vineyard." It wasn't boastful or arrogant. Just matter-of-fact. Harper was confused for a beat, looked at the bottle, then back at Kwesi.

"You have a *vineyard*?"

"Not mine solely. Just part of an investment group. Me and my buddies," Kwesi responded casually. "I could ship you a case if you'd like."

"Ohhh, that's generous of you. Thanks," Harper answered. But suddenly he was done with wine for tonight. He instead found the vase and began to carefully unwrap the flowers. He saw Kwesi watching him closely.

"Make yourself at home. Have a seat," Harper said as he filled the vase with the flower stems and then poured water from the faucet into it. Kwesi took a seat on the couch in the sunken living room.

"Robyn! Your ummm, your . . . Kwesi is here!" Harper awkwardly called out.

"Thank you! Be out in a minute!" Robyn returned. Harper grabbed his wineglass for show and joined Kwesi in the living room.

"Trust me, that means at least another ten," Harper opined as he took a seat on the neighboring easy chair. "Sooo, you from here or . . . ?"

"Born and raised. Went to university in London but spent many summers and holidays with my parents and grandparents here. I claim Ghana more than anything else. You?"

"New Jersey. Born and raised. Live in Brooklyn now."

"Oh, I love Brooklyn."

"You been? Oh cool. Yeah. I heard it's different now than when I was growing up, but change happens. . . ."

"It does." Kwesi nodded along with Harper into more seconds of awkward silence. Harper searched his mind for something else to say.

"So that dude, Abo— Aba— Guy ya? Guy ye . . ?"

"Aboagye," Kwesi corrected.

"Yeah, him. He's the landlord I guess?" Kwesi nodded. "Do you have any idea why the rent has to be paid so far in advance?"

Kwesi brought his broad shoulders into a shrug. "I just met him the other day. Don't know him, personally. It's just the way it is, I suppose. The way it's always been. Some traditions are hard to break."

"So change happens, but not here. . . ."

Kwesi paused to consider Harper's semi-question, semi-statement. "I think the notion is they also figure that Americans and Europeans have money, so they'd rather collect up front. Particularly since much of their wealth has been off colonization," Kwesi responded.

"But Robyn's *Black,*" Harper offered, then gestured between them. "*We're* Black. This guy seems to be screwing her over."

"Some landlords are an unscrupulous lot. But I spoke with him to do what was necessary to get repairs done and stop him from showing up unannounced until he does."

Harper considered Kwesi's words, then nodded. He wished he could find a reply that was better or cooler than "Thanks. Robyn could use the support, I'm sure."

"Whatever Robyn wants to do to keep her business alive I want to support her." Kwesi seemed sincere. "She's a special woman." As if Harper didn't already know that? *Of course, Robyn's special. I married her. Does dude think he's telling me something?* Harper's inner voice was giving him agita. His face was cool, however.

"That she is. No doubt." Harper tried to maintain his calm.

After a beat Kwesi responded with a smirk. "Well, you must have had *some* doubt, right?"

*What?* Dude was looking right in his face with a slight, nearly imperceptible smile. Harper, to maintain composure, looked down at the floor and away from Kwesi's gaze to gather his response. "Well, marriage—relationships are . . . complicated." Harper turned his head to face Kwesi with his final word.

Kwesi lifted his chin, broadened his smile, and nodded. "Amen, bruv. Complicated, indeed. But I'm working hard to make it less complicated as I get older. At least that's my plan." It sounded like he was going to say more like "my plan with Robyn." He didn't, but Harper was sure he heard it.

"I hear that." Harper meant that in more ways than one.

"So . . . what's *your* plan?" Kwesi asked. *Nigga, what?* Harper cocked his head sideways at Kwesi's expectant stare.

"Sorry to keep you waiting," Robyn announced as she breezed into the room wearing a wrap dress you might see Accra socialite women wearing, alluring but not overly sexy. Shoulders exposed, waist accentuated. Kwesi took a beat before pulling his eyes away from Harper, turning to Robyn with a smile and rising to greet the queen in their presence. Harper's eyes lingered where Kwesi had been seated for just a second before he shook it off with a scoff. *This dude . . .*

"No worries, luv. I would have waited longer for this result." Kwesi dropped that compliment like a veteran of relationships (complicated or not). "You look amazing."

She did. Robyn looked as gorgeous as Harper had ever seen her. Her bright multicolored dress hugged her curves, perfectly celebrating her shape. Her cleavage was tasteful and inviting. Kwesi leaned in to kiss her and Robyn gave him her cheek. Harper noted it. *For my benefit?* he wondered.

"I don't want to get lipstick on you," Robyn said, smiling. She turned toward the kitchen. "Oh my God, did you bring these for me? They're gorgeous." *Women really do love flowers,* Harper noted. He was out of practice.

"Of course." Kwesi's smile was brilliant now, beaming at Robyn with pride.

"You look nice," Harper added abruptly.

Robyn started to respond just as Mia entered the room in her pajamas and some DVDs fanned out for Harper. "Is it time for dinner, Daddy? What are we gonna watch?"

"Hello, Ms. Mia," Kwesi said.

"Hi." Mia's response was flat, not rude, but not exactly warm either.

"Doesn't Mommy look pretty?" Harper asked Mia.

"She helped me get ready." Robyn beamed at Mia.

"Uh-huh," Mia responded without looking at Robyn.

"Isn't that sweet?" Harper smiled. "Maybe you can help Daddy improve his look. Get him looking handsome before he hits these Cantonments streets," Harper said. Right away, Mia looked confused.

"You're going with them, Daddy?"

"No, honey . . ." Robyn said quickly.

"I could. We all could go." Harper tried to sound like he was kidding.

"Harper . . ." Robyn cut her eyes at him.

"I'm playing." He looked from Robyn to Mia with a smile. "I'm playing, honey."

"Not funny, Daddy."

"You know we have a whole night planned of kebabs, My Little Pony, and *Supa Team 4,* and we need to get some reading done before bed," Harper assured her.

"Sounds like a full evening," Kwesi remarked.

"Yup." Mia's gaze never left her father in the entire exchange. Harper noticed, pulled his daughter into a loving embrace, and kissed her forehead.

"Y'all have a good time, and we'll see you when you get back."

"Harper . . ." Robyn warned. It was one word, but it communicated so much.

"Oh. Oh. Ohhhhh. Right." Harper too communicated a lot with an economy of words. "Of course. Have a good time. We won't wait up . . ."

Robyn made motions toward leaving. "Mia, come give me a good-night kiss." Mia, who had settled on the couch, exhaled without looking at her mom.

"You come to me," she responded, not budging.

"Excuse me?" Robyn and Harper both snapped their heads around to her.

"Mia. Be nice. And show your mother respect or you can go to bed right now," Harper commanded. She looked at him, did a slight eye roll, and got up.

"You're already on thin ice, young lady." Robyn pursed her lips. Her daughter marched up to her and turned on a fake smile, cocking her head to one side and stepping on her tiptoes to kiss her mom's cheek.

"Bye," Mia said and headed back to the couch with Harper.

"Okay. Remember, your daddy will be going back to New York at some point," Robyn warned. "And it'll just be me and you. Okay?" Mia shrugged without looking at her mother. Robyn headed toward the door as Kwesi ushered them out but then turned back to look at Harper. "You two enjoy yourselves," she said, eyebrows raised on her face. The look in her eyes said, *Your problem now, Harper,* as she headed out of the door with Kwesi.

# CHAPTER THIRTY-THREE

## Jordan

When Jordan crossed through the doors of Little Beach House Malibu wearing dark designer shades and that three-comma lip, she felt satisfied that she'd left absolutely nothing to chance. With the sounds of the ocean's gentle roar in the background and the ambient low-volume Euro synth music playing, the space felt chic and like the right place to set up her very glamorous future. She strode past the bar and through the patio with the same degree of possession and comfort as if this place was also her own beachfront cottage. She tried to ignore the fact that just next door, a few steps down the beach, was Nobu. Weeks prior, it had been the scene of a table of sidecars and Sables leading to an epic night with . . . *No, push that thought away, stay focused, Jordan.*

The reaction of the surrounding patrons was all the mirror she needed—the swiveling heads, the briefly stalled conversations, the looks on the faces of much more famous people trying to figure out how they knew her. She even overheard the star of this week's box-office topper literally say, "Who is that?" in a terrible attempt at a discreet whisper. But that's what Jordan wanted, to shut the room down. When she decided to be undeniable, she was exactly that.

It didn't take long until she saw Evelyn seated at the back corner table, looking at the menu she held in her hand, waiting patiently, just as Jordan had planned it. She'd told the hostess to make her guest comfortable, seated at her usual table facing the ocean. Jordan was going to make an entrance. She walked in long strides, her dress flowing around her, looking like luxury, all the way until she reached the empty seat waiting for her. Evelyn looked up as Jordan approached and did her own double take, her own perfectly set copper face registering shock. She gathered herself and stood up to greet Jordan, reaching her arms out to give her a warm, but nearly reverent hug. Jordan leaned in and then pulled back, letting the flow of the silk fabric draping her body slink its way down to proper position. And there was a reason for the heels after all, as she wanted the height to give her the proper aura. She didn't at all mind if it came across as imposing, in fact, she preferred it. After the long-armed hugs and air-kisses, Jordan took the seat with her back to the view of the water.

"Evelyn, sorry to get in the way of your view," Jordan said with a smile.

"I think the best view, here, honestly, is of *you*," Evelyn said as Jordan casually set her bag down next to her. "Jordan, you look amazing."

"So do you, *Ev.* You look great." Jordan decided to take time for pleasantries. Things were already off to the perfect beginning.

"Well, you know, I'm doing my best. Something about working on East Coast time in Los Angeles takes its toll, you know?"

"I know it well. Reminds me of my many trips for the network. I can't say I'm sorry to have given that up."

"Yeah, you had the right idea. I could get used to this." Evelyn relaxed back into her chair and picked up the menu again.

"Get whatever you want," Jordan offered. "It's on me of course. I just appreciate you taking the meeting on such short notice."

Evelyn looked up and smiled. "It was great timing. I had a trip to LA on the calendar and an open lunch slot. I'm glad we could make it work. And of course, anything for Jordan Armstrong, the woman who mentored me through the wild terrain of the executive ranks."

Jordan couldn't hide the smile that stretched across her face. She had, in fact, mentored Evelyn and so many others. It was rewarding to be able to give back, especially with everything she went through to make it to the top, tough decisions and all. "It has been a long time . . ." she said, releasing a breath of air and memory, all at once. This meeting, this moment was the culmination of everything she'd learned and taught. About television and show business, and everything that could be done better. In fact, she was literally about to burst from all the ideas bubbling up inside her about how to make the show a success. There was no need to wait for the food to come, Jordan was ready to kick it off right now. "So, the notes you gave, on the pitch . . ."

Evelyn raised an eyebrow and then shifted in her seat. "Yeah, I'm sorry, Jordan, that was—"

Jordan cut her off. Apologies weren't necessary. Evelyn had given her everything she needed. "That meeting was *perfect.*" Jordan gave her megawatt smile. "In fact, it was the perfect feedback to unlock the future of this show's success. I got it—*I'm* it." Jordan paused for dramatic effect, having delivered the great "Ta-da!" straight and direct.

"I'm sorry, what?" Evelyn looked confused.

"I'm it. I'm the host. I get it," Jordan corrected.

Evelyn still looked as if she didn't understand what Jordan was referring to. She looked . . . shocked.

"I . . . can't say I know what we're talking about here, J. Did we give some kind of note that—"

"You said—and I remember this clearly—you said, 'why should we care?' And that you needed someone you could sell as a host. That was a perfect point because you were right. The show was lacking specific perspective. It needed a host with an authentic connection to the subject matter. A story. Who could speak to the topics with authenticity and vulnerability—"

"Jordan?" The tone in Evelyn's voice stopped Jordan cold in her tracks.

"What?"

"Jordan." Evelyn took a deep breath. "I've known you for what, twenty years? And, truth be told, I don't even know your middle name other than 'motherfucking,' which, by the way, is epic in its own right."

"And you're saying that to say what, Ev?"

"Just that, you're not exactly the poster child for vulnerability."

"Well, I haven't been, but . . . that doesn't mean that I wouldn't be, or that I couldn't be. I'm willing to bring all of myself to this show."

Evelyn leaned forward. "Okay, so you're telling me that you're willing now, to open the curtains on your entire life? Become a social media fixture? Open yourself to public opinion? Every embarrassing moment, every failure, every upset, every insecurity up for examination? Your love life, your dating history, your family drama, your choice to have children or not have children. Whether or not you're married. All of that . . . and more, by the way, you're willing to share with the entire rest of the world? Right now?"

Jordan took a deep sigh without meaning to. She was ready

for all of this, even some slight bit of skepticism from Evelyn. But in preparing the perfect pitch, she hadn't so much expected a confrontation with the reality of what the show would actually mean for her. She was going to tell her story. Be her story. But she was ready to win, as she always did, and as she would today.

"Look, I get what you're saying. I spent decades running defense for all of my talent, trying to keep them off the pages of tabloids, and protecting what bit of privacy they could hold on to. Believe me, I understand the sacrifice. But that's the least of our concerns here. There's no one better than me to shepherd this idea through the development process, to helm a production, to make sure that we chart, to delight the advertisers and keep viewers coming back day after day. This show is my story. I'm the one who made it to the other side to talk about it. This is what it looks like, Evelyn. I am what it looks like." Jordan felt some cool air hit her back. Fuck, she was sweating. She never sweat, and certainly not in Gucci. She studied Evelyn's face. By now, Evelyn had leaned back in her seat, settled her elbows on the armrests, and made a thinking steeple with her fingers that covered her lips. It seemed like an eternity passed like that before Evelyn dropped her arms, leaned forward again, and finally opened her mouth to speak.

"Jordan, let me just ask you this—*If* you were me . . . *when,* I should say. When you were me, would you have made you the host of a show? With no recent platform, no social media presence, no audience? Would you buy that show?"

Evelyn's words hit Jordan as a bullet would, right to her chest, pushing her backward with the impact of succinct, clear truth. Jordan swallowed hard, and the taste of bile crept up in her throat. She felt nauseous, and woozy. She remembered how she'd been in a flash, the standards she held. The brash callousness required to make the decisions they made daily about talent, especially in front of the camera. *Fuck.* "Why would anyone care? Why should we care?" The words from her meeting in New York began to swirl in her mind, blocking out oxygen. She felt like she could barely breathe, let alone sit there another minute. She needed to get out of there, right away.

"Jordan, are you . . . okay?" Evelyn said, looking concerned. "Listen, I have a meeting with Garcelle's agent while I'm here. Why don't I—"

Jordan looked around frantically, breathing in to keep the tears welling in the corners of her eyes from dropping down. Already, Evelyn was a blur of earth tones in front of her. She scooted her chair back in a loud screech against the floor and grabbed her bag, dropping her napkin on the seat.

"You know what, thank you," she said, fully standing now and turned toward the door. "I've . . . got . . . a . . . thing. I've gotta go. I mean . . . I'll talk to you later."

"Jordan . . . don't—" Evelyn's words barely hit Jordan's ears as she swept past the bar and pushed her shades onto her face to catch the water trailing down her cheeks. But the real tears didn't start until she made it into the driver's seat of her car and shut the door. Then she began to sob.

# CHAPTER THIRTY-FOUR

## Harper

The remnants of Harper's assembled dinner sat in the center of the dining table, and Mia finished the last bits of what was on her plate. He'd just seen his ex-wife off on a date, and adding to the already unbelievable series of events, his sweet daughter Mia was exhibiting disrespectful behavior that he'd never envisioned from her. He poked at his plate, deciding how he was going to address his daughter.

"Mia," he began. She turned to look at him. "Listen to me. I don't want you to be disrespectful to Mom. Or Mr. Kwesi. It's not cool. You're already on punishment. Don't make it worse. Okay?"

Mia looked down at her plate, then eventually nodded without looking at him. Then she slid her seat closer to him and wrapped her arms around his torso to snuggle closer. Harper couldn't help but meet her warm embrace with his own.

"I'm sorry, Daddy," Mia said into his chest.

"You ought to be. You gave Daddy a real scare." Harper kissed the top of her head.

"I know," Mia said softly.

"Daddy loves you and will do anything for you. But you shouldn't be lying to get what you want. Don't ever do that again."

"I'm sorry to mess up work. I know it's important."

Harper tipped her chin up so that he could look in her eyes. He wanted to make sure she heard him. "Work is not more important than you, honey."

Mia met his eyes. "Okay," she said, but her tone was unconvinced, taking Harper aback.

"Wait. No. Is that what you think?"

Mia shrugged. "I don't know. I just know it's important and brings us money so we can live good."

"Live well."

"Live *well,*" Mia corrected herself.

Harper had to take in what his daughter was saying about his priorities. What she felt they were. How that didn't align with what she meant to him. What he'd always thought his priorities were. The truth of the matter was that before Mia called him to come, he wasn't *just* working. Mia's daddy had been making a real connection with her Auntie Jordan. In *love.* Or so he thought. But now, here, he wasn't working, not yet, and it seemed like he'd really set things back with their new chapter. And he wondered if Jordan, just like Mia, had a different view of where she stood in his life.

He let Mia pick the show they'd watch together, and then he'd stop parenting for a little while. So he could focus on Jordan, who, after numerous texts, voicemails, and emails, hadn't responded. He did however get a thumbs-up emoji from Murch in response to his distress signal to delete *that* photo. Harper could concentrate on mending fences with Jordan, then discuss it with Robyn. In the meantime, Kwesi had given him an idea: If Jordan wasn't responding to words, he'd find a Malibu florist to shower her with a much more impressive order than the one sitting in Robyn's kitchen. It'd at least be more than words.

Harper picked the largest arrangement he could find on the florist's website, of white and red roses and greenery, and specified the accompanying note for Jordan, one that he hoped would get him back in her good graces even before he returned.

*Longing to hold you in my arms again.*
*Love Harper.*

With one eye on Mia, who was happily engaged in their movie, he confirmed the order as quickly as he could. He didn't want to make her further confused about his priorities. He was there, after all, to be with her, no matter that she'd called him under false pretenses. He'd needed to see what was happening here, to know how Mia felt, and how she'd been presumably acting out because of it. Something was going on here not just with Mia, but also with his ex-wife.

Robyn was hiding something. Not about her relationship so much, but her business. Up to now, Harper had taken a kind of "I told you so" stance with her taking off to Accra like she did. He had resolved to let the chips fall where they may. But something about seeing her here, once again in this environment, showed him how the motherland did suit Robyn. Things hadn't gotten any better or easier in the States. She had the chance to be reborn here, and she'd taken it despite the stressors that seemed to be mounting. She was managing, but maybe she could use some assistance. Mia certainly could. She had fallen asleep snuggled up next to him. Harper covered her with a throw blanket. He knew he should put her to bed, but he liked having her right there. She was growing up so quickly. And he was only getting glimpses half a world away.

Harper had a hard time believing in a higher power when he was younger. He saw many instances that changed his mind as an adult. And now he fully believed in destiny and things happening the way they were supposed to. So, despite the circumstances that had brought him to Accra, Harper felt he was *supposed* to be there. Be here with Mia and witness Robyn in all her splendor and all her challenges with the restaurant. And to have an opportunity to tell her in person about Jordan. He owed her that. As he tucked Mia into her bed, he felt that somehow, everything would work out in the right way. He'd make sure Mia knew she was his priority, get Robyn sorted, and find his way back to Jordan.

With Mia asleep, Harper showered and settled in to relax on Robyn's couch to check his phone. Still nothing from Jordan. He checked the delivery confirmation for the flowers. It said they'd been deposited at her front door. *She'll get them soon*, he thought, and wondered what she was doing. *Hiking? Having a latte? Journaling? Maybe thinking about me too* . . . Harper sighed. It was driving him crazy not knowing. Harper enlisted the fellas with the group chat. After filling them in, they all agreed in a cascade of advice.

Just keep the lines of communication open.

Tell Jordan you'll be back in a few more days.

Quentin put it more succinctly.

Y'all waited 30 years, what's a few more days?

Communication was the right call. *Why don't I just call her?* Harper hit the button to dial Jordan and got her voicemail, again, except this time, it was full. He followed up with a text that he'd be just a few days longer and hoped she understood. That he wanted to keep the lines of communication open. He wanted to talk to her. It had been two days for him, but it felt like a lifetime ago since he'd spoken to Jordan. At least the Jordan that he thought he was going to spend the rest of his life with. He wanted her to know that she was his priority also.

Harper, finally feeling the effects of travel on his body, lay on the couch, with a pillow under his head and neck, ready to drift off to sleep. The living room lights were already off, and the nearby window was bringing in a soothing breeze. Harper grabbed his sleep mask from the side table and placed it on his head, primed to slide it down over his eyes. He took one last look at his phone and . . . *are those text bubbles?* Finally in his text exchange with Jordan, he saw the three dots of a forthcoming reply. *She must have gotten the flowers,* Harper thought. Excitedly, he sat up on one elbow to see what she'd say. Bubble, no bubbles, bubbles again, no bubbles. It is maddening . . . *technology.* Harper was barely breathing. Finally, the message came through.

Leave me alone.

*What?* Then he received the automated indicator that her notifications were set to silent. *Did she just block me?* He stared at the words in disbelief. *Am I dreaming?* No. The message was clear. Harper's stomach dropped and churned. He read the words again.

Leave me alone.

# CHAPTER THIRTY-FIVE

## Robyn

Kwesi and Robyn had settled into a booth at Nsuom-Nam. Robyn was intimately familiar with this fine dining establishment whose name translated into "food of the sea." She loved to sample the dishes from other creators—Accra's culinary scene was exploding with creativity and perspective. It was inspiring. But Robyn was on edge and already two glasses of prosecco in before they were brought their starter of kelewele, roasted sweet plantain with ginger, pepper, and a touch of nutmeg. The overdue rent for her own restaurant, her daughter's preteen rebellious stage, her ex-husband's unwarranted and unwanted presence, and her current beau leaving town tomorrow, it was a lot—enough to drive her to drink. But if she could manage to relax, this would make for an ideal evening. The setting was beautiful, alive and boisterous with happy well-dressed patrons in their "Friday wear" African print—Ghanaians would proudly display their colors, designs, and style that were completely their own, not influenced by Western fashion. Robyn and Kwesi were about to experience a curated menu, and she was trying her best to enjoy it without being preoccupied by the confluence of stressful circumstances working her nerves. Hence the prosecco. As usual Kwesi was attentive, if not a bit intrusive. Robyn was working hard to distinguish between the two. Maybe the second glass of bubbly would do what the first hadn't managed in mellowing out her insides. Kwesi rubbed her outer thigh.

"You doing okay?"

"Yes. Why do you keep asking me that?" Robyn asked, trying to dampen the edge in her voice.

"Well, because your actions are betraying your words," Kwesi responded.

"What do you want me to say, Kwesi?"

Kwesi placed his hand over hers on the table. His hand was massive, firm, warm, and soft. His touch offered a modicum of calm.

"I want you to tell me what's on your mind. What's going on in there?" He pointed with his other hand to her head.

"I don't want to ruin the evening." Robyn shifted in her seat.

"Well, we're not exactly off to a roaring start." Kwesi smiled.

"And what does that mean?"

"Come on now, luv. There's tension here. And it makes no sense to keep it inside." Kwesi's brow furrowed. "Tell me, should I be worried about your ex?"

"My ex is at least my *ex*," Robyn retorted sharply.

"Robyn . . ." Kwesi's face looked disappointed. "I told you . . . we are *not* together."

Robyn wasn't trying to pick a fight with Kwesi. But the complexity of his circumstances was much harder to accept when her own life felt so acutely unsettled. "No, you just *look like* you're together. For the 'sake of the kids.'" Robyn pulled her hand away from his to make air quotes and then tried to sip her already drained champagne flute.

Kwesi took a deep breath. "I don't mean to bring more stress to your life. I want to be a stress reliever, not make it complicated." His face showed sincere concern.

Robyn closed her eyes to reset for a moment, trying to muster her usual disposition. *Relax, Robyn,* she told herself, then replied, "Well, it's complicated for me. All of it is." With that, she signaled the waitstaff for a refill. "You go on holiday with your wife. Should I be concerned about that? You're not even divorced. How am I supposed to take that?" She turned to Kwesi, eyes pleading for an answer she could accept. He took a deep breath and leaned forward toward her.

"For one it's cheaper," he began, seeming to consider his words. "Divorce is expensive, and we wanted our family unit together. We do some holidays together. Mainly, we do separate things . . . but it took a while. For the kids, they've known there's been a change, but they rolled with it. They see us. So, it's kind of 'divorce light'? I don't know what I'd call it, but for now it's working. She's free to see who she wants as am I. It all works somehow. We're probably the most honest we've been with one another since we've known each other." The freedom of "honesty" resonated with Robyn. Kwesi continued, "That's important. If you're honest with Harper and vice versa everything should be okay. Unless he's an arsehole."

*Harper, an 'arsehole'?* Robyn laughed. "He's not that bad. We've had a better relationship since we broke up. At least . . . more mature." Kwesi seemed to relax as Robyn continued. "And as far as Harper is concerned, I *did not* tell him to come here and play house." Robyn looked at Kwesi to meet his eyes. "That was Mia's doing."

Kwesi nodded. "She misses her dad. I get it. But I want you to know I'm not intimidated by the situation." The tone of his reply was confident and sincere. He added, "I guess it's partially because I understand complexity. But I know what it is and how

I feel about you. It's not easy, but we're honest. Robyn . . . I want this."

"Why?" Robyn wondered aloud. "It's so . . . messy." Kwesi studied her for a moment before replying, his eyes moving across her face in the dim illumination at their intimate table for two.

"I see a beautiful woman who is intelligent, resilient, nurturing, and makes some of the most delicious inventive dishes I've ever tasted. It would definitely make me fat if I wasn't careful." Robyn smiled. Kwesi continued, "I mean who cooks with cocoa butter?" Robyn laughed and blushed a little. "You're a selfless individual. You deserve to get back what you put out in the world."

Briefly interrupting, the waitress brought their second course of the braised oxtail and Swahili coconut fish. The complex aromas filled the air at the table.

"I know who I am and who you are," Kwesi continued.

"You think you know me?"

Kwesi nodded. "I think so. And I'm not trying to replace Mia's father. Harper is Mia's father, but I *do* want to be your man." Kwesi smiled at her. Robyn's insides warmed. She wasn't sure if the prosecco was kicking in or if it was Kwesi's words, his dark eyes, and tantalizing lips that were making her feel this way. But it really didn't matter.

At the end of their courses, Kwesi spoon-fed Robyn their hibiscus sorbet dessert. "Robyn, I want you to believe in us," he said. "I don't care how complicated it gets. I'm not going *anywhere.*" Kwesi caressed the side of her face with his smooth, soft hand. Robyn leaned into his warmth. "I'm asking you to take a leap of faith with us." Ironically, Robyn had said those very words to Harper several times during their marriage—a leap of faith on them, a leap of faith on her, a leap of faith on the future of Robyn's Nest. Harper couldn't do it. He *wouldn't.* She'd doubted herself, doubted her instincts following his lead. She didn't want to be led. Now she wanted to lead.

Despite the tension she'd been feeling all night, Kwesi had succeeded in making her understand more about him as a man. He was very thoughtful, smart, ambitious, driven too—much like Harper—but also attentive, protective, empowering. She felt safe with him. And their sex? *Mmmm . . . yes.* She was planning on getting some for sure tonight, before he left on his trip. Thinking of the work he'd be putting in to make her remember him turned her on. *Is that selfish?* she wondered. *Yes.* And it was about time.

## CHAPTER THIRTY-SIX

# Jordan

The sound of layered guitars filled Jordan's otherwise empty home as the sneaky beginning of the Gap Band's "Yearning for Your Love" cascaded through her surround sound speakers.

*You can't keep running in and outta my liiiife.*

"Shut the fuck up, Charlie Wilson," Jordan muttered back at the voice singing to her. For four days following her debacle with Evelyn, Jordan had been nearly immobile in her bed surrounded by her plushy down comforter and large pillows. The big-ass arrangement of unimaginative roses she'd received from Harper had already started to droop and rot from their position by her door, unmoved from the moment she dragged them inside. If she hadn't wanted to keep people out of her business, she would have left them at her roadside door, right where the Malibu florist deposited them. Her shades were drawn, and food delivery boxes littered her overflowing bedroom garbage can. If she had the energy to roll over and find her phone, she'd fast-forward the song immediately. As with nearly everything, it made her think of Harper, and fuck Charlie Wilson for singing so well as to compound her feelings.

It hadn't just been her playlist of songs trying to reach her. Despite several texts and voicemails from Shelby, Dr. Clark, and of course Harper, Jordan had responded to no one. Shelby's last message an hour ago was a threat to send the police for a wellness check. Jordan couldn't remember when she last showered or when she even looked in a mirror. She didn't want to see the woman who looked like she felt and certainly didn't want the police to either. She struggled to find her phone, first to stop that fucking song from playing, and second to send a preemptive note to Shelby.

I'm fine.

Shelby wrote back immediately, wanting proof of life.

Show me, read Shelby's text.

Jordan typed back, No.

Then I'm getting on a plane.

Jordan sighed heavily. Shelby, I'm fine.

Bullshit. Let me see. Send me a picture.

Call me.

Then Shelby's face showed up on Jordan's phone screen. Of course she declined her call.

Pick up.

I'm not facetiming with you, Jordan typed back.

Shelby rang again. Jordan declined again.

I'm going to keep calling.

Jordan rolled her eyes, knowing that if one person would make good on the threat to take a cross-country trip to break into her place, it was Shelby. "Fuuuuuuuuck!" Jordan yelled into the air.

Hold on!!

The texts stopped for a moment. Jordan took a big swig of water, swished it around in her cruddy mouth. She swallowed to coat her throat so she wouldn't sound like death warmed over. Jordan briefly thought about turning off her phone but reminded herself that wouldn't work, not with Shelby. Best to let Shelby talk, let her hear her voice. After a deep sigh Jordan dialed back. Shelby picked up immediately.

"Hey."

"Hi," Jordan responded.

"Oh my God, you sound terrible."

Jordan sighed loudly. "That's why I didn't want to talk."

"Okay. I'm sorry. I'm just worried about you." Shelby was showing her soft side again. If Jordan could smile—even just a little bit—she would.

"Thanks, Shelby. I'm okay though." After Jordan's string of monosyllabic answers to Shelby's inquiries about her well-being, she wanted the tea.

*What happened with Harper?* Jordan wasn't really in the mood to rehash but she was going to put Shelby on a clock.

"What was so urgent that he had to leave?"

"Something with his daughter," Jordan said flatly.

"Well, you can't blame him for that. He's a parent. And his

daughter was eight thousand miles away, J." Shelby's explanation was accurate, but annoying.

"I *know* that. Everything in me knows that's the logical reason and answer. Still . . ."

"Well, he's coming back, right?"

"I don't know. He left. I don't care."

"Judging from how you sound, you care." Shelby paused. Jordan didn't object. "I bet if he rang your doorbell you would care." Jordan pulled her phone away from her to look at it.

"He hasn't rung the doorbell, so I wouldn't know. Not that I want to have a pity party," Jordan said.

"So why are you? You sound like hell. You haven't answered the phone. You're wallowing. Why?" Shelby pressed her.

Jordan didn't have an immediate answer. "I don't know." Jordan's voice wobbled and began to break. Tears started to flood her eyes. She cried without speaking for thirty seconds and Shelby let her. She gave her space. Then through tears and staccato breaths Jordan confessed, "I'm fucked up, Shelby. I'm really fucked up, but the answer isn't waiting on Harper." Jordan sniffed with a heavy inhale.

"Ohhh, honey. You're right it's not." Shelby's love and concern flowed through the phone. "Are you sure I can't come there? We'll get dressed, have some spa time, get some retail therapy."

"No. I don't want that. I don't want to do anything." Jordan hated how pathetic she sounded. Shelby was one of the last people she wanted to be vulnerable with, but she was giving Jordan grace. To a point.

"Jordan, I know you're working through this, but . . . *this* isn't you," Shelby warned. "Look, go through your process, get it all out, a good cry is necessary, but don't stay there. Get some air, get some exercise, get some sun, and stop listening to sad music."

Jordan really did hope Harper would ring her buzzer, and

stop sending words, flowers, and promises. But she wasn't going to beg him to come back. She'd practically begged him to stay. She *had* begged him to stay. He was either going to show up for her or not. Either way she was giving him her ass to kiss.

"I hear you," Jordan said. "I gotta go."

"Okay . . ." Shelby sounded hesitant. "Are you at least keeping your appointments with Dr. Clark?"

*Dr. Clark? Shit.* Jordan did some quick math thinking back to when she'd had her last appointment. She'd canceled when Harper was visiting, and then after he left, canceled again. "My next appointment is in two days, Shelby."

"Good. And check in with me too, or I swear to God, forty-eight hours from now, I'm going to be in your bed with you."

"Fine. Goodbye, Shelby." Jordan hung up the phone without waiting.

She knew Shelby was right, but it all sounded exhausting. Sure, she couldn't stay stuck, but she just felt so heavy. She didn't want to move, get dressed, or socialize. Not even wash herself. And she didn't have to. It almost made her miss the pull of work, when she was required to split how she felt from what she did. Based on how she felt now, she just wanted to be, to float, to exist. Jordan didn't know who the fuck she was right now. And she had to find out.

"Hi, Dr. Clark." Jordan tried to sound as cheery as she could two days later. She'd kept her appointment but changed it to telehealth to try to keep her promise to Shelby. *Baby-steps,* she thought. Seeing Dr. Clark on a smaller screen was somehow a bit more intimidating than seeing her in person. That didn't seem possible. And there was no candle.

"Hello, Jordan. Is everything okay?" Dr. Clark inquired through the screen with those stylish fucking glasses. *What the fuck? Why is she starting with that?*

"Everything's fine. Why do you ask?" Jordan used her best "curious why you ask" voice.

"Well, you've missed our last few sessions and now for the first time ever, we're meeting via video. Why haven't you been to see me?" Dr. Clark asked.

"Oh, I've, y'know, just been busy. Lots going on," Jordan lied.

"Are you prioritizing your health and yourself?" Dr. Clark probed in her unique way.

"Oh, yes, journaling, that sort of thing," Jordan lied again. She hadn't written a word since Harper left.

"Mmmm. Any new revelations?" Dr. Clark asked.

*Sure. I unlocked painful memories about my childhood that I haven't dealt with. I'm in love with a man who I've loved my entire adult life, who opened my heart, filled it with love, intimacy, joy, and then left an open wound.*

"No. Not really," Jordan said as casually as she could. She looked at the time. She still had almost the full hour to go.

Dr. Clark stared at Jordan through the phone and inhaled audibly. "I see. So, how can I help you today, Jordan?"

"Ummm, I don't know. I was just checking in. It's been a while." Jordan stalled as cheerfully as she could.

"Why don't you come in? I'd really like to see you."

Jordan's stomach churned.

"Ohh, yeah. Of course. Sure. I-I-I'd like to see you too. But video feels pretty good though," Jordan stammered through her reply.

"Well, I can barely see you." Dr. Clark leaned in toward the screen. "Are you on your phone? Are you in your bed?"

*What is this, an interrogation?*

"I'm minding my fucking business, mind yours," Jordan snapped. *Shit.* Whatever small movements Dr. Clark had been exhibiting before this moment came to an abrupt stop and her eyes froze on the screen. *Oh shit, did I say that out loud?*

"I'm sorry. I'm so sorry. I'm just . . . I'm, oh God . . ." Jordan thought their connection may have been lost with how expressionless Dr. Clark had become. "I just, I don't know why I said that." Dr. Clark stayed motionless. "Hello?" Jordan inquired.

After another beat, Dr. Clark blinked slowly, took a short inhale, and licked her lips. "Jordan . . . I understand." Dr. Clark's voice came out measured and remarkably calm. Meanwhile, Jordan's heart was beating quickly, racing with panic. She wasn't ready, wasn't herself. Needed . . . out. "Setting boundaries is necessary. We've been working on that. But if you put them up with me, I can't help you." Jordan felt the stinging in her eyes. She wasn't about to do *that.* She couldn't.

"You know what, you're right," Jordan responded quickly. "You're absolutely right." Dr. Clark nodded and waited for Jordan to continue. She did. "I can't do this on the phone. I'll reach out to your office when I have a better idea of my schedule. . . ."

Dr. Clark leaned forward in Jordan's screen. "Jordan, I can wait and we could schedule it together right now—"

Jordan cut her off. "Yeah, I don't have my calendar in front of me and I have a new temp assistant who is switching me over to another kind of software. It's all very technical—I don't understand it. Generation Z's got it, so I'll have my girl call your girl. Take care . . . speak soon . . ."

Before Dr. Clark could respond with the *J* in Jordan, Jordan hung up. She sat in her darkened room hearing the waves crash up against the shore. Outside, someone on the beach was chattering and laughing with others. The evening sun was softly peeking through her blinds, making the way for night.

*I need to get out of here . . .* she thought, feeling suffocated. Too many feelings, too many thoughts, too much . . . drifting. Dr. Clark couldn't help her—she needed to help herself. The way her father would. Attack the problem, get over it. Move forward. Be rational. She exhaled. Did she have to go in on Harper so badly? Wasn't she the one who told him to leave? *I could have been more understanding, right?* Maybe he was just worried about Mia. *Maybe I took it too personally?*

*Maybe . . . I . . . should read the email he sent,* she thought. Nothing could make her feel worse than her state now.

Jordan went over to her bedroom desk. She cleared the In-N-Out wrappers and Insomnia Cookies boxes off the top of her laptop. She sat at her desk and slowly lifted open the screen like what was inside would bite. *Read it, Jordan. If you cry, you cry; if you get pissed you get pissed. Just open it.* She scrolled through her emails and found the first of several from Harper dated one week ago entitled "US." Jordan swallowed and braced herself for what that meant.

Harper described how he didn't have Wi-Fi and was being driven crazy by not being in communication with her. *Good, that was by design. I'm glad you felt bad,* Jordan thought. Harper went on to apologize for making her so upset and how he didn't want to leave. *Why did you leave, then, when I asked you to stay?* That hurting her was devastating to him. *Hmm,* she thought and softened. But then it went south. "I'm not choosing any woman over my daughter and if that's unacceptable to you then . . ." *Any woman? Any woman?* Jordan slammed her laptop shut before she exploded.

"Nope," Jordan said. She looked back at her bed and as messy as it was, it looked inviting. She'd send her check-in to Shelby. Maybe she'd order sushi. She picked up her phone to find her favorite food delivery service. But there was a text already waiting. One from . . .

Hey Jordan, it's Brian McDonald.

I hope this is still your number. I'm on the west coast and thought about you.

I'm around for a few days and would love to take you to dinner if you're free. Something I want to discuss with you.

*Brian?* Immediately, memories of her relationship with him came to mind. *That smile, those dimples, those hands, that tongue.* Jordan dated Brian over ten years ago. She broke up with him. But she had loved him. For the first time in her life she had considered marrying a white boy. He'd made her think about having some beige babies and taking Mediterranean vacations looking like a family in a Polo ad. But she knew her *Ebony* magazine cover of a brown nuclear family would always lurk in the back of her mind. That wouldn't have been fair to him. Or her. So she broke it off. But now . . . he could break *her* off. Something he wanted to "discuss." Yeah, she liked his approach: respectful. The thought of reuniting with Brian and enjoying all his gifts started lifting Jordan from her funk. *Yes* . . . she thought. *This is exactly what I need.* The saying was: the best way to get over a lover was to get under another. *I'm a bad bitch,* Jordan reminded herself. *I'm desirable. But this time, the pussy leads. . . .*

## CHAPTER THIRTY-SEVEN

# Harper

As six more days in Ghana passed by, with no progress made on the studio pitch, Harper left his hotel gym ready for his reckoning with Stan. Stan, who thought he was in Hawaii—*making progress*—had aligned time zones for a check-in call. In Accra, now, neither was true.

"What the hell are you doing in Ghana?" Stan's voice came through loud and clear on Harper's phone speaker. "You're not supposed to be there until next month . . ."

Harper looked at the phone on his hotel bed and reached for a clean shirt in the drawer. He shook the wrinkles out and pulled it on over his head.

"I know, Stan."

"Is everything okay? With Robyn, with Mia?"

Harper took a big, long breath before responding. That answer was still complicated. "Yes, fine." Harper had no way to gauge how true that was without getting into the details of everything that had happened in his life over the past month. And that was something he didn't want to do now with Stan.

Over the past six days, Harper had been at his hotel, settled in as he would be on a regular visit to see Mia. But this was no ordinary visit. Not only did Robyn think it wasn't a good idea for him to stay at her place, even with Kwesi out of town, but two nights on her couch weren't exactly the most comfortable accommodations Accra could offer. More than that it wouldn't be good to send Mia any mixed messages, especially now. Robyn had clearly stated, "We're not changing for this little girl." Harper agreed. Mia needed to understand that Mommy and Daddy are not together, that Daddy only visited when he was supposed to and *if* he was needed. After the stunt she pulled, best to keep the routine.

Stan paused for a bit, but Harper wasn't offering any elaboration to fill the silence. Stan got straight to the point. "So . . . how are the pitch pages coming?"

"Fine," Harper responded. Stan also didn't need to know that Harper hadn't really worked on it, especially since he'd already blown through the three-week deadline he had promised the studio. Things had gotten thrown off track. *Everything.* He hadn't even gotten real clarity on Jackson and Kendall until he'd reconnected with Jordan. But then Mia called. And he was in Ghana. Something about that, about leaving, about when he left or how he left, had ruined the closest thing he'd had to a "flow." Now every time Harper approached the page, he couldn't focus. Especially not after Jordan had texted him, Leave me alone. It was clear, definitive, much worse than silence. And then she'd blocked him. He was writing their love story. The notes he took while with Jordan, none of it translated without the real-life inspiration. Harper had always been able to compartmentalize, but with no more messages or flowers to send, he'd been in a veritable tailspin and unable to return to authentic storytelling about Jackson and Kendall. So "fine" was certainly not accurate and Stan must have heard it in Harper's voice.

"'Fine' sounds . . . untrue," Stan posited.

"Stan . . ." Harper tried to protest. Even his real reasons didn't sound like a good excuse.

"Look, the studio is hot on this idea of yours. And they are *up* my ass."

"I get it, Stan. I really do. But I have a lot of shit going on with the family."

"Okay. Got it. Is there anything I can do?" Stan asked. Harper thought, *Yes. Find a way to clone me. Two please. One to work on the pitch, another to help Robyn, keep my daughter happy, and send the real me back to Jordan.*

"No. Thank you. I'm handling it."

"Good. Family is most important, so prioritize that. But let me just say this to you—found family is also important," Stan said. Harper sighed as he slid his pants on.

"I know . . ."

"And *I* know what this title means to you. We fought for you to protect your found family, *several* of whom weren't happy with the first go-round of this project."

"I wasn't happy either," Harper said.

"I remember. We got you your shot to protect your vision this time around; so you need to deliver," Stan stated plainly. Harper exhaled hard. "When do you think you'll be done?" Harper shook his head and searched for the right answer.

"I don't know," he finally admitted. Now Stan sighed loudly and paused. Harper's "I don't know" was clearly not the answer Stan was looking for.

"Look, Harp, you have a golden opportunity here, buddy. You need to deliver—and soon—or else they're going to move on. And it'll be out of our hands." The words sat, hanging there in the air. Harper knew his agent of twenty-five years wasn't bullshitting him. He was serious.

Then *brrrrnnngg . . . brrrnnggg . . .* Harper's hotel phone rang, breaking into the silence.

"Hold on, Stan." Harper stepped over to the desk phone and pressed the speaker. "Hello?"

"Good morning, Mr. Stewart, your guest has arrived," the operator said.

"Okay, thanks. Send him to the restaurant please. I have a reservation under my name."

"Very well, sir. We'll let him know." Harper ended that call and turned to his personal phone. "Stan, I'm just not sure. I just—"

"Listen," Stan said brusquely. "I'll tell them two weeks? But you have to give them something. And at this point you gotta blow them away." Stan's voice had a tinge of desperation. Harper knew he was going to bat for him and he hadn't been making it easy. *I can do it . .* he thought.

"I hate to put pressure on you . . ." Stan added.

"Do you really?" Harper half joked.

"Harp . . ."

"I'm just kidding. I'll handle it. Bye, Stan," Harper said before hanging up. On his way out the door, he looked at the wall of notes he'd taped to the hotel room wall, wishing that the ending was clear. As he closed the door, he mused aloud, "Housekeeping must think I'm a serial killer." All his ideas were a jumble and nothing was sticking. His best ideas seemed stupid. Notes that had sounded insightful and entertaining a week ago now felt half-baked. Harper meditated, journaled, and braindumped, sometimes for hours. All his journaling was about Jordan. Jordan who now wanted him to leave her alone. For Harper, this was the worst kind of writer's block. He sighed and threw on his suit jacket while walking down the hallway. Fully dressed now, he entered the elevator to head down and meet his guest.

The doors opened on the ground floor lobby, and Harper walked over to the restaurant where Robyn's landlord was waiting for him. Harper was "inserting himself" again—hoping to have an honest conversation, "man to man," with Aboagye—but all to alleviate stress on Robyn. Even though he didn't say a word about it to her, even though she hadn't spoken about it directly to him, he felt like he had to, that he owed it to his ex-wife.

He had tried all the other ways to help—picking Mia up from school, running errands, pitching in with dinner. Sometimes she'd let him, sometimes she wouldn't. But it pained him to see her stretched so thin, when she was otherwise flourishing so beautifully. It made him rethink his first set of doubts about her coming to Ghana. It seemed like she'd made a good home here, but the way she was doing it was robbing her of the point. She was supposed to be here to have an easier life. And why else take his daughter away from him?

Entering the restaurant, Harper got a look at Aboagye. The man kind of stood out sitting at the coffee bar—colorful outfit, tubby midsection, sunglasses indoors, and already indulging himself with a caffeinated drink of some kind. After some pleasantries and ordering a latte of his own, Harper got straight to the point.

"Listen, sir. I don't know how things work here but what's happening is affecting me in America. I just want to make sure my family has what they need. And that includes the ability to market and promote the restaurant. A leaky roof, flood damage, and a secondhand backup generator is bad for business."

Aboagye sipped his cappuccino. "Maybe your wife can't afford to be there anymore," he said simply.

"*Ex*-wife . . ."

"Ahhh. My apologies. But once a wife always a wife. You are

still responsible for her, no?" Aboagye eyed Harper over the rim of his shades, above the brim of his cappuccino cup. Harper couldn't really argue with that.

"If Robyn thinks she belongs here and can handle it, then she can." Harper was firm in defending her. "I know that much about her. We were married for a long time, and I owe it to her, and my daughter, to see how we can work something out. Man to man."

"Look, brudda, I like your wife," Aboagye said. Harper returned a look of impatience. "Sorry. I like *Robyn.* She is a good cook, but not very good at business." Harper bristled at another man's opinion of his ex-wife's skill set. "Maybe she is 'in over her head,' as the saying goes."

"Robyn is a chef. Not a cook. And she's very passionate about what she does, she's smart, and her heart is in the right place. If the rent is paid you shouldn't have anything to say about her business acumen." Harper looked Aboagye squarely in the eye. Aboagye raised his chin, returning Harper's gaze with a slight grin.

"*Ex*-wife, eh?" Aboagye finished his last sip. Harper impatiently tapped his foot on the bar step. "Look, brudda, as I told Robyn I can rent that space for more than I'm getting now, but she has brought a good service to the area," Aboagye stated matter-of-factly. "So I am inclined to keep renting to her. But the price is the price. If she wants to keep it, then I'll let her stay."

"So, if you get the money—a year of rent in advance—you'll stop harassing her?" Harper leaned forward toward him.

"I'm not 'harassing' Robyn." Aboagye pointed to himself. "I am a businessman."

"A businessman who's holding her hostage by *not* repairing her leaky roof," Harper corrected. "There's also damage to the baseboards and floor tiles from flooding. But I got an estimate on repairs as well as the price of a new generator. If you can't fix it, you're going to pay someone who can. That's your responsibility. She owns the business; you own the building."

Aboagye mulled over what Harper was proposing. "And what happens next year when her business does not turn a profit? I don't want to keep doing this year to year," Aboagye declared.

Harper absorbed what this dude was saying. *Fine,* he decided. *I'll play along.* "Two years' advanced rent." Harper tapped the bar top with his forefinger for emphasis. Aboagye froze slightly as his eyes briefly widened behind his sunglasses. *Yeah. Money talks.* "But everything must be repaired with no disruption to her business AT ALL. And you throw in a brand-new fridge. One that she orders and approves of, and you install it. No more popping by—you leave her alone and let her run things."

Aboagye inhaled through his nose as if trying to smell something deeply as he turned to Harper. "Well, Mr. Ex-husband, do you want to buy the building?" Aboagye challenged.

"I don't." Buying a building was in the past. There was no making up for the fumble four years ago when Robyn wanted that restaurant space in Harlem. Robyn deserved better. So did Mia. Robyn would never ask him to do anything like this, but this restaurant was something she'd built. It was getting all the accolades it deserved because of her passion. Harper could handle this hit. He could do this for her.

"Do we have a deal?"

Hours later, Harper was well into his work as a "helper" for the list of things that Robyn had actually asked him to do. Her requests had been for him to pick Mia up from school and to get dinner started. He knew it was in her anticipation of him leaving. She'd given subtle hints, asking him when he was "heading home" but Harper didn't have an answer to that. He only knew that he was needed here, while at home his life was on the other side of Jordan's now official silence.

"She blocked me, L," Harper said to Lance. Harper was in his rental, parked in the lot at Mia's school FaceTiming. Coach Lance Sullivan was at a Big 10 pro day, watching college hopefuls run, jump, throw, and tackle to prove they had what it takes to get to the NFL Draft, but was taking a moment away for his best friend who was in obvious distress. "And I've tried. I've called, left messages, DMed her socials, sent flowers. She won't call me back," Harper said. "Have you spoken to her?"

"Nah," Lance said. "According to Q, Shelby's had some correspondence. But she's giving everyone the Heisman, bruh." Lance's reference to the man whose statue perpetually gave the forearm was an apropos analogy. *Distance.* Jordan was stiff-arming everyone. And it was somehow his fault.

"Maybe you should go see her," Lance suggested. "Women need assurance. Not maybes. They want security and action. Jordan is no different."

Harper knew Lance was right and looked skyward for answers before sighing. "I get it. You're right. Hell, I wanna see her," he continued. "But I don't feel like I can leave here just yet. Things aren't right."

"Harp, you're there under false circumstances, aren't you?" Lance asked.

"What Mia said, yes. But things aren't right here. And what about next time? And there's going to be a next time. Is this going to happen again if I have to tend to the family?" Harper asked.

"Which family, Harp?" Lance paused as if he was going to let Harper answer. But the question, coupled with Stan's words earlier, caught Harper off guard. With Harper's silence, Lance continued. "Because Jordan wants to be your family. Hell, y'all are already family," Lance answered for him. "At least I bet she feels that way."

Harper looked away from his screen. Lance was right.

"She is . . ." Harper nodded. But how was he supposed to choose? "Do you believe in destiny, L?" Harper mused. Lance looked quizzically at his homeboy, prompting Harper to elaborate. "I know you believe in God, but do you believe in *destiny*? In fate?"

"God, destiny, fate are intertwined in my mind, my guy," Lance answered.

Lance's voice reflected a clarity Harper wished he had. He swallowed a lump in his throat. "I think I have unfinished business here, L. It's not easy to dismiss these feelings I have."

"What feelings?" Lance asked.

"That I'm needed here," Harper said. "My daughter needs help. So does Robyn."

"Mia is your responsibility for sure. I get that. But Robyn's moved on with old boy, hasn't she?"

Harper shrugged at Lance's reminder. It was hard to pretend that Kwesi wasn't an impressive option. "Maybe. I know Mia doesn't like him."

"Of course she doesn't like him. In her mind he's trying to take her daddy's place."

"Did I fight enough for us, L?" Harper posited, asking the question that had been haunting him for days. *What more can I do?* He hadn't figured it out with Robyn, and he couldn't figure it out with Jordan either. "I mean did I do everything I should have done to save my marriage?" Harper asked.

Lance paused and looked at Harper through the phone. Harper knew he was going to get an unvarnished answer from Lance. He wasn't Quentin, but Big L would be honest.

"Do you think you did?" Lance asked.

Harper twisted his lips, then kissed his teeth before slowly shaking his head. The truth was painful but obvious.

"No," he replied softly. "I knew it when it was happening . . ." Harper admitted. "I was . . . selfish. I wanted it my way." Harper could hear both the whistles stateside in Maryland on Lance's end through his phone and the sound of happy children being reunited with their parents as they emerged from the school yards away. They'd both have to end their call soon.

"Harp, you can beat yourself up." Lance squinted into the screen with sincerity. "But you can't go back in time. You did the best you could with what you knew. Things happen, bro," Lance assured him. "You don't think I used to rack my brain on whether I did everything I could for Mia before I lost her? I did the best I knew how to do."

"But what if this is where I'm supposed to be, L?" Harper asked. "What if what Jordan and I had is all there was? What if *that* was the limit of our destiny? What if that was the end of our story?"

"You don't believe that, Harp. Not the way you two have been since undergrad. No way," Lance declared.

"I thought so too. Now I'm not so sure . . ." Harper said. "If this was you and God put you in this situation, what would you think? How would you handle it?" Lance pondered what Harper was saying, but he didn't give an answer. Harper continued, "I'm trying to be a better dude, L. A better man."

Harper looked out the car window to see Mia exiting the building with her classmates. He opened his car door to step out and wave, so that she and her teacher could see him.

Lance finally broke their silence. "'Accept correction, and you will find life; reject correction, and you will miss the road.'" Lance offered the Bible quote as he often did. Harper looked at his phone, at his dear friend. "Proverbs, 10:17," Lance added. "If you think you're there to 'correct mistakes,' maybe you are, Harp. I can't answer because I don't know, but I'd pray on it, do what works for you. Meditate, ask the ancestors, find you a witch doctor. Whatever you think might help. God will tell you. If you ask, he'll show you."

Harper nodded. "Thanks, bruh." Harper threw two fingers toward his screen as Lance signed off. He quickly stuffed the phone in his inner jacket pocket to greet Mia with a hug.

"Hi, Daddy!" Mia sounded so gleeful as she ran over to him, rushing into his arms. Harper smiled back at his daughter, taking her in, as resplendent as always. Mia's the only one who loved him unconditionally now. The feeling was mutual. He loved seeing her every day. *Maybe Mia's call was a call to action for me to try to repair what's broken? My relationship with Robyn? Maybe some part of my destiny was here, in Ghana, with Robyn and Mia? Maybe?*

*But what about Jordan?*

Harper contemplated as he drove himself and Mia back to Robyn's home. And as the questions swirled in his mind, Lance's words from their conversation ricocheted through his thoughts. *Women want assurance, not maybes.* The one thing he knew for sure was that not all of those maybes could be true. And he couldn't leave Accra until he knew which ones were and which ones were not.

## CHAPTER THIRTY-EIGHT

## Jordan

"This place is sexy . . ." Jordan leaned forward toward the candlelit tabletop at the well-appointed Funke restaurant in Beverly Hills. Across from her, Brian sipped his glass of red wine, holding it in the sophisticated yet familiar way that she'd gotten used to when they were dating—and without a ring on his finger, *that* finger, still. *This white boy looks good,* Jordan noticed.

"I think it's still the best pasta in town," Brian remarked, pulling up the menu. "But the fish off the grill is phenomenal."

"Fish it is, then," Jordan volleyed back with an air toast of her sidecar glass in his direction. Somehow, she'd managed to resuscitate her hair and massage at least most of the puff from underneath her eyes. Strategically applied makeup gave a lot of camouflage, and a sexy low-cut black dress did the rest of the repair job on Jordan's confidence. The air down below hit her insides and she squeezed her legs together, feeling a little naughty about coming to dinner so well prepared for dessert.

At the table, they'd already had a chance to catch up on the basics. Brian had some new business venture going on. Jordan spoke in generalities about her numerous projects. And she wondered still, even after appetizers and a near-empty second round of drinks, what had spurred his outreach and how long they'd need to sit here before they could leave and get down to real business. When the waiter came back, Brian took command, ordering what seemed like a sampling of the entire menu, including the pricey grilled whole branzino. Jordan didn't usually register prices for what she ordered, but he was so generous in his selections that she couldn't help but be reminded of his wealth. Brian grew up in a family that had bankers and politicians, and businesses that had been started generations ago.

"You brought me here to spoil me?" Jordan teased with a wink as soon as the waiter left.

Brian tilted his well-coiffed head of dark hair and smiled at her with his eyes crinkling slightly at the corners. "You think I didn't learn anything in the time we spent together?"

Jordan started to warm in her center. She liked how this was going, and so did her body. "As I recall it, you became somewhat of a pro at learning what I like." Jordan held Brian's eye with full intensity as she pulled a sip from her drink into her mouth.

For a moment, Brian seemed hypnotized. He was still like a statue, mesmerized. *I knew it,* Jordan thought. She had him. He drew in a sharp breath and leaned back in his chair. *Oh shit, what's that about?* He was headed in the wrong direction. She resisted the urge to reach for his knee under the table.

"Jordan," Brian said like they were in an office, rather than a dimly lit restaurant. "What I wanted to talk about was this new company. It's a big opportunity and we need the right person, the right woman, who knows what she's doing."

Shock gripped Jordan around her vocal cords. This wasn't at all what she expected. She wanted some rebound dick, not a fucking business opportunity. "Oh. Umm . . . Brian . . . I . . ." She shook her head no, even before she could bring the words to her lips. This wasn't how the evening was supposed to be going. Not down this path. "This isn't where I am right now, professionally," she said. "I'm looking more toward . . ." What was she looking toward? Her pitch to Evelyn had fallen completely flat. Was she really thinking of trying that again? Like a fool? *Hell no,* she resolved. "I'm looking more toward opportunities that are under my own direction."

Brian's face lit up in a way she didn't expect. His response was animated. "See, Jordan, that's just it," he said. "That's exactly what we'd want you to do. Run the whole thing. Exactly what you love. Your vision, a huge operating budget, full support of the board. We're going all in with this and you'd have everything you need."

"What made you think of me for this?"

"You've heard of Dominion Communications, right?" Brian said.

Of course she had. Even those folks who weren't regular readers of the *Financial Times* had heard of Dominion. They were the fastest growing telecommunications company in the country. They were boasting sports, original programming, and world news, all delivered with the fastest speed of any platform on the market, which included home and mobile.

"Uh-huh. They're doing big things in the telecommunications space," Jordan replied.

"Correct." Brian flashed that smile and those deep dimples. "The tech they're using is special, cutting edge, Jordan. All for the best customer experience."

"And corporate profit," Jordan added.

"There's no doubt the company is doing well and snatching up consumers left and right. They're in a great position, but they are looking toward the future and want a leader to help them get there. I told them about you—and you were already on their short list," Brian informed her. "The board asked me to come speak to you personally. There was a hope that with our . . . history, that you might be amenable to considering suiting up again. We know that you've opted for a different professional direction, so we're prepared to incentivize you, *generously.*" He leaned in as if people were listening. "Between you and me, Jordan, you can almost name your package. We just want you in the role."

At this, Jordan leaned forward. From anybody else, she might think this was all gassing up to go to her head. But not coming from Brian. When it came to business he wasted no words and no time. This opportunity was real, and she'd be a fool not to take it seriously. Although this was not good news to her pussy or her plans. Pussy would have to take a back seat tonight. She shifted again in her chair, closed her legs, and leaned forward. *For this shit, I really should've worn panties,* she thought.

"Okay, Brian. I'm listening. . . ."

# CHAPTER THIRTY-NINE

## Robyn

On the second of their shut-down days for the week, Robyn wrapped up the last moments of planning tomorrow's menu with Haniah and the staff. There was no good day to shut down, but to regroup, replenish, and recharge Robyn had to do so. Also to conserve much-needed funds. But today was also a day to have a reality check. Food was getting more costly, some menu favorites had to be replaced or substituted, and some staff were calling out sick more regularly. Robyn's Nest was stretched and its owner was still struggling—trying to make a profit, praying for no rain, and waiting on the city to repair the drainage on the neighboring street. Normally Robyn took obstacles as opportunities and something beautiful usually resulted. Now all she had was frustration. The perennially optimistic Robyn Stewart certainly wasn't seeing a glass half-full right now.

Robyn had met with her accountant earlier in the morning for a "come to Jesus" moment she had been kicking downfield for the better part of six months. She didn't have the funds to drop a year's worth of rent without going into further debt. Some debt was fine, but this was a ship that was literally taking on water. Unless the restaurant started making significant profit Robyn would have to make other plans. She was already paying people out of her own pocket. It was a sobering conversation, one that permeated the tenor of the staff meeting with an onslaught of well-meaning suggestions.

"Smaller portions."

*"Loyal customers will notice . . ."*

"No more fufu from scratch. Use the mix."

*"Can't do that . . ."*

"Raise the prices."

*"It's fair market, but maybe . . ."*

"Faster service, turn the tables over sooner."

*"I don't want anyone rushed . . ."*

"Use tilapia. It's a perfectly good fish . . ."

*"Ugh . . ."*

"I know, Robyn . . . but we must do something. All options need to be on the table."

That piece of advice had come from Haniah. She was just as optimistic as Robyn, but she also kept it real. Robyn knew she had to take her seriously.

"Yup. You're right. Let me take all of this into consideration and we'll regroup tomorrow. Thanks, everyone." The line cooks, dishwashers, and waitstaff all gathered their belongings and headed out. Robyn turned to Haniah to do their usual debrief and saw a look of distress on the face of her closest Ghanaian confidant.

"What's up? You okay?" Robyn asked. Haniah looked away.

"Can we talk?" Haniah said, finally, quietly. Robyn felt an ominous pit in her stomach based on Haniah's tone, but she muscled through.

"Of course. Come to my office," Robyn said, gently ushering her by the arm.

Haniah stepped past her across the threshold and Robyn closed the door behind them. "You wanna sit, have a cup of tea?" Robyn offered.

"No, thanks, Robyn. I don't want to hold you up. I know you're having a family dinner." Robyn gave a slight eye roll and nod. "Plus, I still need to get Mawusi from school." Before Robyn could say anything, Haniah continued, "You're a great boss. Everyone loves you and they want to keep working for you. You have a lot of goodwill with people and they will do anything for you."

"I appreciate you saying that, Haniah. . . ."

"But they have to think of themselves and their families," Haniah continued.

"I understand . . ."

"You don't," Haniah said abruptly, startling Robyn. "I'm being recruited by the Polo Club." Her disclosure sounded unusually businesslike. "And they're talking about doubling my salary."

"Haniah" was all Robyn could muster.

"I know." Haniah's face looked pained. "I love working with and for you, Robyn. You have an amazing vision, and you've built something so very special. I love coming here to work. It's not a job. It's part of my life, my passion." As Haniah spoke, her voice broke with emotion. But I have to think about Mawusi and keeping her at that school. And they just increased tuition."

"I saw that," Robyn said and looked away. The hits kept coming. "Sooo are you telling me because you're giving me notice or are you hoping I can match it?"

"I haven't given them an answer. And I think they're looking at a few other managers."

"They won't find anyone better than you," Robyn declared. Haniah smiled and a tear dropped from her eye.

"Thank you," Haniah said. Robyn stepped toward her to take her hand, nodding her understanding.

"Of course. Thank you for telling me. I know it wasn't easy. Give me a little time and let me know if they put any more pressure on you before you give them an answer. Deal?" Robyn made sure to meet Haniah's eyes. The moment was heavy, but she wanted to make sure they were still in it together.

"Deal," Haniah said. "I'm sorry, Robyn."

Robyn sighed and reached out to hug Haniah. "I understand. I appreciate you."

After Haniah left, Robyn locked up the restaurant and headed toward her vehicle with a heaviness that traveled from her head to her heart. She'd become accustomed to looking at her phone as of late to check messages after work, especially now that Harper had made himself a factor. He'd left her a text message informing her that he and Mia were home, that dinner was being made, and he had something he wanted to "discuss" with her. Robyn sighed, dreading how his "help" would translate today, the thought of what her kitchen would look like after Harper's attempt at dinner, but also whatever he wanted to discuss. She'd been hoping he'd decided on an exit date and was gently pressing the issue with him. Because that's what *she* needed to discuss. Having Harper's extra set of hands around to run errands, pick up and take care of Mia helped *a lot* and it had admittedly been fortifying for Mia, though Robyn was still pissed at her for scaring Harper into coming. *Grow up, little girl . . .* Robyn thought. But *she was only eleven . . . my baby, still. Sigh.* Nonetheless, Harper was in *her* space, *her* life, *her* business and she was ready for him to leave.

Robyn simply responded to his text with OK before getting into her car and noticing a few missed phone calls from Candace. *The time difference* . . . Robyn and Candace were always missing each other. It was only 10:00 a.m. in New York so, the middle of her morning there. Robyn could use a dose of their laughs and good vibes and hoped maybe Candace could talk. She dialed.

"Hey!" Candace picked up immediately, her voice bouncing from her car speakers.

Robyn smiled big. "Hey, Candace. How you doing?"

"I'm all right. How about you?"

Robyn let out a big sigh.

"Lay it on me, sis," Candace declared. She was always a safe place and a good sounding board. Other than Kwesi and Thema, anyone Robyn would tell about the business here in Accra depended on her so it was nice to just be able to reveal things to Candace—to get laughs, perspective, and comfort with no judgment. Though she had her community here, speaking to Candace was home. She caught her up on all the happenings in her life during the past week—the restaurant, Kwesi's situationship, and Harper's disruptive presence in Ghana. It was *a lot*.

"He's gotta go *home*," Robyn announced to Candace's disembodied voice in her RAV4.

"Didn't you tell him the door's always open?"

"Yeah, that was before I got settled and before Kwesi."

Candace laughed. "Dick will do that." Candace's words made Robyn howl out loud.

"I don't mean it like that," Robyn finally corrected, still giggling. "Harper is Mia's father, and she likes having him around. Maybe he should take her this summer."

"That's a good idea. You should come too." Candace sounded excited by the idea. "Just like a week. Let me lay eyes on you and this Ghanaian chocolate man." The thought was a momentary warm one. Kwesi and Robyn hanging out in New York for a week in the summer, showing him off to her friends and family. It had been a while since Robyn had set foot on American soil, saw her friends, her folks. Her parents had been to Accra a few times and she loved hosting them. She'd just started feeling like she wanted to get back to see people and her old familiar places. See America again, even though she didn't miss it so much. But Robyn didn't see any trip that would take her away from Robyn's Nest without it going under or closing, not right now, as things were so tenuous. She was an integral part of its success—her problem-solving, her savings, her stitching together the necessities of one day to the next.

"I wish . . ." Robyn said wistfully. "Did I tell you Kwesi offered to help financially, but I refused?"

"Why?" Candace asked.

"Because I thought I could cover it. I want to do this on my own," Robyn responded.

"Listen, I'm all for independence, but why run yourself into the ground trying to prove a point?"

Robyn took a pause to consider Candace's question.

"Do you know I never lived on my own?" Robyn asked.

"No?"

"Nope. I've always been dependent or in partnership with someone else: my parents, college roommates, post-college roommates, boyfriends, then Harper." The disclosure was something that Robyn had been thinking about, but she'd never spoken it. It felt even more urgent aloud. "I've always had someone to rely on. I always had backup. Now I *am* the backup." Growing up and during most of her adult life, Robyn didn't feel like it was an issue. She was still a great source of support for everyone she loved. But over the years doubt seeped in.

"All that support I had . . . Was I failing the feminist movement? Did I qualify as a strong Black woman?" Robyn verbalized her younger self's thoughts.

"Robyn, please . . ." Candace interjected.

"I'm serious. Was I less of a woman because I chose to allow Harper to lead and to support him?" Robyn pondered. "It ate at me over the years. I was smart and capable, and I could do anything I set my mind to. Most important, I wanted to be an example to Mia. So part of me has something to prove—to myself, to Harper, to the world. And while some of that is scary, I was always looking forward to it. I want to be that lady in that old perfume commercial," Robyn said.

"What lady?"

"You know," Robyn sang, *'I can bring home the bacon, fry it up in a paaaan.'*"

Candace giggled excitedly. "Right, right." Then she continued singing with Robyn, "*'And never let you forget you're a maaan.'*"

"*'Cuz I'm a woooman! Enjoli!'*" She and Candace cracked up laughing.

"Remember that?" Robyn managed to get the words out between laughs.

"Hell yeah. I remember that. Bitches is old." Robyn cracked up further to the point of tears coming to her eyes. They each had to catch their breath from laughing so hard.

"Oh my God. I miss you," Robyn said.

"I miss you too, sis," Candace returned between her cackles. "Ohhh, Robyn, I'm happy for you. I'm happy that you found your way and that you're on your journey," she said lovingly. "But I hate that you're so far away."

"Sometimes I feel like I'm sinking, but I've been managing. And, I have to admit, having Harper here this week to help with Mia, things are a lot easier," Robyn said, returning to her air of contemplation. "I forgot how funny he could be sometimes. Harper Stewart still tickles my funny bone. I'm not gonna lie." She laughed a bit thinking about it.

"Uh-huh. What about with Kwesi there?"

"It's complicated, Candace. I can't be held hostage by Mia who called her daddy in to play police on my vagina. More than that, my future. Whether I'm with Kwesi or not I don't want to end up one of these divorced women who doesn't have a life outside of her children," she said. "You see them, where their child becomes their best friend? Their life, all that they care about. All they have to look forward to. And when their children grow up and move on, what do these lonely women have? Nothing. No. That's not going to be me."

"Some women don't even have that, Rob."

"Amen. I have to do what works for me. At some point I have to think about me and only me. Take a page out of Harper's book. Hell, most men's books. And worry only about myself."

"Whether you're in New York or the motherland, it doesn't make any sense to run yourself ragged. You've been healing. I hear it in your voice, see it in your face, it comes through on your posts. You seem happy so I know you're in the right place, but is running this restaurant too much? Is that really your dream?"

Robyn exhaled and shook her head. "I don't know anymore, Candace. I don't want things to be so hard. I just want to live. Be fulfilled. I deserve that." Robyn pulled into her driveway next to Harper's rental car and realized with a tinge of sadness that her time chatting with Candace was going to have to wrap quickly.

"You do."

"Hey, Candace, let me go. I'm just getting home and have to see what kind of disaster I'm walking into." Robyn put her car in park.

"Oh!" Candace said, sounding alarmed. "I was having such a

good time catching up, I almost forgot why I called you. Harper. Has he . . . said anything to you about . . . anything or *anybody*?"

Robyn looked at her speakers with curiosity. "Anything like what?"

"Check your phone. I just texted you something." Robyn grabbed her phone to find Candace's messages and opened the first one. It was a photograph that she couldn't quite make out without her reading glasses.

"I need my readers."

"Get them," Candace said. "You're going to want to see this clearly."

# CHAPTER FORTY

## Harper

"'*Make me sweaaaat, make me hotaaa, make me lose my breath, make me wataaaa . . .*'" Harper sang along to a Tyla playlist that had him feeling himself in Robyn's kitchen. His dredging bowls of egg, flour, and panko breadcrumbs were also haphazardly placed, leaving remnants all over Robyn's counters. The cutting boards; mallet for pounding cutlets; green sprigs of oregano, fresh parsley, and basil were all dotted around, plus bowls and plates for serving. He had his iPad propped up on a book stand with the chicken paillard recipe he was following on an open web page filled with bright photographs of the finished dish. Harper could pretty much do it by heart, but he didn't want to leave anything to chance. He wanted the flavors and textures to be as good as possible. The fifth piece of flattened chicken was browning in the skillet, and Harper had the tongs at the ready while jamming out and slicing fresh tomatoes and shallots for the salad. He was in a great mood and in his own world when he heard the front door close. He looked up moments later to see Robyn enter the kitchen. She walked slowly and with a reticent look on her face.

"Hey!" Harper greeted her over the playlist. "Welcome home!

"Hi." Robyn's reply was terse. Her energy did not match his at all. *She must have had another stressful day at work,* Harper thought. Nothing that a glass of wine, a good meal, and some welcomed financial relief couldn't cure.

Robyn surveyed the area with a bit of an attitude. "What's going on here?" Robyn gestured at his setup.

"Just making dinner," Harper said proudly. "I know it's a mess, but I'll handle it. Promise. You will not have to lift a finger. You want a drink? Glass of wine?" Harper grabbed a couple of bottles he'd picked up, making sure they *weren't* from Kwesi's vineyard. "I have a red and a white," he declared, holding one up in each hand. Robyn didn't respond. She instead walked toward Harper and turned off the music he was playing, right in the middle of a good lyric.

Harper looked at her with curiosity. "You want to hear something else? I can find something. Or feel free to put on what you like," Harper said, being decidedly unselfish. "It's your house."

Robyn said nothing, made her way over to the stove, and abruptly shut off the burner underneath the browning chicken. Harper looked at her now with disbelief. "Um, is the flame too high? Because that's not quite finished . . ." Robyn turned to him, stood there, and focused on him with an intense glare. "Is everything . . . ?" Harper began, but didn't need to finish. Robyn lifted her phone.

"What's this?" she said calmly, but coldly. Harper studied her face for a beat before shifting his focus to the image on her phone screen. It was a photo. *Oh . . . shit.* It was *the* photo. *That* photo. The photo of him and Jordan that he had taken so carefree and sent so flippantly out of . . . spite, revenge, some stupid tit-for-tat petty high school behavior? The photo that was never supposed to reach Robyn before he'd told her the truth. Well, it certainly reached its intended target, but the reasons behind it already seemed so juvenile and so long ago. Harper saw the look on Robyn's face and tried to explain, but—

"Oh" was all that he could eke out. Robyn remained steadfast and unblinking.

"What *is* this, Harper?" she reiterated. *How does she have the photo?* he wondered, his mind racing through each of the days of the past week. How had he not already had *this* conversation? Harper was supposed to bring it up when he'd first arrived. The longer he stayed, the easier it became to put it off. But he should have come clean. *What an idiot.*

"Look, Robyn. It's complicated—" Harper began.

"It always is, Harper," she said. "It always has been." Robyn shook her head and walked into the sunken living room. All Harper could do was follow and try to gather his defense. "So how long has this been going on?"

Harper's stomach churned as if he were still married to Robyn and needed to explain himself. "Look, it's something that happened . . . I was in LA having some meetings, we had dinner and things happened . . ." Harper said, not knowing at all how to characterize to Robyn those fifteen days that he'd spent living out his dreams of thirty years.

"'Things,' Harper? '*Things*'? You guys had sex. You fucked her," Robyn accused. "Right?"

Harper looked around and stepped closer to her so as not to have Mia hear their conversation. "Hey, can we keep our voices down . . ." he pleaded. But Robyn pressed on.

"When were you going to tell me about this? You're so busy in *my* business you didn't disclose yours?"

"I was going to tell you. It's one of the reasons I came. To tell you in person, before . . ." Harper gestures to her phone.

"What? Before I saw this? You've been here for a *week,* Harper." Harper shook his head, mad at himself for not finding a way to express what had happened and what was happening, what was going to happen if he could stop messing things up.

"Look, I'm sorry. I should have said something before now. But I don't . . . even know . . . what's happening right now with her."

"With *her*? With *you,* Harper. With the *two of you,*" Robyn spit back. "You are *exactly* the same. Hiding information, acting like 'nothing's happening,' 'nothing's going on.'" Robyn shrugged in her imitation of Harper. Harper could do nothing but take the hits that he deserved. "Why not just tell me? We're *divorced.* What the fuck does it matter?" Harper didn't have a defense for his actions. Explaining any or all of it wouldn't justify his silence or the delay. It was just going to sound lame. But he had to try.

"I should have . . . I just . . ." He started gesturing and trying to find the right words.

"Just *say* it, Harper," Robyn demanded.

"Okay," he said. "We spent a lot of time together. Catching up, y'know . . ."

"Fucking," Robyn stated. Harper returned a look of embarrassment at her coarse language. "Stop it. We're adults. At least I am." Harper exhaled. *I deserve this,* he told himself. He had it coming.

"Yes, we were doing that and hanging out and whatnot. It wasn't planned. It just happened and one thing led to another. I stayed out there longer than I had planned because of it. And—"

"And you told your friends. But didn't have the decency to tell me," Robyn said.

"Well, you didn't tell me about Brother Mandingo," Harper shot back. *Lame.*

"His name is *Kwesi* and he's none of your business," Robyn said. "And is that what this is about? I didn't tell you about a relationship I'm having that has nothing to do with you? And your petty ass wanted to show me that you couldn't wait to get with your fucking soulmate?"

"Robyn, please . . ." Harper pleaded with her to chill on the language. But she didn't stop.

"It's a false equivalent, Harper," Robyn stated. Pointing to the phone, she continued, "This woman has been in the background from the *get-go,* waiting for her chance at you. And you with her."

"That's not true. . . ."

"Stop it. Just stop. Do not gaslight me. Own up to it." Robyn's eyes and words demanded a response.

"All I'm saying is I didn't know that was going to happen. The way it happened. Okay?" Robyn squinted back at him. Harper continued his defense. "And I certainly didn't know she would fly off the handle when I said I had to come here for Mia. And now she won't talk to me," he confessed. "She hasn't said anything to me in a week and blocked me." Robyn looked at Harper with no sympathy. No love, but with pity. He knew he sounded pitiful. He felt every bit of it. They stood in silence looking at one another for a few moments before Robyn spoke again.

"So what are you going to do?"

Harper didn't expect that question. "About her?"

Robyn widened her eyes back at him with a shrug, as if to say, "*Yeah, nigga. Her.*"

"I don't really know. Like I said, it's complicated."

"No, it's not. Go be with her. Go be happy. It's what you've been wanting . . ."

"Robyn—" Harper started to explain that it couldn't possibly be as simple as that when Mia breezed into the room wearing her headphones and scrolling on her phone.

"Oh, hi, Mom," Mia said. "Hey, Dad, is dinner ready?"

Harper stood stunned, wondering what if anything his daughter heard of their very adult conversation, but her headphones gave Harper a sense of comfort that possibly she hadn't heard anything at all. .

"Hey, baby," Robyn said to Mia. "Take those headphones off, please. You know how I feel about that . . . And you know the rules."

Mia started to protest, but Harper cut her off.

"Do what Mom says, please. And go wash your hands."

"I washed them already. They're clean . . ." Mia showed her hands to her parents as proof.

"Wash them again, then . . . after you remove your headphones," Harper said sternly. "And then we'll eat. Okay?"

"Fiiine." Mia rolled her eyes, did an about-face and exited the room.

Robyn headed toward her bedroom. Harper called after her.

"Hey." Robyn turned back to look at him with eyes that could kill. "Table this until later?" Robyn scrunched up her face. Harper continued, "And there is something else I want to mention—"

Robyn held up her hand. "There's nothing else to say, Harper, I'm done." With that, Robyn exited the room, leaving Harper with the scent of garlic and the sound of the exhaust fan over the stove.

~

Mia helped Harper set the table. No matter the tension with Robyn, it still delighted him to see his daughter so excited and for them to sit down as a family. She'd been talking about it all day since Harper picked her up from school. Her face lit up with happiness when she learned he'd be making chicken paillard, her favorite dish. And though Harper wasn't the best cook, he could manage to bring a taste of comfort to his daughter. Everything looked good on the plate, well-cooked, flavorful, and it smelled like something he'd want to taste. Harper had even brewed iced tea from scratch and sweetened it with local honey. But despite all his careful preparation, what was supposed to be a relaxed evening was now rife with tension. Harper knew it was his fault. He'd blown it. There had been an opportunity to be straight with Robyn. And yes, she was his ex-wife, but she deserved to know and to hear it from him before anyone else. He had no idea how she got that photo, but now that she had it, he knew very well what it meant—embarrassment for Robyn. And him being selfish, again. Never mind that they were divorced.

There was no easy way to make up for this. But he had to try; that was the least he could do. Harper resolved that before leaving for the evening, he'd make sure he communicated to Robyn about Aboagye and what his proposal was. It wasn't necessarily a peace offering, but he was trying to offer her peace—peace of mind. She deserved that.

Robyn had always been better with the truth and talking things out. Even if she was mad. Even when she'd stumbled upon the picture, and the news of him and Jordan, she was unsurprisingly upset, but metered. *Reasonable. Why has it taken me so long to learn and especially to trust that about her?* Harper wondered. There were still mysteries within him that carried Robyn's name. Even despite these years apart. She was a test he kept failing. Could he ever learn how to love and not damage, to support but not suffocate? Could he trust himself enough to entrust Robyn with the truth? That he meant well, that he wanted the best for her, that he'd really, this time, truly changed. He'd come with the best intentions for her and for Jordan. But if he couldn't get it right with Robyn, how could he ever trust himself to get it right with Jordan? At this point, he should know better. He *did* know better. So, no matter what it took, before he headed back to his hotel for the night, he'd make everything clear, transparent. *After dinner,* he thought. *Let Mia enjoy both her parents and hopefully Robyn could compartmentalize . . . yet again.*

With the table set, Harper and Mia sat playing a game of UNO while they waited for Robyn. Harper didn't dare rush her in his attempt to keep the peace. Once they got past his going behind her back they could get down to brass tacks and he'd give her the news about Aboagye and the rent money. Robyn had a lot of pride, but she wasn't stupid.

"Mom!" Mia bellowed. "Come on, the food is getting cold!"

Harper put his hand on hers. "Honey, give Mom a few more minutes."

"But I'm hungry and it smells so good," she protested, unaware of the adult dynamics at play. Harper reached for some dinner rolls and placed one on Mia's plate.

"Have some bread," Harper offered.

Mia pushed it away. "No, Daddy," she said. "Not before grace."

"Right. My bad." Harper was relieved. *Mia just wanted to say grace.* "We'll just have to be patient, okay?"

"All right," she responded. "Mom! Come on!" she bellowed again. Harper looked at Mia disapprovingly.

"What?" She shrugged. Harper cut his eyes at her.

At that moment Robyn breezed into the room in loungewear.

"Sorry, sorry, I'm here. I'm ready," Robyn said. She looked devoid of the tension she'd left the room with thirty minutes prior. "Everything looks great." Robyn's tone was pleasant and sincere. "Yummy."

"Thanks Ro— *Mom.*" Harper looked at her with a small smile. She returned a small cursory smile of her own. Harper knew it was performative, but he was grateful for it on this night. Why should Mia be dragged into their bullshit? *His* bullshit.

"Okay, shall we say grace?" Robyn asked.

"Yup!" Mia insisted.

"So let's do it," Harper said. "Ms. Mia, please do the honors."

"Okay." Mia reached out her hands for her parents. "Give me your hands, please."

Harper and Robyn offered their left and right hands respectively. Harper looked from Mia to Robyn, who met his eyes after watching Mia bow her head. Robyn held Harper's gaze for a moment before bowing her head and closing her eyes. Harper followed suit.

Mia began. "Gracious Father, thank you for the meal we are about to receive for the nourishment of our bodies. Please bless Daddy's hands who prepared it. We thank you for allowing us to be together as a family. We thank you for Mommy and Daddy, Grandma and Grandpa Stewart, GranGran and PopPop. We also offer thanks to the ancestors who braved the journey to America with strength, resilience, and faith that allowed us to be here today and may those who aren't with us always watch over us including baby Solomon. Our angel."

*Solomon?* Harper's eyes snapped open and his brow furrowed. He looked at Mia, whose eyes remained closed. Harper shifted his eyes to Robyn, who remained locked in prayer as well. *Calm. Calm?* "These blessings we ask in your holy name. Amen."

"Amen," Robyn echoed.

Harper sat momentarily frozen in shock, as he had not heard that name, *Solomon,* out loud in over twenty years. He looked again at Mia, who by now had opened her eyes. She smiled at him and squeezed his hand. "*Amen,* Daddy," she pressed. Harper snapped out of his daze.

"Right. Right. Amen." Harper cleared his throat and squeezed Mia's hand back before letting go. "Good job, honey."

"Yes. Good job, Mia," Robyn echoed. "You're getting better."

"Practice makes perfect," Mia said. "Can I get some chicken, Daddy?"

Harper pulled his gaze away from Robyn to address Mia. He felt like he was suffocating. "What'd you say, honey?"

"Chicken," Mia repeated and pointed. Harper grabbed tongs.

"Of course. Sorry. Do you want a big piece or small piece?"

"A big piece," Mia said eagerly. Robyn spooned salad onto Mia's plate.

"Put the salad on top. It'll make it taste super yummy," Robyn said.

"Yup." Harper smiled awkwardly. He really wanted to ask Robyn "What in the fuckin' hell?" but was in no position to question anything she was doing in her house. Still, he needed to know how Solomon's name was being tossed around so casually yet with such sacredness. "So ummm, Mia, Solomon? What do you know about Solomon?"

Mia smiled with relaxed childish confidence. "Solomon's my

brother," she said with affection. "He died before I was born. But he watches over me now from Heaven."

*What?* "Oh." Harper looked at Robyn, sure that the expression on his face said what his mouth could not. *Really? You told her about Solomon?* Robyn simply looked back at him, a look of defiance in her eyes. She held his glance and didn't look away. There was no mistake here. "I see," Harper said while spooning marinated tomatoes onto his breaded chicken.

Harper watched Mia, who was happily eating, and turned to Robyn, and back at Mia. His appetite had vanished, his stomach was frozen along with the rest of him. He struggled to control his facial expression and push down the geyser of emotion that threatened to erupt from his throat. Maybe he would shout, or cry, or even vomit. There was nothing settled about that name, about that time in his life, in their lives, in Robyn's. Mia's tribute had been so innocent. *Solomon, our angel,* she'd called him.

"You're not going to eat your dinner, Daddy?" Mia's voice touched him even before the warmth from her small hand reached the top of his larger one, suspended holding his fork. Only then did he realize he hadn't moved. He swallowed hard, pushing saliva down his dry throat.

"Of course, honey," he said, grabbing his knife to cut a small enough piece of chicken so he could manage it. He wasn't even sure that he'd be able to eat any of it. But he'd try for Mia. He'd slice and pick off his plate, move things around, soldier through this meal. Because as soon as Mia's head hit the pillow for bed, there was a much more complicated conversation to have with Robyn than he ever anticipated. "Mia, why don't you tell Mommy about that science experiment you guys were working on today." Harper made a maximum effort to sound unaffected.

"Oh my God, Mommy, we made a lamp out of a lemon."

"What?" Robyn reacted sincerely.

Mia nodded enthusiastically. "Yup," she said. "It lit up a light bulb and everything. . . ." Mia was fully engaged in regaling her parents with her latest discovery about the basics of electro-chemistry while Harper forced a smile onto his face and pieces of chicken paillard down his tight, dry throat.

# CHAPTER FORTY-ONE

## Robyn

Robyn drew the curtains together in Mia's room with a sharp pull of thinly hidden frustration. *I cannot even believe this shit* was her honest thought, but as a mother, she used all her available restraint to not show Mia the truth, especially this one. That her father was dating, no, *sleeping with,* his supposed best friend, and moreover that he had the nerve to give her static about telling Mia, her own daughter, about Solomon. He needed to go back home. *Now.*

One day, Mia would become a woman. And as a woman, she would find her heart broken in any manner of ways, from the failures and knocks of life, and from the loss of loved ones. But God forbid she ever experience a loss like that of Solomon. Robyn's loss. Sure, it was also Harper and Robyn's, the loss of their child, but it was Robyn who'd had to bear him, to live with the reality of him inside her body for months. To feel the changes, the promises in each development, the swelling of her breasts to produce milk, the blossoming of her emotions. The radiance of her skin. Robyn remembered how she'd glowed, like she was lit from the inside. She was so happy to finally, finally have that kind of love, to know that hers and Harper's love was so big and epic that it could expand beyond the two of them, that it could go so far as to create a life between them. Robyn was full of love then, when her womb was full with Solomon. And the loss of him, well, it almost destroyed her.

"Dinner was really good, Mommy." Mia's voice floated from across the room, and Robyn turned around, brought instantly to the reality of now, seeing Mia over in her bed, snuggled under the covers, with her hands holding her comforter up to her neck.

"Yeah. Daddy did a good job." Robyn was of course talking about the meal he prepared and the way he was able to steer conversation away from the awkwardness he exhibited when Mia offered her prayer. As soon as Mia had said it, Robyn knew it would be a point of contention. She vowed to give him grace, but Robyn was done accommodating Harper Stewart's comfort level. Robyn stepped over to Mia and sat on the side of her bed, stroking her soft curls away from her face and tucking them neatly under the edge of her bonnet.

"Yup. I'm glad we're all together, Mommy." Mia yawned.

"I know, baby. I know you are," Robyn answered. "Get some sleep and I'll see you in the morning. I love you so *so* much."

"I love you too, Mommy." Mia's sleepy voice sounded like she was already sweetly dreaming and her closed eyes confirmed it.

Robyn smoothed the bedding and stood up to turn off the light with one last lingering glance at her daughter. Outside of that room and the peacefulness that Robyn had maintained for Mia's sake was Harper in the kitchen, making another calamity of the dishes being washed, clinking them together as he placed them from the sink onto the drying rack.

"Hey," Robyn said, crossing over to him through the living room. "You okay?" she asked, referring to his reaction at the table. They both knew it. Harper was great at withholding information, but not so much at masking his emotion in the moment. His energy filled the room and there was no escaping this conversation she'd much prefer not to have.

For a moment, Harper didn't reply, he just kept piling clean dishes onto the drying rack, his back to her like all of a sudden he cared about scrubbing the plates spotless. Harper turned the water off, shook his hands of excess water, and stood still and silent. Robyn stood silently too, giving her ex-husband a moment to find the words he needed to formulate. She also didn't have all night. She was about to repeat herself, but he finally replied.

"Why would you do that, Robyn?"

Robyn took in a deep, quiet breath and looked skyward to gather more grace before replying. "Do what, Harper?" she answered with a question of her own.

Without turning around, Harper tilted his head toward the ceiling to respond. "Tell Mia about Solomon," Harper said quietly, his voice strained and gravelly. Then he finally turned to face his ex-wife. Hurt and confusion showed in his face. "That's a big decision, Robyn. Why would you do that? And not tell me?"

Robyn bit her lip to withhold the obvious quip. But other than to hurt him, to be defensive, what else was there to say that hadn't already been said? Now wasn't the time to throw his own decisions and secrecy back in his face, as much as she might want to. Instead, she maintained her calm, but spoke firmly.

"Harper, that was my experience to share with my daughter."

"Our daughter. And it was *our* experience," Harper snapped. "And—and she said it so casually. It's like you've created a reality for her that I know nothing about."

"There's no reality you're not a part of, Harper."

"Yes, there is, Robyn. She thinks that . . ." Harper caught his breath like he'd been punched in the gut. Robyn knew that feeling, and she started to feel a softening, of empathy. She knew how hard it had been for him, and it wouldn't be surprising if world-famous author Harper Stewart didn't have time for healing, not like this required. She walked over to him, stood beside him, and placed her hand on his arm.

"We both lost him," she said softly.

"Yeah, but why bring that to Mia? She's too young to even understand what happened. And you have her praying on it? She doesn't even know what she's saying."

Robyn felt a flash of anger. "Harper, you don't get to dictate what happens in my home. We thank the ancestors, those family members who have passed on as well as those who are here. And you will never, never understand what I went through and you never will have to. You can't tell me what to share with my daughter, Harper."

"*Our* daughter," he said.

"My *daughter,*" Robyn insisted. "And you are here in the middle of my life, Harper. In my home. And as much as you might want to, you can't make yourself the center of this universe. We are moving forward, *healing* and addressing what's true about the past. That's part of the beauty of West Africa. You can't look away, you can't forget, and you're not supposed to. This is a place of new beginnings, but we embrace the memories too." Harper shook his head and gave a sardonic scoff. Robyn didn't love his reaction but was unsurprised.

"It's not just about healing, Robyn," Harper said.

"You had your work to throw yourself into," Robyn reminded him. "But there was no escaping my own body, the reality that went with me everywhere I went. You have no idea what that was like for me. And you have no right to tell me what I can share with Mia." Robyn hesitated only momentarily. But she'd been bending over backward this whole time to accommodate so much of Harper, even now, even here in what was supposed to be her *own* life. And like a weed, he had already started to take up too much space. She had no idea why the thing she most needed to say felt like it was so hard to say. But still, she said it. "I think it's time for you to head back to your hotel. And then, *home.* You need to go back home, Harper."

Harper's face looked as if he took offense, and he began to protest. "Fine, but I have to say goodbye to Mia—" Harper began.

"No, you don't," Robyn stopped him. "Stop hiding behind her as some self-righteous excuse to overcompensate. Don't worry about Mia. Write her a letter. Send her a text. And go out like you came in. *Sneaky.*" With that, she turned to leave him standing there, frozen motionless in the kitchen. She closed her bedroom door behind her, shut her eyes, and, with a deep breath, closed herself off to the negative energy that had permeated the bulk of her day until she heard the door shut and the engine rev on Harper's rental car.

## CHAPTER FORTY-TWO

# Harper

**2004**

Harper and Robyn found out the sex of their first baby at the end of the first trimester.

Robyn had been indifferent. "As long as the baby is healthy," she would say. Harper of course echoed those sentiments as well, but still, he wanted to know. When they went for the first trimester appointment, the doctor rubbed the wand over Robyn's greased teeny baby bump, and everything looked great. A robust heartbeat was seen and heard on the ultrasound. They both looked intently at the screen and smiled.

"Do you guys want to know the sex?" the doctor asked. Harper eagerly looked at Robyn for approval.

"Go ahead." Robyn looked at her husband with an eye roll and a smile.

Harper gave the doctor an enthusiastic nod. "Yes. Yes please," he said.

"It's a boy," the doctor said. Harper's smile was massive, he kissed Robyn who was just as happy. Even a little teary-eyed, maybe from the news but also from seeing Harper so elated.

She gave him a look of pure love as Harper stood up, raised his arms up like he was a heavyweight champion, and danced around saying "Yes! Yes! Yes!" repeatedly.

"You are going to be awful, spoiling him," Robyn declared.

"Damn right I'mma spoil him, but no worse than you," Harper jokingly shot back. "Momma's boys are the worst."

"I know. I married one," Robyn said playfully.

"What?!" Harper protested, fake wrestling with his wife before showering her with kisses.

Later that night while Robyn lay in bed propped up by pillows, with her prenatal vitamin regimen and a cup of honey lemon tea that her husband made by her side, Harper asked, "Do you like the name Solomon?"

Robyn looked skyward, then smiled. She mused and said it out loud. "Solomon. I think Solomon is beautiful."

"*You're* beautiful. I love you." He leaned in and kissed his wife. Then kissed her stomach. "You hear that, Solomon? Daddy loves Mommy! Daddy loves you too!"

Robyn laughed. "Stop scaring him. He's sleeping . . ." Robyn teased. They were so excited.

In their four-story Harlem brownstone, they occupied the top two floors and Harper had picked the attic for his office. The second bedroom was for their baby boy, where they'd set up a nursery. They were both so full of joy, but Harper was especially thrilled to be having a son. Harper imagined that he would be handsome, intelligent, empowered, and the athlete that his daddy never was. Harper was going to be his protector, his best friend, his teacher. Robyn was going to be the perfect mom—loving and nurturing, but also protective, someone to fortify her son with love, affection, and savory meals. Mia and Lance were already basking in the glow of parenthood, as were Candace and Murch. LJ and Keisha were already in the world and Harper couldn't wait to show off his contribution. It wasn't a competition, but he loved this idea of his chosen family reveling in the joy of their biological families.

Harper and Robyn had already painted the room baby blue. It was a little cliché, but it was their first child, and they wanted the tradition. They had stenciled "Solomon" on the wall to celebrate Robyn's third month of pregnancy, right above where they envisioned his crib would be. Toni Morrison's *Song of Solomon* was one of the first books Harper read that made him think about being an author. What better way to pay homage to a great American writer. In his origin in the Bible, Solomon was "King of Kings," "Lord of Lords," and the Bible's "Song of Solomon" was about marriage and the physical manifestation of love—sex. Harper didn't know that the Bible went there. The thought of exalting his baby boy to know *he* was a "king of kings" was the boost he would need in a world that would regard him as a threat and try to diminish him. With Harper as his daddy and Robyn as his mommy, nothing could stop Solomon from reaching his fullest potential.

As the second trimester began, they let *everybody* know, and all were thrilled—especially the would-be grandparents.

Then the eighteenth-week appointment came. Robyn knew. She felt something was wrong that morning and that was *before* a stream of thick blood dropped into the toilet.

"Harper!" Robyn bellowed. "We have to go to the doctor." Harper heard the urgency in her voice and got them a cab. Robyn was right. The doctor couldn't detect a heartbeat. Solomon wouldn't make it. Harper was in complete shock and disbelief. *How could that be? Are you sure? Check again . . . please,* he pleaded. But it was true. Solomon was gone. Devastated, they held each other and sobbed. The emotional pain was deeper than he could have ever imagined. Harper was gutted. But the news got worse. When the doctors informed Harper and Robyn that they would need to "manage their loss," it meant that Robyn actually had to birth Solomon. They gave her a choice of putting her under and doing a surgical evacuation. But Robyn instead chose option two—to deliver. Harper instinctively shook his head, wanting to protect her, even amid his own devastation. "No, Robyn . . ." he said. "Isn't that going to hurt more? Don't you want . . . ?"

"I know what I want, Harper," Robyn told him. Worried that she wasn't thinking straight, Harper made sure the doctors explained the potential dangers, the pain and risks involved, both emotionally and physically. It would be traumatic. Before the doctor could finish, Robyn held up her hand signaling her to save her breath. "I understand," Robyn said. "I want to do it." All Harper could do was take Robyn's hand and wipe her tears.

When the contractions started at home, they returned to the labor and delivery unit of the hospital to confront the cruel irony of what they would shortly endure. Robyn was incredibly strong and measured. Harper was an emotional wreck. *Be strong,* he told himself. The doctors offered Robyn every comfort they would for any expectant mother, but Robyn refused. She'd read every book on pregnancy, on delivery, already watched every video. She knew. And she wanted to be fully lucid. Having the physical pain dulled wouldn't make her feel any better, she'd said. Harper tried to protest (again) and get Robyn to reconsider, but all she did was look at her husband and say, "Let's get it done. Let's welcome Solomon to the world." Robyn grabbed Harper's hand as if to say *be strong.* Harper stared in disbelief but then quickly nodded. If that's what she needed then Harper had to step up.

Harper admired her fortitude and had to draw on it to get through the procedure. He kept his eyes on his wife whenever she needed eye contact. When she closed her eyes or looked away Harper buried his face in his shoulder to hide his weakness from her. She likely knew he was crying. Her tears fell, but her composure made it seem more like a bodily function than an outpouring of sorrow. Robyn looked toward her stomach for Solomon's arrival.

When he arrived, Robyn wanted to see him. Harper did not. The doctor asked if Robyn was sure, and she repeated that she was. Robyn was sure about it all. The nurse then handed Robyn a bundle the size of a grapefruit, wrapped in a blanket. Harper had to look away. Robyn took her hand from his—not because she was angry or disappointed—but to hold their Solomon. Harper could hear the staff exiting the room, the medical equipment beeping rhythmically, and the sound of his own breathing for several seconds before he heard anything else.

"Hi, Solomon," Robyn whispered through tears. "Welcome to the world . . ." Harper bared down gritting his teeth, and somehow managed not to sob. Tears flooded his eyes and he let them rain down his cheeks and chin.

"Mommy loves you" Harper could hear her say through sniffles. "Mommy loves you so much. And Daddy loves you too." Harper bit down on his lower lip while his upper lip trembled, refusing to conform to his will. *Be strong,* he reminded himself.

"He's beautiful," Robyn said. "Solomon is beautiful." It was unclear if she was directing that comment at Harper, or if she was making a declaration. It didn't matter—Harper just wanted to leave. He just wanted to get his wife home and away from this place.

The nurse came back in after about fifteen minutes. It felt

like much longer. Harper heard her pad over to the bed at a not so intrusive pace. "Hi, Robyn," she said.

Robyn spoke back but it was so faint. "I'm ready," she said.

As Harper heard the nurse's feet head toward the door, he wiped his face clean of his tears and looked to Robyn, who was still staring at the doorway. After a beat she turned to him and spoke with concern. "Are you okay?"

"Am I okay? No," Harper declared. "But fuck, who cares. Are *you* okay?" Harper leaned toward her and embraced her.

"Yup," she said. "It's done. We did it." Harper held her tighter.

He couldn't really speak, managing only an "Uh-huh." Robyn never broke down. She was sad and emotional. It showed in her voice, in her face, and certainly in the days and weeks that followed in the way she walked with all the post-labor effects on her body. She didn't complain, just said it was all just "temporary." Some nights Harper would find Robyn gone from the bed and locked in the bathroom. He'd investigate and ask Robyn what he could do, could he get her anything, how could he help? But she always said in an upbeat voice from behind the door, "I'm okay. Go back to bed."

As time passed, if ever Harper brought up what happened, she acknowledged how tough it was but quickly changed the subject. Harper didn't press. Either she hadn't fully processed everything, or she was an incredibly strong woman. Both could have been (and were likely) true. And Harper didn't know how to help other than to let Robyn be Robyn.

## 2025

Harper lay on the floor of his hotel room. Handwritten notes for his movie pitch were still taped to the walls, illuminated only by the digital clock and the balcony lights from the hotel's many rooms shining in through the window. He had raided the minibar of all the dark liquor they had. Surrounded by the small empty bottles, he was fucked up now and yet still not numb. He felt *everything.* He stared at the ceiling and fantasized about what could have been. The carpet scratched his bare back because he'd stripped down to his underwear without even knowing why. He just had to. He also had to drink. The pain of that very visceral memory had been conjured up tonight from his daughter's simple utterance of "Solomon, our angel." *Mom's angel. Our . . .* Harper closed his eyes tight as more tears formed.

Solomon would have been twenty-one. A college junior. Maybe he would have followed in his old man's footsteps at Westmore. Maybe Northwestern like his mom. Or maybe he would have blazed his own trail. *Yeah . . .* Harper couldn't believe how vivid his recollection was. He wanted to bury it back again. They never should have named him. Harper never should have insisted on knowing the sex. But that was Harper—control the story, direct the narrative. And Robyn let him. She let Harper be Harper. She should have challenged him. But he wouldn't be the writer he had become without her unquestioning support and acceptance. Her sacrifice.

Letting Robyn be Robyn had been good for Harper. *Always.* She was still finding her way when they met and was constantly reinventing herself in the early stages of their marriage. Harper gave her the space to do so, and she seemed grateful, happy with Harper being Harper. She was always encouraging, a rock, making a meal, drawing a bath, buying the perfect sweater, jacket, or T-shirt just because she was thinking about him. She *considered* him. *Always.* Did he reciprocate? He thought he considered her. Her needs, her wants, her desires. He *thought* he did. He knew the buttons to push sexually, they took trips she suggested, he made sure he did laundry, tried to make up their bed, kept their house tidy, rubbed her aching feet. Some date nights took a back seat to his creativity, especially when the muse paid a visit. And she said she understood. She seemed to always want to hold up her end of the partnership. She went above and beyond in doing so, giving and giving and giving. Robyn letting Harper be Harper put him on a path to becoming a world-renowned Pulitzer Prize–winning author. Harper was always first. But for the first time, he wondered what that had cost her, all that giving. Now they were divorced and his heart was broken, while hers finally seemed to be mending. Instead of letting Harper be Harper, Robyn was letting Robyn be Robyn, finally, truly, and that didn't seem to involve him at all.

Had Robyn really been holding on to Solomon's memory this entire time? Through their entire marriage? He'd missed it. Robyn's pain from then was so clear now. The weight of all that strength, all that giving, of putting everyone else first. He hadn't considered her enough. He hadn't been attentive. For *so* long. He'd failed her. He'd been there and still left her alone. And now there was so little he had to give her that she needed. But he had to try.

## CHAPTER FORTY-THREE

# Jordan

On approach to O'Hare Airport, the airplane's flight path was so familiar to Jordan that from the oval window, even a thousand feet in the air, she could identify the neighborhoods below as they slowly descended. Square blocks and brick homes, apartment buildings and structures spoke to the solid middle-class that was the heart of the Midwest and the well-structured foundation that formed the core of her upbringing. Never mind that she sat nestled in a first-class seat, or that a text message from her awaiting driver would be on her phone even before she turned it back on after landing. This was home and it felt good to place her feet on solid ground.

As promised, Brian had arranged a dinner meeting with Dominion's chairman, scheduled for the next evening. The purpose of the trip was not for her to impress them, but rather for *them* to impress *her*, with their best attempts to convince Jordan to make a home again out of Chicago, their corporate headquarters, even if temporarily. As a company, they had problems that only Jordan Armstrong could solve, problems that, as was well known, she had solved for other companies. This meant there was nothing for her to prepare, and nothing to do other than what came most naturally for her. So arriving in Chicago, she was able to focus on what was overdue. A trip to see her parents. By now she'd pushed the memory she'd unearthed on paper back where it belonged. Buried, in her mind, somewhere in a drawer, in the past. It felt good to revisit who she used to be, especially now that she'd remembered why.

"Do you have any checked bags, Ms. Armstrong?" a black-suit-clad man inquired as she approached, heels clacking along the tile of airport floor. She'd spotted him easily as she descended the escalator into baggage claim. Black suit, white shirt, black tie, and a hat even, holding a white digital sign that clearly read ARMSTRONG on a backlit screen.

"No, just the carry-on," she confirmed.

"Fantastic. If you'll follow me, I'll call your driver now to pull up to the curb."

"Okay, then. Let's go," Jordan said.

When the car arrived, the man in the driver's seat briefly turned around to address her in the spacious cabin of the car. "Ma'am, I'm Gregory. I'll be taking you to the Peninsula today. Do we need to make any stops along the way?"

Jordan considered the question. Surely, she didn't need to go straight to the hotel. There were no preparations to make, and she felt plenty good after a first-class flight of only three and a half hours from Los Angeles. "Actually, yes," she said, then gave Gregory the address of her parents' home on Chicago's South Side. "And before we get there," she added, remembering her mother's constant instruction to never arrive anywhere empty-handed, "I'll need to make two other stops, one spot to pick up flowers and another to pick up a nice bottle."

"A bottle of wine, ma'am?"

Jordan smiled. "No. Johnnie Walker." Her dad would clown

her into next season if she showed up with a bottle of wine for him. He'd call her bougie and say she'd forgotten her roots.

"Very well. Three stops. And may I ask your selection of music? I can set the entertainment system to anything you'd like, classical, R&B, pop, jazz, or even white noise, if you prefer."

*This is about right,* Jordan thought. She knew that this experience was all part of the enticements of the position. An easy reminder of what it felt like to be catered to—at least, as an executive, outsourcing the concern for the details of your life to others, letting them optimize your comfort, put you first—so that your focus was concentrated on only one thing: their bottom line.

But what was her bottom line? It was hard to even consider what mattered most now. Everything was so muddled and confused. And better not to ask questions or think. Nothing good could come of it. Her feelings had left her spiraling, and she was relieved to have left those feelings right back in Malibu. A three-hour flight, and she'd managed to outrun them. And the memories of Harper that had been haunting her in every room of her house, in every song lyric, in every moment until she'd left. But this, this felt right, like it was where she was supposed to be. This was how she was supposed to be living, maybe where also. Chicago was a good kind of familiar. She opted for noise, lots of it, so she wouldn't have any chance of confrontation with unwelcome thoughts.

"Put on some hip-hop," Jordan said. "And none of that new trap crap. Give me that classic stuff."

"You got it, ma'am." Jordan could tell Gregory knew the assignment when A Tribe Called Quest's "Bonita Applebum/ Between the Sheets" remix hit the speakers.

"Yass, turn it up, please." Hearing the sound of heavy bass

and syncopated rhythms saturate the air in the cabin, Jordan settled into the seat behind her, hit the button for the back massage, and let her eyes close to enjoy the ride.

By the time Jordan reached her parents' redbrick two-story on Chicago's South Side, she was convinced that the nineties were possibly the best decade in music. Mary J. Blige was still singing hard as hell about "Real Love" when Jordan exited the car to step onto the curb.

"Would you like me to help carry your packages, Ms. Armstrong?" Geoffrey asked, still holding the door open for her with what seemed like all the patience in the world.

"No, I've got it," she replied, pulling the wrapped bouquet of colorful flowers into her arms and lacing her fingers through the corded bag handle carrying the box of Johnnie Walker Black Label. Of course she had it, she always did. And what would she look like having a suited-up white man following her up the steps to her parents' porch? It was too much, and Jordan was in no mood to hear her father's mouth about it.

"Sure thing, Ms. Armstrong. Just send me a text when you're ready to leave. I'll pull the car right up." She tightened her grip around the flowers. She'd picked them carefully, having seen so many versions of arrangements, almost one a day, sent by Harper, all left rotting right by the door in Malibu. Even when she'd tried to leave them outside, someone delivering her food order would bring them up to the door with them; *Too pretty to leave,* they'd say. Ironic. But certainly, the bar had been raised in the selection she'd brought for her mother. *So, thanks to Harper Stewart for that . . . I guess . . .* Jordan smiled and acknowledged her driver, appreciative for having such conveniences. She didn't like to wait, and Jordan *Motherfucking* Armstrong didn't have to wait, not for anyone. Harper evidently hadn't understood that about her. *He'll understand now,* she thought, and just as quickly pushed even the idea of him out of her mind, again. Harper had no business here in Chicago, and especially not living rent free in her head.

"Jordan! Look at you! And those flowers!" Jordan's mother was at the door pulling it open before Jordan even made it to the top step, so clearly excited to see her daughter. Her mother looked a little bit older, but still gorgeous and well preserved, with clear smooth skin and salt-and-pepper hair cascading in curls around her shoulders. She wore subtle makeup as she always did, and a swash of the same deep berry Estée Lauder lipstick she'd worn since at least the eighties. Behind her, Jordan's father became visible in the doorframe, wrapped in a brown-knit collared sweater, wearing his usual cold-weather brown corduroys and a Chicago Bears skully on his head. She was so glad that some things never changed. Jordan was her mother's baby, but her father's daughter. He'd wanted a boy, but made do with Jordan, teaching her the essence of "act like a lady, think like a man." *Steve Harvey learned that shit from me,* her father would always say.

"Hey there, Champ," Jordan's father greeted her with his nickname she'd had from the time she was ten years old—because Daddy wanted her to know she was a winner and to act like it. She was a daddy's girl in just that way then and since. Always setting herself up to land the shot no matter where she was. And she was excited to tell him about her newest opportunity, to see that same pride in his eyes. She needed that.

"Hey, Mom. Hi, Daddy." Jordan gave her greetings and handed over the gifts she brought.

"Oh, Jordan, these are *divine.* Let me find something to put them in right away," her mother said effusively, then scurried off toward the kitchen. Her mother was easy to please. Her father, not so much.

"Let me see what you got here," he said, rummaging his way into the bag that held the scotch. Jordan found herself holding her breath. "Oh, you got that Johnnie Walker. You know I only drink the good shit. What's this?" He pulled the box up out of the bag to examine it.

"It's Black Label, Daddy. That's the good stuff."

"Now, Jordan, Blue Label's the real good shit. You know I know that. But this'll do." And with that he slid the bottle back into the bag. "Now who's that white boy out there with you on the curb? You back with that slick dude from Vermont, are you?"

Jordan had to laugh and shook her head, following her father into the living room. "No, Daddy. He's just my driver. And Brian's from Massachusetts."

"Riiiight. He looked like a Kennedy."

"Speaking of Brian, he reached out to me regarding . . . a new job opportunity. One here in Chicago."

"You're taking another job?" Her mother's voice floated through the room. She came to join them in the living room with a vase of water filled with a perfect arrangement of the flowers that Jordan brought. Carefully, she set it on the table.

"I *might* be taking another job," Jordan corrected. "Dominion Communications brought me in for a meeting to see if they can get a yes out of me for the position."

"Dominion Communications? The cable company? They've been everywhere trying to get us to switch. Commercials, billboards."

"Hell, maybe we should switch. If my daughter's gonna be

running things we can do that." It was clear Daddy's interest was piqued. He was listening intently and nodding slowly to hear the whole story.

Her mother seemed concerned. "A new job, Jordan, really? And here, in Chicago? I thought that you'd decided on Malibu. And that you were taking a break to focus on yourself, honey." The tone in her voice was full of the only question that she didn't ask. *What happened, Jordan?* And once again, Jordan pushed the idea of Harper out of her mind, especially as the answer to any questions. But her mind was defiant. *Harper,* it said. *Harper happened.*

"Like I said, it's an opportunity. A good one. It's a company right in my wheelhouse and I can name my price. They'd handle all the details. I'm sitting down with the chairman for dinner tomorrow."

"That's sounds a-okay, Champ!" Jordan's father exclaimed. "Congratulations." It was the first moment of excitement she'd seen him display since she arrived. "That's my girl. They calling for my daughter, jack. And she commanding *top* dollar. I like that!"

Jordan looked at her mother who had been observing her husband's effusive praise and saw a disappointed look on her face. But she didn't say anything. *As usual,* Jordan thought.

"Mom?" Jordan said. "What do you think?" She wanted her to say something, anything about why she shouldn't be doing this. To say what she'd started to say about Malibu, and leaving all the balance she'd worked so hard to achieve. To say she shouldn't be running away. To tell her where else to find herself when a man had broken her heart. She waited for her mother to be the voice that Jordan had pushed so deep down within her that she couldn't hear it for herself anymore.

"Well," she started, turning her gaze from her husband to her daughter. "I think if that's what you want, then great." She shrugged and continued, "But like you said you don't have the job yet. Let's see what happens." Jordan received her mother's encouraging smile but longed for more.

"Aww hell. She's got it in the bag," her dad chimed in. "So, what're you gonna do about your hair?" her father continued. "That *short* style? That was the power look. Let people know you mean *business*!" He punctuated his observation with a punch to his palm. Clearly his days of retirement hadn't done much to soften the persona he'd developed to propel himself through the executive ranks.

"Aww, honey." Jordan's mother approached to smooth down one of the waves in her perfectly laid style. "This looks so nice. So . . . soft. Short hair is so much maintenance." Jordan stifled any response. She couldn't believe her parents were opining on her hairstyle when she'd just told them she'd been presented with the opportunity of a lifetime. An eight-figure comp package, executive housing, open-ended relocation. And aside from all that, she thought they'd be most excited about having her nearby, close to them again after all these years.

Jordan pulled herself away from her mother's grooming. "Look, all of this is subject to my dinner meeting tomorrow night with the chairman. We'll see what they're talking about and how correct they come."

"You know they better come with them commas," her father said.

"Hmm . . ." her mother said quietly. Both Jordan and her father turned to look at her. With their attention, she continued, still speaking softly, sweetly, but with clear intention behind her words, "The money is wonderful, Jordan, but you just make sure they give you enough time for yourself, and to meet someone nice. It's important, to be able to share your life with someone. Maybe you'll get to spend more time with that young man, Brian? If you'll be working together again?"

"That is the *last* thing on my mind," Jordan muttered under her breath.

"Good. I don't want no beige grandbabies right now anyway," her father chimed in. "Your mother can't wait, no matter what color they come out."

"Having babies is Jordan's decision, not ours." It was Mom's first declarative statement since she commented on the flowers. Jordan didn't have the energy to remind them that ship had likely sailed, or to bring her ovaries into discussion. Quickly, she realized she'd come to do what she needed to do, that her gifts and her news had been sufficiently delivered, and it was an added perk to have a driver waiting outside who could serve for efficiency and as an excuse. So she made her preparations to leave. "Well, I just stopped by to say hello. I'll be back before I leave. And who knows, maybe after tomorrow's dinner, they'll give me a million more reasons to stay."

"No question in my mind. Them white boys ain't stupid," her father said, even more enthusiastically than before. "They know quality when they see it, champ. Believe me."

In sharp contrast Mom looked a bit troubled. "Are you sure you can't stay for a bit? I can make you something. It's no trouble." It was clear she was searching for some connection and some more time to spend with her daughter.

"Maybe later. It was a long flight and I want to unwind a bit."

"Well, get some rest, dear," she responded and embraced her daughter tightly. "Good to see you."

Jordan thanked her mother and pulled herself away from her arms.

## CHAPTER FORTY-FOUR

# Robyn

**9:45 a.m.**

In the restaurant, instead of cooking, Robyn wiped down a table. Robyn's Nest was down a busser today, but Robyn as usual led by example. From time to time, she liked to be at the front of the house, greeting customers, letting them see the owner and operator on-site, doing what she loved. No matter how stressful the job of running this place was, seeing smiles on folks' faces when they tasted what she'd carefully crafted with loving hands made Robyn happy.

Robyn hadn't heard anything from Harper since she left him standing in her kitchen last night. Could he have left Ghana? Doubtful. Mia was upbeat and seemingly still on a high from last night's dinner when she got dropped off this morning at school. "Is Daddy coming to pick me up today?" was Mia's question as she gathered her things.

"I'll find out, baby. Have a great day. I love you," Robyn had said. "Daddy loves you too." Mia smiled. The last comment came out of Robyn's mouth involuntarily, but somehow, she felt compelled to say it. He was her father. And he did love her. He had always been a great daddy. Clearly, he hadn't communicated with her that he was gone yet. *Who the fuck knows* . . . Robyn sighed. *Harper was still . . . Harper.*

"Good morning." Aboagye's voice boomed into the dining room as he made his entrance, snapping Robyn out of her morning's recollection. Leading with his big belly, big smile, and those sunglasses on his face. Most of the staff looked at him with a combination of amusement and derision. Aboagye was like an annoying cousin who always overstayed his welcome *and* wanted a to-go plate.

"Good morning, Aboagye," Robyn said. He smiled, took her hand and kissed it. He gestured toward the front door to a couple of medium-built men in work clothes. "I brought my guys to take a look at your roof. Is it okay for them to bring in a ladder?"

*What? What's gotten into him?* she wondered. *Finally, he's making repairs?*

"Ummm, yeah. But . . ." Before Robyn could qualify her answer, Aboagye was already signaling the workmen to come in and pointing out the culprit in the roof.

"Make sure to cover the counter and floors, gentlemen . . ." he commanded as the crew brought in plastic drapes.

"Wait a minute, what's going on, Aboagye?" Robyn asked.

"Is this a bad time? I can have them come back later if that's what you'd like," Aboagye proposed, more politely than she'd ever heard him.

"No, it's perfectly fine. The breakfast rush is dying down. And I'd rather get it done than not, especially after *all* this time," Robyn said, barely masking her sarcasm.

"I knew that was your schedule and hoping that was the case," Aboagye said with renewed enthusiasm. Robyn grew even more suspicious. Aboagye was acting . . . strange.

"I appreciate it, but why now after all these weeks of

complaining?" she asked. Aboagye opened his mouth and leaned his head back slightly.

"Ahhh, so you haven't spoken to your husband?" Aboagye said, looking at Robyn's confused and crinkled visage. "Sorry. I meant your 'ex-husband.'"

"Harper?" Robyn questioned. "What does Harper have to do with this?" Aboagye squinted behind his sunglasses, took a breath, and stepped toward Robyn.

"He is saving you. He is saving your business," Aboagye reported as he nodded with a smile.

"What?" Robyn was shocked. Aboagye's words made no sense. *Saving me?*

Aboagye explained Harper's offer of covering the next two years' rent. Robyn could see Haniah out of the corner of her eye, behind the bar counter cleaning, but definitely listening.

"He said he was going to talk to you about this the other day," Aboagye reported. "But I have accepted his offer." *The other day?* Robyn thought. So much had come up between her and Harper in the past twenty-four hours that this bit of news should have been under the heading of "things to discuss." She vaguely remembered Harper wanting to discuss *something* last night but yesterday had been so full of emotional outpouring, conflict, and anger that Robyn couldn't hold it all in her brain. *Jesus Christ, Harper . . .*

"Well, he didn't. This is a surprise," Robyn declared.

"Hopefully, a pleasant one for you." Aboagye smiled as Robyn processed. "It is a gift. And a beautiful woman like you deserves it for the wonderful service you provide for your customers. Am I right?!" Aboagye said to the entirety of the sparsely populated dining room. The few patrons looked at each other and then Aboagye with amusement. Some nodded, some smiled, others looked to Robyn for a cue of approval. She was losing her patience.

"Aboagye, please," Robyn said signaling him to chill and quiet down.

He just smiled and let out a big belly laugh. "I am sorry. No disrespect, Ms. Robyn. We will keep things quiet and the disruption to a minimum," Aboagye declared. "Haniah, love? I'll take a cappuccino, extra foam. And some of Robyn's delicious bofrot. So sweet, so tasty." Aboagye looked at Robyn with a smile and raised eyebrows. Robyn turned to Haniah who smiled and began his cappuccino. Robyn turned back to Aboagye who laughed joyfully, anticipating his order. This could not be happening again. Going behind her back? Another secret? Coming out in ways both surprising and disruptive. Robyn started to seethe and then caught herself, finally finding her words.

"You need to leave," Robyn said calmly but with intention in her voice. Aboagye slowly lost his smile and turned his head back to fully face Robyn. He leaned forward slightly to make sure he heard correctly.

"I'm sorry, miss. Did you say I should leave?" Aboagye said.

"Yes. And take your men with you," Robyn elaborated.

"Robyn—?" Haniah said in protest. Robyn didn't miss a beat.

"Haniah, please give Mr. Aboagye his cappuccino to go and make his men a couple as well to go with the bofrot," Robyn said. Then she turned back to Aboagye. "Also to go." Now he looked extremely confused by what was happening. Haniah swooped in from behind the counter.

"Robyn, don't do this," Haniah said as discreetly as she could muster. "At least let them work on the roof."

"Sister Robyn, please listen to your employee," Aboagye said, but Robyn was locked into her messaging.

"Haniah, we have to get ready for the lunch rush, so I have to get back to the kosua ne meko." Haniah looked confused and shocked. Robyn turned back to Aboagye. "Make sure they get what they need . . . to eat. And have your men please sweep away any dust you brought in with you." With that Robyn headed back to the kitchen.

"You are making a mistake, Robyn," Aboagye announced to Robyn's retreating back. "I have other people who want this space!"

Robyn waved goodbye without turning around. "Have a great day," she called out as she walked through the door of her kitchen.

Robyn returned to her task of pounding plantains for today's fufu. But thoughts of Harper and Aboagye conspiring to determine her future and the future of Robyn's Nest was as bitter as the pith beneath the lemon peel she had zested this morning. This grand financial gesture would allow Robyn to see her restaurant thrive in a way that it deserved. Robyn wanted her business to survive and Harper in all his *fucking generosity* could obviously make it happen. Robyn knew she *deserved* it. But it felt like there was a catch. With Harper there always was—something involving him and his needs. Robyn wasn't interested in being caught up in that. She just wanted to live her life, move forward. Her way. On her terms.

Robyn sniffled as she continued pounding the plantains into submission when Haniah came back into the kitchen much more upset than Robyn had ever seen her.

"Do you realize what is happening, Robyn?" Haniah got in her face. "You're going to lose me. You could lose all of us if things keep going this way. You must put your pride aside for a minute and think of others." The kitchen staff stole glances at the confrontation, also looking for answers.

Robyn remained steadfast. "That's all I've ever done, Haniah," Robyn replied. "I need to look out for me and my best interests."

Haniah fell silent but nodded in a way of deep processing.

"Well . . . I'm going to have to do the same," Haniah stated. Robyn simply continued pounding the plantains. Haniah walked to the dining room, grabbed some fresh bofrot on her way. As she passed through the door Robyn looked up at where she'd exited. Now the eyes of all the other cooks and waitstaff were trained on Robyn. She turned her attention to them, unflinching.

"We're going to have a bunch of hungry customers here before we know it. Let's not be overrun and make sure we're on point." Robyn's words made the staff break their trance and get back to their respective duties.

**12:17 a.m.**

At home in her kitchen, Robyn stood at her sink and aimlessly swirled a soapy sponge around the dinner plate as the rain started. She heard it on the rooftop at first. She looked up toward the heavy patter of large, then frequent raindrops banging on her kitchen window. Her heart sank. How could her day get worse? This was how. The roof that Aboagye left without fixing would drip again, leaving another mess to clean in the morning.

It'd been a long day, and she felt it in her body like it'd been even longer than twenty-four hours. It wasn't just the long day at work, or the added pressures mounting in every moment with the staff at Robyn's Nest, or even her blowup with Haniah. It was Harper too. Involving himself like she didn't exist. She still hadn't heard anything from him. Had he gone back to New York? Did he go back to his "just happened" tryst with Jordan in California? Eating goat cheese omelets, drinking lattes, and hitting the fucking hiking trails? Satisfied that he had "solved" all the problems here in Accra? Robyn shook her head in disgust. The nerve of this man to come in, cause disruption and drama, and just leave. He didn't even tell Mia. She was disappointed when Robyn picked her up this afternoon. With all she had to deal with she didn't need that bullshit either. *Fuck you, Harper. Just fuck you.*

Though these weren't the words she left in a flurry of voicemails to his phone, her tone was clear. "I don't need to be rescued by you, Harper Stewart" began one. "I will not be beholden to you" was the gist of another. "You've brought nothing but confusion and disruption and I've had absolutely enough. But you should have the decency to *at least* let your daughter know what you're doing . . ." was part of another. He'd get the messages when he landed, Robyn supposed. But some indication would have been considerate at least. Since he wanted to "help" so much.

After her spat with Haniah she knew that the staff had to be looking elsewhere, and who could blame them? Would they show up in the morning to sweep out and clean up the dining room floor, which she was sure was taking on water at this very moment? She was numb save for the headache that was threatening to add its own layer of physical discomfort.

What was she going to do? Harper's meddling, his presence here in Accra, his insertion into her life and affairs had muddled everything, destabilized her. Because deep down somewhere was the insistent truth that she had felt a small amount of relief when she heard about Harper's offer to cover the rent. She also would be a fool not to admit that it had been helpful to have him pick up Mia from school so she didn't have to disrupt her workday. And even here, at home, it'd been days since she both cooked dinner and washed the dishes because he'd been another set of hands to take half the load. *It was helpful having him here.* With the longest sigh, Robyn had to at least admit that to herself. Helpful wasn't the problem, needing him was.

*He was just trying to contribute.* Robyn knew this, and she also knew that there was something foolish about her own force of pride. She was rejecting his offer, she was rejecting Kwesi's support, she was swatting away every hand extended to her. *Why?* Because she wanted to do it herself? And what good would that do? What did that prove? Since when had she become this person? Someone who got stuck on the formalities of things, who cared about appearances, who missed the point? This wasn't her either. And with that, the slow realization developed within her that by insisting on being the savior in the situation, she was letting everyone else down, herself included. The disappointment brought the first tear to her eye, which welled up in the corner until it slid down her cheek into the sudsy water below. She let the tears fall. Not the first time she'd cried like this—in frustration, alone, confused, along with the rain. *But I don't want to be saved,* Robyn thought. *But maybe I* . . . She didn't get a chance to complete the thought as her doorbell rang. Mia was sleeping and she rushed over without thinking just to make sure there wouldn't be another ring to wake her. She wiped her hands down her apron, rubbing the last of the suds off, and then the last of the tears from her cheeks. She squared her shoulders and filled her lungs with air to pull the door open.

In front of her, a most familiar face, but not familiar in this way. It was him, brown skin, bald head, a shadow of a beard. But distraught, breathing like he'd been running a marathon and soaking wet from the downpour.

"Harper? What are you doing here?"

## CHAPTER FORTY-FIVE

# Harper

Harper hadn't meant to drive to Robyn's house this late, not after she told him to go home. But he needed to speak with her—no, he *had* to, *urgently*.

He'd been in his hotel room packing and thinking, reliving moments of one failure after another, until it had become so much he wept. The way that he felt, he was ready to keep trying, keep showing up at her door day after day after day until she'd accept his help, his hand, his apology. Without this, there was no way he'd find peace.

When she opened the door, he was so thankful to see her across from him, all he could say was, "Robyn, I'm . . . sorry." He could feel the sadness exuding from her. She needed him. She needed him to be there for her in all the ways he hadn't been before. For all the times he'd left her to deal with things alone because she seemed strong enough to handle them. Because she wanted to be brave. But nobody should have to be *that* brave, *that* strong, *that* . . . alone. He wouldn't make her do that again.

"Please," he continued. "Just . . . hear me out." She held the door open but hadn't moved one step out of the way to allow him inside. But she hadn't shut the door in his face either. And if she had, he deserved it. Even if she'd slapped him, he deserved it. He'd take it. He'd take all of it if only she'd just give him the chance now. "I know what you said. And I heard you."

"Clearly, you didn't," Robyn said, shifting her weight to fold her arms in front of her.

"I heard you, Robyn, but I saw you too. I see you. And I didn't before." Robyn held her hand up between them, and opened her mouth as if to protest, but he needed to say it all. And it was one last act of selfishness, but perhaps the one that was needed, the only one that was ever needed. "Please, let me finish," he pleaded. Robyn's mouth closed, and her arms folded again. He took the moment in the pouring rain and continued, "I was just so caught up in my ego, *my* son, my career, my wife, Mia, the life *I* was providing for us. I . . ." but the words trailed off, caught in his throat. And he fought the stinging in his eyes with fists balled up against the corners. But the tears still came down his cheeks.

"Harper, just . . . come inside. Here, come in . . . Take off your shoes, I don't want the floor getting . . ." Harper was already half out of his soaked gym shoes and laid them by the door. Robyn closed it behind him and walked into the sitting room. She sighed loudly, clearly not happy about this development, but he was never more assured that right here, right now was exactly where he was supposed to be. Robyn stood in front of him. She looked pained, annoyed even. In the light of the room, he could see the tracks of moisture on her cheeks.

"Robyn, I'm not here to fight . . ." Harper said earnestly.

"What are you here for, then?" Robyn demanded. "Why are you still here?"

"I just want to help."

"I didn't *ask* for your help," Robyn spit back at him.

"You *never* ask for help," Harper said, voice raised. Robyn just stared at him. "You don't have to do this by yourself," he said, more softly this time.

"I don't need to be rescued."

"You don't *want* to be rescued, but maybe you do *need* to be," Harper said. Robyn shook her head at him, exhaling hard.

"Do not mansplain to me, Harper Stewart," Robyn fumed.

Harper bowed his head, knowing he'd touched a nerve, and softened his tone. But he knew his upcoming words would sting. He pushed them out anyway. It was the truth.

"I wanted you to fail, Robyn," Harper admitted. "I was so angry at you for taking Mia away. I wanted you to suffer here in Africa. I wanted things to be hard for you. I wanted you to have to admit you made a mistake. That you'd have to come back." His confession was to Robyn's feet, but now he raised his eyes to meet Robyn's. She was looking right back at him with hurt, scorn, breathing heavily. "I know you deserved happiness and fulfillment, and I wanted you to have that. But with me. Only with me . . ." Harper could feel the moisture in his nose start to form. His throat was growing a boulder. "I wanted to be the one who brought that to you, but *you* found it. You succeeded without me.

"And I was jealous. And hurt. I should have been able to move on," Harper continued confessing. "I'm the big Pulitzer Prize winner. I'm rich and successful and I could have anyone I wanted. But I couldn't. It was my life that wasn't working without you." Robyn's lips tightened and she shook her head in slow disbelief at what she was hearing.

"It's ridiculous. You've got all you've ever wanted," Robyn countered. Harper couldn't stop confessing.

"You should want to come back to me and be with me. But

you didn't need me. I should have been able to make you happy. And I couldn't. I didn't know how," Harper tearfully admitted.

"I failed you, Robyn. I'm a failure and I'm sorry. I should have done so much more for you and our family other than *money.*" He spit out the word "money" like it was filthy. It felt dirty. But it also felt hollow. He felt hollow.

"But that's all I can give now. You deserve it all. So, I'm asking you, Robyn," he continued. "I am begging you to let me help you. No strings. I just want you to continue what you started here. You belong here, Robyn," Harper admitted. "This is yours and I don't want to—"

And then a loud noise of flesh against flesh, reverberating from Robyn's hand to his left cheek.

Harper felt the sting of Robyn's stiff five fingers *smack* against his face. Hard enough for his body to produce automatic tears, not from pain, but out of shock. Wide-eyed, he looked at Robyn. She was breathing heavily and tears welled in her eyes but hadn't yet fallen. Harper calmed himself, folded his lips in on one another and parted them to speak.

"I deserved that—" Harper began.

*Slap!*

Robyn hit him again. Same cheek, same result. Harper had to take a long, deep breath to calm his defenses. Feelings of grief and sadness mixed with the pain of the strike. Tears rolled. But he wasn't sad for himself. He was sad for what he had caused. He had caused this. He deserved this. "Robyn, It's okay—"

*Slap!*

"Robyn, I'm sorry—" Harper was feeling the pain acutely.

Harper reached his hands up to protect his head. Robyn pushed his head so hard that his neck snapped back. The mush was jarring, painful. But he deserved it. He *wanted* it.

"Robyn, please. Let me—"

Robyn did it again, this time hitting the other side of his head. Harper instinctively went to protect his head and body and reached out for her to stop, but again, dropped his defenses.

Robyn hit his hands and arms with a flurry of both of hers.

"It's okay—" Harper spoke as his body rebelled against the sentiment. His hands and arms were being pummeled and retreated to cover his face and head.

*Whapwhapwhapwhapwhapwhapwhap!*

The blows proceeded like the drops of rain outside on the ground.

Robyn swung and landed hand after hand, forearm after forearm, letting out high-pitched frustration, exasperation, and pain. "I hate you. I hate you . . . I hate you."

"I know. I know. It's okay. I know—" Harper felt every blow, every word.

"Selfish . . . ass . . . fuck . . ." were Robyn's breathless words. Harper's knees hit the tiled floor, his lower back hunched, his arms covering his head from Robyn's scorn. She pummeled his back seemingly with all her might. Harper could feel the physical impact, but the pain was coming from regret, and realization, and sorrow from his heart. The pain he felt was everything that Robyn had ever held back, all heart and emotion attacking him and he held on for dear life. He reached forward for something solid, something to hold on to to anchor him from the onslaught. He reached and felt Robyn's legs through her dress.

*Whapwhapwhapwhap!* She continued, the blows came quicker and stronger, but Harper held on. He pulled himself tighter against the flurry, reaching up to her back, managing to pull his head, neck, and face into her torso, holding on to her, holding on.

"Get off of me . . . !" Robyn fought, another *whap!*

Harper interlocked his arms around her waist as she continued to rain fury on him, with heavy breathing and sweat now mixed with unrestrained tears that dripped on him. It didn't matter.

"Let me go!" *Whap!* "Let me go!" *Whap!*

"I'm sorry, Robyn . . ." *Whap!*

"I don't want your help . . ." *Whap!*

She pounded him with fists. He held on and resisted. He deserved every strike, every nasty word. He'd let her pour it out until there was nothing left.

"It's okay . . . it's okay," he kept repeating, giving Robyn permission. He never asked her to stop, never expressed the pain of it, just took it. *Keep going, Robyn . . . keep going.* He knew he deserved it all. She could do anything she wanted to him, and he would allow it. "I'm sorry, Robyn. I'm sorry, baby . . . I'm sorry . . . It's okay, baby . . . it's okay. . . ." He accepted the wrath. He would not let go of her. He would hold on, no matter how long it took.

Slowly the fists transitioned back to hands. The speed decreased. Her frequency became inconsistent, rhythmless. Robyn's breathing became heavier. Harper could feel her stomach expanding and contracting on his face. The bottom of her breasts were heaving and resting heavily on top of his head. Robyn inhaled and exhaled, fighting to get air back into her lungs. Her inhales quivered; her exhales quaked with sobs. She was sobbing, exhausted, drained. And Harper was responsible. He inhaled and exhaled with her in rhythm. Harper was drained and exhausted also. Harper too was sobbing. But he deserved this. Robyn did not. The darkened room was silent aside from their breathing, sniffles, and the heavy rain pummeling the house, pavement, and grass. Harper remained on his knees, his arms wrapped around her waist, his hands gripping the fabric of her dress, his fingers rubbing and squeezing her hips in a soothing motion. He wanted to try to ease her pain. He needed to try.

Harper felt her hands drape on his shoulders and stay motionless. She was spent, heaving heavy breaths. Harper pursed his lips; they looked to touch and soothe where it hurt on Robyn. He turned his head toward her waistline. He could feel her panty line on his ear and cheek. With his lips, his closest part to her, he sought to soothe and kiss her stomach slowly, lovingly, worshipful and reverent. Robyn's hands on his shoulders were now sliding east and west mimicking the rhythm of her deep breathing and Harper's fingers on her hips. His lips crossed her covered stomach, pelvis, and belly button with the same rhythm. He loosened the hold of his arms around her waist so that he could continue to massage her with his hands, to squeeze love back into her, up the sides of her stomach and her lower back. To his relief, Robyn's hands squeezed back, awake, caressing Harper's shoulders with each one of his kisses and each soothing touch her body received. Harper kept alleviating her pain. He wanted it to subside. He wanted her hurt to dissipate. He wanted to bring her body back into love, into herself, without suffering. For once.

On his knees still, he reached up as far as he could to caress and rub the back that bent over tables, and sinks, and stoves, all the way down to her buttocks where he took each one in his willing hands to squeeze and massage them through the thin fabric of her dress. Robyn's hands moved from his shoulders to slide along his moist head. She rubbed the smooth skin, searching to rediscover its shape, holding on to him as he brought what tenderness he could through his hands. Her fingers made their way to his ears and gripped them, pulled them, squeezing his earlobes between her thumbs and forefingers. Harper continued to cover Robyn's midsection with his lips, his hands running down the back of her thighs down to the hem of her dress and to her calves, firm from standing all day, from serving, from giving. Her skin was soft, bare, glossed with shea butter. His hands squeezed her muscles, released the tension, and moved up the back of her bare thighs to her buttocks again. She was so warm, so soft, and familiar. Robyn let out a heavy moan as her fingers expanded to fan across the back of his skull, her thumbs slid back and forth along the sides of his chin. She cradled his jaw and tugged his face toward hers. Harper rose off his knees to obey, but did not miss kissing her torso, kissing between her breasts, and pressing his lips along her clavicle. As he rose, his hands gripped her dress, dragging it with him up past her waist. He kissed up her neck to her chin that she'd lifted to give him access. When Harper fully stood up and brought himself face-to-face with Robyn, their lips met with no hesitation, no thought or reservation. Messy, wet, barely breathing, but so comfortable. He knew those lips so well, every line, every contour. Lips that felt so pillowy and soft, that kissed him back and that parted to let him enter with his tongue. Inside her mouth, their tongues slid around one another, consumed with reacquainting, twirling in a muscular dance. Her hands came up around him, and gripped him, holding tight to his shoulders, down to his arms, pulling her body closer to his, as if she were accessing a physical memory. Her actions quickly became more urgent and aggressive.

Harper continued to give her anything she wanted. Right now, he was hers for the taking. She, Robyn, could be as selfish as he had been. He wanted her to take and take from him. Anything she wanted, everything. He would oblige without hesitation. Instinctively, his hand went up toward her breasts, and cupping them, he caressed the small ridges of her nipples back and forth with his thumbs. She moaned, softly, a sound he remembered like poetry. Her hands began to pull up his wet shirt that clung to him from raindrops and sweat. Together they moved in a single mass, kissing, feeling the parts of each other they'd already learned, but with a stranger's hunger, with curiosity for the body contours of someone new. He pulled the top of her dress down past her breasts to her waist. She helped pull off her panties. Her hands grabbed at his sweatpants and underwear and yanked the waist down his hips. The erection he'd developed sprung free into the thickened air between them. Harper helped pull his pants down farther, over the flexed muscles of his thighs, high stepping out of his clothes before clinging back to Robyn. They wrapped their arms around each other and locked mouths again. He yanked down her bra straps to free her breasts, and she reached in to pull herself out of each of the cups, one at a time to reveal her engorged nipples and darkened areolas, settling the swaying mounds against her ribs. Seeing that she wanted this now, Harper wasn't going to stop, he couldn't stop. She was going to get everything he had left to give.

With her body, she received the apology he had never offered. They stood in her living room kissing, hands exploring each other's naked bodies, wet where saliva, sweat, and rain combined with their tears. Their midsections connected, grinding against one another, sliding together as Harper's penis searched for an opening. Robyn's hands grabbed him and placed him at her center, wet and pulsating moist heat. He slid inside and she moaned with abandon. Her warmth, her scent, the feeling of her wrapping around his manhood was what he knew, a memory his body slipped toward with ease. As good as she felt to Harper, though, he was not here for himself. He was there for Robyn.

"Give it to me," she said with a throaty whisper as she enveloped his whole ear with her mouth. "Give it to me, Harper," she commanded on hot breath against his earlobe. Harper adjusted his stance, crouching to gain more leverage, to use his back and his thighs, tensing them, squeezing the muscles so hard they trembled, all to give her what she asked for. Robyn tried straddling one of his legs to assist in Harper's stroking. She put one hand on his shoulder and the other on the back of his head, pulling him in deeper and deeper. "Come on. Don't stop . . ." she ordered. He wasn't going to. He didn't dare. He worked himself thrusting, pushing his body into its furthest limits to do whatever she said, for fear that he wouldn't be able to make *this* apology, that she wouldn't give him the chance, that if they separated for even a moment, it would be over, done and undone all at once.

So he kept kissing her, touching her, feeling her, driving love into her, doing anything he knew to give her pleasure. To fight for soft moans from her, to persist in her pleasure blooming here and now, with anything she asked for, *anything.* He'd not let go of her until . . . there was no until. He'd just make use of every moment she gave him.

"Don't stop," Robyn said. "Don't you dare stop . . ." Robyn closed her eyes and moaned and breathed heavy as her rhythm met Harper's. He watched her, making sure she received what she wanted, what she needed. She pulled her leg across to straddle his hips, settling her full weight and passion on his pelvis. Harper steadied himself, maintaining that same challenging crouch using every muscle of his back, his ass, and his thighs to support them, to support Robyn and hold her up, guiding her by her waist. With every bit of his effort, he brought his other hand to hold on to the back of her thigh. He could do it; he had to. The sound now was bodies slapping together, a slapping of wet skin on wet skin, Robyn riding him with a vengeance. Harper staggered briefly but held on. Failure was not an option. Not tonight. Not ever again . . .

# CHAPTER FORTY-SIX

## Jordan

On the eighteenth floor of Chicago's Peninsula Hotel, Jordan stood facing the open lacquered wood doors in the bedroom closet of her executive suite. Her luggage had been carefully arranged by housekeeping, and her favorite business attire was perfectly placed on hangers. She reached a freshly manicured brown hand in front of her to pull down her red Valentino pantsuit that was a perfectly tailored fit.

On the floor of the closet were the black patent-leather Louboutin stilettos that took her frame instantly from a million bucks to a billion. She envisioned herself walking tall and confident into Gibsons Steakhouse, as old school and stodgy as it got in Chicago, where the real money showed up for dinner and the big deals were cut over white fabric tablecloths ensconced within the carved mahogany walls. And the brown of the wood and the service staff was about all the dark brown you'd expect to see in that place. But tonight, Jordan Armstrong would be walking in to make one hell of an impression.

She had already done her research on Dominion Communications' chairman of the board, Charles Farmer, who, according to *Forbes,* had a net worth of $23 billion. He'd served as the company's board chairman for the last five years. He was a serial entrepreneur and most recently had sold a telecom company to Verizon.

Jordan studied herself in the floor-length mirror, measuring herself up to the moment before her. She had not only researched Charles, but also every member of the board of directors, along with its current executive leadership team. Especially the latter since they would all be reporting to her if she decided to take this position. She'd already found pictures of Charles ringing the bell at the New York Stock Exchange, images of him at the White House attending a state dinner, and pictures at the groundbreaking for a research wing at his alma mater, of course named after his family. In fact, their dinner tonight was set for thirty minutes after the landing of his flight in from New York, which of course meant that his flight was also on *his* plane.

Seeing herself in the mirror, all suited up, Jordan felt almost giddy, almost like her old self. She enjoyed that rush of power, of confidence, of feeling like the world was at her fingertips. Her eyes sparkled between the flowing waves of her highlighted hair, split down the middle. *Should I cut my hair?* she wondered. Sure, "casual beach waves" Jordan was a carefree version of her, but as her dad had said, the short hair was the power move. Had she become too soft? At least this job would give her plenty of money, *more money than I could ever spend,* she thought. It'd be money, plus stock options, hours on the corporate jet, legacy. And *a lot* of hours of work. Her mom would be concerned, of course. She never trusted Jordan's decisions, although, all of Jordan's decisions had been great. All except one.

# CHAPTER FORTY-SEVEN

## Robyn

Robyn stirred awake. Her eyes slowly blinked open, first to the ceiling fan oscillating over her bed.

The second thing she noticed was Harper's arm draped around her waist, his raw morning wood pressing against her naked backside. Robyn slept well with him spooning her. They still fit together, even in her bed. Surprisingly. This was *her* bed. *Not theirs and never had been.* She hadn't even shared it with anyone other than Mia occasionally. Yet it felt natural with Harper, at least through the night. But now she was awake and conscious. The midnight rain had given way to a hot Accra day. The passion, magic, and emotion of last night had dissipated.

Third, she and Harper were both naked as newborns. She had to move. She needed to get Mia ready for school, to call to see if Robyn's Nest had any flood damage from last night's rain and Haniah. *Oh, Haniah.* Her trusted soldier, her confidante. She needed an answer about moving to the Polo Club. She felt so bad. Aboagye's presence had pushed her, and Haniah hadn't deserved Robyn's dismissiveness in that moment. Haniah had been on her side from the get-go. She was loyal. Robyn had meant to meditate on the entire matter before Harper's unexpected arrival last night. Now she could feel his deep breathing on her shoulder.

She turned her head and shifted her body slightly to look at him. He was still handsome, still sexy, but in the morning light and the reality of her life none of that mattered. She not-so-gingerly peeled his arm off her to start her day.

"Harper, come on, wake up." Robyn turned 180 degrees to face him, conscious of the density of her unencumbered breasts hitting the mattress beneath her. "You need to get up." She grabbed his bicep and gave it a firm but gentle shake to stir him. She hadn't even looked at a clock, but judging from the sunlight it was later than the usual time she started her routine of ten minutes of morning meditation and coffee. This morning, she was waiting on Harper, who began to stir with a deeper inhale and a groan. Robyn shook him a bit more, "Come on. I'll make you some coffee. . . ." Harper slowly opened his eyes. He blinked awake without the urgency Robyn had wished for but at least he was one step closer to being out of her bed. And that's when Mia entered.

"Morning, Mom . . ." Robyn had heard her daughter's footsteps approaching the door and the sound of the doorknob turning but hadn't thought about her walking in until she actually did. Mia entering her room unannounced wasn't forbidden, but it wasn't routine either. Robyn instinctively shifted her body and sat up, taking a slight beat to quickly cover her swinging breasts. But this wasn't about nudity. Mia knew the difference between nudity and shame. Fully dressed and coiffed for the day, Mia froze upon seeing her parents sharing a bed, clearly naked under those sheets. Robyn's face immediately went hot as she swallowed around her dry throat.

"Mia, what— Good morning— Go pull out the coffee for

me, please—" Robyn stammered. Mia's wide eyes shifted from Robyn to Harper as her lips parted. Out of her peripheral vision Robyn could see Harper calmly propping himself on his elbow.

"Morning, Mimi," Harper said.

"Hi, Dad," she replied after a slight pause.

"You sleep good?" Harper asked. *What?!* Robyn thought. This wasn't the time for small talk. There was entirely too much to explain. *We're not changing for our little girl,* Robyn had said clearly. This was no time to muddy the waters. *Enough with this casual shit.* It was all Robyn could do to stop herself from jumping up and ushering her daughter out of the room.

"Uh-huh." Mia was still in conversation with her dad while she shifted her look back to her mother. It was all so uncomfortable for Robyn. Too uncomfortable.

"Good. Give me and Mom a minute. And check to see if we have all the ingredients for some French toast, okay?" Harper said, like everything was normal. Robyn was mortified.

"Okay," Mia said.

"Thanks, honey." Harper shifted to a sitting position against Robyn's headboard.

Mia took her time before turning away from her parents to exit, clearly capturing a full mental picture of her mother and father before she left. And did Robyn detect a small smile before she turned away? *Ugh . . .* Robyn considered the notion that Mia was happy with what she just saw, and the confusion that would create. Robyn shut her eyes to gather her thoughts and contemplate her next move as Mia closed the door behind her. She could hear Harper sigh and the creak of her bed as he turned to shift his focus on her. Robyn opened her eyes and twisted toward him, only to witness Harper's slight grin. *What is there to smile about?*

"Morning," Harper said. He was studying Robyn's face.

"Sorry about that. I'll start breakfast." As he started to swing his legs out of the bed, Robyn grabbed his arm.

"Wait. What are you going to tell her?"

"I'm not going to say anything other than 'Where's the vanilla, eggs, bread, and a bowl,'" Harper replied far too casually still.

"What if she asks?"

Harper shrugged. "I'll say it was late and Mommy and Daddy had a sleepover."

"Harper . . ." Robyn said.

"Look, we should get her to school. The rest we'll figure out after drop-off. Okay?" Harper calmly pulled his underwear on.

Robyn turned her face away from him before she responded. "Yeah. Okay. Fine."

Harper then pulled on his pants before he exited, making Robyn grateful he'd at least had the wherewithal to gather their clothes off the living room floor before they went to sleep. When he closed the door behind himself, Robyn buried her face in her hands and shook her head, wondering only *why?* She yanked the sheets off her naked body like a Band-Aid on a wound, swung her legs over the side of the bed, and pushed herself up.

Once dressed, Robyn entered the kitchen to hear laughter from her daughter and ex-husband, who were enjoying each other and their choice of morning music. Though it made Robyn happy to see that bright smile on Mia's little face, she knew it was largely the result of something that couldn't be sustained. What would be on the other side once reality set back in? For so long, Robyn just let everything happen "like it's supposed to." She let nature take its course. But now she was feeling more like she had to be proactive about how things worked out. Especially *this* thing.

All three of them loaded into her RAV4 to run Mia to

school. Mia offered her dad shotgun, but Harper gladly took the back seat, sitting between the gaze of his ex-wife and his daughter. Despite her discomfort, Robyn managed to crack a smile and even break into laughter at Harper's imitations, silly riddles, and quick jokes. To the outside world they looked like a happy family. And for a few moments it felt that way to Robyn too.

As they pulled to the front of the school Mia commanded, "Come on and walk me in, Daddy." Robyn was surprised because Mia hadn't wanted to be walked in since she turned eleven. At least not by Robyn.

"You cool with that, Mom? It'll only take a few seconds," Harper asked.

"Sure." Robyn was not going to deny her daughter the pleasure of her dad's company. It hadn't occurred to her until now that Mia probably took pride in showing her daddy "all the way from America" off to her classmates and teachers. Robyn noticed that Mia walked taller and prouder holding her father's hand as they moved down the pathway to the school. *She's a big girl now, but she is always going to be daddy's girl.* She sighed.

Robyn blew Mia a kiss from the car. Standing with her at the door of the school, Harper bent down to kiss her. "Bye, Dad," she mouthed and smiled at him before turning to scamper inside. Seeing Mia so happy, and watching Harper look back at their daughter with pride as he headed back to the car, Robyn sighed heavily again—the familiar knot in her stomach was growing. She had to do something.

Harper returned to Robyn's RAV4 where she remained pleasant, but mostly silent. He opened the passenger-side door for himself and the two of them sat without speaking.

Finally, Harper asked, "You okay?"

"Mm-hmm." Robyn's response was terse. In her mind she knew *this can't continue.*

"She didn't really ask anything about this morning," Harper reported. "She was mainly talking about a quiz she was a little worried about. That's all."

"Uh-huh," Robyn said absentmindedly. Her phone rang then, and Kwesi's name popped up on her screen. *Clockwork.* He always checked in after drop-off. Robyn stared at the display. She felt Harper's eyes looking between her and the screen. After the phone's third ring, Robyn hit the decline button. "I want to take you somewhere," she said. Before Harper could say "okay," Robyn put the car in drive and took off.

"Where are we going?" Harper asked.

"Labadi Beach."

"Beach day," he said with a smile. "Okay."

"It's not exactly that, but it's beautiful," Robyn informed him. "I give thanks and tribute to the ancestors. And I think it would be good for you to do so as well."

"I'm down." Harper smiled and seemed good-natured, along for the ride.

"Good," Robyn replied. "I think it would be good for you to honor them . . . and Solomon." Harper became completely still. Robyn looked over at him. The smile had vanished. She turned back to put her eyes on the road. From her periphery she saw Harper tilt his head down. She turned to look at him again and he began to nod.

## CHAPTER FORTY-EIGHT

# Harper

As Harper and Robyn arrived at Labadi Beach, Harper remarked that the blue skies and never-ending ocean were beautiful, but different in their feel and look from anywhere else he'd ever experienced. It was painful, powerful, and caused an overall malaise. It came over him like a heavy cloak, weighing him down. The spirit of Solomon, maybe the ancestors that had come there before him were all likely present? When Robyn and Mia first moved to Accra, Harper had visited Cape Coast and had gone to the Door of No Return at Elmina Castle. As a family they went to the dungeons where captured Africans were held and chained together, separated only by gender, without regard for language or culture. Stripped naked, they were bathed then shackled again before being thrown into the wretched hulls of the enslavers' ships. Harper felt something there for sure. Many folks on that tour said they felt the spirits of the ancestors. It was heavy. Even though Labadi Beach, more of a tourist area, was miles and miles from the castle, Harper felt a heavier, more personal, more profound part of him, weighed down.

Harper and Robyn stood by the shore, barefoot, holding hands.

"What do you want to say to him?" Robyn asked.

Harper looked at Robyn with confusion. "What do I— What? I thought you were going to lead us in . . ." Robyn just continued to hold eye contact with a gentle expression. "I don't know, Robyn. I don't know."

"Harper, you're one of the world's most prolific writers. Try," Robyn encouraged. More than anything, his loss of words was out of fear of what he'd say. How do you sum up an actual lifetime of words for a son you never had?

"Don't think of this as your magnum opus. Think of this as the first draft. Or your journal," Robyn suggested. Harper turned to Robyn. She spoke his language. She smiled at him and squeezed his hand. He tried smiling back but his heart was too heavy; he was nervous. "Don't filter. Just be honest. Unload, Harper."

After another moment, Harper felt like he could begin. "I always wanted to meet him," he said.

"Tell him." Harper looked at her. She nodded. "Tell him."

Harper looked out again toward the powerful yet peaceful ocean.

"I always wanted to meet you, Solomon," Harper began. "I know I had the chance when you left Mommy's body. But . . . I didn't want to see you like that. I couldn't bear it. That wasn't you. Not the you I saw in my mind," Harper continued. "I imagine the man you'd be now. Tall and handsome. A great combination of Mom and me. Smart. Man, you'd be so smart. You'd have come by it naturally, but Mom would have made sure you were encouraged to discover all your gifts." Harper's tears started creeping out the corners of his eyes and his voice began to quaver. "I think we would have been best friends. We would have had our fights. That's only natural. And you'd tell Mom 'Dad doesn't understand me' and I'd tell her 'Solomon just doesn't get it.' We'd have played catch, you would have learned how to swim, we'd have done Little League baseball, and I would have read to you every night. You would have loved hearing stories. You'd say 'Read another one, Daddy? Just one more, Daddy,' and I'd do it. I never would have said no," Harper continued.

"Good. Keep going, Harper. Keep talking," Robyn encouraged.

"You would have loved my boys. Your uncles. Uncle Lance would teach you football and the Bible, Uncle Murch would teach you how to dance, how to be a leader, and to have integrity and I would rely on them to help me raise my first-born son. I'd get so much wrong, but damn it, I would try. I would try so hard. Uncle Quentin would have taught you the guitar and music and how to play the dozens. Because you gotta have thick skin around Black folks, son. And you gotta be ready with your comebacks. And *spades.* Oh, you'd have to master spades. An absolute nonnegotiable. I'd teach you how to bid correctly, to set people and talk shit. That's basic Black, Solomon. Basic. Black." Harper laughed as messy tears came. "You'd be a great son," Harper said. "You'd have been the best thing I helped to create. Nothing I would write would be better than you. Nothing," Harper declared. He went silent save for his sobs. Harper felt Robyn's hand rub his back.

"I miss you, Solomon," Harper said through a face full of tears, through quivering lips. "I love you, Solomon. You are my angel. You've been there and I haven't paid attention. But it's been you. It's been you all along. Thank you for being there for me. You've probably guided me more than I know," Harper declared. "You're my muse." His tears were a cleansing cry. Harper didn't even try to stop it. A purge. His knees hit the soft wet sand and his body shook violently, heaving. He felt Robyn's much-needed love and support in that moment.

"It's okay. It's okay. You're okay, Harper," Robyn said. "He's okay. He loves you. He forgives you. Solomon forgives you, Harper." Harper couldn't stop sobbing. Robyn knelt beside him and embraced him from behind. Her warm tears dropped on his neck and shoulder. "Let it out. It's the beginning. It's just the beginning. He will give you strength, he will give you wisdom. He will give you love, Harper." Harper felt nauseous, breathless.

"Here," Robyn said, handing him her water bottle. "Hydrate. Come on, baby." Her voice was maternal, loving, soothing, comforting. *Robyn.*

Harper caught his breath, wiped his tears, exhaled deeply. He looked at Robyn, who regarded him with understanding and empathy. They hugged while on their knees, with love and endless support in their embrace, lasting until they pulled back enough for Harper to look into Robyn's eyes. The same eyes that he used to wake up to for over two decades. The same eyes that showed nurturing patience, understanding, and acceptance. Her partially sandy thumbs wiped his tears off his face. Harper wiped his moist nose and upper lip, letting out an embarrassed "Oh . . . God."

"It's okay," Robyn said. "It's okay."

"Thank you, Robyn." Harper meant it deeply.

"You're welcome." Robyn nodded. She handed him a handkerchief, rubbed his shoulder, and leaned forward to kiss his cheek. "Take your time." She abruptly stood and headed back to the car. Harper watched her go, wishing she hadn't left him there. But he also understood why. As Robyn became smaller in his vision, Harper turned back to the ocean, took a deep breath, and let out a verbal and forceful sigh. He closed his eyes and listened to the sounds around him. The seagulls, the crashing waves, and his deep breathing became his soundtrack of his return to himself.

# CHAPTER FORTY-NINE

## Robyn

"How has the trip been?" Robyn asked Kwesi on FaceTime from her car. From what she could see, Kwesi was walking on some kind of university campus.

"Good, ya. Nigel seems to be taking to the University of Liverpool. I'm really wanting him to investigate the Caribbean or back home. He needs some Black influence."

"I guess you guys don't have any HBCU's over there." Robyn smiled at the screen while keeping an eye on Harper, who was making his way back to the car.

"Nah, just tighty-whities. How you doing, love? How's Mia?"

"She's okay. She'll be a real mess when her father leaves."

Kwesi nodded, with a subtle smile. "Mmmm. So . . . Harper is still there, yeah?"

Robyn knew Kwesi wasn't wholly comfortable with that notion. But Robyn also knew he didn't have much of a leg to stand on given his own family circumstances. And now that gave her comfort. Not stress.

"He is. We'll talk when you get back," Robyn said.

"I see. Okay . . ." Kwesi sounded reticent. Robyn knew it was time to give reassurance.

"Hey, I miss you," she offered sweetly. "My feet miss you too." She smiled at the memory.

Kwesi let out a small chuckle. "I miss you and them too," he teased right as Harper approached the passenger-side door. His eyes were bloodshot with tears. Robyn smiled at her phone, said goodbye to Kwesi, and hung up right as Harper reached for the door. He climbed in and closed it, muffling the sound of the ocean and tourists outside.

"Everything okay?" Robyn asked.

Harper nodded. "Yeah, I'm good."

"Good," Robyn replied as she looked out the front windshield. She had something that needed to be said.

"I'm not taking your money, Harper." Harper turned to her. She looked back at him. She wanted him to hear her and see it in her face. "I appreciate the offer, but that's not the answer."

"Well, what is?"

"I don't know, but I'm going to figure it out."

"Whatever it is, I'd like to help figure it out. Together." Harper took her hand. Robyn pulled it away. Harper's brow furrowed. She decided to end the confusion for once and for all.

"Last night was incredible . . . and a little crazy."

Harper nodded. "Yeah . . ."

"But you don't owe me anything. And . . . vice versa," Robyn declared. "I need to move forward with clarity and certainty. The 'married to Harper' part is over for me," Robyn said.

"I get it," Harper said. "Will it make you feel better if we consider it a loan? A no interest loan," Harper said. "You pay me back whenever."

"It's not about that for me, Harper."

"Because of ol' boy—?" Harper began to say. Robyn shook her head.

"'Ol' boy's name is *Kwesi.* And no. It's not because of Kwesi.

It's because of me, Harper. This is about me. You do what you want for your journey, your path, but it no longer involves me. . . ."

"What are you going to do with Robyn's Nest?" Harper asked sincerely.

"Let's take a ride," Robyn said.

"Another one?" Harper joked.

Robyn gave him a playful, not playful side-eye. "Do you trust me?"

Harper returned her side-eye and chuckled a little. "Yes, I trust you. Of course."

"Good, I want to show you one more thing," Robyn said as she cranked up the SUV.

# CHAPTER FIFTY

## Harper

Back at Robyn's home, Harper followed Robyn to her backyard. The giant hammock looked like an inviting place to lay right about now, but Robyn led them both to her small vegetable and herb garden. Harper had noticed it from afar. It was perfectly squared off. About twelve feet in length and an explosion of vegetation. Tall stalks of sunflowers; bushy shoots of leafy green collards and kale; eggplant, plump red tomatoes on vines, various sizes of multicolored peppers; and fresh and fragrant herbs—mint, basil, sage, thyme, lemongrass, and dill. It all sat underneath the guard of a mango tree.

Robyn walked ahead of him, thumbing a green leaf in front of them. She seemed so relaxed, so, at home. She turned to him. Squinting a bit with the sun on her face, she looked beautiful, like a goddess in the middle of a fairy tale. The gentle breeze jostled her tendrils of twists around her cheeks.

"I've been tending this garden since we moved in here," Robyn said.

Harper looked around with sincere admiration. "It's certainly better than ours was back on the Upper West Side," Harper joked.

"Uh-huh. I had to learn the qualities of the soil here, in Ghana. It's different from what we had in our last place, true. It's richer, with more minerals and nutrients. And the sun and water have to be balanced so that everything grows at its best."

"This is incredible, Robyn." Harper was awestruck, and a little confused. For sure, Robyn had a good reason for bringing him here other than to show off her horticultural skills.

"Thanks," she said. "See these leaves?" She pointed to a small cluster of common looking greenery. Harper nodded. "That's sweet basil. It needs a lot of sun and a lot of water to grow well." She picked a leaf and snapped the stem. She brought it to her nose and inhaled deeply. "Here, smell." She brought it to Harper. He inhaled the freshness, the sweet herbal smell of it, unmistakably like Italian food, but here they were in the lushness of Africa, in Ghana. "But this one, see this plant? For as spicy as it is on the palate, it's actually very delicate as it grows." She showed Harper a deep red chili pepper, slim and fiery, hanging on a green peduncle.

"Spicy, eh? You like to cook with that one." Harper made his best attempt at another joke, despite the air of seriousness between them.

Robyn smiled. "Right, a little goes a long way. But it makes a dish better, wakes it up," she said. "But only if you can get it to grow." She let her fingertips graze the vegetation again and then turned back to him. He felt the energy of having her full attention. "You know, gardening . . . it's a lot of work. Getting all these temperamental plants to grow. A lot of sacrifice. You must be consistent, anticipate their needs, read between the lines. You have to pay attention, Harper, and not just in an emergency, because then it's already too late. You tend to this day in and day out, from one month . . . one *season* to the next, year after year. That's the only way it works."

Harper felt his sarcasm bone start to twitch. "Something tells me you're talking about more than just gardening, Robyn."

"You are as smart as you look, sir," Robyn quipped. "You have to make your own garden and love it, tend to it, water it, talk to it, shade it, prune it," she said. "It doesn't need all your attention, all the time, but it does require your consistent presence and care. Sometimes things will happen because of circumstances, climate, environment, critters that want to eat away at it and some who want to help it flourish. It's your job to monitor it, nourish it, and love it. You've been the delicate flower that needed watering and attention and sun. Now it's your turn to be a gardener."

Harper crinkled his forehead and coupled it with a smirk. "A gardener, Robyn?"

"A *dedicated* gardener, yes. To learn how to grow and nurture something beyond your books." Robyn smiled. "To nurture *someone* . . . someone *else.*"

Harper's brow furrowed, but he was listening.

And then with a sigh, she seemed to soften, but her shoulders rounded again. "I . . . am going to be all right," she pronounced. "I've thought about it: I don't need this much. The big restaurant, all the staff, two sittings . . . it's not *me.* I came here for a simpler life, for more time, for healing, for peace. And then I got here and just started re-creating everything from back in the States. What we *think* we need for happiness. What success is supposed to look like. I don't need that, Harper."

Harper took her words in and they made sense. Like the home she had built and the garden she tended to, they were reflections of her. He nodded.

"And what if I could be here more often to support you? Financially and otherwise," Harper asked. "Does that change anything for you?"

Robyn sighed, "If you really want to stay here, in Accra, in Ghana, if you imagine this place as where your happiness is, I can't stop you. But don't do it because you think there's some kind of do-over."

"But, what about Mia?"

"Mia . . . will be fine. She's going through what adolescents go through. She'll get past it and we'll help. We'll always be her parents. We'll always be family. But Harper, you and I . . . we have separate futures."

"So, you're saying . . ." Harper had a hard time finding the words, but he understood the truth. "You're saying that . . . you don't need me."

Robyn took a deep breath. Her eyes held the answer. He had to figure the rest out on his own.

"You're free, Harper. You're free," she said, taking his hands. "And as long as you understand the sacrifice this kind of love takes, you're going to find your way. But get your hands deep in that soil, Harper. It's the only way to cultivate a life. You have to nurture it, sacrifice for it. You don't owe me anything more. But the same might not be true for everyone else in your life."

It was clear at that moment that Robyn was giving him permission. She was releasing him from any self-inflicted obligations to her. But she was also tasking him with fulfilling an assignment. If he completed it he might truly get what he wanted. He pulled Robyn into an embrace in the middle of her garden, closed his eyes, and uttered the words.

"Thank you, Robyn. I love you. I will always love you."

# CHAPTER FIFTY-ONE

## Jordan

Jordan's dinner meeting with Charles Farmer had gone so well that she rolled her eyes as her phone buzzed with yet another message from him trying a flimsy attempt at casual communication, pretending he wasn't pressing for her acceptance of their offer. It was a generous one, worth an easy eight figures over five years, and so rich with cash that she was in Chicago touring a penthouse condominium that she'd only dreamed about even a few years ago. She'd brought her mother along, in part because in her girlhood, they'd always wonder, walking down Michigan Avenue, who it was that lived at the top of those tall buildings, the imposing structures that exuded wealth and control, power and imperviousness. And here they were, in one of those very fortresses in the sky, all windows looking down, all perfectly placed and tastefully decorated in neutral tones. She'd be safe up here, comfortable, ensconced in luxury, and she wanted her mother to know it.

"Jordan, this is beautiful, but do you really want to give up living in Malibu? You were right there on the beach."

"Mom, living at the beach is overrated. It's overcast half the time anyway. With this job, I can go anywhere I want for vacation. I could probably buy an island." Jordan smiled at the thought; she was only half kidding.

Her mother turned from the window and walked over. The sound of her heels clacking along the hard floor echoed throughout the expansive two-story living room. When she was close enough, she joined her hands with Jordan's and met her eyes. "You don't have to do this, you know."

*What else am I supposed to do?* Jordan's mind silently replied.

The real estate agent reentered the room with a brisk stride to the two women. "So sorry, I just had to take a quick call. So, where were we? Oh yes, of course. This is a double-unit penthouse. The prior owners bought the unit below them and expanded through two levels. And it's really impressive how seamlessly this was done. Now you have this massive living room, just majestic, looking down over all of Chicago. And of course you have the views of Lake Michigan." The agent continued her enumeration of the selling points—twenty-four-hour concierge in the lobby of the building, a two-story fitness center, aquatic center, three bedrooms, three and a half bathrooms, an office, and, if she wanted, the owners would throw in some of their art collection and furniture. The art and furniture alone were worth what some of her friends had paid for their entire home back in Los Angeles.

"I like it," Jordan said confidently. With the signing bonus alone, she'd be able to make a healthy down payment, and could move in within weeks. "Mom, you like it, right?"

Her mother's face was unreadable, which was strange for a moment like this. You'd expect any parent to be proud to see their child come from modest beginnings and go all the way to the top of the world. But that wasn't all that her mother wanted for her. "It's . . . nice," she said. "Amazing, just beautiful. But are you sure, Jordan, that this is what you want?"

Jordan rolled her eyes like an annoyed teen.

"Mom . . ." Jordan readied herself to dismiss the trophy wife when her mom stepped in close.

"Honey," she said as she took Jordan's hand with a maternal love and concern. "Is everything okay? Did anything . . . happen?" Mom's eyes locked onto Jordan's, searching for an answer. Jordan wanted to look away. But the softer side wanted to collapse into her arms, confess she was hurting, bawl her eyes out, and get the nurturing that she knew her mom was longing to pour all over her. Instead, Jordan remained steadfast.

"I'm fine, Mom. I know what I'm doing," Jordan insisted. "Trust me. This is great. A great development."

"Okay, Jordan, you've always been your father's child." She smiled weakly.

*Yes, yes I am,* Jordan thought, looking out the window and surveying all the world below.

# CHAPTER FIFTY-TWO

## Harper

Harper and Mia sat in his hotel's cedar garden having tea. They were having a daddy-daughter date. They snacked on plantain croquettes, loaded fries, and macaroons. Mia didn't always have a big appetite, but she liked to taste *everything*. She clearly got her sophisticated and fearless palate from her mother. Robyn had picked out a cute outfit for her: a white dress, petticoat, and beret that sat on the left side of her braids. She looked like a little lady and the waitstaff treated her as such. "What else may we bring you, milady?"

She giggled but tried a proper British accent: "More lemonade, please," she asked.

They simply nodded and humored her with, "Right away, madam." She seemed so grown up sitting across from Harper, who'd put on his Sunday's best, trimmed his beard, and carefully barbered his bald pate. Mia was growing into a beautiful, worldly, and confident young lady. Despite the circumstances that brought him to Accra, Harper was thankful for the unscheduled time he got to spend with Mia—no itinerary planned, no grand trips, amusement parks, or extravagant gifts. Just time spent together. He vowed to come more than just every six weeks. He could do that. He also told a local realtor to keep an eye out for a two-bedroom or a one-bedroom efficiency. Something with a view. It could be a good investment because Accra was on the rise. Plus, it would ultimately be cheaper than paying for a hotel every time. He could stay for longer periods because as Murch (and Robyn) had told him long ago "you can write from anywhere." And given last night's brain dump and *Unfinished Business* pitch pages, that was no longer just a theory. Robyn was also right that he didn't belong in Accra. This was Robyn's safe space, not his. And he was determined to find his own.

Mia knew this would be their "goodbye for now" tea, but she wasn't sad. "I'm gonna miss you, Daddy," Mia said as she dipped her macaroon in her teacup before bringing it up to her mouth.

"Oh, honey, I'm gonna miss you too. Something terrible." Harper put his hand on his heart speaking those sincere words. "I'm glad we got to spend some more time together. You are getting to be such a big, brilliant girl."

Mia smiled bashfully at her dad's compliments. "Thank you," Mia said, studying him. She paused, like she was thinking, deciding about saying something. "Are you . . . going to be okay, Daddy?"

Harper cocked his head and then smiled at her. "You're worried about me, baby?" he asked.

"Yes," she said. "You're all alone in New York." Harper was touched deeply by his daughter's sincerity. She had always been perceptive. Could she tell that he was out of sorts with companionship? "I want you to be happy, Daddy."

"I'm happy, baby," Harper reassured her. Mia looked at him dubiously. It was a look that Robyn would have given him. "You don't think I'm happy?"

"I think you'd be happier if you weren't alone," she said. Harper thought of Jordan. He'd been thinking of Jordan. But it wasn't time to tell Mia, not yet. But he hoped there would still be a need to. He grinned at Mia, marveling at the little woman in front of him.

"Girl, I'll tell you, you are your momma's child."

"I'm serious, Dad."

"I can tell." Harper winked at her.

"Can you be that? Can you be happy?" Mia asked him.

"Listen to me: I am happy. Could I be happier? Yes. And I'm working on that," Harper said. "But knowing how concerned you are for me makes it so much easier for me to get to happy. Thank you for that. It's really sweet and it means a lot to me."

"Okay. You're welcome," Mia said.

"I'm coming back next month too, okay? If you ever need me, call me. But no more crying wolf." Mia folded her lips in on one another, looking like a cute brown Muppet.

"I'm really sorry about that, Daddy." Mia looked down.

Harper took her chin and pulled it up so she faced him. "Hey. I know. Mommy and Daddy love you no matter what happens. Don't ever be afraid to let us know how you feel, what you're thinking. Even if it feels hard to talk about. Just know whatever it is, we can work it out," Harper said.

Mia smiled. "Okay . . ." Then Mia studied him for a beat before asking, "Daddy, do you still love Mommy?"

Without hesitation Harper nodded. He hadn't expected the question, but he probably should have. It was important to assure Mia of the truth. "I do. I still do. I'll always love Mommy. I would not be the person I am without Mommy. But we're not together anymore, Mia. That's not going to change. And that's okay. We're still a family. I'll always be your daddy, she will always be your mommy," Harper said. "And you're always going to be our Mia. You are the very best of Mommy and Daddy. You are special, honey. You understand?" Mia nodded.

"I'm going to be fine, baby," Harper said again, to Mia, and to himself. Mia looked at him like she was trying to believe him but wasn't convinced. Harper paused and pushed himself to dig a little bit deeper. "I . . . just think Daddy has to learn to really love himself," he revealed. "To love and accept himself."

"Is that hard?" Mia asks.

"Sometimes, baby," Harper said. "Sometimes."

Mia contemplated Harper's honesty. Then she picked up her lemonade and swirled around the ice.

"You should love yourself, Daddy," she insisted, then sipped. "Because I love you."

Harper smiled at his daughter and picked up his iced tea.

"That's really good advice, Mia," Harper assured her. "I'm going to. I love you too." Harper held up his glass of iced tea to toast and Mia followed suit.

"Milady," Harper said.

"Mi'man . . . ?" Mia said with a shrug.

"Mi'man?!" Harper said with a huge laugh, echoing through garden.

"I don't know. . . ."

And just like that, they continued their laughter and conversation well into the afternoon.

# ACT III

## CHAPTER FIFTY-THREE

# Harper

Harper wore a black suit and a crisp white collared shirt. He was back in Los Angeles, in the studio conference room to discuss the *Unfinished Business* sequel. Stan was on his right, Harper was in the driver's seat sitting across from Mark and Cynthia, who'd been waiting for Harper's new take on his latest pitch for the sequel. When the meeting began they were pleasant, which in and of itself was good to see because based on Stan's initial reporting they were giving him grief, threatening to "pull the project" from Harper, that they "had waited long enough" and how "ridiculous it was that they were being held hostage" by the novelist being "too precious" with an idea that wasn't really based on his previous work and the like. Harper was not expecting a friendly room. Nor did he worry about it. He was confident in the story. He was going to pitch what he wanted to write, and he was going to convince them they'd be crazy not to go right to production with it. Empowered by his ancestors and the muse that was Solomon, his vision was clear. And they were going to see this with his eyes.

Ninety seconds into his pitch the white folks were riveted and by the time Harper got to the crisis moment in the second act they were hooked. Harper painted a vivid picture of Kendall and Jackson's epic sex scene: "a night of undeniable passion leaving both wondering aloud why they hadn't been together all this time."

"There is legitimate fear on Kendall's part of falling in love so completely and forgetting her type A personality. And that was even *before* she was married," Harper illustrated. "Conversely, Jackson hadn't felt worthy of her. Her running from him post college was not only regarded as a rejection of him, but of his manhood. So, they were two ships passing in the night *until* that night," he said. "But now, Jackson has a lucrative offer on the table to go to New York . . . And not as a sportscaster, but doing the news. His lifelong dream," Harper continued. "'Kendall, I love you. I hate how you upended my career, but you made me an overall better person and man. But now I have to go.'" Mark and Cynthia waited with bated breath for Harper's next words. "Love requires you to be open and display your heart for another without fear of damage or pain. Risking your heart is everything," Harper said. "There's a pathway forward, but will he choose love over career? And will she choose love over her loveless but convenient marriage?" Harper paused, letting the question sit in the room.

"Well, will they?" Mark asked, leaning forward.

"I don't know," Harper said. Then teased, "We'll have to find out. We can certainly answer it at the end of this picture or leave the audience on a cliffhanger. I can give you both versions. One with a run through the airport where she stops him from boarding. And one where he gets on the plane. Or a train."

"Train stations are sooo romantic," Cynthia quipped.

"Totally," Stan added. Harper recognized his impish grin. *They're hooked.* Not that he needed Stan's confirmation. Harper knew when he had a room captivated.

"Well, if you can pull that off, we'd be thrilled," Mark remarked. "People want wish fulfillment in movies. And love, relationships, finding your person is one of the biggest ones. Especially for the ladies." Cynthia nodded in agreement.

Harper chimed in this time. "Personally, I think dudes feel the same way. They just show it differently." He was encouraged by the harmony of consensus in the room. "*And* if we can tap into that male audience . . ." Harper continued.

"And get marketing," Stan added.

"Yes, marketing. Then I think you'll pull in the women *and* the men," Harper stated.

Both Mark and Cynthia exchanged smiling looks.

"Well, I must say this was worth the wait, Harper," Mark said.

"Seriously, Harper. Great job. We are super excited for this," Cynthia conveyed similarly.

Harper smiled and nodded with confidence. "I'm glad," he simply stated.

"We want to pitch this to Damson ASAP. If he bites, we'll want you to pitch it to him yourself in person. Hell, maybe we'll even fly you to London if that works," Mark said.

"Sure. Sounds good." Harper kept his response even-keeled.

Cynthia leaned forward with faux trepidation. "I'm afraid to ask . . . but when do think you'll have a first draft?" she asked not quite sheepishly.

Stan immediately ran interference. "Well, Harper has a lot of commitments: family, travel, his next book," he listed.

"July fourth weekend," Harper said confidently, briefly taking Stan aback. Mark and Cynthia looked thrilled with that news.

"That would be amaaazing," Cynthia remarked toward Mark. "We would be right in time for a potential fall start and would be great for the studio slate."

"Yup. Box-office hits are rare, but this one will resonate with audiences," Mark iterated.

"Well, I'm ready. And I thank you guys for your patience," Harper said and stood up, letting *them* know this meeting was over. He extended his hand toward Mark who was pushing his chair back to catch up and meet Harper's palm.

"Absolutely. Thank *you,* Harper. Talk soon," Mark responded. Harper turned and extended his hand to Cynthia.

"Thanks, Harper, thanks Stan," Cynthia said with a broad smile.

"You guys have a great day," Harper said as he exited.

Stan did his best to do his agent thing, "We'll be in touch, guys, thanks," while keeping up with Harper, who was shooting through the cubicles of assistants and coordinators and past the wall of impressive movie posters. By the time Stan caught up, Harper was already on the elevator with the double doors ready to close. Stan had to turn his body sideways and do a quick side-step to avoid missing the narrowing opening.

"So that's how it's done, huh? Drop the mic and exit?" Stan said.

"You think they bought it?" Harper asked, keeping his eyes on the descending numbers display.

"Dude!" Stan said. "You *crushed* it. They are thrilled!" Stan was effusive. He almost sounded in awe.

"Great," Harper said. "I think they felt it. They got it."

"For sure," Stan agreed. "Hey, do you really think you'll be done by this summer?" He spoke just as the doors of the elevator opened. Harper stepped out first.

"Yeah." Harper moved quickly toward the exit. Stan was in tow, scrambling to match his client's pace.

"You put a lot of work in," Stan affirmed. "And coming to do it in person made a difference. Took some coordinating, but hey, we got it handled."

"Yup." Harper's mind was no longer on satisfying the studio. That part was done.

Stan continued speaking. "You must be wrecked. So much travel in such a short amount of time. What's on your agenda? I hope some sleep."

"Headed to Malibu," Harper remarked.

"The west side at this time of day? You'll be stuck in traffic for hours. What's in Malibu?"

"My destiny, Stan!" Harper responded and walked ahead. "My destiny!"

Stuck in crawling traffic, Harper fervently changed lanes trying to gain an advantage on the 405 south. But it was to no avail. Every alternate route was just as crammed, and his navigation system swore it was showing him the quickest route. Even though he'd left multiple voicemails, emails, and texts and had gotten no response, Harper tried Jordan one more time. "Hey, I'm back in LA. I need to see you. I want to make it right between us again. I'm sitting in traffic, but I should be at your place by like 5:17. I will wait until you arrive. I'm not going anywhere. I love you," he finished. Then, "It's Harper, by the way. Okay. Call me. Or wait for me. Or just give me a chance. Okay. Bye."

At 5:19 p.m. Harper reached Jordan's place. He saw the latest flower delivery from him untouched and wilting at the gate. Had the rest of the arrangements he sent suffered the same fate? He rang her buzzer multiple times. She didn't answer. *Maybe she's working out, maybe she's in the shower, maybe she's sleeping,* he thought, waiting. With no answer, and as more time passed, Harper was coming around to the possibility that Jordan wasn't home. *Was she at a meeting? Out of town?* He walked over to the garage and attempted to look in the window. He had to step on his tiptoes. When that proved futile, he jumped up to see if he could grab a peek. He caught a glimpse of what he thought may have been her Beemer, but the glass windows were tinted and dirty with salt water and sand. Did he know the code of either the garage or the front door? His mind raced. It was a four- or five-digit combo. He'd seen her input it and she may have even shared it with him. Was it her birthday? Was it a name of some sort . . . ? Before he could try something a white minivan pulled up with yellow sirens flashing.

*Oh shit.*

Turns out there's a reason Malibu is exclusive.

"Can I help you, sir?" The white uniformed guard stepped out of the vehicle. His imposing build and buzzcut didn't put Harper at the least bit of ease. With his thumbs looped in that thick black tactical belt, he clearly wasn't there to be helpful. Harper knew the circumstances. He tried his best to explain anyway.

"This is not what it looks like. I know the woman who lives here. She's a . . . friend . . . she's my girlfriend . . ."

"Uh-huh. Is she home?"

"It doesn't—I don't—I'm not sure. I rang the bell a few times. I was just trying see if her car was here. . . ."

"Uh-huh. Do you have her number? Have you tried to call her?"

"Well, yes . . . several times. See, I was here about two weeks ago for like . . . two weeks. Wherever she was, I was. And then I had an emergency for my daughter . . ." The more Harper spoke the more ridiculous it sounded and the more this dude didn't give a fuck about his lovers' quarrel with Jordan. Harper looked and sounded exactly like what he was being taken for—a stalker. *Ain't this some shit?*

"Sir, I think it would be best if you move along. And do not return unless you are with the resident of this house and invited in."

"Her name is Jordan. Jordan Armstrong? Do you know her? We went to undergrad together. Brown skin, beautiful face, long hair, about this tall, great smile, drives a blue BMW convertible . . ." As he kept speaking and looked at this man's inscrutable face the deeper in a hole he felt. *Stalker,* his mind accused. This was a bad look.

"You know what? I'm gonna go. If you see her around can you tell her Harper is looking for—that Harper Stewart—the writer—came by . . . I won the Pulitzer . . last year . . ? Anyway, I'm looking for her . . . just trying to reconnect . . ." Harper was backing up to his car as he was speaking, knowing this was a losing battle.

"You have a good night, sir," the security guard said and he waited until Harper got in his car and drove off.

"Where is she, Shelby?!" Harper was definitely a bit overzealous speaking into his car system as he drove the I-10 east back to his hotel in Santa Monica, having narrowly avoided arrest, or worse.

"Ummmm excuse me? You need to take it down a notch, Langston Snooze." Shelby was going full housewife and undergrad diva on him. How she became the guardian of all things Jordan Armstrong he would never know. "What's going on?" Shelby continued.

"You know damn well what's going on. Jordan blocked me, changed her number, I'm out in LA looking for her like a damn stalker because she won't call me back."

"So why are you calling me?" Shelby asked, dripping with superior attitude.

"Because you know where she is. You could at least call her for—"

"I don't know where she is. And I spoke to her about a week or so ago, but she's been radio silent since," Shelby said conclusively. "And plus, even if I did know, I wouldn't tell you."

"Why not?"

"Because you hurt her. And that's my girl."

"Your girl?! Bullshit. She's *my* girl. You know it and *she* knows it. And furthermore—"

"I'm hanging up. Goodbye . . ."

"Shelby, don't you—" Harper looked at his phone display. *Yup, she did hang up.* "Fuck!" Harper hit the redial button. Shelby picked up immediately.

"You hurt her, Harper. Badly," Shelby began. "I've never heard her like that. Ever. So she's protecting herself. From all of us." Harper took in what Shelby was saying. He knew that Jordan was hurt. He'd never before seen her lash out like she had when he left. He'd experienced her ferocity, her anger firsthand and it had been scary. If he was responsible for that, then he was also responsible for bringing back the woman he loved.

"Look, Shelby, I know I fucked up—"

"You did," Shelby added for good measure.

Harper hated having to explain himself through Shelby to get to Jordan, but he took a deep breath, adjusted his tone, and soldiered through. "Shelby, I know you know how to get in touch with her," Harper began. "And I know you're just protecting her. Please, just tell her I'm in LA and I want to see her. I came back like I said I would. And I'm sorry. Please let her know *I* want to protect her. *I* want to be her safe space. Tell her . . ." Harper got choked up. "Tell her I love her." There was silence on the other end. Did Shelby hang up again? "Shelby . . . ?" More silence. "Aww shit, come on. Hello? Shit."

Then, "Harper," Shelby said with a softening tone.

"Yeah, Shelby?"

"I can't get ahold of her. I'm hoping she checks in soon. If she does, I'll relay the message, okay?" Harper detected a breakthrough of some sort, or at least he hoped for one. Shelby, as tough as she could be, was a romantic at heart. If she believed in Jordan and Harper getting together she'd do what she could.

"Thank you."

As he pulled into the circular driveway at Shutters, Harper reflected on achieving real clarity on the story of Jackson and Kendall. What he and Jordan shared was magic on the page and demonstrated to him how powerful their connection was (and hopefully *still* was). He could not force a relationship between them, but he wanted *her.* Did she still feel the same? Harper had to see. As he'd told Lance, he was trying to be a better man. He also told Mia he had to get some acceptance of who he is. And love himself. Could he do both?

As he crossed the lobby to the elevator he caught a glimpse of the classy bar. He'd be back. He had a whole "Where is Jordan?" itinerary planned. Tonight, he'd come back down and order a sidecar at the hotel bar. Tomorrow he'd head to Urth to have a pistachio latte, he'd take a hike up Solstice Canyon, he'd stop at 1212 for a late lunch all in hopes of seeing Jordan. He would go to Nobu tomorrow night and check to see if the bartender had seen her. She had to be *somewhere.* He was going to keep searching. But for now, he had to unwrap a new gift he got for himself.

When he entered his junior suite, Harper played Sade's *Love Deluxe* on his phone. He stepped into his en suite bathroom and turned on the faucet on the double vanity, unbuttoned the sleeves on his shirt, and rolled up the cuff on his right forearm that was wrapped in plastic.

He dipped his fingertips into the flow of running water, then adjusted the handle to a lukewarm temperature. He carefully peeled back the plastic to reveal his first ever tattoo. SOLOMON. Harper smiled at it, admiring its craftsmanship. It really did turn out great. Harper chose the same font that they had used in Solomon's nursery. Except this one had an angel's halo over the first *O*. It was in black ink but still raw. He had gotten it at a parlor close to Malik Books in Culver City. Harper took care to wash it, dab it dry with paper towels, and moisturize it gingerly with shea butter. He gently massaged SOLOMON with love, care, and tenderness while singing the chorus to the first track. No ordinary love indeed.

Suddenly, Sade was interrupted by an incoming phone call. Was it her? Harper raced to it. No, it was Quentin.

"Yo, Q, what's up?" Harper asked.

"What you doing, joe?"

"I'm sure you already know, seeing as how you and your wife don't keep no secrets from one another," Harper responded.

"Yeah, she told me," Quentin said with exasperation. "So what—you just hoping to run into her somewhere out there?"

"I told her I'd come back. I'm staying until we reconnect. I have to try, Q."

"Harp, this is stupid. You giving real stalker vibes right now. 'Bout to make yourself a news headline. She'll come around," Quentin declared.

"What if she doesn't? What if I blew it, Q?" Harper's voice broke just a bit.

"Then you blew it," Quentin said bluntly. "Move the fuck on. I know that ain't what you wanna hear, but fuck it." Quentin could be eloquent. Just not all the time. "Listen, man, come on back to New York. You already missed the last poker night going to Ghana on some bullshit." Harper didn't like Quentin's characterization but there was no sense debating him. "We want you back home, joe. Touch base. Regroup. We'll figure it out together."

"Q, do you know where she is, man?" Harper had to ask. He leaned forward for good news.

Quentin answered without hesitation.

"Poker night. Wednesday. My house. Don't flake."

# CHAPTER FIFTY-FOUR

## Robyn

Robyn yawned as she pulled her RAV4 into the parking lot at Kotoka International Airport. She'd been making a lot of changes, preparations for this next segment of her life in Accra. Change was exhausting and so was not sleeping. As much as she valued her peace and peace of mind, she'd spent nights tossing and turning, ruminating over the prior weeks' events, trying to sort through the truest desires of her heart. She made a mental note to check in with Thema; she'd need a tonic to replenish her body. She wasn't accustomed to this much worry.

No matter how hard she tried to see it another way, even now, sitting in the parking lot of the airport, her only true regret was not giving Kwesi the full benefit of the doubt before he left. Regret for not believing him when he tried to explain something so complex to her that it took almost two weeks of her own complexities with Harper to fully understand. Kwesi said that he could hold love and connection in his heart for his ex, but also have simultaneous certainty that he did not want a future with her romantically. Now that Robyn had experienced the roller coaster of Harper's visit, that they'd made love even, she more than understood. Their marriage was over and complete. She was certain about Harper, and thus, surer than ever about Kwesi.

He'd given her the space and time she'd requested and had kept in touch while he was away. He'd shown her kindness and consistency, everything she'd asked for. So, she'd been counting down the days until he returned. He told her that he'd be taking a chauffeured car from the airport, but Robyn planned to surprise him with a different welcome.

She stepped out of the car into the daytime sunlight and straightened her skirt. She adored the beautiful Ankara cloth prints; this one she wore today was a Nsu Bura print, which resembled the ripples that formed on the surface of water, mimicking how a single drop reached out farther beyond itself creating cascades of effect into the distance. Robyn loved this print, with meaning as deep as the well it was named for. The future was this—ripples of changes into the distance from a single point. There'd been many moments like this for Robyn, but Mia's call and Harper's visit set into motion a set of decisions that needed to be made. She couldn't wait to share with Kwesi.

Butterflies filled her belly as she walked up to the terminal, heading to arrivals. If she timed it right, she'd catch him just as he was coming out through customs. She fidgeted and touched up her hair with nervousness but soon fell into step with the energy around her, of tour guides bustling about and taxi drivers trying to secure their fares.

When she finally saw Kwesi's face and his tall frame walking toward her, she pulled herself up on the tips of her toes, waving so that he could see her. And his look of recognition, first of slight confusion and then pure happiness, was priceless. Robyn smiled, feeling the happiness stretch across her face, up through her forehead, back to her ears.

He pointed her to her left, seemingly gesturing to where he planned to meet her on the other side of the throngs of family members, loved ones, and business associates also meeting their own arriving passengers. To the side, Robyn noticed the well-suited man holding a white sign with Kwesi's name on it.

Kwesi reached her quickly and wrapped his arms around her, pulling her in close to squeeze her tight. She held on to him with her hands around his shoulder blades and cheek against his chest. She let her body sink into his, and for a moment, time seemed to stand still. He felt so good, smelled so good, sounded so good.

"I didn't expect you, Robyn," he said as he finally pulled away from her. It was almost as if they were the only two people in the world, even within the buzz of the airport.

"I wanted to surprise you." She gave him a smile, a genuine smile. "I'm just so glad you're back. I have so much to show you."

Kwesi laughed. "Well, will we be needing a car?" He turned to the driver standing patiently at attention.

"No, I brought mine," Robyn said.

"Well, then," Kwesi said, turning to the driver. "Thanks, mate, I'd say you could just take off, then, I'll be all set." For a moment the driver looked confused as if he didn't quite know what to do. Kwesi smiled good-naturedly and placed his arm around Robyn's shoulders. "I'm all yours, then," he said, meeting her eyes.

"And I'm all yours," Robyn said, reaching her arms around him and letting her head settle onto his chest as they walked in tandem into the great day ahead.

# CHAPTER FIFTY-FIVE

## Harper

On poker night, the crew was at Quentin's house this month. Quentin was the most centrally located for everyone, including Lance, who had to hit the George Washington Bridge from Alpine, New Jersey, to get there. Harper and Murch were both in Brooklyn, though Murch was coming from a donor meeting in the city. He got a five-million-dollar fundraising pledge from another billionaire to help fund his fourth school that would nestle in the heart of Manhattan. So he was on quite the high. They were all in good spirits. The camaraderie of brotherhood was in the air as were the smells of the gourmet vegan options that Quentin had laid out for them. Between the mac and cheez, oyster mushroom calamari, and the chick'n skewers, Harper swore they were eating real meat. If this was vegan eating, Harper was down. Murch apologized about Candace sharing the photo with Robyn. He *had* deleted it, but Candace had found it, looking for some specific photo of Kellie that she swore was on his phone. Evidently, it was perfect for a passport. She checked his deleted photos and there it was. But Harper told Murch there was nothing to apologize for—he shouldn't have put him in that situation. Harper was the one who should be sorry—and he was. In true Murch fashion, he forgave Harper and they hugged it out.

Quentin had pulled out a new set of poker chips and broke out a brand-new table for them, plus a 1980s playlist with Guy's "I Like" kicking things off into a mixture of Frankie Beverly, Patrice Rushen, Prince, and Chaka Khan. Quentin had been right to push Harper to get back to New York. This was their new tradition: a commitment to get together every third Wednesday of the month, no matter what—Knicks game, comedy show, new bar, new restaurant opening, live music, or just playing cards—like tonight. The fellas were able to accommodate Harper's "emergency" circumstances, but the penalty would be sharing the extent of his excursions and "don't leave out shit." A reset indeed. Quentin made triple sure that Shelby would be out for the evening at whatever event he could send her to. He even offered her the grand master suite at the Spivey Grand so the fellas could speak as freely as they wanted, especially Harp. She said she'd be home by midnight. "Get all of your boy bitch-fest out," she'd told her husband.

Since Harper had confessed so much to the women in his life it was time to do the same with his day ones and fill in the gaps that group texts left. There were lots of laughs, but also "Ohhhh shiiiiiit!," "Nigga what?!," and "THE BOTH OF THEM?!" They were college teens again. The sexcapades were titillating for sure, but the intensity of the feelings that Harper described out loud for the first time took him a bit by surprise. It was one thing to internalize and journal about the experience of having sex *with* Jordan. But it was another to express that out loud to his closest friends, his brothers, and get their honest reactions. They were his confidants, his therapists, his collective conscience.

"Y'all was making love for real, joe," Quentin said.

"God may have been presiding over that union," Lance said. Harper couldn't argue with either of those notions.

Murch simply said, "It just fits." Leading with his Malibu experience Harper thought for sure they would admonish him for essentially going backward, sleeping with Robyn. But they all had a level of understanding. At this stage of life, it was complicated.

"You guys were married for a long time. There's a lot of history," Murch said.

"Shiiit. Do you know how many times Shelby and I sneaky linked before we got married?" Quentin posited, shaking his head. "Hell, that's how Kennedy was born."

"Sometimes those primal feelings take over. Y'all still love each other and that's just a natural extension," Lance declared. "Don't beat yourself up."

"Yeah, let Robyn beat that ass!" Quentin quipped and they all howled with laughter, including Harper.

"Ol' Fifty Shades of Black-ass," Lance chimed in. More laughs ensued.

Harper managed a chuckle and shook his head. These were all his family. Supportive but also holding him accountable. Forcing him to see himself, but also to love and forgive himself.

"We all have flaws, Harper," Murch said. "We're human. We've made mistakes and we will continue to."

"Amen," Lance agreed.

"Plus, you ain't never prioritized any relationship or partner over yourself," Quentin said. "It's who you are." Harper looked at Quentin, wanting to challenge that notion, but the more the words sat out there, the more Harper knew he couldn't refute them. Murch and Lance paused the game knowing a nerve had been touched. "Robyn used to accept it. Jordan didn't. It's pretty cut and dry, joe." Quentin wasn't challenging him. He wasn't baiting Harper into a fight or trying to push his buttons. He was just being . . . Quentin.

Harper nodded. "You nailed it, Q," he said. "As always. But I'm ready now."

"How's that?" Lance asked.

"Yeah, ready for what?" Quentin wanted to know.

"Ready to be a gardener," Harper said simply. They all looked back at him with confusion.

"Nigga, you changing professions?" Quentin looked at him with disbelief. They *all* looked curious but intrigued.

"Q's right. It's always been about me and what I want," Harper began. "It's always worked for my career goals, but not always in my friendships and relationships. It didn't work in my marriage to Robyn. It's not working with these women I'm dating. It certainly won't work with Jordan. I been a little delicate, bitch-ass flower that needed all the watering and sunlight. And I got all of it. Now, if I want back in my life, I have to prioritize someone other than myself. And that someone is Jordan."

Harper looked at his boys, ready for any possible response—clown him, break out laughing, challenge the notion that he could be anything but a delicate bitch-ass flower, whatever would come. It was quiet for a moment. They each seemed to take in Harper's declaration, and they exchanged looks. Finally, it was Murch who spoke.

"Welp, I've heard enough. I think he's ready."

Harper crinkled his forehead. Lance looked at Quentin.

"Yeah. The 'bitch-ass flower' did it for me," Lance said. "How about you, Q?"

Quentin turned to Harper and sighed.

"Yo, what the fuck—?" Harper wanted to know what exactly was happening.

Quentin took a sip of Sable from his glass and nodded.

"Yup," he said. "That's my nigga."

"Fellas! Will someone please tell me what is going on, please?"

"She's in Chicago." *Chicago?*

"She's in Chicago?" Harper echoed. "What's she doing—?"

"What does it matter, Harper?" Murch said.

"For real, man," Lance chimed in. "Go to her. And make it plain."

Harper looked at his boys in a daze. The alcohol, the emotional churning in his stomach, the logic police running scenarios in his head, they all created a dubious countenance on Harper's face and Quentin could tell.

"Don't look like that, Harp," Q said.

"Y'all *all* knew about this?" Harper asked.

"Yup. Even me," Murch declared. "And I kept it to myself."

"Y'all ain't shit," Harper said, half joking.

They chuckled. Lance patted Harper on his shoulder.

"It's time, dawg. We ain't getting any younger. Get back in your life," Lance said. "You know Jordan is stubborn as a motherfucker. She will dig in."

"You have to step the fuck up for this woman. You got to step up for the life you say you want," Quentin said.

"You have to show her," Murch added.

*Women want assurances. Not maybes.* Harper remembered that.

Of all the responses he could have gotten, Harper did not expect this one. He was grateful in that moment that his boys were his boys: supportive, challenging, holding him accountable, and loving.

## CHAPTER FIFTY-SIX

# Jordan

Jordan reached up to smooth down the sides of her freshly tapered haircut. It was still a bit unusual to feel the air against the back of her neck instead of flowing waves brushing against her shoulders. But here she was, in her power suit, perfectly tailored and matched with her stilettos, walking into the office hallway out of the conference room still filled with the top tier of executive management, her direct reports. In just fifteen minutes, she clearly let every single one of them know exactly what time it was with a new sheriff in town. She left them exactly as she'd planned—a little stunned, a little speechless, and with absolutely no question about who was in charge. She was.

"Jordan." Her overeager assistant intercepted her, all sweater set and ballerina flats shuffling along, trying to keep up with Jordan's strut down the hall. "I have four urgent meeting requisitions, one from Charles, and then three of your EVPs: Laura, John, and Chris S. as opposed to Chris P., who you met with yesterday. So I know that you asked me to slot fifteen minutes after your all-hands meeting, but I was thinking that we could just use this time since it's open for Charles at least?"

"No."

"No?"

"No," Jordan repeated simply but firmly.

"You going to say no to the chairman? Jordan, I . . ."

Jordan stopped her strut abruptly. "Michelle, I appreciate your taking initiative, really, I do. But no. The fifteen minutes is a nonnegotiable." And then she turned and resumed her strut, quick and powerful, right through the open door of her office, with Michelle still scrambling to figure out what had happened.

Jordan closed the door behind her and in two swift motions kicked those tall heels off her feet, sending them flying in separate directions. Ahead of her was a clear view of Lake Michigan in the distance from her two adjoining walls of windows. But time was short. She walked over to her carryall, pulled out her makeup bag, and carried it with her into her private en suite bathroom. She placed the bag on the counter and dipped her fingers through the open zipper to pull out her concealer and set it aside. On her phone screen, she opened the timer and set it to fourteen minutes and thirty seconds. She managed to hit the start button just as her vision blurred with all the tears she'd been holding back. By the time she'd sat in her usual place on the top of the toilet cover she'd already begun to cry.

Already she'd stopped trying not to think about Harper. It wasn't working anyway. Holding back tears in meetings, tearing up reading reports and emails. This was the only thing that worked. To let it out before it poured out of her in front of everyone. No matter how full her day was, no matter how far she was from Malibu, even with him blocked, Harper was still in her head and her heart. *I was so stupid,* she thought as the tears welled. But she missed him. She missed him down to her bones. But she'd given all of herself, and he still left. There was no apology to make up for a man who just wasn't ready. And Jordan hated being wrong. Her judgment was the one thing she could trust, but not anymore.

Fourteen minutes later, when the timer rang, Jordan abruptly stopped her tears and wiped her eyes with the crumpled-up wad of tissue in her hand. Sniffing, she stood up and walked over to the mirror to reapply her concealer and touch up her eyeliner and mascara.

She straightened her clothes as she walked out of the bathroom and into her office, retrieving her shoes and replacing them on her feet. By the time she opened her office door again, she was breathing normally and looked almost as if nothing had ever happened. Almost.

"Michelle," she called out to the cubicle ensconced desk in front of her door. Instantly, Michelle swung around the corner with a cup of coffee.

"I'm so sorry, Jordan, I just went to get you a cup of coffee. And your friend is here, an old friend from college and—"

"Jordan."

She'd recognize that voice from anywhere.

"Harper?"

And closely behind Michelle, there *was* Harper. Looking great, but uninvited.

Jordan held her hand out to accept the coffee from Michelle, but her eyes never left Harper's face. "Thank you, Michelle, can you just give us five minutes? Tell my next meeting I'll be right there."

Michelle nodded and scurried in the direction of the elevator.

"Follow me," Jordan said, her knees feeling wobbly now, but not wanting to make any kind of a scene. She walked through the opened door to her office and closed it behind Harper. Her heart was beating so fast but her face remained stoic. Even as she brushed past him heading toward her desk and smelled his cologne.

"What are you doing here, Harper?" Jordan was as clear as she could be. She didn't have time for bullshit and the clock was ticking: four minutes and thirty-seven seconds left.

Standing with his hands behind his back, Harper swallowed, cleared his throat.

"I—Uh, I'm sorry to interrupt your day, but I umm, I wanted to . . ." Harper stumbled.

Jordan's stoicism was downshifting to annoyance that would soon find its way to anger. She too pulled a deep breath in, poised to interrupt, but Harper spoke instead. "I . . . got . . . you lunch," he said, and pulled his hands from behind his back, producing a brown paper bag with grease stains.

Jordan's brow furrowed with incredulous confusion. *Did this nigga just say lunch?*

"Lemon pepper wings," he said. *What the actual fuck?* "Now, I don't know if they're as good as the ones that we ordered from Jasper's back in the day but they're close. Very close. I tasted quite a few before landing on these." He placed the bag on her coffee table.

Four minutes and eleven seconds.

"I'm sure both of our palates have changed quite a bit, but that memory is strong for me, Jordan. Us studying together and us sharing wings."

Jordan did not have time for this trip down memory lane. And she wasn't about to make the time it seemed to need. She made a mental note to get those fucking wings out of here even if they smelled like heaven.

"Jordan, I can't stop thinking about you. I can't stop thinking about everything from the time I met you. From the time you gave me advice on my first girlfriend and my eighth girlfriend. From telling me it was okay that I wasn't gonna be the next Bryant Gumbel. From the time you read my grad school essay and told me I'd be 'a voice of a generation.' I can't stop thinking about what you mean to me and what the fifteen days and thirty years that we've had together has meant to me," Harper shared.

Jordan's brow unfurrowed. She moistened her lips with a flick of her tongue and deliberately checked her Hermès watch. Two minutes twenty-five seconds. Then Jordan saw Harper kneel.

"I want another fifteen days and thirty years with you."

Jordan's heart jumped in her throat and jackhammered. And suddenly time stood still. *What the fuck? What is going on? No, this is not happening now.* But it was happening. Her eyes pricked intensely, and tears that had dried in her en suite pooled in her eyes, blurring everything before her, including Harper. She blinked them down her cheeks. Harper's tears were already running down his face as he reached toward her, holding out a small black box. "I'm asking you not only to be my friend. I'm asking you to be my wife"—*Is that a ring?*—"I'm asking you to let me be your gardener," Harper said. *His what? His gardener . . . ? Is that a fucking ring?* Harper opened the box in his hands and Jordan thought she was going blind again. The glare from the rock made her squint, and blink, and squint, and . . . *breathe, Jordan* . . . Harper kept talking, but it was muffled. Inside, Jordan was lit with emotion.

"I'm asking you to let me be the one who's going to be there for you," she heard Harper say. "To let me be the one who's going to do shit for you. Shit that you want me to do and shit that you're not asking me to do. Let me be the one who makes *you* better. Let me be the one who encourages you and makes *you* whole. Let me be the one who understands you. And when

I don't, I'm going to find out why. And if I don't, I'm going to be held accountable. I'm going to hold *myself* accountable. Let me be the one to dry your tears, not the one to make you cry." Harper continued with his moist face. "I don't just love you, I'm *ready* to love you, Jordan," Harper declared. "I'm ready to really love you."

Jordan was frozen and breathing heavy. Tears had reached her chin and dripped onto the custom carpet. She heard her door open and saw Michelle's feet stop abruptly behind Harper's shoulder.

"Ummmm, Jordan, I'm sorry," Michelle said. "I'm—I'm— Oh my God . . . That's five karats . . . I mean . . . five *minutes.*" Jordan heard her, but she could not respond or move.

"I just redid my makeup," Jordan said finally, looking at Harper.

Harper smiled.

"It looks really good too. You look beautiful," he said. "And I love the hair. So what do you say?"

# CHAPTER FIFTY-SEVEN

## Robyn

Lying still on the padded surface of Thema's treatment table, Robyn folded her hands against her chest and concentrated on the sound of the ocean in the distance. The smell of lemongrass, lavender, and soapy burned sage swirled in the air, familiar and soothing, reminding Robyn that coming to set up shop here at Thema's was the absolute right decision. Even after her decision to downsize and the relief that came with it, exhaustion still stuck with Robyn, and she wasn't herself. Keeping up with preteen Mia was a challenge, but nothing out of the ordinary. And planning for her new, much smaller business had become manageable. There were some late nights with Kwesi, but that was all enjoyment, *all* enjoyment. His support and understanding had helped her bridge the rest of the changes that came along with building her much smaller presence, a beachfront offering with a small menu—letting staff go, signing last checks, selling the furniture and equipment, and preparing to hand the last set of keys over to Aboagye who had the nerve to wish her a "prosperous future" when she told him of her plans. *Cue eye roll* . . .

This was going to be the first step in her fresh start. And more than that, this was the jump-start that she needed. Thema had given her an energetic treatment—a Reiki massage, reading her body and helping unlock the flow of energies that usually allowed her to be a superwoman. So, a strong tonic to go and a possible short meditation would be enough to set her along the path to full recovery of her much-needed balance.

"Okay, my dear," Thema said, pouring her bowl of water into the sink. "You're all set."

Robyn sat up and began to arrange her clothing. "Thank you so much, Thema. I'm really looking forward to feeling like myself again."

Thema raised an eyebrow. "Really?" she said. An unusual response.

"Well, yes, of course," Robyn confirmed. "You always know exactly what to do. I've just been feeling so run down lately, but I know I've been out of balance. And it's my own fault I know—"

"Give me your hands, dear," Thema said as she approached Robyn, who now was sitting on the edge of the treatment table.

Robyn extended her hands toward Thema, who stood in front of her in her flowing embroidered white robe.

"Other side, palms up, please."

Robyn turned her wrists to expose her palms to the air. Thema placed her thumbs on each of her wrists.

"Umm, um-hmmm," she said.

*Um-hmm?* Thema's methods were somewhat unique, but this woo-woo was working overtime. She examined Robyn, focusing, it seemed, on her eyes. Robyn wondered if they were still red and bloodshot, even though she'd started sleeping better in the past week. She hoped that whatever Thema had to say had an easy answer, a cure she could leave with. Tentatively, she asked, "Is there a tea or something, a tonic?"

"Oh no," Thema said. "I don't give tonics to my pregnant patients."

"Your what?" Robyn heard herself say.

"Oh yes, dear, you're pregnant. I'm quite certain of it. You haven't noticed a missed period?"

"A what?" Robyn said again. She didn't know if she'd be able to manage another word. "I . . . I . . . hadn't paid much attention. I'm in perimenopause. It skips sometimes, but I thought I couldn't possibly—"

"Oh, now see, anything is possible, Robyn. It's still quite early, but I would say congratulations."

*When was my last period?* Robyn thought. It'd been before Kwesi left, for sure. She hadn't had it at all while Harper was in town. Oh. *Harper?* But with Kwesi she'd . . . they'd . . . *Oh my God.*

# Acknowledgments

**MALCOLM D. LEE**

Adam Kanter, David Doerrer, Gordon Bobb, Jackie Bazan, and Malcolm Spellman, who told me this series of books was worth pursuing. Thanks, Malc! Mr. Captain America, youknowhutumsayin'?

Jayne Allen, thanks for showing me the ropes. You had me at "Do you wanna win?" You're a great partner and collaborator. Thank you for being on this phase of my storytelling journey. The Zooms, the phone calls, the texts, the three-hour and ten-hour time differences, transcontinental texting from LA, NY, Detroit, Accra, and Cape Town. Thank you!

My editor, Chelcee Johns, for believing in the viability of this storied franchise, for pushing when I wanted to pull and pulling when I wanted to push, for simultaneously challenging and supporting the vision, for being present every step of the way—through sickness and health—for the quick reads, the encouraging Zooms, the phone calls, the emails, the deadline extensions, and the notes that made this first book of mine better.

I could not have asked for a better partner to bring this vision to fruition.

To my ever-supportive wife, Dr. Camille Banks-Lee. You make me my best self. None of this happens without you.

My father, A. Clifton Lee, who is always curious and encouraging of all my endeavors.

To my three sons, Langston, Lennox, and Lucas, who may actually read this one . . .

To my Ghana angels and guides, Sidra Smith and Nicole Amartefeio, who helped make my Ghana experience fulfilling and wonderful!

To Chef Maame Boakye and the staff at Ghastro, for preparing amazing food and allowing me space for my questions.

Nana Stephen Afrah for the Twi lesson—"Medasse Pa, brother!"

Rabbi Kohain Helevi, for the tour and the knowledge of our history and our ancestors.

Renee Neblett, founder of the Kokrobitey Institute—you inspired so much for me. Thank you for the time, the Neem Tree, and the lemongrass, the freshest I've ever smelled!

Ambassador Erieka Bennett, for the official welcome to Ghana at the W. E. B. Du Bois Centre.

The African American Association of Ghana (AAAG).

Kwabena Jumah and Edwina Akufo-Addo Jumah, for being amazing hosts!

Paul Ninson, founder of the Dikan Gallery.

The Ga Fishing Community.

Lori Lakin Hutcherson.

My Georgetown University crew, who helped inspire a franchise: Taj Paxton, Bruce Hamilton, Chris "Bod" Bodiford, Yaphet Smith, Kayode Vann, Daniella Jackson, Kayatanya Henderson, and Chip Simms.

## JAYNE ALLEN

On October 22, 1999, the theatrical release of *The Best Man* film, I was in the fall of my senior year on the ivy-covered campus of Duke University, planning my future. I can still remember the ribbed turtleneck and the red-brown lipstick I wore with a gaggle of my girlfriends to buy our movie tickets opening weekend. We were fascinated by the portrayal of aspirational versions of ourselves—looking up to Jordan Armstrong, laughing with Shelby, wondering if Harper would ever straighten up his act.

If I were to stand before that younger version of me—that newly minted Delta in the red sorority jacket, that young black woman obsessing over whether or not she'd get into law school—and tell her that one day she'd be working as a novelist with the incomparable Malcolm D. Lee on the extension of the same story she'd been so enthralled and inspired by onscreen, she'd tisk her lips, roll her eyes at me, and go right back to studying, thinking she was *supposed* to be a lawyer. But the woman I am today, my lips stretch into the widest smile and my eyes fill with tears as I am overwhelmed by the magnitude of appreciation and gratitude I feel for having been blessed with this opportunity.

As I told Malcolm, I did not have a single bad day working on this book, not even one. Our writing sessions were filled with respect, with depth and honesty, and with so much laughter. I am thrilled that that high energy translated to the page, infused into a story rich with life, truth, hope, and humanity. So, I first would like to say thank you to Malcolm, for entrusting me with these characters whom you have so carefully protected and their stories that you have so meaningfully crafted for over twenty-five years. It has been beyond a dream. It has truly been an honor. Thank you for showing me an even higher level of excellence, such rare air to breathe, of a peak beyond the clouds to reach for. Thank you to Chelcee Johns, our dedicated editor. I will never forget our collaboration across three time zones to trade drafts, even sometimes at early hours in sleeping time, to help bring the best version of this work to conclusion. Your brilliance and openness, your support and encouragement, your fantastic ideas, offered with respect and care, helped craft a work we can all finally stand back from and enjoy.

And as always, thank you to my literary agent, Lucinda Halpern and team, and my editor Amy Baker at HarperCollins, who is my forever cheerleader and was so supportive of me to do this project alongside my other books. Also, as a "recovering lawyer," of course I must thank my attorneys, Peter Nichols and Jay Burkholder. Thank you to my parents, John Sealey and Shermane Townsend Sealey, for absolutely everything, to my family and friends, and to Jeff, who often found himself in a long-distance relationship with me even though I was just a few feet away in my writing nook. Thank you to my community of readers, my Bookstagram family, and to the bookstores and libraries who have been a constant support. I'm so incredibly grateful to have the opportunity to do what I love, to keep learning and growing and offering you my best.

*With love,*
Jayne Allen

# About the Authors

MALCOLM D. LEE is a writer, director, and producer whose directorial work includes his critically acclaimed feature film debut, *The Best Man,* as well as *Girls Trip, Night School,* and *The Best Man: The Final Chapters.* His company, Blackmaled Productions, is dedicated to telling diverse stories that contribute to changing and amplifying narratives of people of color.

Instagram: @malcolmdlee
TikTok: @blackmaledproductions

JAYNE ALLEN is the author of the bestselling *Black Girls Must Die Exhausted* novel series and *The Most Wonderful Time.* Allen crafts transcultural stories that touch upon contemporary women's issues.

Instagram: @jayneallenwrites
TikTok: @jayneallenwrites